Shadows Of Conflict

by
Joanne Leigh

PublishAmerica
Baltimore

© 2004 by Joanne Leigh

All rights reserved. No part of this book may be reproduced, stored in a retrieval system or transmitted in any form or by any means without the prior written permission of the publishers, except by a reviewer who may quote brief passages in a review to be printed in a newspaper, magazine or journal.

First printing

ISBN: 1-4137-3760-9
PUBLISHED BY PUBLISHAMERICA, LLLP
www.publishamerica.com
Baltimore

Printed in the United States of America

DEDICATION

With love and thanks to my sister, Margaret Chopping,
whose help and encouragement helped
me as a writer and who always believed in me.

Chapter One

Snow was forecast for that December even though golden sunshine laid on the Philadelphia rooftops. Businessmen and shoppers mingled in the streets to read the headlines fresh off the press, while in the offices of De La Rey Estates, eight floors above, George de la Rey lit a cigar and sent an acrid cloud across the room.

'Where the hell is Robert? I want my son here. Now these offices are ready, I want him to see where he's going to spend the rest of his working life.'

Herman, his secretary, retreated a few steps and glanced in the direction of Mrs de la Rey for support.

'Now dear,' she said, 'you know Robert's preparing to go south for a while.'

'Yes, Rachel, I heard something of the kind. South? Damned fool thing to be doing. Off to the Jeffersons' again, is he?'

'Yes, but it's hardly again. He hasn't been down there in a long while.'

'The boy's duty is here, specially this time of the year. And he knows I don't hold with him seeing that Jefferson girl. Why now, when I need him here?'

'I should think he wants to see his friends before he begins working for you, George.'

Rachel spoke quietly, reassuringly, aware that her son was journeying south before it was too late to go there at all.

Through the window she could see the hoarding with the company name being lifted into position. From below came the mouth-watering aroma of roasted nuts and she suddenly longed to get home to the comfort of their house on Dale Avenue. She rubbed her hands together against the cold. The heating in the building had not been on for long.

A news vendor shouted the headlines. Not wishing to hear what the papers were so full of these days, she turned from the window. It was evident that matters had taken a turn for the worse and perhaps Robert was indeed foolish to travel at such a time, but then he knew that, was well aware of the growing situation between the states. He often spoke on political matters and she was proud of his views and policies and his growing interest in the affairs of state, though she kept these thoughts to herself. She would never seek to undermine her husband's wishes. She glanced at George, hoping he had calmed a little. It was not good for his blood pressure to be so fraught.

Tucking an arm through his, she said, 'Come, dear, let's go home. The Stewartsons are coming for dinner and I want to organise the meal in good time.'

'I hope we've plenty of whisky, in that case,' he muttered. 'Going to need it if I've to listen to that old fool all evening.'

Rachel smiled to herself. Somewhere a clock struck five. She took a last look behind, pulled the heavy door to and locked it.

• • •

Through the study window, Robert watched the family carriage pull on to the forecourt and Thomson, the driver, open the door and stand aside for the de la Reys. All was not well, he could tell. Herman had warned him, had kept him in touch. He went into the hall to greet them.

'Hello, mother, you look as beautiful as ever,' he said, kissing her lightly on her cheek. A glance at his father's expression told him to go careful and he decided to wait until he had settled down with a drink.

'I understand you're off again,' George said at last.

'Yes, father, I leave quite soon.'

'You'll be home in time for Christmas, of course.'

'I'll try, sir.' A lie.

'The Stewartsons are coming tonight. I want you here with your mother and myself. They'll have Elizabeth with them.'

Robert's heart sank. Elizabeth Stewartson was the biggest bore.

'Now that the new offices are ready, I'll expect you to come back and manage a section for me.'

'Yes, I've seen Herman,' Robert replied, his voice flat.

'Can't do it all myself. You'll make a fine surveyor, then when you're established, I'd like to see you marry a woman like Elizabeth. She'll make a good wife. Can't stand the family, but they're rich. So think about it while you're in Savannah. That's all I've got to say.'

Enough, thought Robert. His entire future had been mapped out in seconds. A warning look from his mother told him to say nothing.

In his room, Robert took out the telegram Herman had handed him. Overjoyed to see it was from Savannah, he tore it open. 'MY DEAR ROB, GET THE HELL DOWN HERE SOONEST. WE ALL MISS YOU.' It was signed Ben Jefferson, December 1860. He scribbled a brief reply, left it for Herman to send, and made a note of what he would require for the journey. He would go as far as possible on horseback. He did not like train journeys.

Pouring a sherry, he slid a cheroot from its case and poked it between his lips.

Through the window a sprinkling of snow covered the streets. A newsboy shouted the latest political developments. Rob listened, aware of the tingling sensation inside him. Lighting the cheroot, he sent a cloud of smoke high into the air.

Two sherries later he strode through the now heavily falling snow, collecting a newspaper on the way. Tension filled the air as young lads lined the walkway discussing their intention to enlist should war break out.

Rob turned up his coat collar against the prevailing wind and headed home. The news headline was not good at all. Things were moving fast, so he would leave on the 14th. Some time later, he packed all the necessities; shirts, neckties, trousers, shaving kit, boots.

When the dinner gong sounded, he tidied his hair with the flat of his hand and checked his appearance in the long mirror. Voices below him told him the Stewartsons had arrived. He sighed. It was not going to be a lively evening. Elizabeth would stare adoringly at him, his father would no doubt encourage her. Perhaps he should have taken her long ago – she wasn't going to let up until he did, if then. A no-win situation. It was going to be a pleasure, however, announcing his date of departure. Might make that irritating smile fade.

Another look in the mirror and he was ready. He closed the door behind him and went down to the dining room.

• • •

Samuel Jefferson liked to watch the sun go down. The Plantation was at its best then, bathed in different colours and tonight was no exception. *Be glad to get between the sheets, though,* he thought. Must be getting old. Today the workload had really gotten to him. He sighed. A man had no right to feel tired at fifty-six, not with such beauty around.

He peered into the growing dusk. Out there was the best cotton land in Savannah, and the Jefferson cotton was purchased at good prices before being shipped off to France and England. Trade was at its peak, so why was he so tense? Because of all the talk of war. Why, they didn't speak of *if* but *when*.

Samuel looked at the house. How long would a Plantation house made mainly of wood survive a war? Then there was his family. Benjamin, his son, who would inherit everything, and his daughter, Jo-Ellen, who would one day marry and raise her own family. Expansion had been on his mind for some time. Another home next to this one would benefit his grandchildren, but with rumours of war, how could he plan anything? As these thoughts passed through his mind, Jo-Ellen ran down the steps on her way to the stables.

'Hey, girly, where you going? Ain't you going to evening prayer?'

'Not this time, Papa. I'm going to see if Rob's arrived. He's due any time now, so I thought I'd ride out and see if he's coming up the track.'

'Like you did yesterday and the day before that, and will probably do tomorrow. Don't you know which train he's due on?'

'He's not, Papa. He'll be riding in.'

Samuel shook his head. 'Do believe the boy's crazy. Why, when I was courting your Mama, I couldn't wait. Hopped anything so I could be with her. He don't seem too eager to get to you, Jo-Ellen.'

She laughed. 'Don't make no difference. I know how he feels, and I can wait it out.'

Samuel ran a hand through his unruly grey hair. The girl had become arrogant. All those fancy ways. Returned to them too headstrong. Never did go along with the idea of sending her to that girls' school in England – and most girls her age wore sensible clothes.

'You letting him see you like that? Ain't you wearing a pretty dress instead of them riding pants?'

Jo-Ellen led the mare out of the stable and threw a saddle over her back.

'Papa, Rob's used to seeing me like this. I'll dress pretty later on.' She mounted expertly and swung the horse.

'Don't stay out too long, it's getting dark!' he called, but knew she couldn't hear as she galloped off in a cloud of dust.

He lit a cigar. On the evening breeze came the sound of the congregation giving forth the first hymn. By rights he should have gone along with Constance. Not like him to miss evening prayer with his dear wife. He felt tired, more so lately and it worried him. What would happen if he could not run the business properly? The Jefferson Plantation was probably the best known industry south of the Mason-Dixon Line. Travellers knew well what it was they looked upon from the road that bordered the Plantation. Farmland stretched for many miles and thereafter cotton fields were all that met the eye. He was proud and justifiably so. The place was run efficiently with an air of peaceful co-operation, the reputation of which was well known outside Georgia. Businessmen travelled a long way to come there and they expected high standards. Well, they got them and it was all down to him.

Samuel turned from the dying sunset and went to the drinks cabinet. Pouring a double, he toasted the air. To hell with rumours, to hell with politics, here's to me, 'cause without me…He tossed back the contents of the glass in one go.

• • •

Jo-Ellen rode flat out, allowing the mare full rein until the lowland was behind and more rocky terrain slowed her to a walking pace. A breeze chilled the air, but she didn't care. She was excited, happy and hopeful.

Her thoughts centred on the moment she would see him again and the memories flooded back. Chasing across meadows – did he know she always allowed him to catch her? – feeling his arms around her, pulling her down, sitting astride her, laughing and teasing, always teasing.

How attractive he was, handsome really. A real man now, having just reached twenty-five. Would he have changed much? Family commitments had prevented his travelling whenever he wished and she knew he was coming this time because of the elections. Well, she thought, negotiating a steep slope, if it takes a political upheaval to bring Rob down south, then well done Abe Lincoln.

How would it be? she wondered. Would he want to kiss her immediately? First they would eye each other, play cat and mouse – she liked that part – then he would probably take her in his arms and literally sweep her off her feet. She looked into the distance where the hills met the edge of the cotton fields, and visualised Rob holding her, his lips on hers, smouldering, passionate.

Spurring forward, she rounded a bend and stopped. Far below something moved, a tiny dot as yet but definitely something. She waited. The something disappeared, then it was there again larger, clearer. She picked her way forward, and stopped again.

She shouted his name and urged the mare into a canter. It seemed an eternity, then all at once he was only twenty yards from her and she dismounted to run the rest of the way until they were locked in each other's arms.

That moment was magic for Jo-Ellen. She took a good, long look. Tall and striking, his voice rich and deep with the northern 'twang,' he scooped her into him a second time, then he was looking at her appraisingly and she knew he approved. At twenty her bosoms were full and firm, her waist small, the pretty girlishness of previous months replaced with a womanly elegance, a state that she had worked very hard to achieve.

'I've missed you so much, Jo.'

'I've missed you too, Rob. It's been too long this time. Did you ride the whole way?'

He chuckled and patted his horse. 'Of course not. We hopped connecting trains and here we are.'

They came to Early Ridge and looked down on the scene that held so many memories.

'Tell me, how's Ben? What's he up to these days?'

'He's fine and longing to see you again.'

'You know, whenever I'm looking at this view, I remember that day we all stayed out too long and your mama was so mad.'

'Yes, and Ben went off alone and you and I ended up in the old barn. He never did find us – at least, I hope not!'

She laughed gaily. That had been such a special day. Having just reached seventeen, she was expected to be at home learning to cook and sew and generally prepare for womanhood and instead there she was running around climbing trees. The sun had set late in the Savannah hills, on a day so tranquil as though promising never to end. Jo-Ellen remembered the prayer she had said to herself over and over – Please God, let it go on forever, keep tomorrow away, please God – because the following day Rob was to return to Pennsylvania. That was why she had allowed him to kiss her, and why they had remained hidden from Ben, for they had later made love for the first time there in the quiet, musty barn. She had loved Rob for years and it was the memory of those blissful moments together that had carried her through the lonely months.

'Doesn't it give you a pang?' he said beside her. 'God, how I've missed it all.'

'Then you should live here and not up there in that big city.'

'My father might have something to say about that, Jo,' he said.

She averted her eyes. All along she and Rob had been kept apart by his family.

'Nothing to stop you living up there with me, though,' he added.

'You know I'd live anywhere you want,' she returned, though deep down she wondered how she would fare without her beautiful Savannah. Having spent six years overseas, she was reluctant to leave Georgia again for good. Yet, one day she might have to. Her thoughts see-sawed constantly between Savannah and Philadelphia. Only twice had she visited Rob there and had not felt very welcome — not by his father, that is. Yet, her dream to become Mrs de la Rey would never be realised were she to remain where she was.

Rob took her in his arms and she lifted her face expectantly.

'How about riding down to the old barn?'

She readily agreed, leaning into him and savouring his masculinity. As they went, she said, 'You hear what's happened in South Carolina? They seceded on the 20th. Isn't that right, Rob?'

He grinned. 'Sure is.'

'Tell me, what does it mean, exactly?'

'It means they don't agree with northern politics or with our choice of president and want to go it alone. They've wanted out for a long time. And if other states take the same attitude, it could mean war, Jo. Folk are already preparing for it.'

'I hate fighting, you know that?'

'I know it. Hey, you sound so English at times. It's fetching.'

They came to the barn and dismounted. It was chilly inside. The winter sun had barely warmed it. Robert made a bed of hay.

'It's beginning to get very dark,' he murmured, peering through the small window. 'Reckon there's not a soul anywhere for miles.'

Taking both her hands he pulled her down beside him. She knew what was about to happen, realised that neither of them would try to stop it. He wanted her, she wanted him. His kiss was at first gentle, then passionate and her lips parted in response, allowing his tongue to explore her mouth. As his hands closed over her breasts, she turned into his arms.

Outside, a sharp breeze rattled the door on its hinges. Inside, they joined together to free all the pent-up emotions resulting from months of waiting and longing.

•••

Ben hadn't expected to inherit Jefferson House so soon. Along came his nineteenth birthday and it was suddenly his. Cantering away, he paused at the top of the hill to admire the white building with its mighty pillars. He was proud to be inheriting it all, though it was presently too large for just the four of them. One day, though, he and Jo-Ellen would require it and probably another like it for their families. How he looked forward to that day, to settling down, to loving a woman and raising children, to building the business together and watching his family raise their own children. What more could a man want out of life? His thoughts flew instantly to Susanne Montgomery.

Ahead he could see Earl staring absently at the numerous white clouds that drifted across the sky. As he reined in, the handsome black face broke into a grin.

'Now, what're you thinking about there, Earl?'

'Hello, Mr Benjamin.'

'Haven't I told you not to call me that? You know I don't hold with all that mister talk.' He tossed over an apple. 'Here, fruit's good for you.'

Earl bit into the apple. His new 'boss' had come to talk about something. He knew the signs.

'I've something important to say, Earl.'

'Sure, go ahead.'

'I suppose you've heard about Abe Lincoln and all.'

'Yessir, I heard, but I don't rightly know what it all means.'

Ben sighed. He was too tired to spell it out. Having taught Earl to read and write, he had hoped he'd worked it out for himself. Truth was, he and Earl had practically grown up together and now they seemed far apart. Nineteen had come along and changed everything. 'What are you thinking about now?'

'Nothing.'

'You're gonna spend your entire life thinking about nothing if you don't watch out, Earl.' Ben yawned, pulled a hand across his eyes. He was exhausted and it wasn't even midday yet.

'How's your ma. I ain't seen much of her lately.'

'Her heart's not good.'

'She out there?'

Earl nodded. His ma had been toiling since sun up.

Ben placed a reassuring hand on his shoulder. 'I'll do something about that. See she gets more rest. That's an order, Earl.'

'Yessir, Ben.'

'You know I'll always take care of her, don't you?'

'How do you know you'll always be there for us?'

Ben ignored the impudent question. Of course he'll always be there. This family had cared for him when Jo-Ellen had gone overseas, had seen to it that he had not been lonely.

'Look, I've mentioned this before to your ma and the way things are going it could become a reality. I want you to be overseer as soon as you're old enough, but meantime I want you to go free, and I want to pay you and your ma.'

'No thanks, Ben. I know you're thinking of us, but me and my mammy like things the way they are.'

Earl looked unsure and Ben knew he was only repeating what Hannah had said so often. *'I heard about so-called freedom but some of them bosses in the north are bad. Best to stay as we are, that way we've a roof over our heads and food in our bellies. Freedom don't always mean happiness.'*

Ben remounted and turned the horse in the direction of the Plantation. 'Okay, but think about it some more. And don't worry.'

He dug in the spurs, not entirely happy with the situation. When he got back he went into the library where his greatest friend was waiting. They had a drink and went riding, grown men now, with a lifetime ahead and several memories to call upon.

'Just as long as things don't get out of control down here,' Rob said grimly. 'If any more states secede, could be none of us will have much of a future.'

'Not a very cheerful forecast.'

'Things are moving fast in the north, Ben. Men are enlisting overnight. Won't be long now before they'll be on the march.'

Ben shook his head. 'I disagree. There ain't gonna be a war. Just a lot of hot head Yankee politicians causing trouble again.'

He smiled as he spoke, always remembering to keep anything political as light as possible. He reined in, his blond hair blowing wildly in the wind.

Rob said, 'You're out of touch, you know that?'

'Maybe, but I've read all the papers and the gist of it is that Abe Lincoln ain't too popular down here.'

'That isn't it at all. Lincoln's just bringing home to everybody the truth. Slavery's got to go, and you know it. Wealth has to be more evenly distributed.'

'So I agree slavery's got to go, but I for one don't want any drastic changes. Life down here suits me fine and now I'm master of the Plantation, I don't want trouble from a lot of hot heads trying to change history overnight.' They rode on in silence before Ben spoke again. 'You seem to be getting really involved, Rob. I mean, this war business and all.'

'Sure,' came the reply, 'Lincoln is the man to show us the way forward. He's a man of vision, surely you can see that?'

'You're sure he'll be elected?'

'Yes, but not because of the true majority but because his opposition's hopelessly divided.'

'A farmer's boy from Kentucky?'

'Yes, you wait and see.'

'How can he be a man of vision? How can the way forward be to stir up trouble between the states?'

'They're doing their own stirring and besides, the time is right. Matters can't go on the way they are.'

'Well, could be Lincoln won't get voted in after all.'

'Oh, he will. Feelings are running high.'

'And you, Rob – will you fight?'

'Looks as though I'll be working in an office. My father won't allow me to do anything else.'

'He'll stop it, you mean? He won't be able to.'

Rob chuckled. 'Then you don't know my father. He knows all the right people, remember.'

'Answer my question, Rob.'

Rob cast him a concerned look. 'Let's wait and see, shall we?'

'So, if this whole thing breaks, what about us?' Ben asked. 'If there's a fight, are you and I going to have to fight each other over this issue? Call that vision?'

'Nope, whatever happens we'll always be friends. Old Abe can't change that. And we can't change what's past, can we?'

Ben grabbed the bridle. 'Come on – let's race!'

They flew over grassland, jumped the fence that surrounded the Plantation and headed towards the river. Neither spoke again about the war.

• • •

It rained all Christmas Day. The Jeffersons celebrated as usual, and Rob stayed on longer than planned.

After his departure, Jo-Ellen's mood became flat and she locked herself away, sparing time only for her brother and it was to him one morning that she turned to confide her innermost feelings.

Looking very mature in a well cut suit, Ben filled a pipe and puffed on it thoughtfully, waiting for her to finish talking.

'I don't rightly know what to say to you, Jo-Ellen,' he said, looking through the window to where Earl was working hard loading the buggy with food supplies. 'I ain't much good with emotional problems. Guess all you can do is wait and see what happens.' He felt a little impatient with her. The Plantation took up all his time and he had none to spare for much else. 'You know Rob's the best friend I got,' he went on, his eyes still on Earl rein-slapping the horse into a steady trot. 'I'd like nothing better than to see you two get together, but give it time.' He turned to face her as Earl moved out of vision. 'You can't hurry these things. He's bound to miss you and then he'll probably make a decision.' If he's free to do so by then, he thought, and if he don't join up with them Yankees, which he's bound to do eventually since he is one.

She took hold of his hand. 'Thanks for listening. I just hope you're right. All this talk of war – suppose I never see him again?'

A grin of disbelief broke the contours of his face. 'Aren't you over-dramatising a little? Just forget it. Look, I've gotta go see to my work. It needs urgent attention.'

He made for the stables. Seconds later, he emerged with the Sorrell and swung into the saddle.

• • •

Jo-Ellen turned from the window. Today she would crochet. It might help get her mind onto a different course. Since Rob's return to Philadelphia, the weeks had passed too slowly for her. After South Carolina had pulled out of the Union she had watched events keenly and now it had been joined by Mississippi, Florida, Alabama, Georgia and Louisiana, and rumour had it that even Texas would shortly secede.

The final blow had come on March 4th when Abraham Lincoln was inaugurated as President, but at least that event produced a letter from Rob at last, rewarding her ebbing patience. His enthusiasm about the new presidency was evident by its content.

> *'My dearest Jo, So much is happening that I hardly have time to myself any longer. There is a great deal of excitement in the City. People are going wild. I took a trip to Washington city to watch the inauguration. Jo, I wish you had been with me.'*

Jo-Ellen smiled at this first mention of herself.

'So large a crowd as we stood in Pennsylvania Avenue under a harsh sun. I was half-blinded by the wind and dust, but it was worth it.

Abe Lincoln looked very solemn, even ill at ease, and there were so many bodyguards and security men. I caught a glimpse of President Buchanan. How old and white-haired he looked. Abe's speech was clever and I feel more confident than ever. Perhaps, God willing, the seceded states will now re-enter the Union.

We enjoyed ourselves last time, didn't we, Jo? I look forward to the next time, hopefully soon, though now I'm tied more than ever to the business. I miss you. Love to you and Ben.

Yours, Rob'

She read it over and over. There was hardly a word about his feelings and she shared the affectionate line at the end with Ben.

She drafted a reply immediately, unable to stop herself from pouring out her heart and soul. Could she come there and visit him soon? When was she going to see him again?

Her worst fears were realised on April 12th. The war officially began, thus delaying any further contact with her beloved. Jo-Ellen was sadder than anyone else, she declared. Rob had been taken from her and she was alone and in love.

Her mother tried to reason with her. 'You have to realise that there's a war on now and Robert's a Yankee. Your Papa won't allow you to see him, let alone marry him some day! And quite frankly, Jo-Ellen, I doubt if the boy will want a Confederate bride.'

'Mama, you forget that I'm also English.'

'Holding a passport don't make you English! And the way you speak don't change anything either. You're a southern girl – just remember that.'

Jo-Ellen felt the tears pricking. She had cried so much lately, it was a wonder there was anything left to come, but whenever her mother spoke like that, sure enough the tears started again. She longed for Rob, to feel his arms holding her.

'I love him, Mama, and I'm going to marry him if it kills me!'

Samuel overheard the outburst. 'Now you listen to me, girly. I won't have a daughter of mine fraternising with the enemy, for that's what they are now. Times have changed. The sooner you realise that, the better it'll be for all of us. Get yourself a southern man, not one who'll one day be pointing a gun at his own countrymen!'

'But, Papa, Rob's not in this war. Neither of us wants it. And he loves me – he's not fighting!'

'Not yet, but he soon will be. It won't be long before Lincoln whips them all into action up there, and even if the boy don't pick up a gun, Jo-Ellen, his heart's in the north and that's good enough for me!' He turned to the whisky bottle and poured a large one. 'Had I known you were gonna lose your head over him, I'd have put a stop to certain things long ago. What'll people think, a young girl galloping off in the night to meet a man – what'll they think? In future, I'll see you're chaperoned. Should've done that a long time ago.'

Jo-Ellen rushed from the room in distress. Papa just didn't understand. Come to think of it, he'd never understood!

To try and calm herself, she sat a while in semi-darkness and pondered love.

• • •

Samuel strolled onto the porch with Constance.

'What's going to happen to us all, Samuel?' she asked. 'What'll we do when the Yankees start fighting us?'

He pulled her close to him. The evening sun cast a glow over the countryside. The air smelt distinctly of wood fire.

'Sh, now, Constance. It's not coming to that. Just look over there. Can you imagine guns and killing in a setting like that? The good Lord won't allow it.'

'I hope you're right, Samuel. I surely hope you're right.'

They remained outside watching the watery sun settle behind the hills. There was hardly a dusk, for darkness followed immediately.

∙ ∙ ∙

April brought with it gusting winds and ceaseless slanting rain.

'Put the buggy away, Earl!' Jo-Ellen called, walking quickly through the wet weather to reach the house. In the drawing room a fire crackled in the grate and the warmth was welcome. No one else was there and this pleased her. She needed time alone to think about her situation.

Susanne Montgomery had been a great help that morning, listening to her and comforting her, but in the end she was still left with the problem. Jo-Ellen stared into the fire. What was she to do? Too often in the mornings she felt sick. Too often other signs told her she was pregnant.

Nothing had gone right lately. Political events made life nigh on impossible. She had waited for another letter, but none came. Now a nagging doubt bred within her mind and try as she may to banish it, it lingered and cast a gloom that she found difficult to hide from her parents.

Constance tried to cheer her up.

'He's probably very busy, dear. I expect his papa's business is expanding rapidly. He'd hardly have time to write letters and all. Well, would *you* have, Jo-Ellen?'

Even Samuel tried. 'The boy's probably taken up with other matters. He might even be at war already. Might not have your letters. Letters get lost these days.'

Jo-Ellen looked through the window and down the track that led towards town. No one came by these days, not the right people, that being the mailman and all. She took a poker to the fire and caught sight of herself in the mirror. How long before she began to show? How long before she would have to wear special gowns?

Constance came in. 'Ah, Jo-Ellen, I asked Jacob to leave the fire on – strange how chilly it still is. When is summer going to arrive, I wonder?'

Jo-Ellen took a deep breath. 'Mama, have you a few moments to spare?'

'Why, of course. What is it?'

'Sit down, Mama, I've something to tell you.'

• • •

Constance cried all night and Samuel refused to speak to Jo-Ellen properly. They blamed themselves for allowing their daughter so much freedom.

By May, the whole town knew and much gossip followed, but as political matters gathered momentum, Jo-Ellen's pregnancy became absorbed into daily life.

The idea first popped into her head on the first day that summer arrived. There was the summer rain, leaving everything fresh and clean, followed by a steady heat that set firmly in. That was when Jo-Ellen made her decision. First she told Susanne, then she steeled herself to face her parents.

'I've decided to journey to Philadelphia,' she announced.

'Whatever for?' Constance managed to keep her voice steady.

'To find Rob and tell him about the baby.'

'You can't go there alone – woman in your condition,' Samuel said. 'I won't allow it!'

'It's dangerous. Don't you realise there's a war on?'

'Only too well, Mama, but I'm going all the same. I can't stand being without him any longer.'

'That's what you think, girly. You're staying put and that's final! And what good's it gonna do you? Is he gonna wait to come and live down here or are you considering bringing your child up a Yankee? I tell you it won't work, Jo-Ellen. Best have the baby and forget the rest.'

She faced her father, defiance in her eyes. 'I'm all grown up now, Papa. I've fallen in love and I'm expecting Rob's baby. All I require now is a husband and I aim to go up there and get me one. I want Rob with me when I have his child!'

'Your Grandma would be appalled to hear you speak so, Lord rest her soul.'

Mention of Grandma Bella Williams made Jo-Ellen pause in her tracks. The old lady still wielded the power to do that, even though she had been dead the past eleven years.

'I'm sorry, Mama, but I ought by now to have my own opinion.'

'Yes, quite right, but this family still retains some rules and regulations. And they won't be forgotten, ever.'

'No, Mama.' Then, 'Tell me some more about her, was she very much in love with Grandpa?'

Constance smiled and cast a knowing look at Samuel. How many times had she been asked to talk about her dear Mama's personal life? Their daughter had reached that age when she needed to know her roots, needed something to romanticise about.

'Very much. Theirs was a marriage made in heaven sure enough. And you should have seen your Grandpa in his uniform, such a handsome man. I swear every woman in Savannah was in love with him.'

Jo-Ellen's face softened. Her eyes sought the photograph of Parker Williams amongst the other family photos on the sideboard. He'd been tall, slim, and striking.

'Let's get back to the present, shall we?' Samuel said.

Constance laid a restraining hand on his arm. 'Sam, there's nothing we can do. Let her go, but make sure she takes somebody with her.'

'All right, but you leave here against my wishes, Jo-Ellen. You should think about the baby, if nothing else.'

She gave him a peck on the cheek. Dear Papa. Did he not realise – that's precisely what she *was* thinking about.

• • •

That evening the Jefferson family sat down to an evening meal of cooked meats and salads. Prayer over with, Ben cut enthusiastically into the small piece of meat on his plate after helping himself to a portion of potatoes and salad. This he washed down with cold wine.

'Steady on, Ben, that's the second glass since you sat down,' Samuel said.

'Had a hard day, Pa, feel I need it.'

'And you, Jo-Ellen, you aren't eating much,' said Constance.

'I'm not hungry, Mama.'

'Remember, you're eating for two now.'

Jo-Ellen pressed a napkin to her lips and rose from the table. 'Think I'll go to my room, I've a slight headache.'

Ben forked the meat from her plate on to his. 'No problem, Ma, I can eat Jo-Ellen's share.'

The meal continued in silence, broken only by the occasional clink of china and cutlery. When the door opened and one of the servants entered, Samuel tutted irritably. 'Yes, what is it?'

'There's a soldier at the door, sir. Says he wishes to speak to Mr Jefferson. I tried to make him wait, but he insists.'

Samuel made to leave the table.

'No, sir, I believe he wants so see Mr Benjamin.'

Ben set down his glass. 'In that case, he will definitely have to wait.' He cleared his plate and finished his wine before sauntering to the door. 'Who the hell wants me at this hour anyway?'

The soldier stood smartly to attention, a youthful figure with the rank of lieutenant. 'Brigadier-General Beauregard sent me, sir. Have you received a dispatch from him yet?'

'Not to my knowledge. Why?' He knew of Beauregard. He was popular and prominent in the news lately for his involvement at Fort Sumter.

'Your presence is requested in the Confederate Army, sir.'

'What the hell!'

'Sir – these papers are to be signed.'

'Papers – what papers?' Ben snatched at them. After a brief glance, he threw them on to the hall table.

Samuel, having overheard through the half open door, came to join them. 'Did I hear you say Beauregard?'

The lieutenant nodded. 'That's right, sir. Says he knows the Jefferson family well.'

'Well, now, what do you know about that? Pierre Beauregard himself. Always thought that young man would do well for himself.'

'I thought this war was for volunteers only!' Ben snapped. The lieutenant explained at some length.

'I know Pierre quite well,' Samuel was saying. 'Guess we should be proud to have our son chosen personally by him.'

'Pa, I ain't going so get it out of your head!'

Ben went directly to the stables and saddled up, feeling sick in his stomach. Everyone knew he was against war, especially his Pa. It was something that happened to other people, the ones who wanted that lifestyle.

He rode as though his life depended on it, anger and frustration spurring him on. He was upset at his Pa's attitude. Anyone would think Beauregard was inviting him to a house party, not a war. Had Pa forgotten that he'd handed over the Plantation work in order to rest up? Who would do it all now? Perhaps he'd even forgotten that his only son might have to give his life, and what for – what the hell for? Things were only just beginning to make some sense. The business was showing a profit and he had the respect of his black workers. On the grounds of who would take on the work if he were not there, he would plead his case. Wars were for men with nothing better to do.

He slowed as Highlands came into view. Curtis, the Overseer, came out to meet him.

'Evening, boss.' He took the reins and led the horse to grassland.

'Evening, Curtis. Miss Susanne at home?'

'Yessir, boss, she in there somewhere.'

The house was cool and quiet. Ben wandered into the hallway and knocked on the drawing room door. Susanne's eyes lit up with surprise as he entered.

'Why, Ben, what brings you here at such an hour?'

He hesitated. God, she was beautiful. He felt like gathering her into his arms and making passionate love to her. Sitting there on the chaise longue, her golden hair tied back, she looked lovelier than ever. His eyes swept over her long neck and large green eyes that gazed into his. Feeling a rush of emotion he found hard to contain, he crossed the room and pulled her to him, kissing her firmly on the mouth.

'Benjamin!' She stepped back from him.

He felt suddenly foolish. His temper dispelled, logic had returned. He squared his shoulders and steeled himself for rejection. 'Dearest, I care for you. We've known each other for some time now...' He stopped. Why couldn't he say it?

'Yes, Benjamin, go on.'

When she looked at him like that, he was speechless. Even the wine he'd consumed with dinner was useless. He could do with a bottle of fine old Irish. That would loosen his tongue. What was she going to say when he told her he was off to the war? She would hardly want to become involved with a man about to leave her, and there was no time left in which to court her properly. Into his head popped the news item he had seen, that for three hundred dollars he could possibly buy himself out. At first he had been disgusted by the fact that rich men were sending in substitutes, but now it didn't seem such a bad idea, though where he'd find such a large sum he had no idea.

'I've received orders to go and fight. I'm to join the Confederate Army.'

Her eyes widened. 'Orders?'

'Look, I doubt if I'll have to go. That is, Pa can pull strings if I ask him to. He knows the general well and somebody has to stay home and run things.'

'But, if you have to go, you surely will?'

Her directness unnerved him. 'Well, yes, I guess so. Beauregard – he's the general – hasn't enough volunteers, apparently, so he's asking the rest of us nicely but firmly to join in. We don't have to but I agree that refusing would be wrong.' He paused. What did she want? Was he handling this correctly? 'However, having given it much thought, I decided that in my case there's good reason not to go. The Plantation, you see, and then there's the labourers…'

He was about to add 'and there's also you' when she said, 'Refusing would, of course, look like sympathy towards the Union, wouldn't it, Benjamin?'

He took a breath. 'Why, yes, I thought so too, you're right.' Goddam it.

'When do you go?'

'I think it could happen within days from now. Susanne – I've come here to ask you to marry me!'

Shocked silence. 'Marriage! But we haven't known each other long, not closely, that is.'

'It's sure as hell long enough for me. Oh, sorry.' He hadn't meant to swear. 'I love you, Susanne. Surely you know that? I've always loved you.' They had known each other since they were children and he had begun to see her on a more regular basis after they had met at a social gathering some months before in Savannah.

She indicated the seat beside her. 'Please Benjamin, sit down.' He did so. 'Now tell me, how do you know you love me? After all, I know you see others.'

'But, you're different.'

Hell, how could he tell her? He had hardly ever touched her and he was always careful to behave most properly. She had perhaps misconstrued this as lack of interest on his part. Truth was, he was scared. With the others it was easy, but he hadn't cared for them.

His mind went back to the day that Rob and Jo-Ellen had made off and left him by the river, and how he had followed them and eavesdropped. Watching them make love in the old barn, it had looked easy enough, but when he later tried it for himself, he had felt awkward and not up to standard. It was always better after a few drinks, at least he felt more confident. Later he took himself to a hodown, met a pretty girl and set about seducing her. He had suggested the barn, thinking that perhaps if it worked so well there for Rob, it might do so for him. The girl, whatever her name was, had considered the barn well below her, but consented nevertheless and he'd found the experience pleasant enough. Discovery of the female body excited him but he never fell in love. After that he had several girls, but no one special – until Susanne. She was sincere, with no doubtful background. She was also a year older than himself and this he liked for she was the same age as his sister.

'Different?' Susanne was saying. 'Tell me more.'

'I want you, I always have.'

He felt considerably embarrassed, but knew it was all or nothing. He was not a man who did things by halves. Intimidated by her gaze, he looked away. Why was he so darned hot under the collar?

'This is all very sudden, Benjamin. I don't know what to say.'

'Just say you'll marry me.'

He waited for what seemed an eternity while she considered. Then, 'Yes, my dearest, I'll marry you.'

He jumped to his feet. 'I can hardly believe it! Let's do it now – let's not wait!'

She laughed at his boyish eagerness. 'No, my parents and yours will want a proper wedding. This war will soon be over, ninety days is what they say and it could be even sooner. You'll be back before you know it. Then we can be married.'

He pulled her to him, his lips claiming hers passionately. No longer was he unconfident. She was his, all his. 'What I'm saying is, can we be together tonight?' he whispered.

She drew away. 'No, Benjamin, we must be patient.'

He kissed her again and her soft lips parted for him, he held her close against him, covered her face and neck with feathery kisses until she sighed and he felt her body weaken.

'Go now – please,' she urged.
Half dazed with longing, he left her.

● ● ●

Susanne went to the window. The sun had long gone behind the hills, casting a red glow over the countryside. Everywhere looked peaceful, hardly a fitting venue for war, she thought, but then people had so often overreacted in the past. She had no head for political matters, but even she knew it would not last very long. Some said days, others weeks.

Her attention focussed on Curtis who crossed her vision and disappeared into the house. Since her father's riding accident, Curtis had been given full power and he had proved himself very efficient. Indispensable, in fact.

She saw her father leave the house, moving with difficulty towards the stables. He was crippled now and unable to do much these days. She thought about her poor Mama. The last few months had been strenuous for her. Curtis had indeed been their strength and quite often their legs as well.

Her eyes took in the acres of farmland that met the edge of the surrounding countryside. One day it would all be hers. She was an only child with parents no longer in good health. Now that this silly war had come to threaten them, anything might happen. She and Curtis could manage for a while, perhaps, but what of the future? He was 25 years old, strong and good looking and she knew he had a woman somewhere in Savannah. Curtis was also a free slave and one day with all the pressure from the north, he might even want to leave her. Short as the war might be, what would happen then? She would be quite alone.

Turning from the window, she returned to her crocheting. Dear Benjamin. A surge of joy filled her at the thought of him. From the moment they had met again she had been secretly his. No other man interested her in the same way. Love had grown silently within and now she was free to give it.

• • •

It was dark as Ben rode along the valley towards the Plantation. He was in no hurry, not even tired. The moon hung large, the air was brisk. He felt unusually elated.

The woman he loved had accepted him. He could even face going to war now. Three months – it was not long. His Pa would have to manage and there was Earl and also Jo-Ellen to help out and perhaps his Pa would appreciate him more when he was not there. Halting at the fork in the road, he decided on the route that led into town. A man needed a drink after such a stimulating evening.

Savannah was very much alive as he cantered in. Noticing a card game in the saloon, he tethered the horse and went to join in. He lost a few dollars and drank plenty of liquor. The room was smoke-filled and he got quickly drunk. Something began to nag at the back of his mind, something to do with the Plantation. After refilling his glass he joined in another card game. Then into his mind popped potato cakes and yams, just before he passed out.

He woke propped against a wall, wandered outside to his horse and slid into the saddle. Walking at a slow pace, he reached the Plantation and crept into the house. There was no one about as he got between the sheets and sank into a deep sleep.

• • •

The rumpus outside woke him. Sunlight streamed into the room and he guessed it was close on midday.

Through the window he saw his Pa with shotgun in hand, and close by another man he did not recognize. Facing them was Earl and his stepfather, Jacob. Jo-Ellen had joined them and they were all talking at once. Ben hurried down the stairs.

'What the hell's going on here?'

'It's Hannah,' Samuel said, his face grave. 'She's been murdered out there on the road.'

Ben glanced at Earl's tear-stained face, and the grief-stricken Jacob. The stranger stepped forward.

'My name's Clem Levi. I run a farm about twenty miles from here.'

Ben nodded. He had heard of Clem Levi.

'It seems,' Samuel broke in, 'that Hannah went alone to her sister's place.'

Ben's memory returned. Potato cakes and yams! He had promised Hannah he would take her in the buggy to her sister's farm. He had promised! The sister was ill and Hannah had to go and so he was going to load the buggy with potato cakes and yams and fruit and take her there.

'On the way back she was attacked. Her heart couldn't take it,' Samuel added.

'Found the woman about a mile down the valley road. She was in bad shape – I mean...' Clem glanced at Jacob. 'They'd done terrible things to her. Brought her back here myself.'

'They? Who was they?' Ben demanded.

Clem shrugged, said he wasn't sure but two soldiers had been on the rampage and tried to raid his smallholding a while back. He'd managed to see them off, said they wore the Confederate uniform. 'Seems one of them was a sergeant name of Foley.'

Angry tears blinded Ben. 'We're grateful to you, Mr Levi.' He put out a friendly hand to Earl. The boy ignored it.

'You should have been there with her! She'd be alive now if you'd kept your word!' he shouted.

'Enough of this!' Samuel lifted the shotgun and said that Ben had not educated Earl to be accused like that.

'It's okay, Pa, leave it now.' What was the use of saying he was sorry? He looked at Earl, into those eyes that were now full of hate, went into the house and slammed the door behind him.

At sundown, when the workers returned from the fields and heard the news, they began a Negro spiritual, their mournful voices filling the evening air and penetrating the space that Ben occupied. He closed his window, could not shut out the sound so he poured the first of several brandies.

• • •

Jo-Ellen meanwhile prepared herself. She would go north. First she would travel by railroad then take a buggy for the remainder of the journey. And she would take Earl with her. Her papa had been right in that one matter. She could not go so far away alone.

'Them Yankees ain't gonna take kindly to a woman and her slave boy travelling together in their part of the country,' Samuel remarked as she packed together a few things.

'They probably won't even notice,' she replied, wondering why he always found it necessary to look on the dark side of life. She had planned her trip down to the last detail, had decided against telling Rob in a letter first. She would simply arrive and tell him about the baby and once they were together again, she was sure he would ask her to marry him. It was also necessary for his family to see them together, in fact, it was of paramount importance. Somehow she had to convince them that she and their son were meant for each other.

On her evening stroll, she went to Earl's hut. Best to prepare him, she thought. It might even help take his mind off his grieving.

Jacob looked up as she approached. 'Come in, missy. Can I get you anything?'

'No, thank you, Jacob. I've come to say I'm sorry about Hannah. We'll all miss her so.' He looked at her with such sorrow in his eyes, she decided to leave it alone. 'I've also come to see Earl. I want him to go on a journey with me.'

Jacob's eyes slid away from hers.

'It'll do him good,' she hastened to add. 'I simply cannot go without him. It's safe too – things aren't as bad as people make out. Jacob – is something the matter?' His silence alerted her. 'Jacob, please tell me.'

'I promised not to until he was well clear,' the old man said. 'He's all I got now, missy.'

She listened as Jacob explained that on the previous night Earl had packed a bag, took some food and left. 'I tried to stop him, missy, begged him not to go, but he wouldn't listen.'

'Go on.'

'I said he wouldn't get far, that there's only trouble for runaway slaves, but he still went. Said he was going looking for the Union army.'

'Oh dear, whatever for?'

'Said he wanted to join with them, said he wanted to kill Confederates. Said he was going looking for Mr Benjamin. Kept saying they'd killed his mammy.'

A cold fear took hold of Jo-Ellen. 'All right, Jacob, thank you for telling me.'

'He's jest angry, missy. You ain't gonna punish him?'

She shook her head. What was the use? Jacob had been through enough. 'No, I'll not report him.'

On the way back to the house she decided that her plan to travel north would have to be shelved for the time being. What seemed like a heavy weight pressed on her as she went up the marble stairs to her room. Earl had surely taken leave of his senses. She prayed he would return to the Plantation. His mission to seek out Confederates and Ben in particular, gave her great cause for concern. Her brother had gone to join the Confederate Army of Northern Virginia.

Quite suddenly the war had become both personal and very, very close.

Chapter Two

That summer Samuel tried to trade wheat and cattle as well as cotton, but his efforts were hampered by poor connections resulting from inefficient railroads. Lincoln had placed a blockade on all southern ports, and this cut supplies to a minimum. Samuel began to worry more and more. He would be hard pressed to keep his business from falling apart.

Jo-Ellen helped all she could, but with Ben and Earl gone, daily life at the Plantation became difficult. More often than not she was forced to take it easy and sometimes spent whole days resting. It was on such a day that she and Constance sat in a shady spot under a sun so hot that the shade did little to alleviate the discomfort.

Fanning herself under a fashionable wide-brimmed hat and sipping cold lemonade, Constance said, 'Why, you'd never know there was a war on, Jo-Ellen. It's so peaceful out there.'

'Papa would disagree with you, Mama.'

'Yes, I must confess I hardly see him these days. Oh, I do wish Ben were here to help out. When I remember how things were this time last year. Last week I went into town to buy some supplies and they cost me twice as much!' She patted her brow with a lace kerchief. 'As for you, Jo-Ellen, any day now there'll be another mouth to feed and you with no husband and all.'

It was said kindly, but found its mark. Any reference to Rob's absence from her life hurt Jo-Ellen deeply. She got to her feet.

'Now, where you off to?'

'I think I'll go visit Susanne. I hear her folks are poorly.'

'All right, but you take care now. Make sure Jacob goes with you.'

Jo-Ellen beckoned to Jacob. 'I'm driving over to Highlands. Help me into the buggy.'

'I'll go along too, missy. It ain't safe for you alone.'

'No, I'll be quite safe. You may tell the master, but only when I'm gone.'

'But, missy...!'

'Do as I say, Jacob. It'll be all right – I'll see you won't be blamed.'

'Yes'm, missy.' He stepped aside as the buggy shot past.

The drive was tiring. The horse took its time in the heat of the day. On the breeze came the sweet fragrance of roses, crab-apple and violets. Jo-Ellen urged the horse faster but it resisted.

If only she didn't feel so restless. There was, within her, a strong desire to do something, not sit around waiting for a baby to arrive. If only women could go and fight for their country, take out their aggressions on the battlefield. She sighed. Having overnight leaped the gap between adolescence and womanhood, she was not sure she was ready. She missed those days running free with the boys. So much had changed. Her whole life, she concluded, had changed drastically. And now she was about to become a mother, inviting sharp criticism and gossip.

As soon as she reached Highlands, Susanne came out to greet her and they went into the drawing room where it was cooler. Jo-Ellen marvelled at the fact that to this day she had not seen all of Highlands and wondered how Susanne managed so well with so few workers.

'I had thought to buy more since Papa's accident but the war has put paid to that idea.'

'And your Mama, I hear she's poorly.'

'The doctor called just this morning. Her heart's not too good.' Susanne poured two glasses of lemonade. 'Ben's asked me to marry him. I said I would.'

This news was met with a squeal of delight. 'That's wonderful! I knew you were seeing each other, but never thought...when is it to be?'

'As soon as he gets back. We haven't told our folks yet.'

'Then I won't say a word.'

'Now, tell me about the baby, Jo-Ellen. I was so excited when I heard.'

'You were? Then you were the only one. You didn't mind my not having a husband?'

'Heavens, no. Why should I? I know how much you love each other. What will you call it?'

'Alexander.'

'And if it's a girl?'

'I don't know yet, but it's not a girl.'

Susanne gave a chuckle. 'How do you know that?'

'I just feel it. The news certainly woke up Savannah. They spoke of nothing else for weeks.'

'You must pay no heed to them. Half the women round here are only jealous, anyway.'

Jo-Ellen rose and moved to the window. It was such a beautiful day. The lawn sloped up to the house and it was the purest green she had ever seen, set off by a colourful array of blossoms.

'Now that you're to be family, so to speak, I've had a brilliant idea. In fact, it's been on my mind for a while.' She faced Susanne, her eyes alight with enthusiasm. 'Why don't you and I – I mean, your Papa and mine, amalgamate?'

Susanne looked puzzled. 'How?'

'Well, we're both having hard times. Together we could run one business – your tobacco and rice, our cotton and cattle. Curtis and Jacob, your workers and mine.'

Susanne was silent. 'Is it possible?' she said at last.

'Of course. Our plantations adjoin each other and it would only be while the war is on.'

It was a good plan, might help solve the labour problem if nothing else, Susanne thought. Ben would be delighted as well.

'It's a wonderful idea. Now all we have to do is convince our Papas of the fact.'

Jo-Ellen tucked an arm round her. 'I'm so excited. Oh, if only Rob were here!'

'He will be, I'm sure.'

'Are you, Susanne, are you really?'

'Yes. I know it's been some years since I met him, but I liked him and could tell he was so in love with you even then. When he hears he's about to be a father, he'll come running fast. You wait and see.'

'And you don't think it strange he hasn't answered my letters?'

'No. They are probably all held up somewhere. They'll get through eventually.'

'That's done me a power of good. Ben is fortunate finding a wife like you, Susanne.'

'I'm counting the days off the calendar. I pray he'll be safe. I do worry about him so.' Susanne raised her glass. 'Come, let's not be morbid. Let's drink to the future and to our business. We must not think the worst, but the best.'

Jo-Ellen raised her glass. 'To the Plantation. Both of them!'

• • •

Just outside Washington, an army was drilling hard under an irate sergeant who knew best how to handle the whooping, singing hordes of volunteers ready to fight for the south.

On the morning of July 5th, Ben rode in, not alone, for about that time volunteers and conscripts poured in from everywhere. Each was dispatched to a section for instant drilling and reorganising.

Ben had little time to think of the things closest to his heart, and it was only at night when his head touched the bolster that he allowed thoughts of Susanne into his mind, bending over him, touching him, and even though they had not yet made love properly, he knew how it would be.

He met several soldiers during those early days, the one he admired most being Thomas Jackson, but the man was an oddball, he had to admit. A West Pointer from Virginia, Jackson rode grim-faced on his white horse, an awesome picture. When Ben was introduced to the man under whose leadership he was to begin his days as a soldier, he saluted smartly and stood to attention. Brigadier-General Pierre Gustave Toutant Beauregard, nicknamed Old Bory by his men, cut a romantic sort of figure. At 43, he had risen sharply to command and rumour had it that he was due any day to become Major-General.

Ben shook his hand, feeling rather grand in his new grey uniform, and with an air of confidence for the first time since arriving in Virginia. Under the harsh lamplight, Beauregard leaned back in his chair, his dark eyes penetrating. A heavy moustache covered his upper lip.

'Private Jefferson, when I issue an order, I expect it to be obeyed!'

Ben blinked. What now?

'You were offered a commission.'

'Yessir, I refused it, sir.'

'When I give the command to charge, you going to refuse that as well?'

'No, sir.'

'Then why didn't you take the commission? Not up to it?'

'Yessir!'

Best not to tell Old Bory that he didn't want any responsibility of command. A few months doing what he was told to do, then he would be out.

'As soon as you've finished your training, Jefferson, I want to see you here again.'

Ben saluted and left. Back at his quarters, which was a tent he shared with Private Elisha Sheldon, he said, 'It was strange, he didn't say much, just stared right at me, sizing me up, then told me to go and see him again when I finish training.'

'Tiny' Sheldon, a large man with an agreeable nature, grinned. 'A good sign, soldier. You gotta go through the sergeant's hands first and anybody who survives that sure is on the ways up. If'n the Brigadier-General wants to see any greenhorn afterwards, it could mean promotion.'

'Except I ain't going to be here that long. The war's not going to last and darned if I want to stay and make a career out of it. Just doing my duty, that's all.'

Tiny shook his head. 'You won't have any say in the matter, Ben. They give the orders – you obey.'

'You mean I'll get a different rank, regardless?'

'A higher rank, soldier. Cain't get no lower than you are.'

• • •

On the evening of July 20th, Ben lay on his bunk, gazing up at the crude canvas that divided him from the humid air and the large bright stars. He felt fit, but very tired. The past days had been given entirely to training, firing guns, and taking orders from the sergeant, whose shrill voice seemed to echo through his head even now. Tiny was on watch and that gave Ben time to be alone, to think. He felt content, even though he was so far from home, from the family he loved and the countryside he grew up in. His thoughts centred on the day he and Susanne would marry and a surge of pride shot through him.

The tent flap opened and in came Tiny. The big man stood at the entrance in his ill-fitting uniform, beads of perspiration on his brow.

'You sleeping?' he asked.
'Nope. You been relieved already?'
'Yep, ain't too soon neither.'
'Hey – you all right?'

Tiny lowered himself on to his bunk. 'Sure – just tired, that's all. Don't wake me till the war's over.'

Ben looked closely at his friend. He didn't look too well. He liked the gentle giant immensely and he trusted him. Their friendship had grown quickly, they had exchanged addresses already and Ben was sure that after the fighting and they were sent home, Tiny would be a regular visitor to the Plantation. At night they spoke of their hopes for the future and Ben learned that all Tiny wanted for himself was a woman, a home and a son.

'My aim is to bring up a boy,' he'd told Ben. 'Sure I want success in my farming business and wealth aplenty, and I've had women aplenty too, but there's one back home I've a mind to marry. None of it will make me happy, though, until I have my boy.'

'Say it's a girl?'

'I'd not complain, but I'd jest keep right on trying for my boy.'

As soon as Tiny's heavy breathing turned to loud snores, Ben stepped outside for some air. A banjo played somewhere and through the darkness came the lilt of an Irish tenor. The familiar 'Dixie' was sung with much gusto, accompanied by laughter, and Ben gathered that morale was high despite the conditions. When the tenor began a love song, slow and thought provoking, he paused to listen to the words.

The music stopped. Men grouped round a senior officer who quietly briefed them. 'Looks like trouble, soldiers. The Feds are pushing in on us at Manassas Creek.'

Ben ran back to the tent as a bugle sounded. Uniforms went on at speed and figures dashed about at the double. He shook Tiny. 'Come on, wake up! The Feds are here!'

Tiny sat up slowly, and with eyes still closed he jumped to his feet and grabbed his kit.

They rallied with the other trainee soldiers from Army headquarters in Manassas. They were about thirty miles west of Washington in northeast Virginia, a strategic location as the village of Manassas lay at the junction of two railroads. One of these led to the

Shenandoah Valley, sixty miles away, where General Johnston commanded a force of some 8,000 Confederates to reinforce the 18,000 that stood ready under General Beauregard.

When a lull came, the silence was like an electric current. Nerves were taut, fingers tense on triggers. Federal forces ceased to advance and bided their time as the main contingent of Confederate forces anchored themselves along the Warrenton Pike at the stone bridge. As Ben waited, entrenched with others in a meandering eight mile line along one side of the Creek, his mind began to race. He'd been trained to kill, but was he ready? When the general gave the command, he would have to open fire on any blue uniform that advanced on him through the morning mist. But would he be able to kill? Only if it saved his own skin, he decided. Shooting out of hand was not for him. And he knew too many of them Yankees. Some meant the world to him – Rob and his family, definitely Rob. He relaxed his grip on the weapon as his friend passed through his mind and a pang of despair shot through him as he imagined Rob on the receiving end of his first unleashed bullet.

A distant drum drew his attention. His grip on the rifle tightened once more.

• • •

A chink of brightness lit the horizon as the Federal Army, led by General Irwin McDowell, advanced towards what they called Bull Run Creek. They moved slowly to the arched stone bridge that spanned the brownish river before it became a stream fringed with marshland and briar.

Ben raised his head to watch. What the hell was going on? The scene before him was a sauntering mass of soldiers, most of them wandering about picking ripe blackberries.

'Christ, this ain't no picnic!' a voice cried. 'What are they up to?'

'They ain't in no hurry, that's for sure,' said another.

It was as late as eleven o'clock when action began. From a distance came a Federal order. 'By the left flank, march!'

From every corner of Bull Run Creek, Federal troops emerged, pouring like ants over the rough, forested terrain, the rays of the morning sun picking out the bright blue of their uniforms. Bullets whined overhead and Ben ducked out of sight.

Beauregard gave the order to fire. Taking careful aim, Ben squeezed the trigger. A faceless enemy running towards him fell. Another soldier fell, then another and another. He stopped firing. Hell!

The Federal attack was strong, their mission to take Richmond, the Confederate capital. Another order from Beauregard to close in and engage in hand-to-hand fighting and Ben left his position to close with the nearest blue uniform, knocking him down with the butt of his rifle. As the man lay on the ground, he shot him at point blank range. Oh, God!

Union cannon hurtled across the Creek into the wood beyond and a thick cloud of smoke covered the area for miles. From out of the murky atmosphere a horse and rider were cut down, his sword flying through the air and landing close to Ben. He picked it up and, after checking that the officer was dead, he blindly lashed out at another blue coat. No more than nineteen, Ben thought fleetingly as the soldier died in agony. When a bullet whined so close to his head he felt it, he threw himself forward and crawled to safety. So much smoke, so much noise.

Across his vision raced a figure and Ben could have sworn it was Tiny Sheldon.

'Christ – what's he doing!' He watched as Tiny moved forward and ducked out of sight. The smoke thinned momentarily but he could no longer see his friend. He waited, praying he was safe. Had Tiny stumbled? Dreading the worst, Ben decided to take a look.

He ran zigzag through the dust clouds and hid behind a clump of foliage. Ahead he could see Tiny lying face down in a pool of blood. Staying low, he managed to get to him. He cradled his head, tried to revive him.

'Hey, don't give in, not now! Remember your boy, remember all your plans!'

But Tiny's eyes were unseeing. Ben covered him with his jacket, tears streaming down his cheeks. 'Goodbye, soldier, I'll miss you. I'll surely miss you.'

He barely remembered running back to join the others. Beauregard's voice could be heard above the din of battle and Ben crouched out of sight to become a spectator to the confusion and disarray around him. Several of their men had run from the field, and he too felt like running away.

An aide rode through the smoke screen with a message and Beauregard paused to read it. Even from there, Ben could tell there was trouble. Beauregard looked desperate. Rumours were whispered down the line. Federal regiments were crossing the stone bridge, and three northern divisions were about to cross the stream. Beauregard's flank was turned. They were considerably disadvantaged.

Ben rubbed a hand across his face and eyes. Only a miracle could save them now. A shout went up, there was commotion to the left. From out of the smoke Brigadier-General Jackson rode in with what looked like thousands of reinforcements. He gave another shout, rallying his men into a strong impenetrable line. This was the chance Beauregard needed, and spirited by this unexpected turn of events, he urged his men to surge forward again to attack. It was late afternoon before the tables were turned and the Federal forces withdrew.

When the firing ceased, the silence was sickening. The dead and dying lay about. Ben dragged himself to his feet, his trousers torn, dust and mud covering him, and blood pouring from a gash in his shoulder. The world spun, the ground came up fast. Someone bent over him, a distant face, a distant voice. Barely conscious, he was lifted and carried into a tent and lain on a bed amongst other troops. The stench was dreadful. He opened his eyes, *this must be hell – it is hell* – his last thought before he passed out.

When he woke, his wound had been cleaned and dressed. A nurse bent over him, soft, warm, feminine. Like Susanne.

'You're in Mathews Stone Field Hospital,' she told him before disappearing from view.

'Take it easy,' said an orderly. 'The nurse is off duty for five minutes. You been out for hours. Been shouting and carrying on, but I had to agree with what you said. It sure is hell. That's what you said over and over.'

Ben lay back, trying to recapture the last hours. Tears pricked his eyes. Somewhere a door opened. The nurse wiped his forehead. 'How are you feeling?' she asked.

He reached for her hand. For him, Susanne was there beside him.

'I'm fine now, just fine.' The tears came then, ran unheeded down his face. He was over his first major crisis.

• • •

As soon as Ben left the hospital, General Beauregard sent for him.

He stood to attention and waited as Beauregard studied some papers on his desk then looked up, a hint of a smile on his face.

'Glad to see you're well again, Jefferson. How's the arm?'

'Not so bad, sir.'

'Good, good. Off for a bit of leave now?'

'Yes, sir.'

'Yes, I put in for that. Insist you go home for a well-earned rest.'

'Thank you, sir.'

Ben watched as the recently promoted Beauregard walked slowly round the desk towards him. 'You helped save my life, Jefferson.'

'Sir?'

'My horse – a shell exploded and killed it. I was unhurt but when I got to my feet I saw a rifle pointing at me and a bullet aiming at my head. But then in you came and cut the Fed down.'

Ben relived the sound of his sword sinking into the youth's flesh. Beauregard was holding out his hand.

'I thank you, Captain Jefferson.'

Captain! Did he want this? 'Thank you, sir.'

'You're where you should be – in the Cavalry.'

As he made to leave, Beauregard said, 'Remember me to your father, Captain.'

Back at his quarters, Ben sat head in hands staring at Tiny's bunk. Captain Jefferson. One battle, hundreds dead, his friend killed, and he was a captain already. How would he live with that? Tiny had said he would be promoted and he was. But what in God's name for? Home – he had to get home, back to sanity. The next few hours were spent preparing to return to Savannah.

...

Earl went north. Northward might lead to an army that would take him. All that first night he travelled on foot and as dawn began to break beyond the distant hills, he found a tree off the beaten track and lay down to rest. He slept well and some hours later, set off again.

Refreshed after eating some food, he pressed on until eventually crossing the line which divided Georgia and South Carolina. Not a soul passed his way as he headed in the direction of Raleigh, North Carolina.

His mammy's words tormented him. Running away carried a heavy punishment. If I'm caught, he kept telling himself, only if I'm caught.

What if he were caught by the Confederates? Perhaps they wouldn't even bother to question him. They didn't take 'niggers' in their army. The Yankees, though, would wonder why a black boy was travelling so far from home. He had no papers declaring him free so they might even think of sending him back. The last thing they would do would be to enlist him. Union forces didn't take 'niggers' either. So what was the point? Running out had been just plain stupid. He couldn't go forward, he couldn't go back. Back home there would be trouble waiting. This thought spurred him onward as the late afternoon sun bore down and dust flew into his eyes.

It was some hours before he heard the train. He panned the horizon, saw ahead a railroad and scrambled down the incline, hiding until the train chugged into view. It passed slowly and he was able to pull himself into the last carriage.

The train gathered speed through the Virginia countryside. Darkness brought a chill and Earl huddled in the corner of the carriage, now and then dozing off. Soon a dash of bright light on the horizon told him that dawn was about to break and he read from an old signpost that they were approaching a place called Manassas Junction.

The train halted and he wondered if there was anybody other than the driver on board. It was some time before he stirred from the carriage. As the light grew brighter, his attention was drawn to what looked like a dark snake moving across the countryside. Soldiers! He could see them clearly now, their leader astride a fine horse and there on the left another spectacle – a mass of people, some in buggies, others walking, most carrying gaily coloured parasols and picnic baskets, making their way over the Creek by way of its bridge.

The soldiers halted, the spectators did likewise. Suddenly there was a loud 'Hurrah!' Someone shouted a command and hundreds of the soldiers charged forward. A sound like thunder rippled through the countryside.

Earl watched, charged with excitement. He had never seen the

Federal Army, had only heard about them, about how grand and powerful they were. Guns fired, cannons boomed, grey uniforms merged with blue. The killing began.

The onlookers, who until now had enjoyed the spectacle, fled back to where they had come, some stranded on the bridge as bullets whined into them. Parasols flew into the air, picnic baskets were abandoned. This sickening turn of events startled Earl as what had been a venue for sight-seeing and relaxation became a bloody mess.

Frightened, he took the opportunity to climb from the carriage and run from the scene. When he saw a farmhouse ahead, he crept up to the window and peered in. On the table was a loaf of bread. Hunger drove him. If he was very quick, he could be in and out without being noticed. He opened the door, grabbed the bread and helped himself to a chunk.

'Hold it right there, sonny.'

Paralysed with fear, Earl turned to face a shot-gun. On the other end was a woman.

'Ma'am, please, I don't mean no harm.'

'Tell me, you on the run? The truth, now.'

'Yes, ma'am. I ran out in Savannah.'

'Where you headed? Canada?'

'No, ma'am.'

'Did they ill-treat you. That why you're running?'

'No, can't say that they did, ma'am. I jest came in for some food, honest.'

'So I see. Look at the mess you made of my bread!'

'I'm hungry, ma'am. I don't mean no harm.'

The woman lowered the gun. 'You know something, boy, so am I. Let's eat.'

She produced cold meats and potato, which Earl demolished and washed down with lemonade.

'You're not part of that fighting going on over there?' she asked.

He shook his head, cramming more bread into his mouth.

'No, of course you ain't.'

'But I saw it all,' he said.

'And I heard it. Was going to shoot the first soldier that set foot in here.'

'Why, ma'am?'

'Cause I don't hold with fighting. When a man kills his own, then the world's got big troubles.'

'But you said…'

'I didn't mean I'd kill him, just shoot and scare hell out of him. I ain't in this war, sonny.' She hesitated. 'Oh, mah name's Emily.'

He shook her hand. 'I'm Earl. You gonna report me, ma'am?'

'Report you? Lordy, no, that goes against everything I feel strong about. I'm anti anything that takes away a man's right to live proper, so you knocked on the right door, Earl. You eaten enough?'

'Yes, ma'am.'

'Then get some sleep. You can use the room at the back.'

Earl was curious. 'You Union, ma'am?'

She placed her hands on her large hips. 'Listen, boy, I got me one son Union, another Confederate. My brother, he's with Jackson's lot and my brother-in-law's fightin' alongside McDowell. If I'm anything, I'm confused!'

He left her sitting by the window, shotgun in hand, her face turned towards the black smoke that curled high above the Creek.

• • •

As Susanne tended the forsythia in the drawing room, Jo-Ellen put the finishing touches to her crocheting. Neither spoke, each caught up in her private world as thoughts of their men and the growing war dominated their minds. Outside, the visibility was perfect and Susanne occasionally looked beyond the maple trees to where the workers toiled in the fields. Her attention was caught by a rider galloping across her vision and she moved quickly to the veranda as Curtis reined in.

'Missy, missy, I thought you should know!'

'What is it, Curtis?'

'I was down in the fields and I done saw me a soldier riding by. So fine and proud and when he waved, I could swear it was…'

Susanne rushed past him down the steps, through the small gate and across the dirt track alongside the fields. Stopping only once to catch her breath, she saw him cantering over the brow of the hill.

'Oh, my!' Gathering her skirts again, she ran until she was in Ben's arms.

'God, how I've missed you,' he whispered, scooping her into him.

She felt his hunger and passion and when he lowered his mouth to hers she responded with every fibre of her body. Ben was home again – nothing else mattered. He covered her face with kisses and held her so close she could scarcely breathe. It was then that she noticed his shoulder.

'You're hurt! What happened?'

'Nothing to be alarmed about, dearest.' But she was alarmed and so he told her how he came to be wounded. 'I was promoted and ordered home on leave.' He handed over his horse to Curtis. 'This is where I want to be. You've no idea how I've waited for this day.'

As they approached the house, the door flew open and Jo-Ellen ran to him.

'Shouldn't you be resting?' he said, hugging her to him.

'Resting's all I ever seem to do. How long you home for, Ben?'

He motioned to his bandaged shoulder. 'Until this is better.'

'Do tell us about the war. We hear so little. Is it as horrible as they say?'

Ben outlined some events, careful not to go into too much detail. Jo-Ellen listened carefully, her thoughts on Rob.

Anticipating another question from his sister, Ben said, 'How about a glass of brandywein to celebrate my homecoming?'

'Of course – Curtis, bring us some and then go tell everybody that the master's home.' Susanne clutched Ben's hand and led them into the drawing room.

Jo-Ellen hung back. They were so in love. 'I'll not have any, if you don't mind. I'll leave you two alone.'

When she had gone, Ben said, 'I've come home to marry you, Susanne. Say you won't make me wait a minute longer.'

She clung to him, happier than she had ever been in her life. More than that, she felt secure. No, she would not wait out the war as planned. She wanted him – now.

'Tonight,' she whispered, 'tonight we'll be together. And tomorrow at the party, we'll announce our wedding day.'

• • •

They chose a beautiful August day. Savannah's faded elegance came alive in a spectacle of colour as folks from miles around arrived with floral displays and numerous small gifts.

For those few hours there was a joyfulness in the air, as thoughts of war were set aside. A celebration such as this was just what they needed to boost their morale.

Susanne glowed with happiness, aware of the admiring looks and favourable comments as she arrived at the church. Interested male glances made her acutely aware of her slender, firm body as she moved slowly down the aisle on her father's arm. He led her with difficulty, but Ralph Montgomery was as proud as any father could be whilst her Mama sat in the front row, a lace kerchief held to her cheeks ready for the tears.

Ben looked at his bride. The sight of her took his breath away. Only one thing was missing today, he thought, allowing a sad moment into his happiness, and that was Tiny Sheldon.

Susanne smiled and placed her hand in his as the Reverend Charles Biddell began the service.

• • •

Jo-Ellen sat at the back of the church watching her brother marry her dearest friend, trying not to show the emotion she felt. One day, God willing, she too would stand before the altar with Rob and she would swear to love and cherish from that day forward, for better, for worse, for richer, for poorer.

The procession filed past and the gaiety began. Music, dancing, food, and wine. She cast around, excited by all the new faces. Her eyes travelled from one to another until they finally came to rest on one man. He had noticed her also, for he grinned and raised his glass to her.

'Sister dear!' Ben bore down on her. 'Susanne told me the news. You and she managing the plantations together. Good idea, though you'll need more workers, especially now Earl's gone.' He shook his head. 'Hell, why'd he go and do a thing like that?'

'Now, don't you go worrying about those things today, Ben.'

He grinned. 'Know something? You're right. To hell with everything until tomorrow, and maybe not even then.'

'Just go easy on the brandy.'

'I intend to. This is one night I want to remember.'

'Tell me, Ben, who is that soldier over there?'

He followed her gaze. 'That's Major Daniel Hunter. I met up with him at Manassas. We hit it off so I asked him to the wedding.'

'Introduce me.'

'What?'

'Introduce me. Oh, he's coming over.'

'Ben – congratulations!' The stranger held out his hand. 'And may I know who this lovely lady is?'

'Jo-Ellen, my sister.' He gave her a knowing look. 'Meet Daniel Hunter.'

She held out her hand and he collected it into his.

'Very pleased to meet you, Jo-Ellen.' She noticed his very blue eyes and the greying hair at the temples, the neat moustache above a generous mouth. A handsome man, she decided, directing her most charming smile his way. 'Ben seems to surround himself with beauty,' he added, releasing her hand.

As Ben excused himself and headed off in the direction of his guests, Daniel turned his attention fully on Jo-Ellen. 'So, I've met you at last. Ben speaks of you often. What a lucky man, and Susanne is a lovely bride.'

'I'm thrilled she is now part of our family. We've been friends for many years.'

'Ben tells me you were once in London.'

'Why, yes, Major.'

'Please, call me Daniel.'

'All right – Daniel. I went to a private tutor in London then finished off my education there at a college for girls before returning to Georgia. I was about sixteen when I saw my family again.'

'I expect you missed them very much.'

'Yes, especially Rob. He and Ben are great friends, too. Rob lives in Philadelphia.' She glanced across to where Ben was talking to a group of well-wishers. 'Ben looks so happy and that makes me happy too. I hear you met each other at Manassas.'

Daniel nodded. 'Yes, in Mathews Stone Hospital. His shoulder was quite bad.'

'And you?'

'Oh – just stopped a bullet in my leg.'

'Oh, my – is it better now?'

'Save for a slight limp, splendid. Shall we have a drink?'

He motioned to a waiter and ordered cognac. Jo-Ellen liked him, enjoyed his baritone voice. The insignia displayed on his shoulder and the gold star on his collar completed the picture.

'Have you ever been to England?' she asked.

'Spent some of my childhood there.' He handed her a glass of cognac. 'Well, cheerio, as they say.'

She asked him to tell her about the war. 'Ben seems to not want to talk about it. Thinks we women should be protected from such matters and I'm longing to know.'

'What can I tell you?'

'What's it like out there? Are the Federal Army strong? Were there many casualties, things like that.'

Daniel set his drink to one side. 'Security prevents me from telling you certain things, but yes, they're strong all right. They've got the financial backing, you see, and the manpower. However, we have the better generals, in my opinion. But Abe's no fool. He's now offering $100 for men to volunteer for a two-year period. That's official.'

'Two years! But, I thought…'

'Yes, so did we.'

'Isn't that serious?'

'It could be. Up until now they've been in for a three month period only. Can't really train a man in so short a time, though. I wouldn't underestimate them. We've been winning so far, but two years, now that could bring real results.'

'So, our men might have to enlist for the same period?'

'Yes. As for casualties, with respect, I don't think this is quite the place to discuss such matters.'

'No, forgive me. I was just curious.'

'Jo-Ellen, you don't seem the kind of young lady to show morbid curiosity. Do you know somebody in this war?'

She lowered her lashes.

'May I know who it is?'

'It's unlikely that you know him.'

'I'm being inquisitive, I know, but I'm privy to many a conversation about our boys' activities. Who knows what I might hear?'

Jo-Ellen hesitated. 'His name is Robert de la Rey. I'll show you a photograph.'

'De la Rey. No, can't say I know that name. The only way to make sure is to get in touch with the officials in Virginia. When I'm there next, I'll see what I can do.'

'That's very kind of you, Daniel.'

'Better still, of course, would be for you to go there yourself, but that may not be possible, yet.'

Glancing down at her tummy, she blushingly said, 'Oh, I see, it's not due until September.'

'And your husband is Robert de la Rey?'

'He's not my husband.'

'Forgive me, I didn't mean to embarrass you. He's the young man from Philadelphia?'

'Yes. After the baby's born, I may journey north, that's if I haven't heard from Rob before then.'

'You think he's still in Philadelphia?'

'I've no idea. I know nothing of his whereabouts at present.'

He offered her his hand. 'I wonder if I may stand in for that lucky young man and escort you this evening, Jo-Ellen?'

She was taken aback. What was there about this personable young major that she found so charming? She fancied mostly everything he asked for he probably got.

'I should be honoured.'

'That's settled, then. You know, if you do come to Virginia, I'd be delighted to meet you from the train.'

He called the waiter and topped up their drinks. Jo-Ellen felt very uplifted. This stranger had come into her life and brought with him the promise of contact with Rob.

It then occurred to her. 'Daniel! I forgot – Rob will be fighting for the north.'

His eyebrows lifted in surprise. 'I see. How interesting.'

'I'm so sorry, I'll understand if you change your mind.'

'Why should I? However, it will be to Washington you'll have to go, not Virginia, and I'll definitely have to meet you. Washington's in a dangerous situation, caught between Virginia and Maryland. You can't wander about the place alone.'

She listened attentively as he outlined some important facts. No wonder her Papa had been so against the idea.

'I'm sometimes in Washington, myself. When I'm next there I'll make some enquiries for you,' he added.

'Then I'll watch the mail with great interest from now on.'

He offered his arm. 'Now, I may have a wounded leg but I can still dance. Would the most beautiful lady in the room care to?'

The music began and he guided her on to the dance floor.

Chapter Three

Rob tossed the report on to the desk. God – he felt like bursting, he was so bored. It had been so bad lately he had even considered assisting in the war effort, not that he had any intention of ever fighting, but anything was better than this day-to-day monotony in his father's firm.

Heavy rain streaked the window panes. The once crowded streets were unusually empty. Only newspaper offices buzzed with activity these days and his own offices were busy since there had been a general increase in immigration. Other corners of industry had been hit severely, though, with so many young men away from home. Running an office of colleagues and secretaries, he discovered after only three months, was teeming with frustration and non-fulfilment and a nightmare sense of failure.

His relationship with his father had suffered more than ever. Often it was at breaking point. They argued over the business, over politics and about the war, but mostly over emotional matters. Elizabeth Stewartson being the last straw. At every opportunity she came to the house for meetings contrived by their families and there was never any doubt what was uppermost in her mind. He doubted if she'd ever had a man. An inhibited female, straight-laced, speaking and smiling to order, she lacked both personality and sex appeal, which only served to make him yearn all the more for his vivacious Jo-Ellen.

That was another thing – there was no longer any contact. He had written letters, warm and sincere, about his longing for her, but with no response he'd begun to sense indifference. Did she feel so strongly about Savannah that she could withdraw her love? Were her feelings for the south stronger than her feelings for him? If he and Ben could remain friends throughout, why couldn't they? Why were women so damned difficult? All along, their ideas on the political structure of the south had differed widely. Jo-Ellen had seen nothing wrong in keeping slaves, her argument being that she had been brought up alongside them, had laughed with them, had even been punished with them. He'd always accepted that, except when he'd learned that Ben had taught Earl to read and write. Now *that* he'd objected to. It was illegal. And now? Silence from Jo-Ellen. Impulsively, he hit the buzzer. Lighting a cheroot, he waited. No reply. He strode down the corridor to Herman's office. One of the female secretaries followed him in.

'Herman's out for a while,' she told him.

'Any idea where the letter from the attorneys is?'

'Herman had it last. Could be in his briefcase. He often tucks letters in there.'

When she had gone, Rob slipped the catch on the briefcase. Inside was an assortment of documents. He was unable to find the letter he sought but something else, something familiar, caught his eye. He lifted out the envelope. On the outside was his own handwriting and it was addressed to Jo-Ellen. As he tore open the flap, there was a movement from the doorway. 'Ah, Herman, what's this doing here?'

'I didn't post it, sir.'

'That I can see. Why not?'

'Your father instructed me not to.'

'My father! I should have known. Am I allowed to know why? I mean, as the author of the letter, I feel I have certain rights!'

Herman made to reply, but Rob went on. 'No – let me work this one out, and you tell me if I'm wrong. With the outbreak of war my father made it clear to you there was to be no more contact between Jo-Ellen and myself, his plan being to stop all letters either way and also to encourage meetings with Elizabeth Stewartson. Then, with no contact, either Jo-Ellen or I would lose interest and I would turn in my loneliness, to Elizabeth. How am I doing, Herman?'

'Good, sir.'

'Now, how many letters have been stopped? How many have arrived I'm not aware of?'

'Four leaving, three prevented coming in, sir.'

'Three! I want to see them!'

Herman shook his head. 'I had to destroy them, sir.'

'Unread?'

'Unread.'

'You kept this one. Any reason for that?'

'An error, sir.'

Rob strode from the office and out to where the family carriage waited. To the driver he said, 'Take me home.'

Lunch had just finished when he burst in.

George pressed a napkin to his lips and moved away from the table. 'What on earth are you doing home at this hour, Robert? No work to do?'

'Not any longer, father.'

'Oh? Has something happened that I ought to know about?'

'Where's mother?'

'She's lying down. Got one of her headaches.'

Rob closed the door. 'I just resigned!'

The old man's face went white and red in turn. 'What's that? Look, if there's something you don't agree with, son, let's talk about it.'

'There sure is. I don't agree with having my letters intercepted!'

George let the napkin flutter to the floor. 'Letters?'

'Yes, father, and I don't mean business letters, either. I mean the ones I wrote to Jo-Ellen.'

'I see. You found out. How?'

'What difference does that make? Herman had nothing to do with it, I discovered it by accident.'

George seated himself. 'It's for your own sake, Robert. A man like you don't need a Confederate bride.'

'That's a decision I shall make. *I'll* have first say in who I choose for a wife!'

'You think your mother and I would accept a southern girl for a daughter-in-law?'

'I don't give a damn. I happen to love her.'

'Huh, you only think you do. Just because you knew each other as children. I always thought it wrong to mix with them southerners. You should spread your wings more, son, gain some experience before making such dramatic decisions about your future.'

'And you consider Elizabeth Stewartson as spreading my wings?'

Flinging open the door, Rob took the hall stairs two at a time to his mother's room. He paused before entering to calm himself. His father had really done it this time, had given him the wherewithal to leave for good. He could get away from the stringent rules of No. 57 Dale Avenue forever.

He found his mother lying on her bed. Her headache was almost better, she said, as long as it didn't get any hotter. Was anything the matter – why was he home so early? He explained. She was shocked.

'I'd no idea. But don't hold it against your father. He thinks only of your happiness, Robert.'

'You expect me to believe that? He never liked Jo-Ellen, whereas you always did. Father dislikes anything south of the Line, yet he does most of his business there. Why, two of our largest contracts are with Georgia folk. Such hypocrisy!' He stopped. 'Sorry, mother.'

She squeezed his hand, assured him he had a right to be angry. 'Go and find Jo-Ellen, tell her what has happened.'

He sighed. 'Is she hasn't tired of me by now.'

'Then go and put it right. If she loves you, she'll be waiting.'

He moved to the window to stare out thoughtfully. 'I'll surely do that, mother, but first I aim to straighten out my life. I'll write to her and if she'll still have me, I'll go down and see her.'

'Good. Now what will you do to straighten out your life?'

He turned to her concerned gaze. 'I hear McClellan's got the Potomac. I'll see if I can join him.'

'McClellan? But why get involved in the war – I thought you were so against it. You might get yourself killed!'

'Now, mother, I've no intention of getting killed.' Be there but not a part of it, he thought. Get a good commission – that was the secret. A future Senator might get on rather better with a war record behind him.

Rachel lay back, a weak smile playing at her lips. Robert would know best what to do. At heart a Lincoln man, a devoted Republican, he was obviously torn in two. In love with a southerner, and his best friend also a southerner. When it came to duty, his loyalties were in the north, when it came to love, his desires lay in the south.

He took her hand in his. He could not tell her that he wanted to get as far away from his father's firm as possible, that the boredom was killing him. It would only hurt her. He bent to kiss her cheek.

In his room he packed his belongings, his thoughts on Jo-Ellen.

There was still hope. She was still his. First, though, he would contact George McClellan, a man he admired. They had met once at a house party in Washington and McClellan had paid him much attention. Then there was Governor Floyd, a man who could and would pull strings in Rob's favour. It shouldn't be too difficult to find him, get a commission one way or another. A man could get anything he wanted if he tried hard enough.

Whistling a tuneless melody, he poured a large whisky and lit a cheroot. Things were at last moving along. The war might well be over by the time he got involved, then in no time at all he'd be on his way home complete with badge, uniform, and background. The fact that he had not done any fighting would be of no consequence once he got a foothold in Congress.

Several days later, he left home and journeyed to Washington. His father said nothing. His mother cried. These matters were thrust to the back of his mind as he joined the Army of the Potomac as Major under the leadership of Major General George McClellan.

...

Just south of Washington Flats, not far from Manassas, the Confederate Army, under the new leadership of General Joseph Johnston, dug in its heels and waited. Theirs had been a major victory at Bull Run and this shot in the arm for morale was still in evidence when Ben rode in eight weeks later to take up his new command.

He was greeted by Lieutenant Thaddeus Crisp.

'Sir! Glad you're well again, sir.'

'At ease. Yes, I'm fit, thanks. Four weeks of wedded bliss does a man the world of good. You married, Lieutenant?'

'Not yet, sir, but I'm hoping to be. Nice little blonde back home.'

'Where's home?'

'Missouri.'

'Ah – yes, I read about Wilson's Creek. A sound victory for us.'

Ben seated himself behind the desk. 'Right, Lieutenant, bring me up to date.'

Thaddeus Crisp, a tall, lean young man with good features, coughed lightly before speaking. His blond hair curled over his collar and freckles covered his nose. Good humoured eyes gazed steadily from beneath bushy eyebrows. Ben liked him, in fact, was reminded of Tiny Sheldon. God, was that only eight weeks ago?

'There's been no full scale fighting, sir, only a couple of skirmishes not so far from here, but with small losses.'

'And what's our general like?'

'Johnston? Shrewd, likeable.'

'Anything else?'

'I'll let you know when I've seen action with him, sir. I've been with General Beauregard, as you know.'

The Lieutenant handed over a document. 'Seems we're about to be joined by a couple of strays from Jackson's bunch. They arrived half an hour ago.'

'All right. Bring them in.'

Crisp saluted and left. Ben gazed critically round the small office. He preferred a battlefield, he decided. Confinement was claustrophobic. The office had belonged to a previous captain, who was killed in action. It was sparsely furnished, a large map hung on one wall, and a portrait of Jefferson Davis dominated another.

The door opened and Crisp brought in the new arrivals. The taller of the two men held out his hand. 'Major John Barnaby, Captain.'

Ben shook hands. 'Pleased to have you with us, Major.' He glanced at the other man, a sergeant. 'I understand you were both with Jackson.' The sergeant nodded lethargically.

'Still am, Cap'n. Came adrift after Bull Run. Been trying to get back ever since.'

'You been without a division since July?'

'No, Captain,' said Barnaby. 'We tied up with Jeb Stuart, but we're due to rejoin Jackson's Brigade as soon as we can.'

Ben turned to the sergeant. 'Where you from, Sergeant?'

'Atlanta – sir.'

The 'sir' was an after-thought.

'I know it well. I'm from Georgia.' Ben watched the impassive grey eyes. 'You ever been to Georgia, Sergeant?'

'Can't say I have, sir, no.'

Still the eyes never wavered or altered their expression and Ben had the distinct impression that the sergeant probably killed with the same indifference as the lack of expression on his face and the empty tone in his voice.

'You admire Jackson?'

'Very much,' came the reply. 'Saved the day and sure saved my life. Made sure them Yankees didn't get the Creek. I thought my time was up when I got caught in cross fire and then in came Jackson with his men. Gave me time to get out of trouble and stay out. Ol' Stonewall sure earned his name.'

Memories of those moments were still fresh in Ben's mind. Moving to the map on the wall, he said, 'I believe Jackson is somewhere here. Tell me, Major, why are the Yankees biding their time? This fellow McClellan – what do we know about him?'

'I hear he's a stickler for discipline. He orders thousands of recruits then complains that he hasn't enough. The men he trains must get very restless, that's all I can think. They're up on the Flats now, no doubt itching to get into this war, but their general's reluctant to take the initiative. Some say he's yellow, I like to think he's merely over-cautious.'

'A typical West-Pointer,' the sergeant remarked with mild sarcasm.

Barnaby glanced at him. 'We musn't underestimate the man.'

Ben agreed. He liked John Barnaby, a distinguished man with a dark complexion and greying hair. A good soldier, he thought, relying as usual on first impressions.

'Let's drink to that.' He went to the small cabinet and produced a bottle of cognac. 'Here's to peace and to you getting back to your division.'

'I'm sure looking forward to the day, Captain.'

Ben knew the feeling well. He was missing Pierre Beauregard already, the General having fallen out with President Davis and been dismissed.

He finished his drink and waited for the two men to leave the room. 'Lieutenant, you didn't notify me of the sergeant's name.'

Crisp thumbed through his notes and smiled apologetically. 'Beg your pardon, Captain. It's Foley, Sergeant Leon G. Foley.'

...

So much was happening that Rob rarely found time for personal matters but when most soldiers were tucked down for the night, he remained awake and composed letters to Jo-Ellen. In these he expressed his love for her and explained all that had happened in Philadelphia. Two such letters were drafted and Rob decided to send them the following morning so that no further delay was incurred. He called in a young lieutenant and handed them over.

'Make sure they get your urgent attention, Lieutenant. I'd hate to think you'd overlook them.'

The soldier grinned and tucked them away.

'What's your name?'

'Custer – ah, George Custer, sir.'

'Background?'

Custer made to speak.

'Stand to attention!'

'Yessir!' He drew himself up, not a large man, but a powerful looking one, his flowing blond hair framing a bronzed, finely sculpted face.

'Age?'

'Twenty-three, sir.'

'Seen much action in this war?'

'Second Lieutenant in the 2nd US Cavalry Manassas, sir.'

'I see. At ease, Lieutenant.' Rob knew all this already, had checked the man out but liked to establish his authority. 'I understand you're ex-West Point, too.'

'That's correct, sir.'

'At Manassas you showed much courage, I hear.'

Custer looked past him, said nothing, then as an afterthought, said, 'Received an arm wound, that's all.'

'You imagine that gives you leave to dress like that?'

Custer glanced down at his uniform. 'Sir?'

'Two buttons undone, shirt sleeve scuffed, boot unlaced...' Rob paused. 'Do I make myself clear, Lieutenant?'

'Ah – perfectly, sir.'

Rob stepped outside for some air. It was fresh, there were no clouds in the sky, promising to be another hot day. His thoughts dwelt, as usual, on his parents. Since his arrival in Washington he had thought of them constantly and lately feelings of guilt nagged at him for leaving home so promptly. His anger had gotten the better of him again, but having now written his letters to Jo-Ellen his mood was again mellow. He longed for word from her. Was she thinking about him? What was she doing right this minute?

He lit a cheroot and drew on it deeply. One day, his own son would stand tall and strong beside him, proud of his father, he would make sure of that. When the war was over, he told himself, he would get a good post in Washington, get into Congress. With a supportive wife and a family he would go on upward, to the top, into the White House perhaps. He thought about his father's words. Would his marrying a southern girl jeopardise his career? Not once the war was over, surely. The north were going to win – they had to. Now that the two-year term was coming in, how could they not? Anyhow, he would convince Jo-Ellen to give up the south, get her to leave it all behind and live in the north. That should be enough to convince his peers. He thought about Custer, envied him his past glories and certainly his West Point background. It was what a man needed most to get a quick foothold on the promotion ladder – unless he knew the right people.

Rob gazed across the Potomac where a mist, catching the early morning rays of the sun, rose from the water in spirals. Get the fighting over with, put them Confederates in their rightful place, and off he'd go.

Life was panning out suddenly, the way ahead seemed clear. He tossed away the finished cheroot as from inside a bell trilled. A message was coming through.

• • •

Alexander de la Rey was born on September 25th, 1861.

Constance was as thrilled as Jo-Ellen, but nonetheless she worried that the child was fatherless and she declared to Samuel that if the worse came to the worse, *they* would bring up the child.

'That won't be necessary, Mama! I intend to do that myself. I'm quite capable.'

Samuel lit a foul-smelling pipe and puffed on it thoughtfully. 'That why you're still intent on going off on some mad-brained journey just to find a man who's plainly lost interest in you?'

'Samuel!' Constance gave him a warning look. He spoke his mind far too often these days.

'It's all right, Mama. I know what you both are thinking, but I still intend to find him. He's a right to know about his own child.'

'And if he doesn't come to you, Jo-Ellen?'

She turned to her father defiantly. 'Then, Papa, I'll have to think again, won't I?'

She pranced off to her room. Calling for her new maid, she said, 'Close the door, Louise. I want to talk to you.' The young Negro did as she was bid. She was a timid girl but was very good with Alexander and Jo-Ellen had faith in her. 'This is what you must do,' she told her. She had received word from Daniel Hunter that he had some important news for her and that when she was ready, she should journey to Washington where he would meet her. Now that October had arrived, she did not care to delay any longer. Her priority now was Alexander but her life remained unfulfilled without Rob to share it. Never again to feel his arms around her, holding her close, added up to a futile future. She was sure that when Rob learned about Alexander, he would want them all to live together, war or no war.

The birth had been a simple one and she felt strong now. She would miss her child, knew she should be there to love and care for him properly, but how would she ever find Rob if she did not go while she was able? Daniel's words drummed through her head. 'Washington is in a dangerous situation.' A time might come when it was impossible to journey north at all.

If only she had received word from Rob. His work would not have prevented him from writing, and letters, though taking longer to reach their destinations, arrived eventually. There must be something else, something of which she was unaware and it was because of this uncertainty that she was willing to leave everything behind and begin her search. Deep inside, she knew she would never find real happiness if she remained in Savannah without Rob in her life.

With deliberation, she apprised Louise of her plans and made her promise to care for Alexander. 'My Mama will take care of him at night, you just be sure and look after him daytimes.'

She left feeding instructions and spent the rest of the week preparing, beginning a programme of grooming until she felt she was ready. On the last evening she held Alexander to her and watched over him as he slept. She would not be gone away long, she told him in whispers, she was going to find his Papa.

The next day she said her goodbyes. It was a tearful occasion, even her Papa was emotional. As Jacob drove her to Charleston Station, a late October sleet fell.

Some hours after her departure, a letter arrived at the Plantation. Samuel recognised the handwriting. It was from Robert de la Rey.

• • •

On the train, Jo-Ellen took stock of her situation and checked her papers and belongings. Her passport was in order and she had told Daniel of her expected time of arrival.

She had managed to obtain some Confederate dollars, as well as a small supply of Federal money and had chosen her travelling clothes with care. Alone in the carriage, she ate a light snack from her lunch pack and settled down to doze. Hours passed before she woke with a start. Through the window she saw that darkness had become dawn and that the sombre greyness had become a bright glow, promising a fine day. The countryside woke up slowly, untouched and permanent. It seemed inconceivable that out there in the rugged solitude a war raged.

A watery sun rose high above the tree tops as the train neared Washington City. The station was crowded as she stepped on to the platform, the mass of bodies punctuated by blue uniforms. She saw then that Daniel had indeed come to meet her.

'Jo-Ellen, allow me.' After seeing that the luggage was taken care of, he offered his arm and led her into the street where she had her first glimpse of Washington. As they travelled in the buggy towards city centre, Daniel said, 'I almost didn't make it here today. Had to go help sort out the aftermath of Ball's Bluff.'

Jo-Ellen had heard about the battle from the bill boards.

'I got back just in time.' He grinned at her. 'General Johnston wasn't too pleased when I told him I wanted to meet a beautiful young lady in Washington.'

She felt a rush of gratitude. It was good to see him again and she thought he looked even more handsome in his dark pin-stripe suit than in uniform.

She booked into Willard's Hotel and Daniel left her to settle in so that she may rest before bathing and changing into an elegant gown to meet him in the lounge that early evening.

The hotel lived up to its reputation. The food was excellent, the service efficient despite a shortage of staff. As she sipped an after dinner liqueur, she said, 'Daniel, I want to thank you for meeting me and for being such a good friend. I'm so fortunate to have you.'

'I'm the fortunate one, Jo.'

She looked up at him. No one called her 'Jo' – no one except Rob. 'You don't mind, I hope,' he said, reading her mind.

She smiled. 'No, not at all.'

'Tell me, Jo, what are your plans?' She had not yet asked him for his news and he found this odd.

'I'm not sure. I don't want to be away too long from my son. No longer than a month, if that. Therefore, I must find out where Rob is soon and also try and visit his parents in Philadelphia.'

'I see. Tell me about your baby. What did you call him?'

'Alexander Robert. He's very beautiful. He has Rob's green eyes.'

Daniel gazed thoughtfully at his fingertips. 'And you insist on journeying to Philadelphia?'

'Is that too ambitious?'

He nodded. 'I was thinking that a trip there might not be a good idea given that the fighting is so close, but you might get away with it if you go soon and leave soon.' He raised his glass. 'Another liqueur?'

'No, thank you, Daniel. I'm tired and think I'll go to my room, if you don't mind. But tell me first, what news do you have of Rob?'

At last. 'I hope I haven't raised your hopes too much. I was able to find out something, however. I gather that Major de la Rey...'

'Major?'

'Yes, it seems he joined McClellan on the Potomac.'

'Then he's not far from here?'

'No, his division is sitting just twenty miles away.'

Twenty miles! And there she was thinking he was with his parents in Philadelphia. She had been nad've enough to think that Rob had ignored the war as so many others had. 'How will I get to his division, Daniel? Am I able to merely turn up there and ask to see him?'

'I'm afraid not. It's unlikely that the Union Army will allow women anywhere near their camps.' He leaned forward. 'Jo – your papers, are they in order?'

'Of course, why?'

'Because I'm in contact with some highly placed people in Richmond. Sometimes they come to Washington to mingle with the Union Army officials.' He gave a boyish grin. 'Spies, you know.'

'Really?'

'I may be able to introduce you into those circles. It's possible we may find out something about your major.'

She felt a wild pang of excitement. The idea certainly appealed to her sense of adventure.

'If I can get us an invitation to one of these gatherings, then we'll most certainly attend.'

'What if somebody suspects where I come from? And it could be dangerous for you too, Daniel.'

'So far I've been safe.'

'It's not known you fight for the south?'

'No. I mingle with journalists most of the time, have in the past been mistaken for one. And even if I were discovered, nothing would be done.'

Jo-Ellen was rivetted. 'How can you be so sure?'

'Many southern sympathisers spend their time in Washington. As for you, though, if indeed you do find Robert, or information about him, then you'll be on your own. I, of course, will not be able to assist you further.'

She nodded. 'Of course, Daniel, I'll never mention anything about you – ever.' She giggled. 'Your English is so posh at times.'

'Which is probably why I enjoy so much freedom here, as you could, Jo.'

He took her hand in his. Colour rose in her cheeks and slowly she withdrew her hand. 'Thank you, Daniel. I'll be grateful for any contacts you make for me. Now I must leave you.'

Rising to his feet, he said, 'I'll come for you in the morning and we'll get started. A few enquiries in Washington first, of course. Goodnight, Jo.'

She allowed him to escort her to her room and closed the door somewhat reluctantly on his smiling face.

• • •

It was quiet and rather late when he stepped outside for some air after booking a room at the same hotel. Rain had soaked the pavements and he turned up his collar against the brisk wind. He was not tired, merely in need of light exercise. He also wanted time alone to think.

A new feeling had taken him over. He'd experienced it only once before, but not in such depth. Mary-Lee had been a pretty little thing, had given herself completely when he had declared his intention to join the military, but he had never really loved her, not the sort of love that took a man through life. He'd known the difference at an early age, his parents the living example of what marriage and happiness were all about.

Things were different this time, he thought, crossing the road out of Fourteenth Street. What he had interpreted as friendship, casual interest or even protectiveness, as can overtake a man in the presence of a beautiful woman, had now revealed itself as much, much more.

As he walked, the night air revived him and rain soaked him through.

• • •

On the banks of the Potomac, the Union Army under George B. McClellan was busy reorganising itself. Having suffered defeat at Bull Run, every effort was being made to ensure that the next campaign was successful. Five hundred thousand volunteers duly arrived and it was expected that the new commander-in-chief would lead his new force against General Johnston in Manassas before winter made the roads impassable.

With typical reticence, McClellan decided instead to use the time to drill and train his recruits thoroughly. He called to his quarters various officers to brief them, among them Major de la Rey.

Rob faced the general expectantly. McClellan, not a tall man, held himself stiff and proud. His nickname of 'Little Mac' suited him.

'Been reading 'Harpers Weekly,' Major. Peculiar business, this Trent Affair. The British have us with our hands tied on this one. What do you say?'

Rob gave a light cough. He was well versed in the matter and had no difficulty finding an answer.

'I say the president had no alternative, sir. Britain would have recognised the Confederacy as an independent nation had he not given in. Those two commissioners, Mason and Slidell, they had to be released. No question of it.'

'Quite so, Major. As you know, there's one hell of a Rebel army at Manassas. I've been deliberating whether or not to go in and rout them out.' Deep in thought, McClellan went on, 'I want Richmond. We must demoralise the Rebs by taking their capital, send them running back to the Union, that's my ambition. Taking Richmond will be a giant step towards that goal.'

He paused. Rob waited. Things looked as though they were going to be moving at long last. 'So, I'm toying with the idea of advancing first on Manassas then on to Richmond. What do you say, Major?'

Rob's mind raced. For weeks the men had been pushing for action. For weeks McClellan had merely watched the army grow in size, and they had wasted the fall. Now winter had arrived and it was feared they may have to wait out the spring before they moved, if then. What did he have to say? Goddam it yes, yes, yes!

'Seems like a damned good idea, General.'

'Yes, doesn't it?'

McClellan tucked his arms snugly behind his back. 'Now that Jeff Davis has been elected for a full term, he's pushing hard for recognition from England and France. If England does intervene, we'll be beaten, no doubt about it. That's why we've stepped up our military requirements, Major.' He grinned. 'When he heard the news about Davis, Old Abe probably shit himself!'

Rob grinned to himself. There was no love lost between the general and Lincoln.

'Thank you, Major. It was a pleasure talking with you.'

Rob saluted and left, excited that there was to be some action. There was only one way to get the war over with and that was to get on with it.

Only a day after the interview, McClellan scrapped all plans to attack Manassas. Disappointment grew in the ranks and especially in Rob. The weeks crawled by. In mid-December, McClellan fell ill, supposedly with mild typhoid, and he left to spend time with his wife and to rethink strategy. This only served to make Rob more restless. There was less action there than in his father's office, he decided, and time began to hang heavily.

The air smelt of wood fire as he stepped outside for a break. A gentle snow covered the countryside, which looked like a picture postcard and the grey sky warned of more to come.

A glance at his pocket watch told him it was still early. Everywhere was deadly quiet. Tonight perhaps he should go in to town. What was the sense in hanging about any longer? It might ease the boredom. It was almost Christmas, after all. And celebrations would be in process. A drink, some company, and perhaps he'll see things in a better light. It occurred to him that it was exactly a year ago that he had left Philadelphia for Savannah. One whole year of his life had slipped by.

Back in his office he drafted a telegram advising headquarters of his intentions then called in Custer.

'You off duty tonight, Lieutenant?'

'Yes sir.'

'Feel like a trip to town?'

Custer grinned. 'Soon as you like, sir.'

Night brought with it a cold wind and ice formed on the roads, but despite this they rode into town where they found a blaze of lights, music and cabaret. Rob enjoyed his good humoured companion. They found a whore house on the outskirts.

'Just what we need, Major.'

That was an understatement. Rob did need, had been doing so for too long. Since Jo-Ellen there had been only three brief encounters with local females. Custer mistook his hesitation for reluctance.

'You gonna wait outside, Major?'

'Lead the way, Lieutenant.'

Custer chose a young black girl, while Rob settled for a blonde. 'Ain't fucked a nigger girl since I was sixteen,' Custer whispered before they parted company.

Rob indulged himself on those several trips to town, feeling the inevitable easing of tension in those hours of escape with his amiable friend.

On his return to camp one evening, a cable was handed to him. His father had suffered a stroke. Hell, the last thing he wanted was to see his old man so soon. His mother probably needed him there, though, and so he immediately asked to see the general. After obtaining permission, he prepared to journey to Philadelphia.

• • •

Washington City with its community of 60,000 people, could hardly have been described as anything other than a provincial capital, yet it excited Jo-Ellen's imagination as she and Daniel rode together in carriage and pair along tree-lined avenues. True, she had seen many unimpressive buildings and it was disquieting to see the Negro slums, but a drive along Pennsylvania Avenue or Fourteenth Street where other elegant carriages ambled past, more than made up for these lesser features.

The carriage stopped before a grand looking residence on Washington Square and Daniel assisted her to the sidewalk.

The Lodge was well known in Washington social circles. The lull in the fighting had given officers an opportunity to get together to discuss their own involvement, the main venue for this being The Lodge, and being so close to Richmond, it was not surprising that folk from both sides mingled there freely, albeit ignorantly.

Daniel pointed discreetly to several southern sympathisers in close contact with Union officers and Jo-Ellen concluded that their hostess, Catherine Lacey, had an unusual assortment of admirers. She discovered that in order to be invited there at all, one was expected to set aside political preferences and simply enjoy.

Catherine's eyes lit up when she saw Daniel. 'My dear friend! It's so long since I've had the pleasure.' When she saw Jo-Ellen, she said, 'Oh, please do introduce me.'

Jo-Ellen was taken with her beauty, the high cheek bones, the dark gleaming hair, deep lively eyes and when she spoke, her voice soft and refined. When she left them to greet a new arrival, Jo-Ellen said, 'My, she's a domineering personality, isn't she?'

'A mystery to most people. Once seen, never forgotten, though. Most of the top generals know her well.' Daniel led her forward. 'Come, I'll introduce you to a few of them.'

General McDowell was a sombre figure of a man and a mild disappointment to Jo-Ellen who had read about his recent exploits and imagined much more charisma. Generals Meade and Patterson arrived in full uniform, their blue contrasting with the gold and navy of the general décor. Jo-Ellen looked keenly at each one, wondering if they might know of Major de la Rey, and she listened most carefully to any snippet that might give her a clue to his whereabouts.

As the champagne flowed, she relaxed and began to enjoy herself fully. Conversations interested her and she joined in the laughter and when she was not dancing with Daniel she allowed at least two other young men to lead her on to the floor. All the while she was careful about her manner of speaking and slipped up only once when she exclaimed, 'Why, I do declare!' after Captain Antony Wilson of the Ninth Division accidentally spilt some wine. The captain was so fascinated by her that he paid no heed and merely whirled her so many times that the room turned and her head swam. Daniel came to her rescue and escorted her outside, where the moon was large in the sky and the atmosphere delightfully romantic.

'You look very beautiful, Jo.'

She felt herself blush. 'Thank you, Daniel. It's been a very stimulating evening.'

'I'm pleased. Did you learn anything?'

'Only that I'm confused.'

He chuckled. 'While you were dancing I asked Catherine if she knew of your major. She seemed not to have heard of him but that doesn't mean he isn't here. Not even Catherine knows them all.'

Eventually the guests began to filter away and they prepared to leave. Catherine saw them to the door.

'It was wonderful to see you, Daniel. Now, tell me before you drift away, are you still fighting for the south?'

Jo-Ellen tensed.

'Of course, Catherine. Did you think I'd change my mind?'

She smiled. 'Well, we must not forget that you were commissioned into the Federal Army first, must we?'

'So was Lee, so was Magruder. We all resigned.'

Catherine turned to Jo-Ellen. 'All the best officers were once in the Federal army. What a blow to their morale, losing men like Lee.' She placed a friendly hand on her arm. 'And you, Jo, I take it you are from the south as you know Daniel so well.'

Lost for words, Jo-Ellen fought to regain composure. 'We – are old friends and I'm not political. I mean, I find war so distasteful.'

'What Jo means is like yourself, Catherine, she sits on the fence.'

Catherine beamed. 'I'm so happy to have met you. Take good care of her, Daniel, she's quite lovely.'

In the carriage, Daniel asked the driver to take the slower, longer route homewards.

'Catherine worries me. All those prying questions,' Jo-Ellen said.

'Don't worry, she's harmless.'

'But she guessed. She would never have spoken so had she not fathomed out where I'm from.'

Daniel chuckled. 'I happen to know her sympathies lie with the Confederacy. She was just making sure of you.'

As the carriage ambled along Nineteenth, a light wind blew and Jo-Ellen drew her cape closer around her shoulders.

'There were spies there tonight,' he said.

'How do you know?'

'I just do. Ah – here we are.'

He helped her to the sidewalk, and led her inside. Spruce and holly festooned the hotel lobby and mistletoe adorned the chandeliers.

'You'll be returning to Manassas soon, I suppose, Daniel,' she said, walking with him to the elevator.

'Yes, it's quiet at present, but something might break around the festive season. The general will think I've deserted if I don't show up soon.'

Jo-Ellen felt a momentary sadness. 'I want more than anything to be home for Christmas. I must leave for Philadelphia at the earliest possible moment.'

'You do know, don't you, Jo, that were it not for my duties, I would most certainly accompany you?'

This surprised her.

'You mean all the way to Philadelphia?'

'As far as would be reasonable, yes. I'm worried that you'll be travelling alone.'

Laughter from a group in the corner of the hotel foyer broke the tension.

'That's the Willard brothers,' Daniel told her. 'Having their usual early celebrations.' He focussed his attention on her once more. 'Let me know how things go, if you manage to contact your major.'

'I surely will. Thank you for everything, Daniel. I'll miss you. I would have been quite lost without your help.'

'I must confess to having selfish motives, Jo.'

Her eyes became trapped by his where she detected an unmistakable message. She felt herself colour.

'Will it be dangerous at Manassas?'

'Only if the Feds surprise attack us.'

'You think they might?'

'Hard to say.' His hand reached towards her. 'A clever change of subject, Jo.'

Somehow she avoided contact with his hand. 'You're very dear to me, Daniel, but surely you know that…'

'No – say nothing more. Perhaps I'm speaking out of turn, but I'm compelled to.' He glanced round. They were alone, though he lowered his voice. 'Should things not go according to plan, should you find yourself alone, well, know that you're not alone. There's someone at Manassas who loves – who cares – deeply for you.'

She took a shaky breath as his strong fingers closed over hers and lifted them to his lips as though to seal a promise. She found she could not look away from those eyes. He was like a magnet, this tall, sensuous man and she was sure that if she stood there a moment longer, trapped by the fire in his eyes, she would burst into flame. The arrival of the elevator broke the spell. She moved quickly towards it.

'Take care of yourself,' she said, her eyes misting with emotion.

'I will. Be happy, Jo.'

He looked at her long and intently as though to memorise her face forever, then abruptly turned and left.

In her room, Jo-Ellen lay mulling over the events of the past days, Rob's face passing in and out of her thoughts and her mind racing as it concocted conversations with him until she woke in the darkness.

That morning she would make enquiries at Manassas, she promised herself, and then move on from Washington to Philadelphia. If she did not do that soon, she might never be home in time for Christmas.

Somewhere a clock struck 2 am. She sank into a shallow sleep, her final thoughts of Rob, of Daniel and of her child in Savannah.

Chapter Four

Ben read the letter that had arrived from his Pa. The news shocked him. Jo-Ellen had always been headstrong, but how far did she think she would get with such a mad-brained scheme? Probably only as far as Charleston, he decided. She would never change. God help the man who married her.

His thoughts now on Rob, he wondered where he was, what he was doing. The letter ended with Samuel's hopes that they would be together this Christmas. Not an easy task, Ben thought, to get permission again for a few days leave. Yet he would try. It would be a joy to spend the holiday with Susanne and his family and hopefully his nephew. With luck, Jo-Ellen might even be there.

His audience with General Johnston did not go well. Too many men taking liberties lately, the general grumbled. One victory and you think the war is over? Ben stood to attention waiting for the inevitable refusal. Johnston fixed him with steely eyes under thick eyebrows, the light picking out his bald head.

'Be sure and get back soonest, understand? I'm running an army not a merry-go-round.'

With no time in which to warn Susanne of his arrival, Ben made the journey once again to Savannah, armed with various gifts which he set under the Christmas tree. Happiness overwhelmed his heart and mind so intensely as he looked at the fire crackling in the hearth and decorations in every room. Carols accompanied the clink of glasses as Samuel gave a toast and even he was visibly moved by the unexpected presence of his son.

That morning Ben walked with Susanne in the grounds inhaling air brisk and clean and flavoured by the aroma of wood fire and chestnuts.

'Pity Jo-Ellen never made it home,' he said, his attention on Louise walking Alexander.

'I worry so about her yet I expect she is just fine.' Susanne tucked her arm through his, noting his tense expression as he thought of his sister. To bring his thoughts to more joyful matters, she said, 'I'm considering doing voluntary work. What do you think?'

'Sounds good to me. Have you the time?'

'I'll make time. The soldiers need clothes and so I'll knit and sew and send them off to the war. At least it will help keep them warm.'

Ben's attention see-sawed between Susanne and baby Alexander whom he could hear gurgling even from there. He could not help the anger he felt inside. It was downright selfish of Jo-Ellen not to be there for her child. His thoughts also centred on Sergeant Foley and how frustrated that he, Ben, had felt having the man within arm's reach and being unable to do anything about it.

'Ben, you look so pensive,'

'Take no notice. I'm happy beyond belief,' he said, clutching her hand in his.

'You're missing Jo-Ellen and I do understand, but don't worry. I feel she's all right, truly.'

'You just said you worried about her.'

'Of course I do. We're living in such uncertain times, but she wanted to go and we must help her by not thinking negatively. And we mustn't let it dominate the time we have left together.'

'You're right. I won't mention it again.' His lips closed over hers and they walked on in silence. There was so much he wanted to say about how he was hating this war, how impatient he was to stay home for good to live a normal life with his family. More than anything he wanted to start a family of his own.

Inside the house, a roaring fire greeted them and they sat watching the logs burn to dying embers only to be stoked again by Jacob. Soon the presents would be unwrapped and they would spend the remainder of the day eating specially hunted partridge, a surprise gift from a neighbour, and tasting mulled wine.

Ben wound his arms tightly around her, kissing her long and passionately. 'You know what I'm thinking?'

She gazed into his eyes. 'Yes, I know that look, but tell me anyway.'

'I'd like a son, like Alexander.'

'Someone for him to grow up with? I was thinking along similar lines myself.'

Together they rose and went up to the privacy of their room. In the low light he kissed the soft swell of her breasts, felt the wild pounding of her heart as she surrendered to tides of passion too strong to resist, before abandoning herself to a rush of joy and elation.

• • •

Jo-Ellen's desire to get to Philadelphia and home again in time for the festive season was not to be realised. Her travel plans were hampered from the start. Trains were not connecting and twice she tried to leave Washington, only to find herself back again and having to start over. As many trains as possible had been commandeered by the military, leaving only a skeleton service for Washington's frustrated passengers.

It had been touch and go during all of this whether or not to continue. Her attempts so far to gain access to, or information from, the Potomac headquarters had led nowhere. She was told nicely but firmly that the Union Army had moved their position twenty miles away and that it would be futile to try and see any of the officers. She sighed. The authorities had been less than helpful and she finally tired of it all and wished herself away from the hubbub of city life. Against her will she remained at Willard's, alone now that Daniel had returned to his duties. Boredom began to replace the excitement of previous days and frustration that she could not leave the city.

It was then that fate took a hand. The Northern Central railroad that went through to Pennsylvania was stopping off at Baltimore, from where she would be able to connect directly to Philadelphia. She was suddenly faced with a major decision. Either she finished what she had started out to do, or gave up and hoped to find a suitable connection back to Charleston.

With only a few days to go before Christmas, it was an agonising decision. Missing Alexander's first Christmas was not part of the plan and she regretted having started the journey in the first place. If only she had listened to her dear parents! It was obviously useless to go back now, though, for if she began right this minute she would never arrive in time.

Having made up her mind, she stayed at an Inn to refresh herself before the final stage. It was there that she celebrated Christmas with a good meal and a bottle of fine wine. The owners, a delightful elderly couple, made her very welcome and this lessened her loneliness. Thereafter, it took three days to reach Philadelphia and she alighted from the train eager to finalise the last part of the journey. A buggy ride outside of town soon brought her to the de la Rey residence, an imposing building set in rural scenery.

Memories flooded back as the buggy rattled over the cobbled forecourt and drew to a halt. She approached the house with trepidation, remembering the cool reception she had received from George de la Rey. To her surprise, she found the door open.

She called out. There was no reply and so she stepped inside. It was quiet and certainly warmer, a welcome contrast to the chilly December air.

'Hello!' she called again.

A door at the far end of the corridor opened.

'Do excuse me for walking in…' she said to the woman standing there.

'Who are you? I'd no idea anybody was here.'

Jo-Ellen felt a quickening of her pulse as she recognised Rachel de la Rey. A diminution of what she remembered, there were still traces of beauty in the familiar features, though the once golden hair was now tinged with grey and the lines in the ageing skin now permanent.

'Jo-Ellen Jefferson, Mrs de la Rey.'

This brought a look of incredulity to Rachel's face. 'Jo-Ellen? But, how is it you're here?'

'I came via Washington. It wasn't easy. The war has disrupted everything beyond belief and I became stranded. I finally caught a train and here I am.'

'You poor child, you must be exhausted. Come into the drawing room.'

Rachel led the way into the spacious area which smelt faintly of lavender. Jo-Ellen took in the familiar room. It had hardly changed in all that time. An enormous picture, a landscape in oils, still hung over the heavy mantelpiece, and the two vases she had admired still occupied their same position.

'I'm afraid all I have to offer is Bourbon until the maid brings in the shopping. That's where everybody is – I sent them off to do the chores. Jessie must have left the door open by mistake. I shall reprimand her for her clumsiness.'

Jo-Ellen refused the Bourbon, said she preferred tea.

Rachel rang a bell and a servant brought in tea and cake.

'You look so grown up, Jo-Ellen, I hardly recognise you. The last time, let me see, we came to Savannah on a business trip.'

'Yes, and before that I came and visited you here.'

'Tell me dear, have you heard or seen anything of Robert?'

'No, he's the reason I went to Washington City, but there was no word of him.' She suddenly felt a wave of tiredness wash over her.

'He was here. My husband had a stroke and Robert came to see us over the festive season. He went back a few days ago. You only just missed him.'

This news annoyed Jo-Ellen. Had she been fobbed off in Washington when they told her the Union Army had moved on? The only place Rob had moved to was his home, it seemed. Which told her that they had been within a few miles of each other.

'I'm sorry to hear about Mr de la Rey. Is he getting better?'

'He's not at all well.'

Jo-Ellen wanted to get the news over with. 'Mrs de la Rey...'

'Please, call me Rachel.'

'I've something to tell you. In September I gave birth to a son – he's your grandson.'

She felt wanton, waiting for judgement to be passed. A long silence followed while this news sank in. When Rachel spoke, her voice sounded strained. 'Does Robert know about this?'

'No, as I said, I've been unable to contact him. I wrote several letters, but it seems they either did not arrive, or he ignored them.'

'He would never do that!'

Rachel rose and moved to the window, her hands clasped in front of her and Jo-Ellen wondered if she had been too hasty. The news had plainly caused distress.

'I'm sorry, Rachel, I didn't mean to upset you.'

Rachel turned towards her and said, 'It's all right. You are perfectly entitled to come here and tell me this wonderful news that I have a grandson. But you, my dear, had to bear it all alone.' She hesitated before adding, 'Robert did not receive your letters.'

'How can you be sure?'

'Because my husband intercepted them. That was why Robert left and joined the armed forces. He had written to you also, but no letters were allowed through.' She returned to her seat. 'Now I see how very cruel it was. Robert loves you, dear, but he was made to think you no longer cared.'

Blind anger was a strange emotion to Jo-Ellen and she grappled with it as best she could. No words were adequate in that moment. She was justifiably angry but relieved as well. Rob did care for her after all. What a sad, futile situation! One thing was certain. Her journey had not been a waste of time. Any doubts in her mind were swept away by Rachel's confession. She rose and went to occupy the space Rachel had left by the window, her bosom heaving as she fought to maintain her usual composure.

'Mr de la Rey never approved of me, I know,' she said softly, 'but Rob and I intend to marry.'

'I know and you both have my blessing. Come, Jo-Ellen, sit by me.'

Rachel's arm slid around her. In her hand was a letter. 'According to this, he is about to move south with General McClellan.'

'Where south?'

'He's probably not allowed to say.'

'Is he going to fight? Has he already done so? Is he well?'

Questions poured forth. There had been so much talk lately about this campaign and that skirmish. Some of the stories were true, others grossly exaggerated. Rachel read the letter aloud. It implied that McClellan was master-minding something in which Rob would no doubt be involved...the fighting was dragging on longer than predicted...many brave soldiers had lost their lives...the romantic image of a victorious army winning a major battle and ending the war quickly was now a thing of the past...this new mission was to be their most adventurous so far. The letter ended with his love.

'He is well, which I thank God for,' Rachel said, tucking away the letter. 'And he is so handsome, dear. You should see him in his uniform.'

'That's my dearest wish, I can assure you.' Then, 'May I see your husband?'

Rachel grappled with the question, then said, 'Of course.' She rose and led the way up the stairs to a room at the back of the house. George was propped against several pillows, a pair of spectacles on his nose. He set aside the book he was reading.

'This won't upset him, will it?' Jo-Ellen said discreetly.

Rachel shook her head. 'It will probably do him good, if anything.'

The old man gave a grunt of impatience. 'What's all the whispering about? Who is this young lady?'

Jo-Ellen moved closer. Illness had robbed George of the good looks she remembered. His hair was greyer, his face pallid.

He looked appraisingly at Jo-Ellen. 'Well, aren't you going to introduce me?'

'It's Jo-Ellen, dear. She's come all the way from Georgia to see us.'

'Jo-Ellen!' George stared at her as though he had seen a ghost.

'I'm sorry you are ill, Mr de la Rey. Is there anything I can do?'

'Do?' He reached for her hand. 'You're beautiful, young lady, isn't she, Rachel? Are you here for long? Rachel, see if there's any champagne.'

'Now dear, you know what the doctor said.'

'To hell with the doctor! This is the best cure I know – a pretty girl and a glass of champagne.' To Jo-Ellen he said, 'Well?'

'I'm not sure how long.'

Rachel pulled a bell rope and when the servant arrived, she ordered two glasses of champagne.

'Mr de la Rey, there's something you must know. You have a grandson. His name is Alexander.'

The old man's mouth dropped open to speak, then clamped shut again. 'A grandson?' he said at last. 'Robert said nothing of this.'

'Robert doesn't know,' Rachel said.

'Doesn't know? Why in hell's name doesn't my son know he's a father?'

'Because certain letters did not reach their destination.'

George placed a hand to his head, his eyes on Jo-Ellen. 'I guess you know. I've been lying here for weeks thinking about little else. Can you forgive an old fool – can you find it in your heart?'

'I already have.'

'I never wanted him to marry you, or anybody else who didn't come from his environment. I introduced him to several young ladies but they made him unhappy and I came to realise after he'd gone away that you were the one, it was always you. Can you understand that I couldn't accept it, you being a southerner and all?'

'I'm still a southerner,' she replied. The enemy, in fact. The war had truly divided them.

'I know it makes no difference now. It's what makes people happy that counts.' He took hold of her hand. 'I hope you'll not go home yet. I want time with you, we both do, don't we, Rachel? I'm to blame that you're not wedded to my son and I aim to make it up to you.'

Jo-Ellen felt the tears prick at the back of her eyelids. How could she go home now? These good people needed her so much. She had missed Christmas, there was no point in rushing now. George looked ghastly, Rachel pale and tired. Judging by the state of the railroads, she would be unlikely to arrive for the New Year celebrations, anyway. She looked at them both. Their imploring eyes tore at her very soul.

'I'll be pleased to stay and help out all I can.'

George lay back, relieved. Rachel brushed away a tear.

'Good,' he said quietly, 'just what I'd expect my future daughter-in-law to say.'

• • •

It was February before Earl finally departed. He had planned to rest up for only a few days but as time passed, he had no desire to move on. The food was good and he enjoyed working for Emily.

He had chopped logs to last the winter, had stacked them neatly in the barn, dug the earth in readiness for vegetables, and fixed the wooden fence that surrounded the house. In return, Emily took care of him and there had grown up between them a silent bond based on mutual trust and friendship.

Earl knew he could not stay forever. He approached Emily one day, watching as she thrust and turned pastry on the board.

'Emily, as much as I want to stay on, I got to go.'

Without turning from her work, she said, 'I know it, Earl. Still want to find the Union Army? You're headed for trouble there. They don't take black boys in their army.'

'I know, but I've got to try.'

'If that's what you wants to do, then you must do it.' She turned to him, her hands covered in flour. 'I'll miss you.'

He left her then, took the Manassas Gap Railway to Strasburg and journeyed to Winchester, from where he travelled on foot to Kernstown. It was a long journey, not without danger. The sight of a black boy travelling alone was not readily accepted. Icy stares and questioning looks followed him wherever he went, and on one occasion he thought he was going to be caught. Had he not run so fast he would most certainly have been.

In Kernstown the unimaginable happened. He found an army gathered under the leadership of General James Shield, and there he came to remain.

• • •

Rob's optimistic forecast of an early move did not materialise. The Confederates had evacuated the Manassas area, had fallen back to another defensive position south of the Rappahannock in readiness to defend themselves against the intended Federal campaign.

McClellan, having embarrassed the government by not attacking in time resulting from a trick the Confederates played on him, set up headquarters at Fairfax Courthouse. There he devised a brilliant plan to sail his army down the Chesapeake Bay, land at the sandy Peninsula between the York and James Rivers and then push northwards, into Richmond.

The plan seemed foolproof. He called in his officers. One, Major Robert de la Rey, could hardly wait to get started.

• • •

In his Richmond headquarters General Johnston seated himself and directed his attention at the soldier before him.

'At ease, Captain. So you wish to join Jackson in the Shenandoah. Any particular reason?'

Ben shifted his weight from one foot to the other, unwilling to tell the General the truth of his intended mission.

'Well?'

Had he chosen the right moment? Johnston seemed very impatient. Here goes, he thought, this had better be good…

'I hear he's short of men, sir. I'd like the chance to help out.

Wouldn't mind seeing the Shenandoah either before I die, sir.' He met Johnston's gaze across the desk.

'I've had orders from our new Chief of Staff, Robert E. Lee, to go and back Magruder in Yorktown,' Johnston said, thoughtfully. 'It's only a temporary measure to deter McClellan as long as possible, so I'm not sure we can spare you, Captain, and that's a fact. You just had leave with your family.'

'A few days over the holiday, sir.'

Johnston continued his scrutiny. A good soldier, if not an enthusiastic one, he thought. He'd heard good accounts from General Beauregard about Jefferson and he trusted his opinion. Jackson was pathetically short of men, it was true.

'Have the Feds reached Yorktown yet, sir?'

'Almost, despite various delays. Our job is to keep them there to protect Richmond at all costs. Magruder needs us urgently. You ever been to Yorktown, Captain?'

'No, sir.'

'Pretty place, damned pretty. Magruder would sink with all hands if I don't go down there and back him.'

'Yes, sir.' That was it, then. This one chance to track down Foley was about to escape him.

'We don't usually allow our men to transfer out on a whim.' A pause, a light cough. 'But on this occasion I agree. I owe Jackson a favour. Get back to us as soon as you can. That's all, Captain.'

As he left the General's office, Ben felt like punching the air. He had no idea what he would do if he found Foley, but find him he must. Discreet enquiries on his last visit home had disclosed what really happened on that day when Hannah rode to visit her sister. Foley had probably emerged from the trees, had overpowered Hannah on that lonely stretch of road, raped her and beat her until her heart gave out. This vision had tortured Ben since and he prayed that Foley would live through the war long enough for them to face each other, man to man.

Several hours later he prepared to leave Richmond to join Thomas Jackson's First Division of the Stonewall Brigade.

• • •

Daniel Hunter estimated they had sat too many weeks at Manassas waiting for the rumoured attack that never came. Bad for morale, he reckoned. He knew that General Johnston was impatient, and had not been at all surprised when the General gave the order to evacuate. Now he had learned from his private sources that the Federal army planned to ship a massive force down Chesapeake Bay.

He surveyed the wall map. The General had ordered a move to Rapidan. He moved his fingers down the map, tracing the presumed journey the Federal Army would or could take. The Federal Army might float down the Potomac and head straight for the Peninsula where General John Magruder was. He bet even further that Johnston would decide to join forces with Magruder at Yorktown – either that or go back up and help strengthen Fredericksburg. He grinned to himself. Either way, they would not be remaining for long in Richmond.

Ben entered, closed the door behind him 'Just popped in to say goodbye, Major. I'm off to the Shenandoah Valley.'

'You're what?'

Dan felt envious. He would swap anything for the beauty of the Shenandoah.

'I'm joining with Jackson – my own request. And it's not for long – I'll be back.' Ben held out his hand.

'How did you manage it?' Dan asked, shaking hands.

'Caught Johnston on a good day. He was reluctant to let me go, of course...'

'Of course...'

'...but he agreed, saying he didn't like to release one of his best men, etc. etc.'

Daniel shot him a disbelieving look. 'Johnston said that?'

'You can't complain, Dan, not all of us are allowed to flit to and from Washington.'

Into Daniel's eyes came a look of apology. 'I guess I can tell you now. I met your sister in Washington. I wanted to help out.'

Ben sat down slowly. 'You mean, you knew where she was all the time?'

'I promised not to tell. Couldn't break a promise to a beautiful lady, could I?'

'Now why on earth would she do that – I mean, not want to let us know she was safe.'

'She needed complete security. So we kept it a secret.'

Ben chuckled. 'Very cosy. She still in Washington? Can't be safe for her there alone.'

'I agree. She actually wanted to go and see Robert's folks in Philadelphia.'

'She what!' Anger took hold of Ben. 'Has she left her senses?'

'Don't go worrying – I guess she's headed for home by now.'

'I surely hope so. Did she find Rob?'

'Not that I know – I'm waiting to hear myself.'

Ben looked at him curiously. 'You're waiting to hear? Why in God's name isn't she at home taking care of her child! And you know, Dan, she's left Susanne practically alone to run the Plantation? They're supposed to be partners, for chrissake!' He took a deep breath. 'Sorry, it's just that I need to know she's safe – Rob too.'

'You and he are close?'

'Best friend I got and hell, I've a cute nephew, too. Alexander. And Jo-Ellen isn't even there for him.' Ben stood and thrust his hands deep into his pockets. 'Can't wait to start a family of my own. Damned if I'd not be there, either.'

'Look, I'm sorry – I should have put you in the picture sooner.'

Ben waved this aside. 'Forget it. I can tell you now, Dan, I've a letter from Susanne telling me she's pregnant. I'm going to be a father!'

'Hey, that's marvellous! Let's have a drink to that.'

'Looks like the baby will arrive in September.' Ben took his drink and downed it in one go. 'I'll not do what Jo-Ellen did. I'll not leave my child behind.'

'Do I take that to mean you'll not re-enlist?'

Ben looked away. He knew the present situation only too well. Things had become desperate in the south. A large selection of soldiers in the present army were only one year volunteers and their term was about to expire. Jefferson Davis was about to bring in the Conscription Act and in order to avoid the stigma of being a conscript, men were flocking to re-enlist as volunteers for a much longer period.

Ben felt torn. Part of him knew he should remain in the army yet he yearned to get home to the Plantation for good. In June his own term would expire and he had a big decision to make.

'I'm a one-year man,' he said. 'The Plantation can't run itself for much longer. Susanne, Curtis, and Jacob find it too much. How do I know that Jo-Ellen's on her way home? What if she isn't?'

Daniel shook his head. 'You think you can leave just like that? It won't be easy. Sure, some soldiers have pulled out, but they'll be traced eventually and things are made tough for them. The army has a way of catching up with absentees. As for me, I guess I'm fixing to stay a while longer.'

'You haven't anyone back home waiting for you, Dan?'

'No, ageing parents and a dog. Haven't found the time.'

'You haven't found the right girl, you mean. It's time you settled down. A man can't live alone forever. When I get out of here, I'm putting my all into marriage and the Plantation.'

'I'll see to it I take your advice some day.'

Ben pulled open the door. 'Say, you wouldn't be having romantic notions about my sister, would you?'

Daniel grinned. 'That transparent, am I?'

'Wide open. All I can say is may the best man win.'

They shook hands again. 'Get back as soon as you can, Ben. We'll be on the move shortly. Can see us moving to Yorktown.'

'Got it all worked out as usual. You'll make a fine general some day.'

'Tell that one to Johnston, will you?' Dan said as the door swung to.

He glanced reluctantly at the paperwork on his desk. Right now he would prefer to be writing letters to Jo-Ellen. He tried to estimate where she might be.

Hopefully she was back in Savannah with her family, but if she isn't? Confound the war. He couldn't bear the thought of her out there alone.

He felt a pang of remorse. She would never be his. The child would never be his. Wouldn't it be better for all concerned if he were to forget about her? Finish off the war and then go on home. Home – where was that? He hadn't seen Baltimore for so long. His family were there, but that was all. When he'd left Maryland years before to stay in England he'd been just ten years old, and nineteen by the time he returned to America and settled in Virginia before deciding to join the army. Back home – that could mean any one of three places.

A knock on the door and Second Lieutenant Wilcox entered. 'Sir, the general wants to see you.'

'We moving on, Lieutenant?'

'Think so. Could be Yorktown, sir.'

'Should suit you, Lieutenant.' He knew Wilcox had at least two women in Yorktown.

'Yes, sir. Pity we can't bring our women into camp with us, Major.'

'Quite so. Inform the general I'm on my way.'

The lieutenant saluted and left. Daniel paused to reflect. Best thing he'd heard all day – women in the camp. A vision of Jo-Ellen sitting in the chair opposite, smiling, talking, laughing, filled him with pleasure. How could he ever consider trying to forget her?

An hour later he received orders from Johnston to go on ahead to meet up with General Magruder in Yorktown.

Chapter Five

Matters were not as Ben expected when he arrived in Shenandoah. Jackson's command had bivouacked, many of the soldiers feeling the effects of the cold weather. And there was an urgent lack of food and equipment. He noticed also that many had only half supplies and often no shoes on their feet.

It did not take long to locate Thomas Jackson. The General, looking tired, peered at him in the half light.

'At ease, Captain. I heard you were coming over. Good to have you with us. We met before, almost a year ago, I believe.'

Ben recalled clearly. Jackson had been a colonel then, after which on July 2nd, he made brigadier and the famous brigade was formed. It was clear that the war had taken its toll since he had been made a general. Jackson sagged in his chair, dark rings circled his eyes, his brown hair was unruly, his usually trim beard long and straggly.

'Briefly, Captain, I'm informed that there are just four weak Federal regiments under General Banks and I hear that General Shield has been recalled and his men have turned. Tomorrow, we go in and take advantage of all this good fortune.'

Ben was silent, knowing that this might be all he could expect in the way of information from the man not known for lengthy explanations in military strategy.

'So far the Union Army have been on our heels along the Valley. This is our first decent rest for some time. Shield pushed us till we almost dropped.' Jackson added.

Hoping to press him further, Ben said, 'How come Banks and Shield have so few men, sir?'

The question was ignored.

'Colonel Ashby Turner informs me that the Feds have moved to Blue Ridge to join McDowell. I'm going in there with all I've got to wipe out what's left of them, Captain.'

'How many are we, sir?'

'Over 3,000. Yes, yes, I know it's not much, but it's enough to see Banks off. Captain, you're to report to General Garnett for further orders. He'll he leading the Brigade against Banks.'

'Yes, sir, may I ask a question, sir?'

'Another question?' Jackson passed a hand over his eyes. 'What is it?'

'Some weeks ago, a sergeant name of Foley joined my division at Manassas.'

'I remember, go on.'

'I take it he's rejoined your command, sir?'

'Yes, Foley's here. He's with Garnett now. Is that all, Captain?'

Ben saluted and left. Outside the night closed in. It was chilly, the stars were bright in the sky. The men about him looked beaten and slept wherever they could.

Those who did not sleep hardly spoke, sat watching and waiting, eyes red and swollen with fatigue, faces pale in the moonlight. Fires flickered amongst the various groups as Ben wandered about, talking quietly to some of them. One youngster sat alone by a tree, rifle at the ready. No older than seventeen, Ben thought, remembering his own seventeenth birthday. He and his sister had climbed trees that day, and Jo-Ellen had scraped her knee and torn her dress. Trying to sneak into the house without being seen had been impossible. Ma had been very angry.

'You not wanting to rest up, soldier?'

'Yes, Cap'n, I'm dog tired, but I can't sleep. I close mah eyes and I seen them damned Yankee Blue Bellies a running at me, so I stays awake.'

Ben placed a reassuring hand on his shoulder, and moved on to a group nearby. One soldier slept in an upright position by a tree, the others threw dice.

'You men all ready for the fight?'

'You bet, Captain,' came the reply. 'We're laying bets right now how many Yankees we can lick each.'

'You look all beat.'

'Yep, we're beat all right. Been riding and marching along that goddamned Valley just trying to keep out of range. They say that

Shield turned but Banks ain't far away. Can smell 'em from here. But the men are ready, Captain. The Yankees'll run like hell when they see real soldiers coming at 'em.'

'That's the spirit.'

Ben wandered over to where Richard Garnett was addressing his men. A man of inner strength, was the General. Ben had heard various accounts of him before he'd come to command the Stonewall Brigade under Jackson. His attention moved to a small group of men nearby and when he saw Leon Foley, he moved quickly out of sight. The officer with him was John Barnaby. Several soldiers slept not far away. No sense in rushing in now, he decided. He would wait and approach Garnett early morning. Best thing everyone could do was sleep. Conserve energy.

He found a dry spot beneath a tree, pulled his great coat around him and knew nothing more until dawn.

• • •

The entire camp came alive to the aroma of coffee and corn bread. Ben ate then went in search of General Garnett who introduced him to several officers, amongst whom was John Barnaby.

'Good to see you again, Captain. Seems we're destined to meet.'

Ben shook hands, relieved that Foley wasn't around.

The Brigade rallied and morale seemed to be much higher that bright morning. The chilliness was still apparent but a watery sun heralded spring.

On the morning of March 22nd, General Garnett and Colonel Ashby led their divisions forward.

• • •

The Valley was quiet. Jackson ascertained that Banks had been joined by Shield once again, and that they were now just a few miles ahead. The Brigade were to chase Shield instead of being chased by him and pleased enormously by this turn of events, and refreshed by a night's sleep, Jackson motioned his men forward.

The Confederates moved swiftly. Ahead lay Kernstown. Ben rode close behind Garnett. There came the sound of cannon and then the unmistakable thunder of cavalry. Jackson reined in to listen.

'Ho, there, Captain! Ride across and see how Ashby's faring!'

Ben made off to where Turner Ashby engaged James Shield in battle. As he reached the top of the rise and looked upon the battlefield, he realised in a flash the proportion of opposition that Ashby faced. Ashby had estimated the Federal Army to be greatly outnumbered even by Jackson's under-sized force, and Jackson for once had accepted this. Instead, Shield's men numbered thousands, and these were supported by newly arriving reinforcements. Ben rushed back to report.

'Ashby's heading into a trap and Garnett's men are outnumbered, sir!'

'Right – follow me, Jefferson!'

Jackson swung his mount and headed towards a group of Union soldiers, some mounted, most on foot. All these he despatched quickly by wildly cutting them down into a bloody mess with his lance. Stomach churning at the sight before him, Ben dutifully followed. Jackson was on a mission of his own.

'Now, save yourself, get off the battlefield!' yelled Jackson, as he galloped towards the distant trees to give assistance to Ashby. Ben sank to his knees, unable to obey the command immediately. His senses reeled, gunfire and shouting filled the air and he wondered if Garnett and Ashby had survived now that Jackson had been able to warn them. He stared around. Most of the Confederate side had gone; the dead and dying lay wherever he looked. He had to find cover before the Union boys found him.

Summoning up some energy, he moved quickly forward, stopped, listened. Another sound, unlike any other that day, caught his attention. A voice, or was it only the whistling of the wind in the trees?

He moved to the top of the rise and peered over. Ahead of him was a strange sight. A black boy was kneeling, head bent, hands behind his back. Standing over him with a gun at his head was one of Garnett's men.

'Now, you Yankee bastard, know what I'm gonna do? What I do with all Yankees – specially niggers.'

Ben tensed. It was Foley.

'Now then, boy, I'll let you up nice and slow and you're gonna beg for your life before I kill yer.'

As Foley moved off the boy, Ben stepped in.

'Foley, what in hell's name are you doing here? Why aren't you out there assisting your men?'

Foley swung round. 'Well, now, if it ain't the nice Captain. Heard you were hereabouts. I got us a nigger here to play with. Imagine that, Captain. A nigger in the Union army. Seems they ain't too fussy. You hold him down while I cut off his balls!' He swung a bottle to his lips and drank long and deep. 'Bourbon, Captain?'

'Let him go, Foley. That's an order!'

The sergeant sniggered. 'Oh, yeh? Don't tell me you're a nigger lover.'

'Let him go – now!'

'Well now, sorry, Captain, but I ain't about to let this here wretch go free. He's the enemy and we're sworn to kill the enemy, ain't that right?'

'Not when it's plain bloody murder, but then perhaps you're familiar with that lifestyle.'

Foley cocked the pistol in Ben's direction. 'What do you mean by that?'

'Remember the slave woman in Savannah?'

Foley lowered the gun. 'How'd you know about that?'

'Never mind. I came a long way for this moment. Give me the gun.'

'Yeh? What you gonna do, Captain, kill me? You into killing off your own men?'

The boy rose slowly to his feet. 'Ben, is that you?'

Ben turned at the familiar voice. 'Earl?'

The boy pulled off his cap. 'Sure is. Didn't recognise you behind all that dirt and that scraggy beard.'

'You don't look too good, either.'

Foley seized his chance. He lunged forward and grabbed Earl's gun. With both weapons on the two men, he said, 'Say your prayers, you both have seconds to live.'

From the distant hilltop came the sound of gunfire. Whether it was Union gunfire or a stray bullet, but a heaven-sent bullet whistled past Foley's head, enough to startle him. Ben brought up his foot and sent him flying and while Earl looked on, they rolled in the dust, hitting and tearing at each other. Retrieving one of the guns, Earl took careful aim and fired. Nothing. He fired again. It was jammed. An unfortunate blow from Foley's fist sent Ben into a stunned heap. Foley picked up the other gun and pulled Earl down, pressing the weapon to his temple.

'Say goodbye, nigger boy.'

Ben came to, dived with all his might at the unsuspecting Foley and the bullet meant for Earl lodged in a nearby tree. Ben shot Foley dead at close range.

Earl staggered over, helped Ben to his feet.

'I'll be okay,' said Ben, 'A bullet grazed my leg and Foley did some damage, but I'll be fine.'

'You gonna make it?'

'Yeh – try and stop me.'

'You saved my life, Ben.'

'Forget it.'

Earl looked at Foley's body. 'You're supposed to kill Union soldiers.'

'I know it. Looks like I'll have to pay one day for killing one of my own instead.'

'No, you won't. Not if we get a move on. They're sounding full retreat on both sides.' He pointed due south. 'Come on, that's the way we're heading. We're all done here.'

Holding each other up, they pressed forward, a strange combination of blue and grey.

'What the hell are you doing here, Earl? Who took you into their army?'

'General Shield. I gotta tell you, Ben, I was looking for you. I wanted to kill you.'

They walked until the sun set in a haze on the purple horizon. Darkness soon came. Ben peered into the distance. 'Hey – we walking to Savannah or something?'

'I know a place where we can put up. It's some thirty-five miles from here. You up to it?'

'Has it a fire and a bed?'

'Sure has.'

'Food and drink?'

'Yep.'
'What are we waiting for then?'

• • •

It was a long, slow walk. Gradually they put the miles behind them. When their food supplies ran out they ate dried corn in the fields. At night they slept under the stars, using their coats as blankets. On the night of the third day they saw Manassas.

In the moonlight, Emily's house looked mysterious. Earl led the way round the back. When the light within dimmed, he tapped on the door. Emily appeared, gun in hand, her face a mask of awe when she saw the two soldiers on her doorstep.

'Lordy, jest look at you now. I know'd you'd be in trouble soon as I let you go, boy.'

She fed them and showed them where to bathe. She dressed Ben's wounds and as soon as he found the spare room he fell into a deep sleep.

'You can rest up here for a few days, Earl,' Emily said as soon as they were alone. 'Your friend isn't well enough to travel and by the look of it neither are you. You going back there?'

'No, I'm through. As soon as Ben's able, we're heading back to Georgia. I'll probably be going back to trouble, but I'll face that when I get there.'

Emily studied him proudly. 'You're all grown up, you know that?'

She placed an affectionate hand on his shoulder and he gave her a big hug.

• • •

March 29th was brisk, chilly. Jo-Ellen longed for home; the very thought of Savannah caused her heart to lurch. Having remained in Philadelphia because George had taken a turn for the worse and she could not leave Rachel on her own, she then found out that her means of travel were curtailed indefinitely.

After making extensive enquiries into the state of the railroads she found out she could get back to Charleston in a round-about fashion and one morning she bade the de la Reys goodbye and set out on the journey home.

Guilt lay heavily on her. What kind of a mother was she not to be with her son during those important early months? From letters received from Samuel and Constance, she learned that her son was well, though she sensed her parents' disapproval. Although their grandson had received the utmost care and attention, they wrote, nothing could replace the presence and love of the mother.

Jo-Ellen longed to hold Alexander in her arms again, and to look upon familiar faces and places, instead of trying to fit into the insecure lifestyle she had been forced to live in the north. People were different there, she decided, as someone pushed roughly past. Certainly less courteous.

The journey from Philadelphia was harassing from the start. Most of the trains on the Ohio-Maryland railroad were being used for prisoners of war and those allocated to passengers were travelling at half their normal speed, so that she lost much precious time. At one point, she almost changed her plans completely and went back to Washington. She doubted the logic of that decision, however, as Rob's division was heading south. And south was where she wanted to be.

An hour passed and still the train did not move. She longed for a hot bath and a meal. How long was she to sit there, how long in fact was this war going to dictate the comfort and happiness of ordinary human beings?

'Mind if I share with you?'

A woman settled down opposite. Jo-Ellen helped lift her luggage to the rack above.

'How much longer are we to wait?' said the woman. 'I swear I spend more time on trains these days than anything else.' She untied her bonnet, revealing tied back dark hair. She straightened her shawl and smoothed her gown.

'Yes, I've been trying to get away from Philadelphia for several days,' said Jo-Ellen.

'That where you live?'

'No, I come from farther south.'

'I'm from Massachusetts. At least I was born there. Went to Washington City to train as a typist and here I am, wandering the country looking for the war most of the time.'

'Are you a correspondent?'

'Heavens no. I nurse, not that well, mind, but I try and put myself wherever the fighting is.'

'How wonderful.'

'It's something that was thrust on me, I guess. Something happened back in Washington which led me to believe I could be of assistance to our boys. Happened just after Bull Run. I saw boys no older than fifteen fall dead by the wayside.'

'How dreadful.'

'I was sitting at my desk in Washington, when remnants of McDowell's army staggered back from Virginia. Pouring with rain it was. Never forget it. I looked down Pennsylvania Avenue and there they all were, all collapsed on the sidewalks and lawn. The President must have had quite an eye full as well. That's when I saw the miracle.'

'Miracle?'

'Women, some old, some young, came from nowhere. Tended the soldiers' wounds, gave cups of coffee and food. Some of the poor devils were barefoot, their feet torn and blistered. The biggest miracle was me, I left my job and joined those women. It was like I had no choice. One youngster smiled at me and held on to my hand and I just knew what I had to do. I been tending them ever since. Now I'm on my way to the Peninsular.'

Jo-Ellen listened with increasing awe. 'I expect nurses are in short supply.'

'Certainly are. By the way, my name's Mary Bacon.'

'I'm Jo-Ellen.'

'Well, Jo-Ellen, seems we'll be travelling companions for the next few hours. That's if we move at all. Last time this happened, we were told to evacuate the train for wounded soldiers.'

She sat back and closed her eyes. Jo-Ellen took the opportunity to think about her own situation. By the look of things she may not get further than Yorktown and a connection to Charleston would be down to pure luck, so that any hope of arriving in Savannah within the next few days seemed dashed. She had been foolish to suppose she could return to Georgia as freely as she had departed from it. There were now blockades to consider, for one thing. Daniel had been right. She had pushed her luck by going to Philadelphia.

She looked at her companion, whose heavy breathing betrayed sleep. When she wakes, she thought, I'll talk to her, ask her all I need to know. There was something about Mary Bacon she liked; the capable hands, the intelligent eyes and direct manner.

Having settled the matter in her mind, she too closed her eyes.

• • •

By the time they arrived at the Peninsula, they were friends. More often than not soldiers had boarded their trains and more often than not the two women had been not only interrogated at some length, but eventually left stranded with no transport at all, their only course of action being to put up at inns or hotels. This had been increasingly difficult, as many had been taken over by troops and used as hospitals. Once a thriving business, the hotel industry, especially in smaller towns, had become one of the first casualties of the war.

Their train eventually shuddered into their final station. As they collected their belongings, Mary Bacon said, 'How can a journey have taken so long, Jo-Ellen, yet I don't mind, having had such stimulating company as yourself.'

'That's how I feel, too, Mary. It was a pleasure meeting you.'

The older woman turned to her. 'Jo-Ellen, I didn't ask where you come from.'

Jo-Ellen hesitated. 'From Savannah. I expect you can tell by my voice and also my name.'

'I should so like to keep in touch when this war is over.'

'Me too. What will you do now, Mary?'

'I'm off to find a field hospital. There's a battle going on and I have to be there.'

They exchanged addresses and Mary made to walk away. 'You know,' she said, 'I realise you have your baby to consider, but are you sure you want to go home when your man's probably hereabouts?'

'You think he is?'

'From what you told me, it's very likely. Remember, your son is in safe hands, your man probably isn't.' Mary held out her hand. 'But take no notice of me. Goodbye and safe journey.'

With determined strides, she walked away, leaving those words drumming through Jo-Ellen's head. To give up now would render her entire trip meaningless. She took a deep breath and followed the retreating figure.

'Mary! I've changed my mind!'

They found a buggy and went to a hotel outside Yorktown. The hoarding hung down and the building smelt dusty and dirty. After settling in, they sought out the nearby field hospital. This turned out to be an old hotel which had been converted.

'Where's the fighting?' asked Jo-Ellen, aware of the silence.

'It's out there somewhere,' came the reply.

As soon as she was able, Mary assumed the duties of matron, directing all matters except amputations. Jo-Ellen watched in admiration as she gave out orders, skilfully tended to patients' needs and generally ran herself off her feet. Many of the wounded were Union soldiers and Jo-Ellen searched daily for Rob, praying he was not among the hordes of near dead loaded from the wagons being used as ambulances.

Supplies soon began to dwindle. The fighting had been going on for almost a month, each day bringing another batch of wounded from both sides until it became evident that if fresh supplies did not arrive from the Sanitary Commission, there would be a state of emergency at the hospital.

Jo-Ellen's rations were cut by half but she did not mind because often she could not face eating. It was when they were at rock bottom that supplies finally got through. Fresh bandages, morphine, food, and drink duly arrived and the staff had a small celebration, sparing time out for a glass of brandywein. The hospital diet was potato and gruel and bread pudding, and often tea. On special occasions the soldiers were given fruit. Morale gradually picked up, while Jo-Ellen took on more duties, those being to feed the patients and help dress the wounded.

As she became accustomed to the smells and sordid sights, she was able to separate her working life from her private life, what there was of it. Tiredness overtook her often during the daytimes. Dark circles formed round her eyes and she lost weight. Whenever possible she wrote home to let them know she was safe. 'Soon,' she wrote, 'I shall be there with you all.'

It was this thought that kept her going.

SHADOWS OF CONFLICT

•••

McClellan chose two men to accompany him as they left Fort Monroe that brisk morning. The fragrance of jasmine and morning glory hung heavily on the air as Rob and Custer rode alongside their general. The colourful surroundings told that spring had arrived suddenly, but each man knew that this serenity would soon be torn apart and the freshness replaced by the pungency of cannon and gun smoke.

Halting close to where the Confederates were known to be entrenched, McClellan said, 'You scout to the left, Major. Lieutenant, you off to the right.'

Rob dismounted and tethered his horse, moved forward a few hundred yards to some boulders, and climbed up. Below was a mass of grey uniforms. The line of men was thin and he estimated that if the line were consistent, the Confederates were inferior in number. He waited several minutes before reporting back.

'I believe that if we surprise attack now, sir, we could wipe them out. They'll never hold their line.'

'And you, Lieutenant?'

George Custer agreed. 'I think we should go in right away, sir.'

McClellan strode to and fro in thought. 'The line might appear to be thin, but I saw Confederates moving about and there looked to be thousands of them. The thin line might be a trick. Don't know this fellow Magruder too well, but rumour has it he can be devious. So, let's not be too hasty.'

Custer shot Rob a look which read: here we go again.

'I want our men entrenched,' McClellan was saying, 'I don't think we should attack yet.'

'But General, we could waste valuable time!'

'We might, Lieutenant, but I'd rather waste time than lives.'

They rejoined the division and set about carrying out McClellan's orders. The troops threw up earthworks, dug trenches, graded military roads. After installing siege guns, McClellan sent a message to President Lincoln that they were vastly outnumbered and that he urgently required General McDowell's corps to back him.

Lincoln's reaction was one of anger. McClellan had more than enough men, he insisted. To further the point, he sent General McDowell to guard Washington City and with him went 30,000 of McClellan's men.

• • •

Several days passed with no sign of action. Rob was frustrated to bursting point. It was now common knowledge that the Confederates were low in numbers, that Magruder had pulled off a successful bluff. It was also known that General Johnston was about to arrive with massive reinforcements. Still McClellan hesitated to move.

The siege dragged on into weeks. It rained heavily. Hundreds fell sick with tick fever. Food supplies were low and the men became exhausted.

On May 3rd almost a hundred Federal guns were at last in place before Yorktown. McClellan planned his bombardment for May 5th. That night the Confederates intensified their fire. By the following day they had all vanished.

Lincoln blamed McClellan for hesitating. The General merely declared a victory for the Union. The Confederates had pulled back to Richmond. McClellan decided to follow.

The Confederate Congress fled and Richmond prepared for disaster as the Union Army got closer. McClellan once again hesitated, convinced his army was outnumbered. This gave General Jackson time to lead his men on to the Peninsula to join in the defence of Richmond, and again save the day for the Confederacy.

• • •

The fighting was intense. Rob cleverly issued orders that enabled him to stay out of the main line – until he and his men were driven into a cornfield facing a Confederate attack.

Bullets whined overhead as he pressed forward, urging his men into the line of battle. As he ran towards the shelter of some trees, he caught a bullet which shattered his collar bone.

Dazed with pain and striving to remain conscious, he lay there helpless, praying that someone would get him out of there. No one came. His men were in the heat of battle. Meanwhile, he was in a disastrous situation. It would only be a matter of time before he was spotted by the enemy, who were heading his way. Fighting off the black mists that came in waves, he willed himself to stay awake long enough to crawl to safety.

His shoulder bled badly, his horse was gone. In the distance blue uniforms clashed with grey as Union mortar rained into the Rebel lines. With great effort he managed to get to his feet and find a tree to lean against before making for some foliage and sinking down out of sight. If he could just make it behind his own lines, get some help.

The sound of a footfall had him reaching for his gun. It was not there. He had dropped it in the cornfield! Another footfall, closer this time. He looked on helplessly as from out of the foliage stepped a Confederate officer, gun in hand and lance swinging from his hip.

Sweat broke out over his body. This was to be his final moment, his life ended by a Confederate bullet. No honour, nothing. He cowered, waited for the impact. His eyes followed the revolver directed at his head, and the two legs clad in grey tucked in black mud-caked boots.

The officer bent down, searched his pockets. 'Hey there, Major, what's your name? Your name!'

Rob was so terrified he couldn't speak. He felt himself lifted up and there came the distorted view of the trees as he hung upside down over the officer's shoulder. Stray bullets whistled past, until he was lowered against a tree.

'You should be okay here, Major.'

He closed his eyes, felt nauseous and thirsty. The officer pressed a water bottle to his lips. Through the trees was the welcome sight of the hazy sun.

When he later came to, the sun had gone. There was a chill in the air and he could not be sure whether the glow on the horizon was sunset or oncoming dawn. His jacket had been torn off and his shoulder bandaged. He glanced around. He was behind Federal lines. In the distance came the sound of gunfire and cannon but finally there was blessed silence. He tried to move but pain wrenched through his body. He closed his eyes, dreaming of a hot meal and a bath. He was alive, someone had saved him and that someone had been the enemy.

Or had it all been a dream?

It was some time before Federal soldiers came by. Someone knelt beside him, a shout went up, another face – a familiar one – then George Custer spoke. 'The arm's bad, Major. You lost a lot of blood, but you'll make it. Who in hell's name bandaged you? Hey there – bring the Major in – ah – gently now.'

He was lifted on to a makeshift stretcher. 'Shambles, Major,' Custer went on. 'First Magruder duping us, then Jackson arriving from the Valley to back Johnston. All clever moves. And we almost had Richmond!' He shook his head. 'Lincoln'll shit himself over this one!'

• • •

Treating Union and Confederate as equals, Jo-Ellen was gratified to find that some of them became friendly with each other and would chat cheerfully to her as she worked.

'Hey, sister, I done heard a southern drawl that tells me you're from close by where I come from.'

'And where's that, soldier?'

'South Carolina, ma'am.'

'I know it well.'

'There yer are – told you fellas so.'

'God dang it, and I thought you were from Washington, ma'am,' said another.

'I know that also.'

As the days passed, Jo-Ellen saw the urgency for new recruits at the hospital. The only other staff were two orderlies, three women who appeared as untrained as herself, and a doctor-cum-surgeon who wielded the knife all too readily. The rooms were cleaned regularly but were over-crowded. Dried blood and urine were constant companions on her visits to bedsides and the stench of unwashed bodies and vomit mingled with that of the dead and dying was forever with her, even when she spared herself a few moments outside for some air. At the end of each day she returned to her small room, refreshed herself and tried to eat.

When the Confederates finally pulled out of Yorktown in defence of Richmond the fighting all but stopped, and it was on the morning of the Confederate exodus that they brought in a new wagon-load of wounded.

Rob smiled at the nurse as she expertly bandaged his shoulder and made him comfortable.

'Thanks, what's your name, nurse, mind if I ask?'

'Mary Bacon. Now you rest up, soldier.'

Mary checked the list and hurried off to find Jo-Ellen. 'There's a soldier in section two you'll want to see. A Major de la Rey.'

Jo-Ellen's heart pumped wildly. 'Is he...?'

'He's going to be fine. Got a shoulder wound but he'll be up and about in no time.' Mary gave her hand a friendly squeeze. 'Go see him.'

• • •

He was surrounded by the dead. Rob's eyes took them all in – so many of them. He had to get out of there. Getting a bullet had really set him back. Damned if he could remember much, but one thing he did remember and it had been no dream. That Confederate officer. He had saved his life. Why?

'Nurse!' No reply. 'Nurse Bacon!' He wanted to ask how long he had been there. Moving in and out of consciousness had caused him to lose all sense of time.

'Nurse Bacon!'

'Will Nurse Jefferson do?'

The voice was familiar. God, he must be in pretty bad shape.

'Rob, my dearest Rob.'

There is was again. Of course, it was all part of the same dream. Jo-Ellen had been on his mind constantly and now his mind was playing harsh tricks. He turned his head, saw the face peering down at him. He blinked – the face did not go away. Had he died?

She kissed his forehead then his lips. 'Rob, it's me, Jo. I've come to take you home.'

With his free hand he touched her as though she were not real. He brought her hand to his lips and held it there. 'How in God's name did you get here, Jo?'

Overflowing with emotion, she wanted to tell him all at once, about their son, about how she had sought endlessly for him.

'Quickly nurse – I need you!' Mary's voice broke the spell. 'Amputation!'

A soldier, blind and confused, cried out in pain. Jo-Ellen hurried to assist, held the soldier down, soothed him as best she could. No older than Rob, she thought, her heart wrenched beyond endurance. She'd had enough. It was time to leave. She had stayed away far too long but now her mission was complete. She looked with affection at Mary, who had been so instrumental in finding Rob.

Their eyes met in unspoken understanding. Mary knew the time had come, as they collected the blood soaked bandages and moved on to another patient.

• • •

As the sun spread fingers of eager light across the floor of the bedroom, Susanne rose early and planned on a long walk, a plan that was not to materialise.

Curtis was calling out. Something had happened. She ran along the hallway to the drawing room and there found her mother in a state of confusion. She drew her gently into her arms.

'Mama – tell me what's happened. Curtis, get some brandy. And is the doctor on the way?'

Elizabeth tried to calm herself. She had taken her husband's breakfast in as usual – she preferred to do that herself – and suddenly he fell forward. She called to Curtis and did not remember any more.

Susanne had long known it was a matter of time before her Papa would have to take to his bed for good. Now that the time had arrived she felt unprepared for it. Ralph Montgomery had been such a lively man all his life, and it had been a fear of his that he would end up an invalid.

When the doctor came out to them, Susanne asked to see her father. He looked from one to the other.

'Elizabeth, Susanne, I'm sorry. He went peacefully.'

Elizabeth collapsed. Susanne was horrified. Her dear Papa, dead? Her Mama lying in a dead faint. 'Doctor – have you something to help us? Mama isn't strong enough for this!'

Elizabeth took to her bed and there she remained, her sole reason for living having been taken from her.

Following that dreadful experience, Ben had come home, the one joyful occasion among the many sad days. Susanne was watching the sunset, her mind tortured about her Papa, when two figures appeared on the horizon. As they drew closer, and she saw who it was, she ran to them and embraced them. She had never seen two such pathetic creatures. For two weeks Ben occupied the rear bedroom. Progressing well under the supervision of the family doctor.

'My dearest,' he said one morning, 'I feel almost ready to leave this bed and resume my place in yours.'

'No, Ben, the doctor says you are to stay in here a while longer.'

'We'll see. Come and sit here by me.'

She snuggled into his arms. 'I long for our baby,' she whispered. 'We'll call him Jamie, if you don't mind.'

'Jamie Jefferson. I like it. And there'll be no wars for him to fight.'

'Tell me it will soon be over.'

He kissed her. 'Sure – just a couple more months.'

'Ben, will you be going back there? But, of course you will.'

That question had been pounding through his head on the journey home to Savannah. 'No, my love. I'll not be going back. I know it could mean trouble, but I can't leave you, not now. I want to be here when our son is born.'

'They'll come looking for you, won't they? I mean, isn't it desertion?'

He held her to him. Of course it was desertion. Him and thousands like him.

Neither spoke for a long time as they watched the last of the sun blend into darkness. Not a sound came from the inky blackness that came to claim the countryside. It was altogether a different world down there in Savannah.

Chapter Six

The buggy ambled down the track and stopped in the Plantation forecourt. Rob assisted Jo-Ellen down and made a casual assessment of the scene before him.

'Hasn't changed a bit,' he said.

'Did you think it would?'

He smiled. 'Nope, guess not.'

It was a clear, balmy day. Summer had arrived with its deep blue skies, the rivers were low and the earth dry. Everywhere smelt wonderful, everywhere looked untouched. There still remained that lazy peace and slow pace of life. On the breeze came the familiar sound of Negro singing.

Jo-Ellen thought her heart would burst with happiness. Hazy and lazy. How often she had held that vision in her mind as she toiled at the field hospital. Her eyes wandered towards the barn and the lake, both visible through the trees.

'Here at last,' she said half to herself.

Curtis and Earl were the first to greet them. 'Miss Jo-Ellen, Mr Rob! Good to have you back!'

'Go tell Miss Susanne we're here, Curtis.'

'She with her Mama. Mr Ralph – he passed away and the missus has been ill since.'

'Oh no! How sad. Ralph Montgomery is dead. You remember him, don't you, Rob? Come on, let's go find the family.'

•••

Ben, having left his bed for the day, limped over to his sister and gave her a big hug. He took Rob's hand and grabbed him to him. 'What a day this is!' The two people he loved most in the world were back safe and well.

For the next few hours Plantation life stopped. Word soon got out that Jo-Ellen was home. Louise brought Alexander to them and Rob proudly held him up for all to see.

'Alexander de la Rey. Has a certain ring to it. Can see him in big business in Pennsylvania with a name like that.'

Samuel took Rob aside. 'You goin' back there, boy? You gonna continue fighting for the Union?'

Rob nodded. 'I have to, sir. What would you do?'

'Confound it, I'd get the hell down here to my wife and child. I'd not fight on the other side – you know I don't approve of that.'

'I'm the enemy, you mean.'

'That's right, you're the enemy. Won't make for a good marriage. Remember that.'

'I will, sir, but Jo-Ellen knows what I'm about. And she loves me.'

'She loves you, yes, but she also loves the south.'

'I know that.'

'As long as we understand each other, boy.'

'Just doing my duty.' He grinned to himself. As long as he could remember, Samuel had called him 'boy.'

'Can't ask a man to do more than that, I suppose.'

Susanne threw open the door and ran to her friend. 'I saw the buggy outside and knew you were here! My, you've lost weight, and you still look so beautiful!'

'And you, Susanne, have put some on,' Jo-Ellen said.

Susanne glanced down at her swollen tummy. 'Ben's over the moon about it.'

Taking Rob's hand in hers, Jo-Ellen said, 'You remember Rob, don't you?'

'Of course. I remember meeting you when we were all youngsters playing together.'

He kissed her cheek. 'It's good to see you again. Our condolences for your sad loss.'

'We're so sorry. Is your Mama all right?'

'She's resting. It will take time.'

While the women engaged in conversation, Ben urged Rob into the adjoining room.

'I've made up my mind, Rob, I ain't going back.'

Rob did not reply. Ben had matured, he thought, the haggard look sat well on him.

'I thought of you often when them Yankees came at me. It hurt, you know, that we were actually fighting each other. Every time I pulled the trigger, I thought about you, Rob. What the hell would I have done if you were out there, too?'

'I did, too,' he said at last. 'I looked for you. Heard you were with Johnston. Heard he got hit at Seven Pines. You'd have been there, too, wouldn't you, if you hadn't been here?'

'Yes, and I guess you don't approve of my decision.'

Rob shrugged. 'I'm not here to judge you, Ben.'

'I've seen too much. Some of it was unbearable. I expect you know what I mean. I admire a man who can take that on board and go back for more. Me, I can't. Perhaps you're made of stronger stuff.'

Again Rob did not reply. He poured another brandy.

'We're going to have to put this business behind us,' Ben said, accepting another drink. 'You're staying here with us, aren't you, Rob? I mean, Alexander's going to grow up here?'

The message in his eyes was plain. Rob might be a Union man, but his son belonged to the south.

'Jo and I are discussing it. We want to be with the folks we love, and I pray the war doesn't last much longer. However, I've not made up my mind entirely. Jo wants to live on the Plantation and for now this is where we'll stay until I get well.' He raised his glass. 'Here's to us.'

He made to depart, tucked an arm round Ben's shoulders. 'Take care, won't you, old friend?'

Rob went through and managed to entice Jo-Ellen into another room. He drew her into him. 'We'll be married soon as we can get a preacher to do it, Jo.' His lips came down to meet hers. 'I'm the luckiest man alive to have a woman like you.' His eyes burned into her body. 'I want you – now.'

A distant noise caused her to giggle. 'Bad timing, Rob. The others are not very far away.'

He held her tightly to him. 'Goddamn it.'

'Can you be patient, sir?' she taunted him.

He slanted an amused glance at her. 'I'm not sure. Never had to wait for a maiden before.'

He lowered his head and claimed her mouth again.

'Oh, Rob, we've the rest of our lives together, haven't we?'

Her self-doubt startled him. 'Of course. Why so doubtful, my love?'

'I pray you haven't ever to leave me.'

He sighed. 'That's something I may not be able to avoid. I have no control over when I go back.'

She knew then. He said 'when' not 'if.' He was going back.

'You know, I'd not be alive today if it hadn't been for the Reb officer I told you about. Odd, isn't it? I thought I was a dead man, instead he carried me to safety.'

She lowered her lashes, unable to say the words in her head. 'It's good to know that men aren't all killers.' To change the subject, she added, 'Do you think the war will ever come this far south, Rob? Do you think it will come to Savannah?'

'Don't rightly know the answer to that, dearest. It's what the Union want, surely, for we have to take Richmond sooner or later and then it will be a matter of time before we head farther south. But, let's not talk of that.'

He felt torn, wanting to take her away from the world for those blissful moments. There was no avoiding the inevitable. He had to return to his division to be alongside his colleagues. News via the press, together with graphic pictures courtesy of Thaddeus Lowe, of some 80,000 soldiers under General McClellan having established themselves at White House Landing, had been constantly on his mind. The rain-swollen Chickahomany River had parted some of the force from the main body and they had been attacked by the Confederates, resulting in 10,000 casualties. This news had stunned him. The war might last longer than he at first envisaged. This was not part of his plans at all. Furthermore, the leadership of the Confederate Army, following the wounding of General Johnston, was now in the hands of Robert E. Lee. This was not good news. His thoughts flew to George Custer and his men. They would begin to see his constant absence as having abandoned them if he did not get back soon. It would not look good on his record were he to remain in the south too long. The press might not be too kind when at some future date he sought office.

Through the window he saw the acres stretching far into the distance. Earl and Curtis were talking together. Ben was with his mother, and Susanne was chatting to Samuel. Rob felt at peace there for the time being. All in good time he would go and face what lay ahead.

'I refuse to wait any longer, woman,' he whispered. 'Come on, let's creep upstairs.'

They went to their room and locked the door. Her body shook with an urgency that intoxicated her as he kissed her passionately, his fingers undoing the buttons on her blouse and loosening the garment so that it fell from her body, exposing her hard nipples. He took them into his mouth, trapping, tantalising, drawing moans of excitement that quickly brought an erection which he drove into her, transporting them to a land of pure joy.

Afterwards, she lay wrapped in his arms while he drifted in and out of sleep.

'Tell me, Jo, do you love me?'

She frowned in the half light, surprised at his moment of insecurity.

'Yes, with all my heart.'

'And I love you. I did not think it possible to love another human being so much.'

She rejoiced in the words she had waited so long to hear. The past months had been erased – all that really mattered now was that they were together.

She hung onto that thought in the darkened room. She could not bear to think past the moment.

• • •

The wedding was a quiet affair. There was no desire to go away on a honeymoon, both agreeing that to be in Savannah was their dearest wish.

Rob tried to persuade his parents to come down on a visit, but Rachel insisted that George was not well enough to travel in such uncertain times, and so he promised that they would journey to Philadelphia as soon as it was possible for a second wedding, and of course they would take Alexander with them.

Life for Jo-Ellen during the following weeks was exciting and happy. Samuel had given as his wedding present the annexe to the house, a little used section which he had renovated and refurbished, and this together with taking care of Alexander, kept her busy so that thoughts of the war and of her own past involvement began to fade.

Southern morale soared. Following the Seven Day Battles in June under their new leader, the tall and handsome Robert E. Lee, they began to consider themselves invincible. This was reflected in day-to-day conversations and in the press. The future for all in the south appeared much more secure, regardless of growing costs and the gradual decline in living standards.

On a hot late July day, Jo-Ellen found Rob in the study scribbling notes. Placing her arms round his neck, she said, 'You seem so preoccupied, Rob. What are you doing?'

'Writing of the war so far. In these pages is a first hand account.'

Her eyes lighted on the words 'Bull Run.' 'Oh – were you there?'

His expression changed. 'Jo, please go and do whatever you have to do. Leave me to finish this.'

His tone hurt her. 'Aren't you sick of the war? Don't you want to forget it? Instead, I find you going over it in detail. Why, Rob?'

He swung round on her. 'You needn't trouble yourself with it. Have you nothing to do?'

'Yes, I've something to do!'

'Look, this is history we're making, Jo. Do you realise that there's not one clear account of the action out there? It's only thanks to Lowe and his balloon corps that we have up-to-date details of it all. Look at these pictures – they're incredible. The most interesting part, though, are the politics involved. I'm going to do a piece on Simon Cameron, William Seward and Thaddeus Stevens and I aim to get Ben in on it as I'll need his account of Bull Run.'

He turned his attention back on his work and did not hear Jo-Ellen leave the room. She found Susanne downstairs, her figure full with the expected baby.

'My,' she said, fanning herself, 'This weather is just too overbearing for me in my state.' She stopped her vigorous fanning. 'Is something the matter, Jo-Ellen? You look upset.'

'Just preoccupied, that's all.'

Susanne plopped into a nearby chair. 'I have to admit I'm wishing the time away. There's so much to do with Papa gone and all.'

'Is your Mama up and about yet?'

'Yes, but she's lost interest in everything. I don't know where we'd be if we hadn't joined forces. Earl and Curtis work so well together and between them they're practically running the Plantation. Once this baby arrives, though, I'll be able to take on much more.' She stopped. 'There *is* something wrong. Do you want to talk about it?'

Jo-Ellen picked up the discarded fan and seated herself.

'It's Rob. He doesn't seem interested in the Plantation. I know he helps Ben sometimes but his heart isn't in it. He's writing all the time about the war and I know that any day now he'll want to go back.'

Susanne placed a reassuring hand on her arm. 'It's what he wants to do, you know that, Jo-Ellen. Rob isn't a farming man any more than Ben is in big business. Rob's heart is in the city and surely if he wants to write about the war, it isn't harmful. His interest is politics, isn't it?'

'Yes, I know and you're right, but somehow he's different lately. His manner – it's so angry sometimes. And the only time I see him become enthusiastic is when he's writing down those awful happenings of the war.'

'You mean, he's ignoring you, is that it?'

Jo-Ellen gave a weak smile. 'I'm being silly, I guess.' She wanted to say things that ladies did not say to each other, that when Rob made love he was no longer gentle, that she felt frightened sometimes and didn't know why. But she said none of these things. 'I watch him pore over those notes as though his life depends on it. And he's grown so restless lately, as though he's itching for some action, as though he's bored. There – I've said it. I know he loves me and Alexander, but I feel that he misses being with his men.' Her eyes misted. 'Deep down I feel he will never settle here. His heart's in the north as mine is in the south, and that's where he wants Alexander to grow up –in the big city. We have differed so on that subject lately.'

'I'm so sorry, it must be very hard for you. And I do understand, truly I do.'

'You do?'

'Yes, sometimes I see that expression on Ben's face, and I dread to hear what's in his mind. He hates war, and that is a real comfort to me, but he also feels he has deserted and although he doesn't want to go back, at times I think he may do so just to ease his conscience.'

'Why doesn't this awful war end, so we may all live together in peace!' Even as she said it, Jo-Ellen knew that was not the problem. The war was not to blame for the differences between her and Rob.

Susanne left her to retire in the heat of the day, and Jo-Ellen remained by the window, her heart and mind racing. What was this fear she was experiencing? Something deep inside, a subconscious dread.

Louise brought Alexander to her and the sight of him chuckling cheered her up.

'A letter came for you, miss.'

Handing Alexander back to her, she took the envelope and tore it open. Her heart missed a beat when she saw it was from Daniel. It was brief, advising that he was safe and well. No mention was made of Rob, but she knew well enough that it had been Daniel who had saved him that day. He had remembered the photo she had shown him, had given her back the man she loved. Tender thoughts and feelings filled her as she tucked the letter away.

The following day Rob worked in the study, dividing his time between helping on the Plantation and his writing, so that she saw little of him. When negative thoughts crept into her mind she thought of her days in Washington. Had she really met Union Generals McDowell and Patterson? What an exciting time it had been and she was sorely tempted to tell Rob about it but she had made a promise to Daniel and intended to keep it.

As they walked together one morning in the sunshine, Rob said, 'I've been thinking about our future – yours, mine, Alexander's – and was wondering where it would be better for us to live, here in the south which is now reeling economically, or in the north where people are thriving.'

'I thought all was well down here –'

'It was beginning to look that way, but thank God there's been a sudden about-face. These past few weeks have brought a sharp decline in standards and it'll get worse before it gets better. Europe probably won't give the Confederacy the recognition she wants, no matter how hard Davis tries, and without their backing, the south could lose out completely.'

Jo-Ellen stopped walking. 'What did you say?'

'I'm only talking facts.'

'You said thank God! You're gloating about what's happening

down here, Rob. You seem to revel in the fact that we're going to lose the war. Well, I don't think we will and I hate it when you talk like that!'

She moved off and he caught at her hand. 'Jo- listen to me.'

She turned to him, trying hard to compose herself.

'I'd like Alexander to grow up in a better environment.'

'A better financial environment, you mean! But that doesn't always guarantee happiness. And don't write off the south so quickly, Rob.'

'My dear, I don't mean to be unkind, but I'm not going to lie to you about what I see as inevitable. We must be sensible. I've no intention of allowing my family to live in hardship for the rest of their lives, and if we remain here, hardship is what we'll have.'

'You exaggerate, surely.'

He smiled. 'Perhaps, and perhaps I should not have spoken of it. Come, let's not argue.' He bent to kiss her and she tucked her arms around his waist. 'Let's go inside.'

Louise approached as they entered the house. 'Alexander's sleeping,' she said. 'And there's another letter for you, miss. I left it on the table in the drawing room.'

Jo-Ellen felt the colour hit her cheeks. Rob said, 'Another letter? Who are they from, Jo?'

She tried to ignore his searching eyes. 'Just a friend of Ben's. His name's Daniel Hunter.'

'A friend of Ben's. A Confederate, does that mean?'

'Yes.'

He stared at her. 'And why would this friend wish to write letters to you, Jo dearest?'

She gave a nervous chuckle. 'He's a good friend – Ben's really taken with him and he was so good to me in Washington.' The words were out before she could stop them.

'Washington!'

She felt herself go icy in the heat of the day.

'He wouldn't be an officer, by any chance?'

'Well, yes, he is.'

'So you spent your time in Washington with Confederates?'

'Daniel is hardly the whole army, Rob, and I was there searching for news of you. He helped me.'

'Hah! This gets better! He helped you to trace me? Now why would he want to do a thing like that?'

She was speechless, like a child before a stern headmaster.

'This officer seems very attached to you, Jo.'

The note of sarcasm in his voice did not escape her. His eyes flashed. 'It was this officer who saved my life, wasn't it?' His hand gripped her arm.

'Rob, you're hurting me!'

'That Major was hell bent on saving me, and why? Now, I'm not saying I'm not grateful for my life, what man wouldn't be, but I can only guess why a man might go to all that trouble for you, and that's because he's in love with you.' His grip tightened. 'What the hell's been going on behind my back!'

'Rob – that's nonsense! He did it for Ben, as well.'

Pulling her roughly to him, he said, 'Let's leave Ben out of this, shall we? Why haven't you spoken of this man before? I've been home some weeks now, how is it I come to know of him only by accident?'

'Because it isn't important!'

His eyes narrowed. 'He means nothing to you?'

'Beyond being a good friend, as Ben is to you, no.'

For a few moments the expression in his eyes scared her. Then, 'Forgive me, Jo. Sometimes a man can dream up the darnedest things. Must be love.' His lips curled into a smile and he kissed her. 'Go to your room and get prepared for me.'

'But, Rob...!'

'Do it!'

He took her hungrily and she returned his passion as best she could, unprepared for the near violence that his jealous nature had provoked. Afterwards, he said, 'There's nothing I wouldn't do for you, Jo dearest.'

'Then stay here, live in Savannah. We'll be happy, I promise!'

He swung round on her. 'Please don't disobey me. Don't ever ask that of me again. My mind is made up and as my wife you will go with me, wherever it may be.'

Smarting at his brutish tone, she replied, 'The war will never come here, we'll be safer here, surely.'

'I've strong doubts about that. You southern people have your heads in the sand. The war will come here, believe me, and when I send for you, you'll come to me, understand?'

He pulled himself off the bed and began preparing for dinner. 'Wear your blue gown tonight, Jo. I like to see you in that.'

Then he was gone, leaving her alone, sad and disappointed, her energy spent. The change in him frightened her. How much longer had they together, how much longer was she going to be allowed to live in her beloved Savannah?

In the solitude of her bedroom she quietly sobbed.

•••

Several evenings later at dinner he announced, 'Jo, dearest, I've received orders to report back.' He smiled at her. 'I've a duty to be there. I'm no longer considered a wounded man.'

'I expect you're relieved. I've seen you're not happy.'

'I'm happy with you, Jo, but I can't hide away and pretend the war doesn't exist.'

'I don't expect that. But, am I to lose you again, after all we've been through?'

'Of course not. It will be for only a short while. When I leave the army, it will not be because I didn't report back.'

'Like Ben? Is that what you're saying? He wouldn't like to hear that.'

'I wasn't referring to Ben, but men have simply gone home. I can't be one of those men, Jo.'

An idea occurred to her. 'I'll do what you've always wanted – I'll go with you. I'll settle in Philadelphia.'

'Good! At last. I'd like nothing better. However, you have to choose a better time. The north is being attacked constantly by Lee's men. Until we see him off, you'll be safer here. Then I'll send for you.'

She had tried. And failed. Everything was to be on his terms and she had a faint idea that anything she offered would be rejected. The subject was not referred to again. She tried to put from her mind his impending departure, making the most of the precious days left to her.

A final telegraph and she realised that Rob had been making urgent enquiries. He was to report for duty at the earliest possible moment.

On the eve of his departure she lay in his arms in the quietness of their bedroom. When he was able, he told her, he would send for her and Alexander and take them on that trip to Philadelphia, then they would make plans to settle there.

She clung to him all night, hardly sleeping, cherishing every moment until dawn broke with the new day. When the final parting came, she took to her room and nothing would induce her out of it for two days. When she did emerge, her eyes were red and swollen and her faced drawn with sadness.

• • •

Samuel Jefferson died suddenly one Sunday morning. He fell asleep in the chair and when Constance took him some refreshment and failed to wake him, she called for Ben.

'Get a doctor!' he ordered.

'No need,' Constance said, half to herself. 'I know my Samuel's gone.'

Ben put his arms around her. 'Ma, go into the house. I'll see to everything here.'

'No, I've been by his side all our married life, I'll not be leaving him now.'

'All right, Ma.' He called Earl. 'Go tell Curtis we need him to take over my duties today. And don't tell Miss Susanne, yet.'

Ben set about making arrangements. 'When the doctor comes, Ma, I advise you to take a sedative. It'll help you.'

She shook her head. 'No – all I need right now is Jo-Ellen. Where is she, Ben?'

He had been wondering that, too. Since Rob left, he had seen little of his sister. She had busied herself on the Plantation as usual, but kept to herself at all other times, and rarely joined them for dinner in the evenings.

Jacob said, 'I seen Miss Jo-Ellen in the stables.'

Ben hurried outside and found her grooming one of the mares. 'Seems you've got more time for them animals than you have for your family, Jo-Ellen.'

She looked up, startled. 'Ben – I didn't hear you arrive.'

'How long you been over here?'

'Most of the morning, I guess. If it's the work you're worried about, I finished it all.'

'Hell, it's not that. I know full well you pull your weight around here.' He paused. 'I've some bad news for you.'

She turned pale. 'Rob! It's Rob, isn't it?'

He put up an impatient hand. 'No – it's not Rob, it's Pa.'

'Papa!'

'He – died – this morning.'

Tears gushed from her eyes. 'Papa dead! Oh no! Where's Mama? Is she all right?'

'She needs you badly right now. I know you've had a hard time of it lately, but now you're needed. Rob's fine, I'm sure. Ma isn't and she needs you.'

'Yes, of course. I've been selfish, I know, but I'm all right now.'

That evening, Ben broke the news to Susanne. She was heartbroken, having loved Samuel like her own father. Constance refused to eat or rest, preferring instead to keep busy 'until she dropped' rather than give in to her grief.

That night, Ben was awakened by Susanne's cries.

'It's the baby – it's starting early. Quickly, get somebody!'

Tearing to the stables, he galloped into the night to fetch the doctor. Two miles down the road he reined in and pounded on Doctor Winfield's door. 'Doctor – come quickly! My wife – the baby!'

...

They waited outside the delivery room for what seemed an age. From inside, Susanne's cries broke the night silence while Ben paced to and fro praying quietly. The nurse was the first to appear, then the doctor came out.

'She's fine,' he said. 'A difficult birth, though.' To Ben he said, 'You may go in and by the way, you have a daughter.'

Ben laughed aloud. 'A daughter! And I was going to call her Jamie.'

'Then do so. It's a lovely name,' Jo-Ellen said.

Susanne lay against the pillows flushed and exhausted. Ben took her hand in his. 'Dearest, thank you, thank you. We've a beautiful daughter.'

'Let's call her Jamie Elizabeth Jefferson. I do so like the name,' she said.

Jamie Jefferson came into the world on August 28th 1862 as Robert E. Lee's men were facing General Pope's confused troops at Second Bull Run.

• • •

Jo-Ellen pushed the sun hat to the back of her head and dabbed at her brow with a lace kerchief. It was surely going to be an Indian summer. Late September and still so hot.

She lay outside the annexe, which was some way from the main house, but she could see Ben quite clearly appearing and disappearing through the doors. In fact, there was much activity from that quarter.

Settling back, she closed her eyes and relaxed her body. It was the only way to keep cool on such a humid day. It wouldn't surprise her if the skies clouded over and a storm hit them later. Movement, even that of using a fan for her face and neck, only made matters worse and she wondered how Ben could rush about so. True, there was work aplenty, but a certain amount of time each day should be set aside for relaxation.

Her thoughts flew to Rob. She had not heard from him since he'd left. Every day she tried to trace the route he might have taken, either from details in the newspapers or from the rumours flying around Savannah. All she knew was that the Federal Army had recently marched from Washington towards Lee's forces, apparently farther north. There had been talk of a major battle, but no further details had been published and fears for his safety were uppermost in her mind.

Turning her head and opening one eye, she saw Susanne hurrying into the house. She tutted to herself. Her friend had been up and about for only a month and should not be bustling around like that. Perhaps they were organising the small birthday treat for Alexander, which was what she ought to be doing, not lounging about so.

If only Rob were there, she thought, glancing up at the clear sky. He should be there for his son's first birthday. And he would be lying beside her, stroking her arm, or perhaps fanning her cheeks and she would allow him discreet kisses, never taking her eyes from his. Or they might have gone strolling beside the lake where it was cooler, arms tucked about each other, until the dying sun reminded them it was time to return to their son and spend a few hours together before Alexander's bedtime. These joyous thoughts brought a smile to her lips and transported her into her own private and beautiful world.

'Good afternoon, Jo. I trust you are well?'

Standing over her was Daniel Hunter. She leapt to her feet.

'Daniel, how wonderful to see you.' She allowed him to kiss her cheek and hold her close for a few seconds.

'I've ridden a long way for that,' he said.

Ben and Susanne joined them. 'We decided not to tell you. Thought we'd let Dan surprise you.'

'He did that all right!'

'Let's go in the house and have a cool drink,' Ben said. 'You can tell us all your news, Dan.'

As they went, Susanne whispered to Jo-Ellen, 'I like him. Isn't he handsome in uniform?'

'Louise, take the children upstairs so that we may talk alone,' Jo-Ellen said.

'Not before I see this little fellow.' Daniel lifted Alexander into his arms. 'My, you're a fine young man.' He peered into the crib where Jamie was sleeping. 'And this is your daughter, Ben?'

'Sure is. You can take them now, Louise, and will you ask one of the servants to bring refreshments?'

'Did you come specially to see us?'

'That's right, Jo. I take it you got my letters?'

'Yes, I was pleased to hear from you.'

Daniel appeared ill at ease, or so Ben thought. He took this as a signal to leave. 'I'm sure you two have a lot to talk about.'

'No, don't go yet. What I've come to say concerns all of us, especially Jo.'

'Is this about Rob? Is that why you're here?' Jo-Ellen faced him, her voice unsteady. 'Tell us what you've come so far to say!'

Daniel lowered his gaze. 'I saw him – at Antietam Creek.' His eyes found hers. 'Jo, I saw him fall. Soon as I was able I went to see to him but the smoke was so thick I could only take a quick look. I'm afraid, though...'

She stared at him wild-eyed. 'You mean, Rob's dead?'

'Yes, I think it's entirely possible.' He glanced at Ben. 'I'm so sorry,

Jo, to come here with such tragic news.'

She burst into tears. 'Sorry! You and your men kill my husband and you say you're sorry?' She rushed from the room. Susanne followed her.

Ben pushed agitated fingers through his hair. 'It's unbelievable. Not Rob.'

'I know how close you all were, how you must be feeling.'

Dazed, Ben said, 'Don't take note of my sister right now, Dan. She'll hate anything in grey for a while and that includes me, no doubt.'

Daniel sat down, placed his head in his hands. 'There's more.'

'Go on. I'm listening.'

'We were at Sharpsburg, dug in at the Creek and the Feds arrived, thousands of them.' He hesitated, choosing his words carefully. 'During the lull, my men were short of coffee, so they took the opportunity to fraternise with the Union boys and do a swap with some tobacco. One of my men came back and said that a major had been asking questions, wanted to know who commanded our division. When it was known to be me, he apparently asked more questions.'

'A major? Who the hell was it?'

'Robert de la Rey. He wanted to meet me. So I went along to meet with him. I held out my hand to shake but he just stood there, eyed me up and down. There was no mistaking what he was thinking.'

'So, Rob went back there and into battle. Who was in command?'

'He rode in later with Burnside's 9th Corps. They attacked us across the bridge, but Hill's men got the better of them. We managed to drive Burnside back to the Creek. It was the bloodiest day I've ever seen. We were outnumbered but we managed to hold our lines. I was so proud of our men, and am lucky to be alive.'

Ben said nothing, turned to stare out of the window. He felt guilty, always did these days. It sickened him to hear what other men were going through. Rightly, he should have been there with Daniel at Antietam. He'd felt bad enough reading about Second Bull Run, and now this.

'That's not all. Jo was almost right when she said I killed her husband.'

Ben turned. 'You sure you want to talk about this?'

Daniel leaned back against the soft leather headrest, his face pale and drawn. 'I don't want Jo to hear any of this, you understand. You have to promise me, Ben.'

'Okay, I promise.'

'When I went to meet the Major, he asked me outright if it had been me who carried him through the lines at Yorktown.'

'You did what?'

'I'll tell you about it some day. I said yes it was me, and he looked at me coldly, said that although he was grateful for his life, he would just as soon shoot me down right there. Then he accused me of paying court to his wife.'

Ben made to speak but decided against it.

'I replied that I did indeed find Jo attractive, but I respected her marriage and her love for him and, therefore, there was no basis for his accusation.' Daniel paused. 'He then said, "Are you saying, Major, that you, a Confederate, are an honourable man?"'

'Hell, what happened then?'

'I went back to my quarters and the next day we went into battle. I saw him, he saw me, but Major de la Rey appeared to be fighting his own war. He left his men and came charging right at me. He stopped, took aim and fired. His eyes were filled with hatred, or was it jealousy? Fortunately for me, he missed. Gave me time to take aim too, but for the first time I couldn't pull the trigger, Ben. That hesitation gave him the edge and I thought it was all over as he made to fire again. Then one of my men, Dougall McIntyre, shot him down. When I last saw him, the Major was lying in a pool of blood.'

'But you had nothing to do with that!'

Daniel shook his head. 'The man who killed the Major was my friend. Dougall knew he was saving me from having to do it myself.'

'I see. Go on.'

'I went back later, as I said. The sight was sickening. Some of the bodies had been stripped, some of the dead were left naked but when I looked for the Major, I couldn't find him. I guess his men removed his body. I searched around, but there were so many dead, so many pieces of bodies.' Tears filled his eyes. 'I never want to see that again, never. After that, I begged leave and rode here as soon as I could.'

'Thanks, Dan, I'll never forget what you did for us. It couldn't have been easy.'

'And Jo?'

'She'll need time. It's a shock but sooner or later she'll come round.'

'And you, Ben, are you staying here in Savannah?'

'Yes, for as long as I can.'

Daniel stood up, straightened his frock coat. 'I guess I ought to be going.'

'Where to?'

'I'll put up in town for a couple of days then go on back to Richmond.'

'Hey, why not stay here?'

'No, under the circumstances I'd rather stay in town.'

They walked out to the stables where Earl worked on the mare. When it was ready, Daniel mounted.

'By the way, Dan, how's Johnston?'

'He'll live.'

'I'd send my regards, but you haven't seen me, right?'

'Right. Take care of Jo for me.'

When the dust had settled and horse and rider had disappeared over the horizon, Ben went inside the house, distraught about Rob. He hesitated in the hall to try and compose himself. He had to be strong for Jo-Ellen's sake. Daniel's words had rid him of his feeling of guilt, however. No longer did he feel a great burden on his shoulders. The Picture Book War was in reality a departure from sanity, and he wanted no part of it. Rob had such high ideals yet he had lost his life, not fighting honourably for the Union, but for a private reason which had little to do with the war itself. Far better pistols at dawn, he thought, making for the drawing room, where he knew Susanne would be. 'Damned if I can see the sense,' he muttered to himself.

Susanne slid into his outstretched arms. 'Poor Robert, poor Jo-Ellen,' she said.

'Poor Alexander.'

'Yes. I've been dreading hearing that news. When you were away I thought I'd hear it of you. It's unbearable, Ben.'

'Ssh – don't talk about it. I'm here, my love. I'm not leaving you.'

She buried her head in his shoulder. 'Tell me again. Please.'

'I promise, nothing and nobody is going to make me take part in this bloody war!'

• • •

Jo-Ellen, dressed in black, emerged from her room the following day. Constance watched, her heart sympathetic as her daughter sat down at the breakfast table. She felt concerned. Jo-Ellen was behaving in an extraordinary manner. She had cried more the day Robert had left than she had since the news of his death. Perhaps shock was like that. She would have a word with the doctor at the first opportunity.

After they had eaten, Jo-Ellen took Ben aside. 'Tell me, where's Daniel? Why isn't he here?'

He was surprised. 'In the circumstances ...'

'To hell with that – he should be here! I want to see him. Tell me where he is.'

'At the Savannah Hotel, but...'

'Thank you, Ben.'

Changing into riding pants, she went to the stables and saddled the Grey. As she picked her way through the small market, music drifted from the Casino and bar. The main store where most of the groceries were purchased was open for business, and so was the whorehouse at the end of the street. Savannah was busy that afternoon.

Jo-Ellen paid little attention to these diversions as she made for the hotel, an imposing structure on the outskirts of town. Tethering the horse, she stepped inside. The man behind the desk moved to serve her.

'Good morning, have you a Major Daniel Hunter staying here?'

The man looked at the ledger. 'Indeed we have, miss. May I have your name?'

'Just tell him a friend wishes to see him.' She smiled. 'A surprise, you see.'

She waited patiently. The lobby was well kept, though rather small. An attempt at renovation had been made in places. She turned at the sound of his footsteps.

'Jo – why didn't you give your name?'

'I thought you might not wish to see me.' She paused to take him in. He had not long been awake by the look of it. He wore a casual shirt and trousers, hurriedly put together, and his hair was unkempt.

'Forgive me, I slept late.' His eyes twinkled. 'You look as lovely as ever.' He led her to a seat in the corner. 'May I offer you some refreshment?'

She declined. 'It was perhaps foolish of me to come, but I couldn't allow you to leave Savannah without seeing you once more. I want to apologise for my behaviour. It was unforgivable of me.'

He smiled. 'There's no need to apologise.'

'That's very kind. When do you leave for Richmond?'

'First thing in the morning.' He reached out towards her. 'I'm so sorry for what happened. I know how much you hurt inside.' His eyes sought hers. 'Jo, I know this isn't the right moment to say what I have to say.'

'No, please don't. It isn't right.'

'Right? I'm not sure what's right any longer. All I know is that under other circumstances I could bide my time. However, I've to go into battle again and who knows what the future holds, or whether we'll meet again?'

'Don't say that.'

'You can walk away if you wish, but I'm going to say the thoughts that are in my head. If I could make you happy again I would. It isn't possible yet, of course. If God allows me to live, I'll be back for you, Jo.'

'I am so lucky to have your friendship, Daniel.'

'Friendship? You must know I feel more than that.' He took a step towards her.

'No, please don't.'

He stopped himself from sweeping her into his arms. He had said far too much, and at such a delicate time had indulged himself when he should have thought only of her feelings. Yet, there was so little time left.

On an impulse she leaned forward and kissed his cheek. 'Take good care of yourself, Daniel. We'll all miss you. And thank you so much for coming to see us.'

She made to leave, and it was almost more than he could bear. 'Jo, always remember I love you. When the hurt goes away, if it ever does, I'll come for you.'

His words of love still floating in her head, she left the hotel and when she looked back, he was still there watching her. As she galloped away, his voice reached her on the wind.

'Don't forget – I'll be coming for you!'

The wind caught at her face, the sun climbed high. Filled with an overwhelming sadness, she was aware of tears rushing down her cheeks, for Rob, for herself, and now because she may never again see Daniel.

At the top of the rise she stopped to look at the panoramic view beyond. How she loved this beautiful land. The war had not come to Savannah. It must never come there. She urged the Grey forward and as she approached Jefferson House, the sun stood high and proud above it, highlighting the gold and mauves of the fall. Pride swept through her at the very sight of it all. She had lost the man she loved but she still had so much. Alexander, Ben, Susanne, her Mama, Jefferson House, and Daniel.

Louise came out to meet her and she took Alexander into her arms and held him high above before drawing him close to her breast. A new energy flowed through her. She would devote her entire life to her son, bring him up with love, mould him in his father's image. No more going away and leaving him. She had gone through that, had come out the other side, not unscathed, more mature, wiser and at the end of it she was still without Rob. Fate had dealt a bitter blow.

Without a word she climbed the stairs to her room and lay Alexander in his crib. The house was so quiet that she could hear distinctly the wind rustle the trees. An unusual calm settled on her. Before, she had needed to cry, to scream her anger at the unfairness of life. Now, despite everything, she felt composed. The reason for this was evident. She no longer felt alone.

Chapter Seven

Unrelenting rain fell over the Hagerstown countryside. Piles of furrowed mud lay along roads and tracks, driven there by the uncompromising wheels of buggies passing to and fro.

Laura Hilton alighted and paid her driver, waiting while he rein-slapped the horses forward. Hoisting her mud-spattered skirts, she climbed the house steps out of the rain.

Music and a high-pitched giggle, both familiar and irritating, caused her to hesitate before pushing open the front door. That woman was still there. Laura tilted back on her heels, her mounting anger tempered only by her father's laughter. Perhaps she ought to remain where she was rather than interrupt them.

Nothing had gone right that day. She had woken with a headache, following a night of troubled sleep – who could rest knowing that not far away some of General Lee's men roamed the countryside? – after which she had learned from one of the servants that Marilyn Beauville was going to visit that day.

Her eyes focussed idly on the creaking sign above her head. Its large letters required a re-paint. 'Hilton Heights' now read 'Hilton Heigh.' Again came the laughter. How long was her Papa going to entertain this time? The huge door suddenly swung open. Sebastian Hilton grabbed her arm.

'Ah, Laura, come girl, come with me.'

She stepped back, startled. Her Papa had been drinking.

'Where to, Papa?'

'You'll see, you'll see.'

Before the door closed behind him, Laura caught sight of Marilyn Beauville. Sebastian paused to dab at his brow with a kerchief.

'Are you all right, Papa?'

'Hmph? Of course!' He rounded on her. 'Where in God's name you been, Laura?'

She hesitated.

'Well?'

'I went to visit Lizabeth.'

'Haven't I told you I want you here when Marilyn comes to visit? It's better that you wait on her than those gossiping servants.'

Which was why she had journeyed to Berkeley Springs to see Lizabeth. She followed him to the buggy.

'I want to drive out to Frederick,' he said.

'Frederick, whatever for?'

He gave her a warning glance. 'I need supplies from the sutler's store.'

'But, Papa, surely one of the servants…'

'Not this time. Don't question me, girl!'

Not only the sutler's store, she thought.

'Papa, there are soldiers in Frederick.'

'That's right. A few stragglers left over from the Union Army. They won't bother us. Scared of them, eh?'

She shook her head.

'It's them Rebs we have to look out for,' he said, 'but I hear tell Lee's taken them all back to Virginia, so I think we'll be safe for the time being.'

Not all of them, Laura thought. Lizabeth had seen real evidence of that, had told her all the local war gossip, for Lizabeth's brother was a captain in the Federal Army of the Potomac and Lizabeth also read as much as possible about the war itself. Many of the Confederates had by all accounts moved from Frederick to Hagerstown, right where they lived! Her Papa might consider them safe simply because Rebel forces had left the Sharpsburg area the previous day, but there was no telling how many deserters remained, or how many soldiers from both sides were out there pillaging and attacking innocent people. Lizabeth had told her some sordid tales, and yes, she was indeed scared. Not that she would let her Papa know it since he frowned on what he saw as cowardice. She had to think like a man in such matters.

The buggy started forward and Laura settled back for the ride, feeling fatigued from her excursion into Berkeley Springs.

She glanced discreetly at Sebastian as he lashed out at the horses. He looked frantic. She had guessed right, too. They not only called at the sutler's store but paid a tedious visit to the expensive gown shop on the corner of Main Street. Tedious, because the gowns she saw and wanted she could not afford, and the one her father bought she had to stand in for ages while it was pinned. For Marilyn.

Later that afternoon they took the scenic route back towards Hagerstown. Laura said very little. She not only felt worn out but was disappointed at her Papa's behaviour. He was like a love-sick young man, and he was far from young. At fifty, shouldn't he be a little more adult? And did he really love that woman? Did he suppose she loved him? An ageing man and a twenty-eight-year old woman? She glanced at him again, but he seemed not to notice anything other than the road ahead, while the whip cracked under his hand.

The lane they turned into was flanked by fields and trees; gorse and bushes now turned gold with the arrival of the fall lined the lane, and the rain had left a fragrance which reminded Laura of earth and pine. To her it was beautiful and peaceful. Hard to believe that not far from there, only days before, hundreds of men had fought and lost their lives. She shuddered. Where the bodies had lain, there was now green grass covered with russet leaves. How she hated this war. It was destroying the very fabric of their lives, and Maryland society in particular resented this latest intrusion by General Lee's commander. Laura struggled to remember his name – Longstreet. This General Longstreet had actually been in Hagerstown, had brought the war to their very doorsteps.

They negotiated a bend in the road as the sky turned into a glowing red and the sun slipped lower towards the edge of the hills. With luck, they would be home before sunset. Only three more miles to go and at the rate her Papa pushed the horses, it might be even sooner.

Laura saw it first. It looked like a hat, but in the half light it was difficult to tell. 'Papa, slow down. Look there.'

Sebastian slowed, narrowing his eyes to take in the soggy black article Laura pointed to. An officer's hat, sure as anything, one of those soft wide-brimmed types. Not such a surprise. There had been plenty of them around the last few days.

His attention diverted to something else. He reined in sharply.

'Looks like something in the ditch,' he said. 'I'll go see.'

'Careful, Papa, it may be a trap.' She had heard of such things, soldiers pretending to be dead, then attacking the poor victim who showed them sympathy.

'Stay right where you are, girl.' He tutted irritably. Laura seemed to thrive on drama. Time she was married, he'd thought so for some months. He moved closer. Someone was definitely there. An officer, judging by the insignia on the hat, if it was his. He studied the body. It had no uniform, in fact, there was little clothing, just a torn shirt and underpants.

'What a goddamned mess.' He knelt down to take a closer look. The familiar stench of death made him nauseous. The soldier's face was blackened by mud and blood. His hair, was it dark? – hard to tell – was matted. He certainly looked dead. He placed an ear to the man's chest. Something was happening inside there – he might be just alive. How had he gotten there? They were at least two miles from Sharpsburg, even farther from the Creek. Had this young fellow crawled that far? Did the hat belong to him? The hat was Union, but the soldier might not be. He beckoned to Laura.

'Looks like this fellow's almost gone. Help me lift him. We must get him to the house. Can't leave the poor devil here to die.' Even though he may be the enemy, he thought.

Laura helped lift the soldier into the buggy. Her heart reached out to him as she lay him down. He was the most pathetic creature she had ever seen.

Sebastian slapped the horses into action. The journey was bumpy and Laura cradled the young man's head against her bosom. She did not care about the smell or the fact that her gown was caked with blood and dirt. She dipped her kerchief into the water bottle and wiped his face. As his features became clearer, she saw fine bone structure and a well shaped mouth. She touched his hair, pushed it gently off his face. It was good, thick hair. He wore no boots or socks. Lizabeth had mentioned that soldiers robbed the dead and wounded. Whoever he was, he had obviously experienced much pain and torment. She held him very carefully against her. She would not let him die. She, Laura Hilton, would make sure he survived. The war, for him at least, was surely over.

•••

It was almost dark when they arrived. Marilyn came out to meet them, her face creased into the familiar smile. When she saw the figure slumped in the back of the buggy the smile disappeared and she recoiled.

'Ugh – who is that? Why, he's almost naked!'

Sebastian handed Laura the reins. 'Here, tether the horses for me while I call one of the servants.'

Johnson, the manservant, carried the soldier three flights to the spare room at the top of the house. Sebastian decided it was for the best, just in case he was a villain.

'Never can tell these days. Won't be easy for him to do mischief up there.'

He planned to make discreet enquiries about the young man, especially if he pulled through, which he doubted. The fact that he wore no uniform made the whole thing very difficult. Only hope was to wait until he came to, and then question him. The fellow might not be who he seemed. The hat might not belong to him. They were all presuming far too much too soon. Especially Laura. The girl was fondling him as though he were her very own.

'Have you thought what you're going to do if he's Confederate?' Marilyn asked later, when she and Sebastian were alone in the drawing room.

'Turn him in, naturally. We don't need that kind of trouble round here. I don't begrudge him the right to a bed under my roof, but if it ever came to that, I'd turn him over to the Federal authorities.'

Marilyn sat languidly on the chez longue. 'Did you find what you went into town for, dearest?'

'Sure did. I took Laura with me so she could try on the gown for you. Must say it looks very grand indeed.'

Marilyn sat up abruptly. '*She* tried on my gown?'

'Only so the seamstress could make sure it was perfect for you. After all, you and Laura are pretty much the same dimensions.'

A smile of satisfaction lit her face again. 'Oh, I don't mind really. It was so sweet of you to go all that way and just for little me.'

He sighed, more with relief than anything. Why in God's name these two women couldn't get along together was beyond him. It was surely jealousy. Typical of women.

'Now, I really must be going, Sebastian.'

'Going? Already?'

'Why yes. It's getting late and I have to rise early in the morning.'

He crossed the room, arms outstretched. 'But dearest, I thought you were staying over tonight.'

'I want to, but I am so very tired and if I stay I'll not get my beauty sleep, will I?' She giggled. 'Anyway, I have to rise early, I told you.'

He was suspicious. 'You going somewhere special?'

'I have to see that old Mr Brewster about a business matter. I could only get an early appointment.'

'I see. He causing you trouble again?'

She looked away. 'Only the usual. Seems I owe him money, but you're not to worry, Sebastian dearest.'

'But I do worry. Just let me know how much and I'll settle with the old bastard for good.'

'I will if it ever gets out of hand.'

'Then stay tonight. For me.'

'I would, but you know that once I get comfy with you, Sebastian, I never want to leave.' She gave him a provocative look and kissed him lightly on his lips. He pulled her to him.

'Stay, Marilyn,' he begged. 'I need you tonight.'

'And I you, dearest, but we must be sensible. You don't want me to look worn out tomorrow afternoon, do you?'

He had forgotten. Tomorrow they were to journey to Berkeley Springs to attend a function given by his old friend, Jasper Lee. He wanted Marilyn to look her very best as this was to be their first public appearance together. Until now, he had been discreet, showing Marilyn to only his close friends, people he trusted. Now the time had come to be more open.

'All right. I'll take you home,' he said.

'No – one of the servants can do that. After all, you also need your beauty sleep.'

He slapped her bottom playfully and she giggled, slipping out of his clutches in order to rearrange her hair and clothing.

'The gown, Sebastian, have you forgotten? I may have it tonight?'

He smiled. 'Of course.' He pulled a bell rope. 'Johnson, I want you to take Miss Beauville home. And take this parcel. See they both arrive safely.' To Marilyn he said, 'I'll call for you tomorrow at noon.' He blew her a kiss as Johnson assisted her into the carriage and pair.

In the house he doused the lights. How strange the sudden silence. He missed her already. Yawning, he mounted the stairs to his bedroom. Perhaps he should go and see the young man, but surely Laura had done that. Early tomorrow he would see him and by that time, Doc Adams may have arrived. That's if the man lived. By the look of him he may not make it through the night. Maybe they should have left him out there to die. Bringing him home hadn't achieved anything. He shook his head, reprimanding himself for the thought. No, bringing him home was a humane act. Especially if he was a Federal Officer.

'Couldn't take the chance,' he muttered to himself. 'Wouldn't be able to live with myself if I found out later I'd left a Federal officer to die.' Wouldn't be able to live with myself if Governor Floyd got wind of it, either, he thought.

Pulling off his boots, he lay on the bed, his need for Marilyn growing by the second.

• • •

Marilyn waited until the carriage disappeared from sight before hurrying into the house. It was quiet. The servants were either asleep or off duty. She couldn't remember which. Relieved to be home, she went up the stairs to her bedroom to unwrap the gown. She slipped out of her clothes and pulled the gown over her head and in front of the long mirror eyed herself with satisfaction. It was beautiful. Blue, with gold lace, pinched at the waist. Devastatingly beautiful.

The clock struck eleven. She pushed her hair into place, sprayed cologne over it and poured a small brandy. Vince was usually on time. He was due at any moment. At the sound of hoof beats she pulled aside the heavy drapes to reveal a black stallion and Vince in his familiar black cloak. Her heart beat wildly as she watched him tether the horse and enter the house the back way.

'Vince – my love!' She ran to him and he enfolded her in his arms.

'Here, let me look at you,' he said. 'A beauty beyond all doubt.'

'My new gown. Do you like it?'

He stood back to admire it. 'Perfect. Wear it for me tonight?' He pulled her close again. 'Not this minute though, darling.'

'No,' she whispered. 'I just wanted you to see it. Isn't it the most beautiful gown in the world?'

He smiled to himself. It must have cost a fortune. Never could he have afforded such a luxury. The fact that Sebastian Hilton had purchased the gown did not bother him at all. Hilton could foot all the bills, while he and Marilyn enjoyed the fruits. Indulging Marilyn financially, or anybody else for that matter, was not part of his future plans.

'We're still going to the midnight ball?' she asked.

'Yes, ma'am. It was some task but I finally made sure of the guest list. Nobody we know is going, and besides we'll all be wearing masks.'

She was satisfied. Wrapped in the arms of her lover, the world was a wonderful place. And she trusted this tall, dark, and extremely handsome man. If he said it was safe to be seen together that night, then so be it.

He let go of her and moved to the drinks cabinet. She took him in with hungry eyes, enjoying his broad shoulders and long athletic body. The small neat moustache covering his lip lent the finishing touches to his chiselled features. She sometimes thought she was in love with him, really in love. He certainly satisfied her sexual appetite. Sebastian, on the other hand, was a poor substitute, a bungling fool who on occasion she did her duty for. How else could she obtain such expensive gifts and eventually hope to own Hilton Heights? And it suited her that Vince knew of Sebastian's place in her life. At least she had no reason to ever lie to him. If only it were that simple with Sebastian.

Slowly, seductively, she undressed just how he liked it, hardly taking her eyes from his, watching his enjoyment as she gradually uncovered her body. Placing his drink on the table, he moved towards her and pulled her roughly against him. She groaned, warm and vulnerable in his arms. He lifted her to the bed and, undressing quickly, he climbed in beside her. He slid easily into her and she welcomed him with every fibre of her body, arching her back, groaning, moaning and crying out. She knew that this turned him on, and Vince gave her all she desired, for he knew her inside out – when to hold back, when to let go, when to tease. She was all woman, his woman, and for those moments together as lovers, his world took on a pleasant meaning.

Afterwards, they lay for some time as Vince dozed. Minutes later he woke, bright and alive.

'Come my sweet – to the ball!'

She laughed gaily and he pulled her from the bed, catching her lips to his. They bathed and dressed, Marilyn humming a happy tune as she again stood before the mirror and admired herself in the gown.

They took a carriage and pair and drove south east. The night was chilly, though inviting. Half an hour later, against a backcloth of bright stars, they saw the venue for the ball, its lights spreading across the vast lawns. Shadowy figures flitted across the windows and the scene lent itself to splendour as music from the main ballroom echoed through the hills.

•••

Miles away in Savannah, the sinking sun poured orange-red fingers across the library floor as Jo-Ellen used what remained of the dying natural light to read her book.

Raising tired eyes, she listened for any sound that may forewarn her of danger. She had become accustomed to doing that of late, but as usual there was only the silence. Setting aside the book, for the light was now gone, she rose and went to the window. Quiet – everywhere was so quiet. Even Alexander was sleeping.

Outside was a stillness that was almost unnatural. Barely a leaf stirred. Under the old oak were still the remnants of the small party she had given for Alexander's first birthday. Her brother had protested. 'A party? So soon after Rob's death? How can you, Jo-Ellen?'

Poor Ben, how torn he must be feeling. How at odds the war had placed him.

'I know it seems heartless, but Rob would have wanted this for his son.'

'But it's only days.'

'Don't you think I know that?' He was right. It was literally days. Rob had been killed on 17th September, she had heard about it on the

23rd and on the 25th she acknowledged her boy's birthday. It had not been an easy decision but she was in no mood to constantly defend herself to her brother.

Turning from the window, she lifted a photograph of Rob from the bureau. His cheerful face brought tears to her eyes. They were the first she had shed. Perhaps she was over the shock now, perhaps she would be able to give vent to her feelings properly. If only Ben would try and understand. She had needed to go on as though nothing had happened and it had helped.

Somewhere a door banged. Through the window she saw her maid leave the house. Moments later she appeared in the doorway. 'Miss Jo-Ellen, shall I draw the drapes? You're standing there in the darkness.'

'Yes, please, Louise. Is Alexander still sleeping?'

'Yes'm.'

'Good. I shall retire early tonight. My eyes are sore from reading.'

'You do look tired, miss, I hope you don't mind me saying so.'

Jo-Ellen smiled at her. 'Of course not.'

'And since you've eaten so little lately…it's since that awful day, miss.'

'Hush, Louise. I know I've not been looking out for myself but I'll be all right.'

'It was the shock. Your Mama said so. She's been so worried about you.'

Jo-Ellen waved to her dismissively. Louise was getting above herself. 'Then the next time you and my Mama get to talking about me you must put her mind at rest instead of gossiping. Now, go about your work, please.'

Pausing by the long mirror, Jo-Ellen studied her face intently. At twenty-two, it was a mature face. Attractive, though care-worn. Her fair hair fell loosely around her shoulders, her eyes were bright and healthy. With her fingers, she scrubbed at her cheeks to draw more colour into them.

Grieving was a debilitating business, she thought. It prevented rational thought, banished hunger and sleep and generally took one over. How long would it be before she would wake, if in fact, she slept, and think with pleasure on the day ahead, instead of longing for Rob or yearning to hold him close? It would take time, certainly more than the few days that had passed. Possibly years. Her love for him had been too deep, her marriage too short for her to get over his death so quickly.

Turning sideways, she was pleased to see that her figure was trimmer than ever. She had certainly lost weight. Her time in the field hospital had seen to that. She did not hear the door open.

'Jo-Ellen, will you be joining us for dinner this evening?'

Constance wanted company. Since Samuel had died, she felt lost, alone. Her husband had been her life, now her children must be her saviour. Jo-Ellen could at last identify with that.

'Yes, Mama, I think I will.'

'I'm so pleased. We've all missed you these past days.'

'We?'

'Why yes. Ben has joined me on occasion. He misses you so.'

Jo-Ellen said nothing, knowing that Ben was far too caught up in his own problems to have missed her that much.

'I expect you think Ben has been a little hard on you, but it was because of the way you spoke to Daniel Hunter and then rushing off after him like that. It was so impulsive of you and Ben thinks only of your well-being, dear.'

'Mama...!' Jo-Ellen caught herself in time. What was her Mama talking about? And what was the use of arguing? Let her say what was on her mind. Better now than over dinner.

'Ben's concerned about you. It's very hard for him, staying loyal to the memory of Rob on the one hand and being so very fond of Daniel on the other. The war has wreaked havoc on us all. In many ways you both have so much in common.'

Jo-Ellen listened patiently. How often she had heard it all before, how Constance had never approved, how since their childhood she had tried to gently discourage contact with Robert de la Rey, only to find her words falling on deaf ears. Ben had experienced the lectures first, then when Jo-Ellen had returned from the school in England, and the three of them had gone around together, Constance had on many occasions voiced her disapproval on the grounds that they came from very different backgrounds, that they had very different values. Neither she nor Ben had heeded anything their parents ever said when it came to Rob and it was all academic now, she thought, as her Mama off-loaded her thoughts and feelings, her voice as always gentle.

'What's done is done, I suppose,' Constance said finally. 'Nothing can change it. You've had a terrible shock, dear, and we all want to help.' Her face brightened. 'I'm delighted you're dining with us. I shall enjoy the evening all the more for your being there.'

Ben came in for dinner, nodded agreeably in Jo-Ellen's direction and took his seat. Jo-Ellen was hard put to it to read his thoughts. His general countenance was pleasant enough though she detected in his questioning eyes that he also had plenty to say to her.

'Are you well, sis?'

She inferred from the endearment that he had already forgiven her for her outburst. 'Yes, very well,' she replied, helping herself to some cold meats. She noted the sparsity of the food on the table.

'Not only is everything very expensive,' said Constance, 'but the shops are practically empty. As for meat, salt is too dear to buy and so much of the meat in the shops is not edible.' She paused. 'This on our table tonight is from a good neighbour. If there's one good thing to come out of this war, it's found us some very good neighbours in our time of need.'

Ben shot his sister a knowing look.

'And the drought,' Constance continued, 'why, that has only exacerbated the problem. Old Jonas Darby over at the Pike told me that the price index has more than doubled and that the economy is now at its worse.'

Remembering what Rob had once told her about the economy in the south, Jo-Ellen said, 'I know it, Mama. I've long thought we should give up providing cotton and produce food instead. Everybody I know is doing that.' She lifted some corn bread and sweet potato on to her plate.

'Well said.' Ben took a long sip of wine. 'Said the same thing myself to Susanne. Soon as we can, we're raising food.'

Constance frowned at him. 'Samuel worked so hard producing cotton. It would be wrong not to carry on his good work.'

Ben disagreed. 'Ma, I'd not consider it save that we'll all starve to death if we don't do something soon. It makes sense, don't it?'

Silence followed. Jo-Ellen glanced at her Mama. She was still grieving for her husband - they had spoken without thinking. Perhaps she would see sense later on.

'The papers say that Abe Lincoln is going to give freedom to all slaves if the south don't rejoin the Union by 1st January coming,' Ben said, taking a second helping of sweet potato.

'What!' Constance placed a hand to her head. 'My, what is it all coming to? Does that mean we'll have to let ours all go?'

'Over my dead body.'

'Ben, don't say that!'

He grinned at his sister, finished his wine and sat back, a satisfied man. 'Food shortage or not, that was fine, Ma.' To Jo-Ellen he said, 'You free for me this evening, Sis?'

She agreed. There were things they had to discuss and she wanted to assure Ben she was ready to go about her duties once more and so she joined him after dinner in the study where he was reading a copy of the 'Tribune.'

'Says here that the age limit for conscripts is going up to forty-five. Forty-five!' he said.

She closed the door and took a seat opposite. 'And what of you, Ben?'

He lowered the newspaper. 'You mean am I going back? I told you I'm not. Why ask?'

She gave a shrug. 'Just wondered. They're looking hard for deserters now. They've got men who go and get them and make them go back.'

Ben set aside the newspaper, rose and stood before the mantelpiece. 'You seem to know a lot about it.'

'I also read the newspapers.' She had done little else lately other than read the war news. She had even read all of Rob's memoirs of the war. His account of First Bull Run was excellent, even she had to admit. Had Ben really gone through all that? Deep down she did not blame him for not wanting to return.

'Let me tell you, big sister, it says in the newspaper that one white male on every plantation may be exempt from going to fight.'

She raised surprised brows. 'Why, that's wonderful, Ben. So if they come looking for you, you can just show them the article.'

He noted her sarcasm. 'If they come looking for me, I take it you'll tell them you've no idea where I am. Lost in battle, and all that. You're waiting with baited breath for news of me. Understand?'

She gave a mischievous smile. 'So much for new Congressional laws.'

He drew from his pocket a pipe and proceeded to fill it with tobacco. 'That's not why I asked to see you. I wanted to discuss the future of the Plantation. Now Susanne and I have started a family, we plan on more and will need more room.'

'But you have Highlands.'

'Not for long. Susanne's thinking of selling it off one day.'

'But what of her mother?'

'Her Ma's not well. My guess is she'll not live out another winter. And what if Curtis gets itchy feet? The way things are going I don't see him staying around too long. Where would we get another like him?'

'Have you spoken to him? Asked him outright?'

'Nope, not yet. But even if he remains Overseer, Highlands is too much for us.'

Jo-Ellen stood up. 'Wait a minute, Ben, whose idea is this, yours or Susanne's?'

'Mostly mine.' He puffed thoughtfully on his pipe. 'We can't afford Highlands. We need to be under one roof. The cost of living presently is robbing us, but with the money we get from the house we can all live here. Pa spoke of expansion and he got it well under way, but only on paper. I aim to continue his ideas, make this place enormous, so our kids can grow up decently. With Earl overseeing for me, I can grow food for us all. If corn is getting scarce, then we'll grow it!'

'I see.' Jo-Ellen wasn't sure what kind of a reaction she was supposed to have to this news. It sounded as usual very simplistic.

'I hope you do see. I didn't want to go ahead without consulting you first.'

'Why not?'

He frowned. 'Because you're in on it. It's your home, as well – or aren't you interested any longer? You and Susanne were getting along well working the two Plantations.' He waited for her reply. All that had been before she went away, and she was away too damned long. 'Well? Don't tell me you're not going to be part of it.'

'I hope you're not about to start on me, Ben,' she retaliated.

'No, no. I'm grateful for all you've done since you've been back. I guess I need to know you're not going away again.' He exhaled a smoke ring. 'You're part of it all, you and Alexander, specially now.'

'Now that I'm alone?' She smiled. 'I'm flattered that you're both including me, especially since Rob had plans for me to go and live up there with him. I'd have gone, you know.'

'Yes, and as his wife you'd be expected to. But that's no longer the case.'

'No, it's not. Of course I'll be here, Ben. Savannah is my home.'

He was visibly relieved. 'And Alexander's a southern boy. His place is here.'

'Yes, with Jamie.'

He grinned. 'So we'll pool our resources and try and make this the most successful plantation in the south. Pa would have been proud and I know it's what Ma will want. I intend to employ more workers if I can.'

'More?'

'If we have another twenty or more, then I'll definitely be exempt.' He tapped the newspaper. 'Says so in here. I intend to build up so much that this food shortage will be a thing of the past.'

Folding her arms, Jo-Ellen said, 'There are one or two things you're overlooking, Ben. For a start, who on earth's going to want Highlands at a time like this? Another thing, people are getting rid of their workers, or losing them overnight, and yet you think you'll be able to hire them? How?'

'There'll be a few problems but I'll overcome them. I can't be negative, Jo-Ellen. Pa taught me to think positive and that's what we need right now.' He tucked the newspaper under his arm and headed for the door. 'I must return to Susanne.'

'How is she? Where was she tonight?'

'She's fine. Had dinner with her Ma. Baby's fine, too. Things will soon be back to normal soon as Susanne's strong enough.'

Jo-Ellen went to her room, her mind stirred with new ideas. Rob would have encouraged her to survive the best way she could. Hadn't he wanted to take her to live in the north because the economy was bad in the south? She now had the opportunity to do something constructive about that instead of merely running away. She could help make all their lives better only she would remain in her beloved Savannah.

That night, she slept soundly for the first time in weeks.

...

Laura rarely left the house and more particularly the top floor unless it was to go and fetch for the soldier. She was sure now that he was a soldier. Why else had he been lying in that ditch with a bullet wound in his head?

Doc Adams duly arrived, checked him over, and spent considerable time tending him. He called several times more and then declared his patient on the mend.

'A miracle. By rights he should be dead, but it was not his time, no indeed.'

'You'll not be calling again, doctor?' Laura asked, hardly able to believe his words.

'No, not unless something unforeseen happens. You've been a good nurse, Laura. I don't foresee any trouble for the young man. Still no idea who he might be?'

She shook her head. 'Papa has enquired locally, I believe, but so far hasn't found out anything. So many men must be lost or missing, believed dead.'

Doc Adams finished his brandy and picked up his briefcase. 'Won't be long before he opens his eyes and begins to take part in life again. Take it easy, Laura. He'll feel lost at first, so be patient. If you should need me again get a message through to Hagerstown, for that's where I'll be for the next week or so.'

She showed him to the door. 'Thank you, I'll do that.'

'Maybe Washington will have some information.'

'Yes, maybe.'

'Weather's turned for the worst.' He turned up his collar and stepped through the doorway.

Laura went upstairs and found the soldier propped against pillows, his eyes closed. She opened her book and read for a long time until she was drowsy. Several hours passed and she was wondering whether to go to the study for a break, when the soldier's eyes flickered open. She leaned over him. 'Hello, can you see me?'

He stared at her. 'Who are you?'

'Laura Hilton.'

'And where am I?'

'Maryland. Just outside Hagerstown, to be precise.'

'Hagerstown?'

'Just north of Sharpsburg. Where you were fighting the enemy.'

He frowned. 'That what I did – fight? You mean there's a war on?'

Laura sighed. He had lost his memory. A common complaint with some soldiers, wanting to shut out the horror of everything. It rarely lasted, apparently, so she was not too worried.

'You want to try and remember your name?'

He shook his head.

'There was no uniform, no identity, you see. It was all stolen I expect.'

Still he said nothing.

'We found a hat with the insignia of major in the Federal Army. Was it yours?'

Again silence. He closed his eyes. Laura took comfort in the fact that he spoke like a northerner but that did not mean he fought on the right side. Many of those northern boys had their hearts in the south. At least this one was alive and was going to get well. She gazed at him affectionately. He was about the best looking man she had ever seen. Dark hair framed a strong face. When he opened his eyes she saw that they were large, green and expressive.

'Don't you know anything about me?' he asked.

'Only that we found you lying in a ditch way outside Sharpsburg. You don't know who you fought with?'

'No.'

'What about your folks? You must have a family somewhere. A woman, perhaps. Are you married? And that scar above your eye, did you get that in battle?'

He managed a grin. 'Are you always like this? Asking questions all the time?'

She felt herself colour. 'Why no, that is, I just want to help. We all do.'

'We?'

'My father, Sebastian Hilton, and Doc Adams who's tended you these past weeks.'

'This house, it's your father's?'

'That's right.'

'I owe you all my life.' He smiled weakly at her. 'Laura – I may call you that?'

'Yes.' She gathered up some dirty linen. 'Time you rested. And you must have a name. For the time being I'll call you Ray. It's easy and you look like a Ray.'

'Hey, that sounds fine.'

She laughed. 'Maybe I hit on your real name!'

'Laura, how long have I been here?'

'About four weeks.'

As she opened the door to leave, he said. 'Thank you so much for everything.'

'It's the least we could do.'

'Tell me, what's this war about?'

'Oh, slavery mostly. Listen Ray, you're much too weak to hear about that now. I'll tell you when you're stronger. I have to warn you, though, if it's found out that you're a Confederate, my father intends to turn you in to the authorities.'

'Confederate? They the enemy?'

She smiled. 'Depends how you look at it. Longstreet and Lee were in Hagerstown a short while ago. Seems some of Lee's men are still here.' His blank expression prompted her further. 'They are generals, Longstreet and Lee.'

From the doorway she took a long look at him and pulled the door quietly behind her.

He lay staring up at the white ornamental ceiling, at the oil paintings on the walls and the elegant furniture carefully arranged around him. Strength had returned to his body. He longed to walk again, to see the rest of this house and smell the freshness of earth and grass outside. He tried to move his legs. They hurt. Who the hell was he? Had he been fighting a war? What was he doing in Maryland? Did he know Longstreet and Lee? Did he live in Maryland? No answers came to his questions. Did he have a family or a woman somewhere? Four weeks – perhaps he had no one for wouldn't they have contacted him by now?

'Have to get well so I can find out about myself,' he muttered. He touched the bandage around his head. That hurt, God how it hurt. The room spun momentarily. He felt sick. He closed his eyes and slept.

∙ ∙ ∙

The battle was still vivid in his mind. Daniel closed his eyes against the ghastly images of long nights of screams and moans, of dead and dying, of limbs being severed on the spot by surgeons with saws, of corpses left by the roadside swelling ready to explode.

Fortunately for the Confederacy, General McClellan had not attacked when the great opportunity had presented itself otherwise things night have gotten a lot worse. Instead, the little General had dug in and waited and General Lee took the opportunity to withdraw over the Potomac, otherwise Daniel would not be there now.

Such good fortune did not happen often. After the dramatic ride to tell Jo-Ellen of her husband's death, he had returned to his division in Virginia, a changed man. He wasn't alone. All who had been at Sharpsburg, or Antietam, as it was also known, had a blank look about them and merely went through the motions of soldiering as though their minds were still there in that sunken road they had since named Bloody Lane.

Daniel looked through the window of his office headquarters in Richmond, unable to dim the persistent images that passed through his mind of that morning when the Confederate Army of Northern Virginia had made their way into the wooded area north of Sharpsburg on the Hagerstown Turnpike. He had felt uplifted. He had not only slept well, but had eaten a substantial breakfast, and the fact that he had dreamt of Jo-Ellen all night, or so it seemed, made him feel grand as he rode slowly along the lane. The sun was not yet up and the sky was clear against the reds and greens of the Maryland countryside.

Only days before, General Lee had led 40,000 soldiers across the Potomac into Maryland in the hope of eventually gaining a foothold in the north with an added hope of persuading England and France to recognise the Confederacy. Daniel had been optimistic in the extreme about this. Lee's plan to capture the Federal rail centre at Harrisburg was splendid. This would sever Washington's links with the west. Splitting his army into sections, Lee had taken up position along the crest of the three-mile ridge, east of the town of Sharpsburg. That was when Longstreet had seen McClellan's men pouring over the countryside. They had all been there, even General Jackson, freshly arrived with his men from his capture of Harpers Ferry. Jackson was a real hero that day. Capturing that Potomac crossing had opened up a supply line down the Shenandoah Valley for the Confederacy. That day, at Sharpsburg, Jackson had successfully led the Confederate left division in the first attack against Major General Joseph Hooker's First Corps. After that, the fighting had escalated, only quieting down a day later. A pleasant break, Daniel recalled, amidst a bloody battle. The worst part had been in the sunken road, watching his men being cut down by Union fire until the road had rapidly filled with bodies two and three deep.

Poor Jo-Ellen had lost her husband that day. Would she ever get over that? And he, Daniel, had done so little to help her. How could he have talked about it to her when Rob had lost his life, not in battle, but because of his hatred and jealousy?

She must never find out. Far better to let her think that he died honourably.

In the small cracked mirror on the wall, he straightened his frock coat and pulled his hat straight. The thought of Jo-Ellen that day had helped him through and he was now comforted by the fact that she had come after him before his departure from Savannah, had taken it upon herself to visit him at his hotel. Did that not indicate that she cared a little?

Despite the gloomy memories of Sharpsburg, he managed his first smile for days. He would keep his promise very soon. One day, when this bloody war was over, or even before that, he would go down there and claim her for his own.

• • •

Laura felt proud of herself. The young man in her care was progressing well and it was all down to her. Daily she waited on him, and some nights she lost precious sleep in order to see to his comforts.

December had arrived, cold and bleak and she threw some logs on to the fire and waited for the flames to take hold. Two and a half months had passed since they had taken Ray into their home. Twice she had thought about journeying to Washington to try and find out about him but both times something happened to prevent her from doing so. Besides, half of her did not want to find out. Once the mystery was solved, once he found out about his past life, he would leave. And she didn't want that now. Her father persisted.

'Time you did something, Laura. How do we know he isn't the enemy? How do we know he won't attack us some day?'

'Papa, he won't.'

'You can't ever be sure. Do something, girl, and quick.'

'Yes, Papa. I'll look into it next week,' she'd reply, making sure that next week never arrived.

Watching the flames lick over the logs, she let her imagination run away with her. If the truth be known, Ray had probably known many young women. Just the publication of his face in the newspaper would most likely bring hundreds of replies. What was his background? Who were his parents? Which State was he from? Did he have any close friends? Had he trained for the army? If so, where? She knew how very easy it would be to trace his background once she put her mind to it. The fact that Sebastian had not come up with any information was because he was so taken up with other matters he had not given enough time to it. The fact remained that Washington probably had a file on Ray.

'Them pants are army supply you can bet your life on that,' Sebastian remarked to her one day. 'A civilian wouldn't wear them, and this young man looks like the fashionable kind to me. He wouldn't wear them unless he had to. He's army all right.'

Laura was unable to argue the point. Men's underpants were not her domain, her knowledge of such things was truly limited. All the same, her Papa had obviously accepted that Ray was a soldier.

'If you say so, Papa.'

'I do say so. We've got ourselves either a young hero from McClellan's army or a Johnny Reb willing to murder and steal his way around the countryside.'

Laura fell silent. She differed so much from her Papa in her opinion of the Confederates. Lizabeth had told her that general opinion of them when they entered Maryland was of a band of ragged, dirty soldiers, yet bearing a determination and a bravery that the Union boys lacked. Laura had cautioned Lizabeth not to speak so blatantly. What if they were overheard? Might not such a remark be used as evidence that she was perhaps a southern sympathiser?

Lizabeth had scoffed at such an idea. 'It's general opinion. I'm not the only one to say so. Anyhow, I find some of them southern boys attractive.'

Sebastian's voice jolted her back to the present. 'Just do something soon. Laura, otherwise I'll have to do it myself. Won't take long to contact the papers. Might even get in touch with Floyd.'

'Governor Floyd?'

'Yes.' He looked at her keenly. 'Any objections?'

'No, of course not.'

But it would be the final straw. Governor Floyd would know what to do. Ray's identity wouldn't remain a secret for long once he was involved. Perhaps she ought to take the initiative quickly. She excused herself, and hurried from the room.

• • •

Sebastian straightened his cravat and looked again at his timepiece. Marilyn was late. In front of the long mirror he surveyed his corpulent figure. Perhaps he should heed Doc Adams' advice and lay off the drink. His face was redder than usual. High blood pressure, the Doc had said. Well, maybe he was right, but a man needed a good slug of whisky sometimes. This was one of those times.

He poured himself one and tossed it back, eyed with disappointment his empty glass and poured another.

Somewhere a door closed. Footsteps mounted the stairs to the top of the house. Laura. He could almost set his clock by her movements lately. She drove him crazy, always had done, but over this soldier she was worse than ever. Anyone would think they were lovers the way she cared for him.

It had been a cruel twist of fate that had given him a daughter instead of the boy he yearned for. When his wife had produced Laura and then died afterwards, his world had collapsed. He tried to love the child but it was impossible – she had killed his beloved Lillian. How could he avoid the resentment that followed? That Laura had grown into an attractive woman had not gone unnoticed by him, however. She had blossomed well, very like her mother. It had also not escaped his notice that she was well read and intelligent. Yet, none of this cheered him for long. It had been Marilyn Beauville who had eased the burden he carried. When she came into his life, some of the bitterness had left him. His new mistress became the all-important feature of his life. With Marilyn he would one day have the son he craved. She and the boy would inherit everything.

He looked out of the window. Looked like snow was about to fall. Christmas would soon be upon them. Laura had better get a move on, find out who the fellow upstairs was so they could send him back to where he belonged. There was no place in their lives for this stranger. Perhaps then he could concentrate on settling down with Marilyn.

A carriage drew up outside the house. She had arrived. He took another look in the mirror and went downstairs to greet her.

•••

Laura warmed herself by the log fire in the drawing room. Through the window, about an inch of snow covered the courtyard and she was relieved that she did not have to go outside. She had sent Johnson into town with one of the maidservants to order and buy all the groceries for Christmas and she had taken that opportunity to give him a list of gifts she had in mind to buy. In past years she had gone to town herself, but then there had been no soldiers lurking about.

She yawned. It would be impossible to deny she was tired. Loss of sleep these past weeks had robbed her of her usual glow and that morning she had taken herself in hand and groomed herself from top to toe. First she manicured her nails, then bathed and powdered her body and brushed her hair until it gleamed. Finally, she put on her warmest and prettiest dress and covered her shoulders with a shawl.

A sound from behind startled her. In the doorway was Ray, leaning awkwardly against the wall for support.

'Ray, you shouldn't be out of bed! What'll Doc Adams say?'

He took her supportive hand in his and shifted his weight on to her. 'He won't say anything because we won't tell him.'

She lowered him into the chair. 'And you'll catch cold. Here, take my shawl.'

He chuckled. 'No, Laura, it looks prettier on you. I'm fine, really.'

'You'll catch your death.'

'I doubt it, but I could die of boredom. That ceiling upstairs isn't at all entertaining.'

This brought a smile to her face. 'I know it must be frightful lying around all day but how else will you recover?'

His smile was affectionate. Couldn't she see he *was* recovering? Slowly he had exercised his legs as he lay in bed, and gradually he had been able to sit up, then stand and eventually walk.

'How come you got down those stairs on your own? Suppose you had fallen?'

'Well, I didn't. I have to do things by myself now.' He held her gaze. 'Laura, I've much to thank you for. Had it not been for you…'

'No, Ray, please…'

'Had it not been for you, I'd be dead. I know you've been sitting up most nights tending me. So, now I'm feeling better I intend to do for myself so you can get your rest.'

For something to do in that emotional silence, she held out a sprig of holly to him. 'Look, Ray, aren't the colours rich?'

Her cheeks flushed as she spoke and she averted her eyes so that he couldn't see the effect he was having on her. She had recently groomed him, had cut the excess growth of hair from his neck, shaved off the straggly beard to reveal vital good looks. Green eyes gazed unwaveringly into hers then he, too, looked away, turning his attention to the erratic flames in the hearth.

From outside came the sound of horses' hoofs. 'I must go and greet Papa,' she said and made to open the door. 'You'll be all right here on your own?'

There was no reply. Ray was staring in that thoughtful way of his into the glare of the fire, as though all the answers to his inner conflict were about to materialise.

• • •

Laura took Sebastian's cloak and hung it up. He glanced towards the servants' quarters. 'Where's Johnson?'

'Still in town. I do believe I ought to have gone along to supervise.'

'No – the roads are dangerous. There's ice everywhere.'

She took this as an uncharacteristic gesture of paternal affection.

'Besides, I need you here to help me. Marilyn's coming over tomorrow.'

Her previous thought unceremoniously dismissed, her spirits sank.

'She'll be spending Christmas Day with us. I'll entertain grandly for her as usual, so make her feel welcome. Understand?'

Laura did understand. Christmas had been snatched from her. 'Did all go well in Berkeley Springs?'

'Fine, splendid food and good malt whisky.' A smile of pleasure lit his eyes. 'Marilyn looked magnificent. They all thought so.'

She supposed the 'they' to mean all his sycophantic cronies. Jasper Lee was the world's greatest 'yes' man, given to creating false impressions rather than telling the truth, and she imagined that those so-called friends of Sebastian's had conveniently forgotten about his dear departed wife who had once been their devoted friend. She had doubts, though, that Marilyn had been so readily accepted by them. If they were insular and insincere in one direction, they were surely insular and insincere in another.

'That's nice, Papa.'

He shot her a doubtful look. 'I want to talk to you about that young man.'

'Yes, Papa?'

'I want him out of here.'

'But, Papa...'

'As soon as possible. We've done our bit for him, saved his life, now he should find out who he is and go back to where he belongs.'

'But, Papa...'

'Don't keep saying that! Do as I say, Laura. If your mother were here, you'd have to.'

Mama wouldn't expect a wounded soldier to leave the house at such a time, she thought.

'I want to get the ball rolling by publishing a picture of him, send it to The Times, the Tribune and so on. Someone out there must recognise him.'

'Yes, Papa.'

He stood before the fire in the study rocking to and fro on the balls of his feet, a satisfied gleam in his eyes. He did not notice Laura quietly leave the room and return to the drawing room. Neither did he notice the tears in her eyes.

Chapter Eight

The dream took many forms. Jo-Ellen had woken in the early hours, had risen to fetch a glass of water and had fallen into a deep and disturbing sleep into which the images of war penetrated.

She had run through cannon fire towards the forest, the leaden heaviness in her legs preventing her from getting anywhere. After much effort, she came to the edge of the forest, and was confronted by thousands of dark blue uniforms all pointing their fingers at her and laughing. She woke bathed in perspiration, relieved beyond relief to be in her bedroom instead of on a battlefield.

She bathed and changed into riding breeches, shirt, and boots. Today she would relax and go for a canter. Through the window Earl was already at work. There was no sign of Ben and her mother had apparently not risen yet. In her mind she relived the dream. It was horrid, too horrid for such a beautiful day.

Her attention was drawn to a noise on the distant horizon. A cloud of dust lay across the countryside. She called out to Earl and he went to see what it was.

'Riders, miss. Several of them, coming this way!'

Her tummy muscles knotted. Rumour that Union forces had ridden into Savannah in past weeks worried her, but it had only been a rumour. The dust cloud grew in intensity and her heart beat wildly. Was the rumour about to become reality? She went outside to join Earl.

'Uniforms, miss. Grey uniforms.'

A sigh of relief escaped her as a group of about twelve Confederate riders came into view. Her thoughts centred on Daniel Hunter. Had he kept his promise and returned to Savannah? But even from there, as they reined in, she could see that the leader was a captain and a stranger.

'Earl, to be on the safe side, go and warn everybody there's army on the premises. Then go and hide.' She nodded her head dismissively. 'Just in case, you understand.'

Earl needed no further warning. Overseer he may be, but that did not make him safe. He had run away from these men, had fought against them. Without a word he moved off in the direction of the house.

The leader dismounted and bore down on Jo-Ellen. He was young, officious. Tipping his hat, he smiled briefly. 'Good morning, ma'am'

'Good morning, Captain.'

'Pardon us for disturbing you, ma'am.' His eyes took in her riding clothes. 'I hope we're not delaying you.'

She smiled charmingly. 'Not at all. Can I be of any assistance, Captain?'

'This the Jefferson Plantation?'

'It is.' Her voice felt shaky and she prayed that he hadn't noticed, but his attention was taken up by the retreating figure of Earl.

'Where's the nigger boy off to?'

Jo-Ellen continued to smile. Already she disliked the Captain. 'He's doing a chore for me.'

He nodded, apparently satisfied. 'May I know who you are, ma'am?'

'Jo-Ellen Jefferson.' What did these men want? They all looked rough, their uniforms dirty from riding and their faces covered with several days' growth. The Captain pulled out a document.

'Got an order here, ma'am.'

Jo-Ellen took a steadying breath. Oh God, they had come for Ben. 'For Captain Benjamin Jefferson. Is he hereabouts?'

Replacing her smile with an expression of concern, she said, 'My brother? Have you news of him?'

'You've not seen or heard from him?'

'Why no. We are all so worried in case something has happened. This war, so many young men killed or simply gone missing.'

The Captain began to look impatient.

'I do so hope, Captain, er...'

'Pike.'

'I do so hope, Captain Pike, that you'll let us know of any news concerning my brother.' She paused. 'He's not in any trouble, is he?'

'I'm not at liberty to discuss anything with you, begging your pardon, ma'am.'

'I see. Well, if you would keep us in touch with any news, we'd be so grateful.'

The Captain's expression softened momentarily. 'Of course, ma'am.' His eyes wandered in the direction of Jefferson House and with a curt nod of his head, he turned and remounted. 'If you see or hear anything of your brother, I'd be obliged if you would contact me at division headquarters.'

'And where might that be, Captain?'

'Richmond. Good day, ma'am.'

She sensed as they rode off that he was suspicious, she also knew that she should have offered them all refreshment. But what if Ben had ridden out from Highlands at that moment? And there was also Earl to think of. Ben had told her about Leon Foley, how they both had to kill him. Word must be out that Ben had gone missing since that day. Suppose they had been seen together, he and Earl. Was it possible that they were looking for Ben to question him about the murder, as well as to take him back to fight?

When the dust cloud had settled, she went inside the house and up to Alexander's room, no longer wishing to ride. His large eyes gazed into hers and he put out his arms to be lifted. Gathering him to her, she said, 'When you grow up, little one, you'll never have to fight. There'll be no nasty men with guns, no wars - never, never.'

She hugged him to her, her heart strings tugged almost beyond endurance.

• • •

'They were here?' Ben's face turned pale. Jo-Ellen had never seen him look so frightened.

'No need to worry. I saw them off. A group of them led by a Captain Pike.'

'Pike? Never heard of him.'

'That's not the issue, is it? What's going to happen, Ben, if they come again and you ride in behind them? Any excuses on your behalf will be useless, won't they?'

He thrust his hands deep into his pockets. 'I'm grateful for what you did, Sis, but now I'm worried sick. Susanne needs me here now more than ever.'

'Yes, we all do.'

She wandered outside. Overnight it had grown chilly. Pulling her cape closer round her, she strolled across the grounds. Today she would put in a full day's work.

She actually felt like it. For so long she had lacked enthusiasm.

This Christmas will be different, she told herself. Last year she had been away from the people she loved, but that won't happen ever again; in future she will stay with her family in Savannah. Her heart went out to Rachel de la Rey. She'd had so much heartache already, and then to hear that her beloved son had been killed. Jo-Ellen had often thought of asking her to journey down to Savannah but would her husband be well enough? George had recovered from his heart attack, but how was he since hearing the awful news about Rob?

She set her eyes on the distant hills, their pastel blues and mauves attractive against the pale sky line. How she looked forward to the festive season. Their family had been diminished by three but two had been added since. Alexander and Jamie were about to experience their first Christmas surrounded by a complete family.

The main difference, she supposed, was the food shortage. Money was also a problem. It now cost seven dollars to buy an item that cost only one dollar two years before. Which was why they ought to get a move on, put Ben's plan into action so that a year from now, war or no war, there would be plenty of food on the table and money in their pockets.

Over by the house Earl moved into her vision. She quickened her step towards him.

'Go get Curtis. Mr Ben and I want to talk to you both.' His puzzled expression brought a smile to her face. 'Don't worry, Earl. It's good news. You'll like it. Oh, and bring Jacob, too.'

He hurried off. There was no time like the present. It would stop Ben from dwelling on his problems, too. Mama would understand in time when she saw their fortunes rise. The children had to be fed properly, Constance was always the first to say so.

She hummed as she went inside to find Ben, her spirits lifted, her mind positive and sharp.

• • •

Susanne rose early that morning. Jamie was crying and she went to settle her down. Deciding not to return to her bed, she got on with her day. Ben found her in the study.

'You look tired, Susanne. I heard Jamie raise the roof in the early hours. Think she'll be a soprano when she grows up?' He stood close behind her and she turned into his arms. 'It's chilly in here,' he said as she snuggled against him.

'Yes, I'll make sure the servants light all the fires today.'

'Do we have enough fuel?'

'Surely. We must be warm, regardless of cost.' All Susanne cared about presently was the fact that her family was together for the festivities. Even her Mama was fighting her frailty in an effort to join them on that special occasion. Susanne welcomed it, knowing deep down that her Mama's health had been worsened by Ralph's death. She had begun to wonder if the old lady would recover, when she had emerged smiling from her room asking to see her grandchild. The change that had come over her as she held Jamie in her arms had made Susanne cry with happiness.

'I spoke to Jo-Ellen about Highlands,' Ben said.

'I'm pleased. Does she mind – our wanting to live there?'

He grinned. 'No, in fact she's quite enthusiastic.'

'I'm relieved.'

Sensing something else, she said, 'Ben, is there something on your mind? You seem so very preoccupied.'

He had agonised over telling her, had rather left it because of her condition since Jamie's birth. On the other hand, if those soldiers returned and found him, how much greater would the shock be then?

'Yesterday, some soldiers came by asking about me. Seems they're rounding up deserters in earnest now. Jo-Ellen saw them off but they could return.'

'Oh, God!'

'Now, Susanne, I'm only telling you so you can prepare yourself but there's little to fear, I'm sure.'

'Little to fear! What would they do to you, Ben?'

Having heard that the army shot deserters, he felt disinclined to reply.

'I can tell by your silence that they mean to be harsh. What's to happen to us?'

'Nothing, dearest. You forget that Beauregard spoke very highly of me.'

'Beauregard! You said he wasn't in command now. How could he possibly help you?'

'Shh - you'll upset yourself for no good reason.'

He was beginning to regret speaking to her. 'You also forget that a man can buy his way out if he's a mind to. Three hundred dollars is a lot of money to us right now, but it would be worthwhile to keep me here. Also, my love, one white man per family may remain behind if it's found he's needed more by his family.'

She sighed against him. 'Paper talk! That's all that is. Do you really think, Ben, that having served as you have, the authorities are now going to let you go?' She affected her voice. 'Of course, Captain Jefferson, we do understand how you feel. Don't bother to come back, we know you'll be of more use to your country at home with your wife and child.'

The words hurt, she knew, and she suddenly pulled away from him and went to the window where the sunlight filtered in soft waves through the louvres. 'I'm so sorry, Ben, I'm just frightened. You won't face reality – you never have.'

'I know, I know.' He knew she was referring to, not only his being a deserter, but the death of Leon Foley. That was something that would not go away. Yet, how had they been able to tie him up with it? No one but Earl had been on the hilltop that day. 'I either give myself up and face the consequences and God knows what they might be, or remain hidden always glancing over my shoulder. And how long for? Those men need only make enquiries hereabouts to find out everything they need to know about me.'

A sob escaped Susanne. He went to her, tilted her chin and forced her to look at him. 'Hey, we have to look on the bright side. Christmas is upon us. How about it?'

She dabbed at her eyes with a kerchief. 'Yes, perhaps I'm being over-silly. Perhaps they'll never come back.'

'And perhaps the war will grind to a halt. Who knows?'

In those moments both knew that only one course was open to them. This coming New Year, Ben might have to give himself up.

• • •

'I just rode in, sir.'

Daniel looked with misgivings at the snow-covered Lieutenant.

'Good, Lieutenant. Are my orders being carried out?'

'Yes, sir.'

'Hardly the best time of the year to be told to leave your home, is it, Lieutenant?'

'No, sir.'

Daniel turned to look at the white wilderness beyond his window. Sometimes his job was undeniably dreadful. Having to urge the good people of Fredericksburg to abandon their homes before the Federal Army attacked them, had been difficult for him. Reports that old, feeble women and very young children were trudging aimlessly through the snow with their few belongings, distressed him. Six thousand people were suddenly homeless. Even as he waited, General Lee was positioning his 75,000 men along the six and a half miles, commanded by Jackson, Hill, and Longstreet. Before them lay the task of beating back the 120,000 Union soldiers under General Burnside, presently crossing the Rappahannock River in an effort to occupy the town. Cannon fire had already exploded inside Fredericksburg. Much of the town was on fire. Rumours of Union looting had reached their ears. Any time now, he thought, rubbing his hands in an effort to warm them, the fight would begin in earnest.

He was growing so tired of the war. Already thousands of men had died, almost as many had been wounded. What he wanted more than anything else, more than a top promotion even, was to spend time in Savannah with Jo-Ellen. Instead, here he was making ready to attack yet again.

It had been over two months since he had last seen her. Sometimes, he thought, turning from the window and taking up his hat, sometimes a man had to conduct his own life, give Fate a big hand, make things happen. Soon as this fracas at Fredericksburg was over he would put in for some leave, not just a couple of days but some real leave during which he could concentrate on his personal life for a change. Once he had paid his family in Maryland a visit, he would journey to Savannah and see Jo-Ellen.

A smile lifted the corners of his mouth as he made ready to join his division at Marye's Heights.

• • •

The snow was settling fast. From where he stood, Daniel could see Fredericksburg with the Rappahannock flowing south, the town itself occupying an open plain on the west bank, surrounded by a curving range of hills. He shielded his eyes from the glare. Not so very far away Federal troops waited to cross the river. General Burnside had replaced McClellan, and Daniel was sorry. At least they always knew where they stood with little Mac. How was this new general going to react?

From somewhere came the refrain 'Star Spangled Banner' and this was taken up with the popular 'Bonnie Blue Flag.' Daniel listened nostalgically. It was a favourite of his. Loud cheering and laughing could be heard above the cannon that hurled every so often into Fredericksburg.

'Lieutenant, tell me what's happening.'

He listened as his first lieutenant told him that Federal troops occupied the east bank of the river. Daniel knew this, knew that occupation had taken place as early as November 17th but he liked to have his men outline what was going on; that way he could see more clearly in his mind's eye what was likely to take place.

'They presumably wanted to surprise attack us, sir, but something delayed them.' The Lieutenant grinned. 'Sure as hell wasn't the little general's fault this time.'

Daniel lifted his field glasses. 'No, James, I think I'm going to miss him today. Those pontoon bridges went into place only at the last moment. I wonder why the delay?'

'Town's on fire, Major.'

'I can see that.'

'Yes, sir. I hear tell that Federal troops have looted the place. Bastards.'

Through the glasses Daniel watched as a surge of blue uniforms rallied on the banks of the Rappahannock.

'Where's General Jackson's second corps, Lieutenant?'

'Holding the right flank downstream, Major.'

Daniel kept his eyes fixed firmly on the activity before him. 'Those Feds are preparing to attack. Could happen any moment now.'

He panned the countryside where the Confederate Infantry were dug in. It had stopped snowing. A mist rose in the distance making further surveillance difficult.

'Weather's gone haywire – fog's coming up,' he murmured.

'That's all we need, sir.'

'Might be to our advantage, Lieutenant. At least they won't be able to see our positions so easily.' Daniel lowered the glasses. 'We're in a very advantageous spot.'

He could hardly believe their luck. The Infantry had taken up positions behind a stone wall at the edge of a meadow. If the Union forces attacked, they would have to cross that meadow first. 'It will be interesting to see if Burnside attacks us here at Marye's Heights.'

'Think he will, sir?'

'I'm praying he will. He might if he's ordered to. Strange, isn't it, James. Little Mac wouldn't, order or no order. It's a death trap, anyone can see that.' He lifted his glasses once more. 'Things get better and better.'

As he spoke, four divisions under General William Franklin began an attack on General Jackson's division. Daniel focussed rapidly on the action. There was Old Stonewall astride his horse, sword held high.

'Jackson's wearing a new uniform.'

'Sir?'

'Nothing, Lieutenant. Make ready for battle!'

They waited, impatient to make the most of their advantage. Someone gave a command. Federal troops poured into the meadow and into the low range of hills where General Longstreet and the 24th Georgia waited. It was at that moment that the fog, until then a Godsend, lifted.

'Better and better, Lieutenant! See how the sun is picking out the blue uniforms? We can't miss!'

The Federal troops, in full view of the Infantry, were half way across the meadow when they were fired upon. From that moment on, it was a one-way battle. Within minutes many of the Federal troops lay slaughtered and Daniel was appalled that Burnside had sent his men to certain death. Not one of them had managed to reach the stone wall.

The battle raged, then stopped as suddenly as it had begun. Confederate soldiers took that opportunity to strip the bodies of uniforms and boots, and as night drew on, bringing with it cold wind and more snow, stretcher-bearers groped their way through the carnage to bring out the wounded.

Daniel remained with his battle-weary men huddled in a spot out of the wind. That morning the sun rose on frozen, naked Federal corpses. Only the occasional gun shot could be heard above the coughing and sneezing and cries of the dying.

He stood up, stretched his legs. He longed for a hot drink. A brightness lit the horizon. The town was blazing in the distance. An uncanny silence hung in the air. Was the battle over, or was this only a pause? As he reached for his glasses, a shot rang out. Sniper fire. He swung his glasses to locate it. Another shot. Pain seared through his arm.

'James – I'm hit!'

The Lieutenant dived at him, dragging him down. His head swam and there was no more pain.

• • •

Governor Hubert Floyd adjusted his necktie and flattened his thinning hair with the palm of his hand. Turning sideways, he eyed himself in the looking glass then took up his cane and left his house on the corner of Seventh Street and strode through the light snow past the National Hotel and along Pennsylvania Avenue.

Despite the cold, there was a number of people about, and traffic on the Avenue was moving, though slowly enough to enable Hubert to take discreet note of the various Congressmen in their carriages. By rights he should be in a carriage, the President would expect it, but his dear wife had been on to him lately about his growing corpulence and so he had begun to walk whenever it was possible.

Hubert took a look up and down the Avenue. Trouble with this idea was he might be late. As soon as an empty carriage came by he would hail it. How quickly everything had changed, he thought. At the outbreak of the war, the City had become deserted. Willard's Hotel, usually full of guests, had all but emptied as residents packed up to flee from the instability of living in a city full of southern sympathisers, and the Avenue itself had become ghostlike. Now, he was pleased to see that Washington was filling up again and recently when he had popped into Willard's for a drink, he had been cheered to note the many arrivals, some of them quite distinguished. Life, it seemed, had begun to slot back into place.

At the other end of the Avenue stood the White House, gleaming in the watery sun, which was striving to break through the cloud. Hubert could imagine the President behind the drapes, his brow furrowed, his mind on the serious business of war. And right opposite, the War Department, where momentous decisions were being made that very moment.

A carriage drew alongside. Hubert hailed it.

'Ah, Mr Floyd, sir, tired of walking?'

As they went, Hubert took stock of the situation. The President wanted an audience with him about the emergence of the casualty lists. Both Sharpsburg and Fredericksburg had landed on his desk. The numbers were colossal. At Fredericksburg alone Union losses were over 12,600. His mind dwelt on some of the names that had confronted him. Good men, good friends, some of them. And it had become his job to deliver the sad news to their relatives.

George de la Rey, for instance. Hubert had been reluctant to journey to Philadelphia to break the news of his son's death at Antietam. Guilt had long rested heavily on him where Robert de la Rey was concerned, since back in '61 the boy had written to him, had begged for a commission in McClellan's army. Well, he could hardly refuse, could he, knowing that young de la Rey had political leanings. Several people with political clout had pushed Hubert to offer the boy a commission, a good one at that, not least McClellan when he heard. De la Rey had made an impression in the past so that when the young man had been made a major Hubert was not at all surprised. A man with de la Rey's education and background did not have to go through West Point, not in Hubert's opinion. Give him a strong position in the army, let him show what he's made of, and one day he could be running for a top job – possibly *the* top job. West Point might turn out good soldiers, but not necessarily good presidents.

George had taken the news badly, and given his recent illness, this was not good. The accusing look in his eyes had not gone unnoticed by Hubert. As for the boy's wife, he had planned to go and see her but so far the war had prevented it.

The carriage drew to a halt.

'There we are, sir. Good day to you.'

Hubert entered the building, handed his coat, hat and cane to the doorman and went in to meet with the President.

• • •

The hospital where Daniel was sent was dismal and cold. He lay amongst horrific stench. His arm had been bound. A nurse stopped by to see him.

'Major, how are you today?'

'Alive by all accounts, nurse.'

She smiled. 'We brought you in here rather than send you back to Richmond.'

'Where am I?'

'The Potomac Inn Hospital, Washington.'

Daniel lay back. Washington! 'How long have I been here?'

'Five days.'

'What date is it?'

'The twenty first, Major. You were in a bad way.'

Exasperated, he tried to collect his thoughts. The twenty first? What in hell's name had happened in the meantime? Beside him a soldier chewed on some bread and butter. On a plate lay boiled potatoes. There was a bowl of farina gruel, a mug of tea and something that resembled bread pudding. About ten yards away a surgeon was amputating a gangrenous leg. As battle-hardened as Daniel was, he found the screams terrifying and closed his eyes tight. Tomorrow he would ask to leave. He would discharge himself if need be.

'Here – try and eat something, Major.'

He looked at the plate of potatoes in her hand. They were a strange colour. Most of the inmates had suffered either scurvy or diarrhoea and Daniel thought twice about eating. Surely hunger was better than illness, yet he was undeniably hungry. He would never complain again about the usual army field rations of salt pork and beans, hard tack and coffee.

'Nurse, what news of Fredericksburg?'

She stopped to think. 'The Federal Army have withdrawn across the river.'

He sat up in a rush. 'What? When?'

'Now lie back. You'll do yourself harm. Two nights ago, I believe.'

The rush of adrenalin was what he needed. They had done it! They had protected Fredericksburg.

Slowly the strength flowed back into him, His work was done for now. He could get on with his life. He was going to go and see Jo-Ellen. He felt contented. Tomorrow couldn't come quickly enough.

Chapter Nine

As the year of 1863 opened, Laura began to relax her attitude towards Marilyn. For once, she did not mind her presence in the house. It served to keep Sebastian's attention from focussing on Ray's identity, for while Marilyn was with him, his mind was devoid of rational thought.

All over Christmas and part of the New Year, Marilyn had been coming and going, giving out her orders and generally irritating Laura but Laura coped, realising how necessary the woman was at such a time. The house, with its many cavernous rooms, was large enough to absorb them both and this also gave Laura time to think.

That she was getting closer to Ray there was no doubt. Often she noticed how he watched her, and then he would smile at her, his eyes full of approval. Her new hair style, recently purchased gown and general improvement in her person, drew his attention and she continued to work hard at this, hoping with all her heart that he would remain at the house forever. Sebastian was still the difficulty, though she noted that so far, Governor Floyd had not been brought into the matter.

As she watched the maid make up Ray's bed with fresh linen, her thoughts dwelt on her Papa's disapproval. Surely he had noticed Ray's attention towards her? Would he be pleased or not?

'Mary, when you've finished here, see to my Papa's room.'

Pausing long enough to check on her appearance, Laura went into the study where Ray liked to read his newspapers. His eyes lit up when he saw her.

'Laura.' He paused reflectively. 'You look lovely.'

Colour filled her cheeks. 'Why, thank you, Ray. And so do you!'

Rising to his feet, he caught at her hand and gave it a gentle squeeze. 'I feel so good today. No more limping and you know what? I feel like going riding.'

'Horses, you mean?'

'Yes, I saw them this morning when I did a tour of the grounds. I guess I can ride, though I can't remember having done so.'

'Then ride you will, though I think we ought to ask Doc Adams first.'

'Nope. Made up my mind. How about coming along with me? You can keep your eye on me.'

'I plan to. You didn't think I'd let you out of my sight, did you?' She linked her arm through his. 'And promise me there'll be no galloping. Just a gentle canter only.'

His arm curled around her waist as Sebastian appeared in the doorway.

'And where are you two off to?' His gaze rested on Ray's arm.

'Papa, I didn't hear you come in.'

'So it seems.'

'We're off to exercise the horses, Papa.'

Sebastian stood aside to let them pass. 'You appear to be fit and well again, young man.'

Ray hesitated in the doorway. 'Yes, sir, thanks to you. Soon as I can I aim to be on my way. I've taken up enough of your time and hospitality already.'

Sebastian allowed him a rare smile. 'Least we could do. Don't rush off on my account, young fellow. Get well first. I can imagine you're more than keen to find out about yourself. Loss of memory's a cruel blow, yes indeed.'

Laura stared at him. Was this her Papa speaking?

'It's all right, Papa, Ray has it all in hand.'

'Has he now?' He eyed her knowingly. 'Well, you two run along and enjoy your ride.'

Laura shot him a curious look. Was he getting softer in his old age? He seemed pleased that Ray and she were getting along so well. Perhaps an acceleration of what must surely be going to happen if she had her way, might turn the tide right in her favour.

In the stables, Ray chose the large Grey and he mounted expertly and turned the horse's head. 'Seems I've done this before,' he said.

On the Gelding, she fell in beside him, gaily talking as they broke into a slow trot along the straight track leading from the house. A weak January sun eventually broke through the thin cloud mass as they cantered over the meadow and Laura felt a rush of extreme happiness. Life was suddenly so beautiful. Beside her was this smiling and handsome man, just the sight of whom sent her heart palpitating wildly and her thoughts reeling out of control.

All of a sudden he reined in sharply.

'What is it?' she called.

'Just then something happened.' Pausing to relive the moment, he added, 'It was only a flash, but I saw myself riding across a meadow and with me was...'

Slowly he dismounted. Laura did likewise. 'What, Ray? Who was with you?'

'I'm not sure. A man. No idea who.'

Relieved, she said, 'Something in your subconscious trying to get out.'

He nodded. 'It was very real.' He caught at her hand and kissed it. She involuntarily retreated a step. 'Forgive me, Laura, but when I'm with you I feel so—contented.'

Her hand still clasped in his, she moved towards him, her heart thumping. 'And I with you.'

'Really?'

His arms wound round her, securing her against him and she leaned into him aware of the hard contours of his lean body. His hand brushed away the stray tendrils of hair from her face as he brought his lips down to meet hers in a gentle kiss. Her world shunted to a halt.

'Oh, Ray...' Her lips parted, allowing his tongue to probe her mouth, and she felt swept away on a tide of emotion so strong that tears of joy sprang to her eyes.

'My dearest Laura.' Their mouths met again, this time with brutal passion, until he broke the spell. 'Laura – I don't know who I am or if I can offer you anything...'

She placed a finger to his lips. 'I know, Ray, I know.'

'All I know is I have these feelings for you.' He looked into the depths of her eyes. 'I love you, Laura, it's crept over me until I can't think straight any longer.'

His lips found hers again and their bodies responded together until she felt she would burst with desire. His kiss left her in no doubt of where they were headed. She barely remembered how they came to be lying on the soft leaves; only his tender caresses and whispered endearments made any sense. When he took her, this her first time, she cried out.

Afterwards, he said as they clung to each other, 'Dearest, you're cold. I felt you shiver.'

It was true, she did feel chilly but had been hardly aware of it.

'Let's ride to the house,' he said. 'We'll open a bottle of fine brandy to celebrate our happiness.'

They rode home, neither speaking. Both were keenly aware that a major turning point had been reached in their lives.

• • •

'You love him?'

Colour filled her cheeks at the delightful thought of it all. 'Yes, Papa, I do.'

'Then, girl, you must have him.'

Her lashes shot up. 'Papa – you mean it?'

She looked at him with new eyes. He actually agreed with her.

'I mean it. A man would have to be blind not to have noticed,'

'Then you'll not pursue your idea of publishing his picture?'

Sebastian chuckled. 'Ah, so that's what's been troubling you, is it? Scared that Floyd might discover who Ray is and break the spell?' His hand came to rest on her arm. 'You have my blessing. It's time you were wed. If the young man feels the same about you then it's not for me to object.'

Her arms wound round his neck. 'Thank you, Papa. I'm so happy, I could burst!'

Embarrassed by her sudden embrace, Sebastian took a step backwards. 'I would warn you, though, that should the fellow discover his background himself, you may have to let him go. What you're doing, Laura, is very dangerous. After committing himself, he may well find himself unable to carry out his desires.'

She had thought about this and it hurt. 'I'm aware, Papa.'

'Good, as long as you are. I'm giving a party this weekend. I aim to announce my intention to marry Marilyn and I hope you'll be there with Ray when I do.'

'Marry? But, Papa...'

'No buts. Surely I don't have to ask your permission?'

She smiled. She was being silly. 'No, Papa. I wish you every happiness.'

He took out his pocket watch. 'You must go now. I'm expecting her at any moment.'

Sebastian waited for her to leave and poured himself a small whisky. Things were moving along better than he had planned. The very person he had thought a nuisance was actually helping sort out his major problem. Laura being his major problem. Ray had come along in the nick of time. Laura would be taken off his hands and he would be free to replace her with Marilyn. Marriage and a family were now his main priorities. Together they would sell Marilyn's home, the Grange Manorhouse, and expand Hilton Heights and with Laura out of the way, he would be able to settle down. Fate had sent him Ray.

Thank goodness he had not looked into his background. Far better that matters remain as they are. Once Ray was married to Laura, surely any past life would be insignificant. Hopefully, he would be entirely happy and would not care any longer. As for Ray's military background, once the war was over, and that could be sooner than they knew, no one was going to bother. Most probably his name was on the casualty list, and that would be an end of it.

He lit a cigar and sent a cloud of satisfaction into the air. The party was going to be quite an occasion. First he would go and pick up the engagement ring then he would announce to all his intention to make Marilyn his wife. There would surely be some shocked faces. Many had been close friends of Lillian's but perhaps when they saw how happy he and Marilyn were together, they would come round.

Refilling his glass, he contemplated the threatening clouds on the horizon. More rain was forecast and with this sudden cold spell, it could mean snow as well. But, what the hell, it could do what it damned well liked for all he cared.

The future for him looked to be very bright indeed.

• • •

On January 20th the weather broke and the sky poured forth torrential rain. Marilyn inserted the key into the lock aware of the uncanny silence surrounding Grange Manorhouse that afternoon.

She pulled the bell rope and waited. A door opened.

'Ah, where the hell you been to, Idah?'

The black girl bobbed a curtsy. 'I done been on mah own here, Miss Marilyn, 'm.'

'What? Where are Ephram and Sims?'

'They gone, Miss Marilyn.'

It was what she had feared. All this Emancipation talk, and now the servants had left her. Not that they were slaves. Despite her South Carolina background, she had embraced the lifestyle of the north. Having lived in Maryland for fifteen years, her employees had always been free to come and go and now they had done just that.

'And what of Josy?'

'She here, miss.'

'Good.' Josy was indispensable. She helped bathe, dress, and generally spoil Marilyn. 'Send her to me.'

Idah hesitated. 'She went to town, says she'll be back around six, 'm.'

In time for dinner. Marilyn heaved a sigh. 'Very well. Bring me a drink, will you?'

'Your usual, miss?'

'Yes, make it a double.'

In her bedroom Marilyn changed out of her damp clothing. Her temper that day had been less than moderate. Vince hadn't been in touch with her. All she'd had from him since the night of the ball were a few red roses.

She consulted the calendar, trying to estimate where he might be. A business trip, he had told her, though when she asked him about it he cleverly changed the subject, but she suspected he might be in New York. She had long felt that he was involved in something. Several times he received telegrams and letters, all of which he carefully concealed from her and what annoyed her most was his indifference towards the situation between them. A little jealousy over the fact that she often stayed with Sebastian would encourage her but Vince merely shrugged it off. Was he going to be that submissive when she told him that Sebastian was hinting at marriage?

Was she to interpret his indifference as a lack of feeling? She shook off that notion. His lovemaking surely told her otherwise.

Pulling a cache from her hair she shook her head so that her hair fell loosely about her shoulders. If only Sebastian did not expect her to make love with him. She could handle anything but that. Initially, it had not been so bad, but as her love for Vince had grown, so had her revulsion for Sebastian. Excuses were no longer enough. Sebastian would soon see through that. He was now giving a party, for a surprise so he said, but he'd also mentioned marriage. Was this party to announce their engagement? She could hardly bear the thought. Having to go through all of this was cruel yet how else could she get Hilton Heights? To be owner one day of such a grand property and all the money involved would surely elevate her position in society. Therefore, marriage to Sebastian seemed to be the only answer, the only way to prevent Laura from inheriting. She sighed deeply. She would give anything to find another way.

As she made her way into the dining room, the seeds of an idea crept into her mind and began to grow. The very next time she saw Vince, she would discuss it with him.

• • •

'It says here that Governor Floyd from Washington wishes to come and see me. I wonder what about?'

Jo-Ellen, warming herself by the fire in the book-lined study, popped the letter back into her pocket and waited for some reaction from Constance. There was none.

'Mama, you hear me?'

Constance paused in her crocheting. 'I was miles away just then. Did you say something?'

'Yes, Mama. Where were you?'

'I was remembering the time when Samuel took me to the theatre in New York a few years back. We stayed at the Fifth Avenue Hotel on 23rd Street and we saw, 'The Governor's Wife,' at the Winter Garden.'

'Well, talking about governors, Floyd himself is on his way. I wondered what he wants.'

'Isn't he the one who wrote to you about Rob? Seems to me that's what it's about.'

'Now why didn't I think of that? According to this letter, he's due here today.'

'Today!' Constance thrust aside her work. 'Glory be, now you tell me. We must prepare ourselves. I wonder what he drinks, what he eats?' She pulled a bell rope. 'Louise, we're expecting a very important visitor. Please prepare some snacks and make sure we have whisky and Bourbon.'

Jo-Ellen grinned to herself as her Mama hitched her skirts and bustled after Louise into the adjoining room. She supposed she ought to feel the same way but the arrival of Governor Floyd neither excited nor interested her, save for his possible reason for calling.

As she pondered this, a noise outside drew her to the window. A carriage had drawn up, as fine as any she had seen in Washington, and climbing out was the Governor himself. She recognised him from pictures she had seen in newspapers. He was a popular man in his own circles, she recalled, had much political clout as well as the ear of President Lincoln. Her Mama would know this, had always been impressed by authority.

Louise appeared in the doorway. 'Governor Floyd, miss.'

The large man standing behind her beamed and held out his hand. 'It was worth the trip all the way down here, Mrs de la Rey, to see such a splendid house and to also meet the wife of one of the finest young men I ever did have the pleasure of meeting.'

She shook his hand and wondered if he was always so gushing to people he met for the first time. And how well had he known Rob? She offered a seat and asked what he would like to drink.

'Bourbon, straight,' he replied, placing himself in an armchair.

She nodded towards Louise who moments later returned with a tray laden with refreshments and delicately made snacks.

'Now, let me tell you why I'm here,' he said when they were alone. 'It's my duty to try and locate as many families of war victims as possible, and having already seen George and Rachel de la Rey, I made up my mind to come to Savannah first opportunity I got. Though I must say,' here he glanced sheepishly at his drink, 'I'm surprised you prefer to live down here.'

'It's my home, Governor Floyd. Always has been, always will be.'

He swallowed his drink. 'Quite so.' There was a short silence. She guessed what was on his mind. Robert de la Rey, the young and promising future candidate for the Senate, had taken for his wife a southern woman. Did he not realise that their decision to marry had occurred to them long before this silly war?

'Your husband was a fine man, a fine man.'

She smiled. 'Why, thank you, Governor.'

Hubert reached forward and sampled a snack. 'When I met your husband back in '61, he impressed me greatly. Had a fine mind, kept talking about his aims and ambitions.' He looked at her intently. 'Had he lived, he might have gone right to the top, even I could see that.'

'Oh, you think so?'

'I know so. I've a keen eye for such people and I wasn't the only one to say so.'

Jo-Ellen offered him another drink and waited until the Governor had eaten more food.

'I'm very flattered that you had such a high opinion of Rob. And thank you for coming to see me.' She supposed this to be the right reaction. She had learned nothing, and sensed that this was a visit he made to everyone, a kind of apology, a 'thank you for your husband and for his ultimate sacrifice' visit.

Constance interrupted them 'Please do forgive me, Jo-Ellen, I'd no idea you were entertaining.' She turned her most charming smile on to Governor Floyd who stood to greet her.

'Not at all, dear lady.'

'Mama, let me introduce you to Governor Floyd.'

Constance offered her hand. 'Delighted, Governor.'

Jo-Ellen, keen to end this charade, rose to her feet and the Governor took the hint. Moving towards the door, he said, 'I really must leave you two delightful ladies. It's been a pleasant afternoon. However, I've one or two appointments to attend to before I journey back to Washington.'

'Before you go,' said Jo-Ellen, darting a look at Constance, 'I've something here that might interest you.' She produced the diary and waited while he thumbed through it. 'My husband wrote it. It's a detailed account of the war up to the end of last August.'

He scanned the pages quickly. 'Mrs de la Rey, if I promise to take great care of this, may I borrow it?'

'Of course, as long as I get it back eventually.'

He assured her she would and they watched from the window as he climbed into his carriage.

'My, what an honour. The man is positively charming,' Constance said in her musical voice.

'Mama, he's only doing his job. Besides, he wouldn't have bothered at all had Rob been Confederate.'

The smile left Constance's face. 'Dear me, yes, I'd forgotten. He's the enemy, isn't he?'

With irony, Jo-Ellen said, 'Yes, Mama, he's the enemy.'

'I wonder why he wanted that diary?' Constance went off tutting to herself and muttering something about handing over the book to the enemy.

Jo-Ellen settled down to write a letter, intent on next paying a visit to Susanne. She had much to tell her. Much that concerned Highlands.

● ● ●

Vince drew Marilyn into his arms and kissed her. Late for his appointment with her, he knew the quickest route to her heart was a long, passionate kiss.

'I began to think you weren't coming,' she whispered close to his ear.

'Now why'd you think that, darlin'. I told you how busy I've been of late.'

Before she could ask questions, he went on, 'Get me a large drink, honey, will you?' He had thought to bring her a gift, something to keep her sweet, but time had not allowed. 'And how's my darlin' been faring?'

He sipped at the brown liquid. It was strong, just how he liked it. And he needed it badly. For several days he'd been bartering between members of the War Department and a certain contact who had not been named. This had irritated him beyond measure. After all, he'd argued, if he'd no idea who he was dealing with, then there was an element of danger in it for him but his colleagues would not budge. Just supply the guns, take the money in payment and get lost, they told him. Cronies of Stanton's, no doubt. He knew all about Stanton.

It had all been rather sloppy and not to his liking but now he had the money, he felt marginally better. He tossed down the drink and handed the empty glass back to Marilyn. 'Pour me another, honey.' He was weary, needed a break, and who better to be with than Marilyn? His other woman in Richmond was too far off at present.

Marilyn waited until he had relaxed a little. She had never seen him so tense, so strung up. And she was no fool. Something had delayed him and she intended to find out what it was, but later.

With deft fingers she stroked his forehead, massaging his scalp and easing his neck and shoulders. His eyes closed, his head tilted back and gently she planted her lips on his.

'Feeling better?'

'Much.' Then, 'What do you think, honey, how about we...' He motioned towards the bedroom.

'In a while, my sweet. I've something to discuss with you first.'

He tensed. One thing he couldn't stand was a curious woman and Marilyn's curiosity often amounted to plain nosiness. If she asked again about his 'business' then he would have to get tough, put her in her rightful place once and for all. She would still be there for him. Marilyn needed her sex as much as he did. No harm would be done, just a man showing his woman who was boss. He closed his eyes again, preparing himself for what might come.

'It's Sebastian,' she said.

Vince gave a sigh of relief. 'What about him?'

She explained about the party, that it was probably to announce their engagement. At this, she expected some kind of positive reaction. She got none.

'I was thinking, Vince, as I don't aim to marry him...'

'Whyever not?'

Her lashes shot up and she stopped her massage. 'Why not? What kind of a question is that?'

'Now, hold on honey, it's a perfectly reasonable question since you want Hilton Heights. How else will you get it?'

'That's what I want to discuss with you, because I've come up with an idea.' She began to pace up and down. 'What if I get engaged, let everybody know that I'm to be Mrs Hilton. In the meantime, Sebastian writes up his Will in my favour and then before we can tie the knot, he has an unfortunate accident?'

Vince stared at her, placed his drink to one side and topped it up from the bottle. 'An accident? How?'

'Oh – I'm sure you'll think of something, darling.'

His hand snaked out to fasten on her arm. 'Now wait a minute. What are you scheming?'

She stepped back from him and he released her. 'You want what I want, don't you? Money and power? Well, all that will come with Hilton Heights. Unless your new line of business is sufficient?' She looked at him with suspicion.

'What I do is none of your business!'

'Perhaps not, but if you want out then say so. I can find me a man at any time, someone who'll appreciate me and what I'm offering.'

Vince controlled himself with difficulty. Damn the woman – she was right. 'You know I'm not going anywhere,' he said, his tone flat. Best to let her think he was hers completely, calm her down. The last thing he wanted was to lose his share of the takings.

'Good. You'll have to plan something that won't arouse any suspicions. Meanwhile, I'll deal with Sebastian in my own way. I'll let you know when to strike. Are you with me?' She placed her arms round his neck. 'Well?'

He drew her to him. 'I'm with you but I can't see that you'll get everything unless you marry him. What's the difference, Marilyn? Whether you do or don't if you're planning on ridding yourself of him?'

She gave a wry laugh. 'The difference? Can't you guess? With things the way they are, I don't have to sleep with him, just keep him sweet when it suits me, as if that isn't bad enough. But as his wife, he'll be in total control over me and my body. I don't want that, Vince, and surely you don't either!'

She looked into his eyes for some sign that he cared.

'Of course I don't, but I'm just being practical. As his widow you'll surely come in for the lot. As his fiancee, you probably won't. He's got a daughter, don't forget.'

How could she forget? The girl had been a nuisance since day one.

'She's bound to get her fair share, if not more, especially if she isn't married,' he added.

Marilyn sighed. What he was saying held a ring of logic and truth. Perhaps she ought to marry Sebastian after all. It wouldn't be for long. Once he was dead, she would be free to be with Vince, and Vince would have to do what she wanted afterwards, to keep her quiet. And they would both be wealthy. So long as no one became suspicious.

'Let me worry about Laura and Sebastian,' she said. 'All you have to do is kill him. Can you do that?'

Her voice sounded miles away. The whisky was blurring his mind.

'Yes, I can do that.' So what, he'd killed before for lesser reasons than this. Once he had his share of anything Marilyn put his way, he would be off. His work took him away usually to northern parts where his contacts in business were multiplying. One day, he wouldn't come back, simple as that. The war was keeping him in whisky, cigars and gambling money, but it wasn't enough. There were bigger fish to fry and it did not include Marilyn.

He lifted her into his arms and carried her up the stairs to bed where their lovemaking echoed the urgency and passion that such violent thoughts as murder evoked.

• • •

The late afternoon glow was deceiving. It was, in fact, windy and cold, and rain streaked down, turning the countryside into a swamp.

Daniel reined in to look down on Jefferson House, a sight he thought he might never see again during those tumultuous last battles. It was later than he planned – 25th January – his journey to Savannah beset with many delays. When he left Fredericksburg, the Union Army were bogged down somewhere in mud, while the Confederates were in their trenches across the Rappahannock. It was with high spirits that he had left his division to set out towards Savannah, to take the leave he had promised himself for so long. He travelled as inconspicuously as possible in civilian clothes, his arm still bound and hidden beneath his overcoat. To minimise the delay, he had slipped into South Carolina and came out by way of Hilton Head.

'Walk on.' He savoured every moment of the remaining distance between himself and the Plantation. To his right was Highlands, its acres of land stretching far beyond his capacity to see. A sluggish yellow river wound away to his left, skirting ploughed fields and grand looking houses.

Later, he thought, he would call on Ben and Susanne. For now, all he wanted was to see Jo-Ellen, to hold her close, to feel her small body against his. A wry grin touched his lips. Such dreams, for that's all they were, had kept him going these past months. That she was still grieving for her husband, he had no doubt. He would have to be mindful of that, but surely even Jo-Ellen would come to realise that life had to go on.

He stopped the Grey and tethered it. There were lights on in the house. A side door opened and a young black girl came out.

'Don't be alarmed,' he said. 'I'm here to see Miss Jo-Ellen.'

The fear in the girl's eyes disappeared. 'She inside. I'll go tell her.'

'No, let me do that. I want to surprise her.'

Louise hesitated. Her mistress would be angry if she did not alert her in time. She eyed the gentleman. He seemed all right but some of them northerners were schemers. Then she remembered. This gentleman had come to see Miss Jo-Ellen before. She hadn't recognised him out of his uniform. And that uniform had been grey, she was sure.

She beckoned to him. 'Follow me, sir.'

The warmth of the house fire was welcome and as Daniel stepped into the great hall, a feeling of nostalgia overtook him. This was where he and Jo-Ellen had stood together six months ago.

A door opened, a bright light filtered into the hall as Constance came out and went straight into the dining room. Daniel stood out of sight, then pushed open the drawing room door. An exclamation of delight sent Jo-Ellen hurrying towards him, her hands ready to grasp his in welcome.

'What a wonderful surprise! Why didn't you tell me you were coming?'

She allowed him to kiss her cheek, allowed his arms to embrace her.

'How are you, Jo?'

The words he had rehearsed so often for this first meeting escaped him. He felt almost tongue-tied. He had longed for this moment, wanted it to last forever but it was over too soon. Not at all as it was in his dreams.

'My, you look so different out of uniform, Daniel.' Her eyes took him in. He was even more handsome than she remembered and looking fitter, or was it slimmer? She noticed his arm and touched it gently with her fingers. 'What happened? Were you badly hurt?'

He told her everything she wanted to know. When she asked how long he was to be in Savannah, he said he was not sure.

'I hope you're staying for dinner, that you haven't arranged to dine elsewhere,' she said, ringing the bell for Louise.

He said that he had no such arrangement.

'Then, Louise, bring in the whisky and be sure to set an extra place.'

When Constance came back they were involved in deep conversation, Daniel about his adventures and Jo-Ellen about the Plantation. She said nothing about Governor Floyd's visit, or about the diary. Anything concerning Rob she preferred not to discuss.

Daniel rose to his feet to greet Constance. She was quite taken with him. Ever since that first day at Ben's wedding she had thought well of this Confederate officer, so that when Daniel insisted that she remain there with them and join in, she was pleased to do so. They discussed the war, Alexander, Susanne and Ben, and also Jamie. When Jo-Ellen mentioned that they might sell Highlands, Daniel listened intently.

'It's become so expensive for them and requires full time work. Susanne hasn't been able to do much lately and now Ben may have to report back.'

Daniel had known that might happen. Not many officers took off from the war, never to return. They were generally tracked down, some had even been shot for desertion. If Ben returned of his own accord, the chances were that he'd be accepted and nothing more said. Lee was not a vindictive man. He had none of the sour qualities of Jackson, who had shown himself intolerant of such behaviour. Lee would caution Ben firmly and that would be an end of the matter.

'We plan to expand this house, try and build up our work force,' said Jo-Ellen. 'Highlands will fetch quite a lot on the market even now, if we can find a buyer, though who would take such a chance at a time like this is beyond me.'

Daniel's eyes never left her face, except when Constance put in a word and then his concentration would revert to her. Over dinner the conversation continued. Without Ben, Jo-Ellen said, the whole plan might collapse, causing considerable financial loss to them all.

'If the war ended then so would our problems eventually, but if Ben does go, heaven knows how we'll cope.' Turning to Daniel, she added, 'Tell me that you think it will end soon, Daniel.' Her tone was light but there was an expression in her eyes that tugged at his heart.

She looked so beautiful in her high-necked blouse, her fair hair framing her sweet face.

'I'd like to, but how can I lie to such a lovely lady?'

She lowered her lashes, aware of Constance looking from one to the other. Did she approve or disapprove?

'Thank you for a delicious meal, Mrs Jefferson.' Daniel's words eased the awkward silence and they adjourned into the drawing room to enjoy the remainder of the evening. It was then that it occurred to Constance to ask about Daniel's sleeping arrangements.

'I still have to take care of that,' he replied. 'It will be simple to find somewhere in town.'

'But it's so late.' She turned to Jo-Ellen. 'Surely one of the spare rooms?'

When she had left the room to organise matters, Daniel said, 'I hope my coming here hasn't inconvenienced you, Jo.'

Her smile encouraged him. 'No, I'm pleased to see you. Now, I expect you're tired so I shall go up to Alexander and then to my own bed, so goodnight, Daniel. Louise will arrange breakfast for you.' At the door she paused. 'Please do help yourself to another nightcap. It will help you to sleep.'

Alone, he obediently poured a small brandy and took it with him to his room, finding it beyond him to describe the feeling that had overcome him so strongly in those moments. Feelings of extraordinary happiness, of total security and comfort, of having come home. A lump came to his throat and water to his eyes and he steeled himself against all that. It had been so long since he had felt such emotion.

Before settling down, an idea so wonderful, so complete, came to him.

When Constance came in so say goodnight, he was fast asleep.

●●●

The diary was loaded. Written by an educated man, but then Floyd knew that already. There wasn't much he didn't know about the son of George de la Rey, and Robert had put his heart and soul into the diary by the look of it. It contained every snippet of the war up to and including the beginning of Sharpsburg. Sad that this promising young fellow had been killed at such an early age.

Historically, the diary had punch, might even fetch a few dollars were it ever published. This thought interested him. That might be one way to repay the widow. She now had a son to bring up and would no doubt welcome the money. As soon as he got back to Washington he would set the wheels in motion, see if the editor of The Independent showed any interest.

Floyd glanced around the hotel room. He had put up in northern Virginia on the last leg of his journey. Tomorrow he should be back at his desk, all being well, and tomorrow he would report to the President about the grieving widows and parents he had visited. Until then he had to put up with another night of oil lamps, bowl and pitcher, and yellow soap. There had been no joyful side to his life lately. One sad story after another, one hotel room after another. Sometimes the food had not been to his liking, overcooked slush some of it. Tobacco had been difficult to come by and one hotel barely had any alcohol. Frankly, he couldn't wait to get back to Washington.

Tucking the diary away, he went downstairs. The young lady in the foyer had been most charming when he arrived, flirtatious even. On this occasion he had not given his proper name. 'Hubert Floyd' would raise eyebrows so close to home. No, he wanted a bit of privacy this night.

'Can I help you, sir?'

She was lovely, about nineteen years old, with large bosoms and a sexy walk.

'I was wondering, would you join me for dinner this evening?'

Her eyes grew large. Floyd prayed she had not recognised him.

'Why, yes, I'd like that, mister. Providing I can get time off.'

The voice let her down, but Floyd wasn't bothered with voices at that moment.

'I'm sure we can arrange something. We'll eat in my room, then? Be there at six?'

She grinned. 'A bit early to eat, ain't it?'

'We won't eat until eight. I take it you like wine?'

'I sure do.'

'Then be there at six sharp.'

Chapter Ten

Was it possible to have feelings for two men at the same time? Jo-Ellen wasn't at all sure. How could she love one man so completely, if part of her had feelings for someone else? She had read somewhere that it was possible and besides, wouldn't Rob have wanted her to get on with her life and not remain alone forever more?

Daniel had been at the Plantation for almost ten days, during which time she had tended his shoulder, and reorganised her work routine so that she had plenty of free time with him. There was no doubt about it. They were getting closer every day, so much so, that she dreaded the day he would return to his division.

Constance had noticed. She could always tell when her Mama looked at her in that way she had, her eyes and frown asking a silent question that Jo-Ellen knew sooner or later she would have to answer.

Through the window she looked at the high moon set in a cloudless sky. The stars shone like crystal balls, clear and clean. Daniel was with Constance, chatting after dinner. Her Mama always liked to do that. Dinner was a sociable affair and did not end with the last course, not for Constance. Jo-Ellen, on the other hand, had excused herself and gone to her room. She needed to refresh herself, change her gown, brush her hair.

A light tapping came on her door and she quickly opened it. Daniel offered his arm. 'Care to? It's a beautiful evening.'

They strolled around the Plantation until he stopped and placed a gentle hand on her shoulder. 'Jo, listen to me, I've an idea which excites me just thinking about it. I hope it has a similar effect on you. Jo- how would you feel about me buying Highlands?'

Shocked silence.

'You, Daniel, but why?'

He gave a chuckle. 'For many reasons. You need the money, don't you? The likelihood of a stranger taking it on is remote. I also like the idea of being your neighbour. I worked on a farm in Virginia when I was a lad, so I'll know the ropes. You said that no one in his right mind would buy it now. Well, that's true, since I haven't been in my right mind since meeting you.' His eyes softened. 'I also want to be near you. If you disagree, then I'll forget the whole idea.'

Her lip quivered. 'Daniel, it's wonderful of you to want to help us but I can't let you. You would lose your money. Highlands is expensive and quite unsellable in this war.'

'I am not looking to sell it on. You forget that I will want to settle down some day. And could you bear to see Highlands go to somebody who might not care as I would?'

She shook her head.

'Think about it, Jo, that's all I ask. Speak to Ben. If he's not keen, then we'll forget it. I can afford it, you can name your price.'

His arms reached out for her and she leaned into him. When his lips came down on hers, gentle and persuasive, she did not resist. This dear man had brought the answer to a major problem, and yes, she did like the idea of having him for a neighbour. There was no war when Daniel was there with her. He made her feel secure, he made everything come right.

'Well?' he asked. 'Is that a yes?'

'Yes, it's a yes.' She gave him a huge smile. 'Oh, please, Daniel! It will be wonderful!'

He held her to him, kissing her temples, her cheeks, her lips. There was little she could do to prevent him, little that she wanted to do.

Their final hours were saddened by his impending departure. They did not speak again about Highlands.

That night, Jo-Ellen was relieved that her Mama was present. Had she not been, she felt sure she might have given herself completely.

...

'Laura – this President Lincoln, is he for or against slavery?'

Laura inclined her head. 'Seems he's against, Ray. Why do you ask? You've read that he's freed the slaves.'

'Yes, but emancipation extends only to those slaves whose

owners are still fighting for the southern cause, and that in the States that have remained loyal, it doesn't apply. That's why I ask, Laura. How can that be right?'

'I don't rightly know, dearest, I don't understand it.' She grinned at him. 'You going to get all political again?'

He did not reply but returned his attention to the newspaper, which carried an article on the slave issue. As he read the words he felt images of his past, as though much of what the article was saying he already knew. Lately, he had begun to remember, tiny things only in flashes, but it was encouraging. Only that morning he had ridden one of the horses and knew that he was an excellent rider with a love for the animal and sure enough that same vision had come of galloping over the meadow – but with whom? Again, when he read about the war, he felt he knew much about it. Some of the news did not surprise him at all. Mention of General George McClellan had alerted him and the image of a small man with sharp features came to him instantly. Had he seen a photograph of the general somewhere?

He set aside the newspaper and took Laura's hand in his. 'You'll be the most beautiful woman at the party tonight, Laura. Wear your blue gown for me? I like to see you in that.' Another flash. Where had he heard those words before?

'I'll wear it just for you, Ray.' She sat beside him. 'Am I as beautiful as Marilyn?'

He found this amusing. Laura and Marilyn were constantly in competition. He had to admit to himself that he'd had a pleasant shock when meeting Marilyn for the first time and she had shown herself to be both flirtatious and charming. How such a woman could contemplate taking up with a man like Sebastian Hilton was beyond him.

'Definitely,' he replied. They were so very different from each other. To compare her with Marilyn was impossible, he thought, gazing at her earnestly. Laura had a peaches and cream complexion, with large gentle eyes and a wide kissable mouth. Her round features were framed by a mane of reddish brown hair, her voice was girlish but educated and soft. Marilyn, on the other hand, gave the instant impression of having lived her life to the full. Her features were sharper, handsome really, her hair bleached, and she wore makeup, lots of it. Her figure was more developed, and her voice was womanly with a husky quality. Only her high-pitched laughter irritated him. He much preferred the softness of Laura, her naivety, her willingness to please. Given time, she would develop into a fine woman, and she pleased him physically, though he'd had to show her how. Again, when he lay with Laura, a distant memory of another woman nagged at his mind. Probably lain with several, he decided, watching as Laura left him to arrange the flowers in the window recess. If only he could remember one of them. Another thing nagged at him. How old was he? When was his birthday?

'Lizabeth wants me to go with her to Frederick to shop. I said I might.'

'Lizabeth? Your friend?'

'Yes. I want you to meet her, Ray. She tells me so much about the fighting. Her brother's in the Potomac Army. She's so proud of him, always boasting about his latest battle.'

Ray frowned. 'The Potomac? I read about that recently.' And it had seemed familiar, personal even.

'I expect you have. It's constantly in the newspapers. That General McClellan ran it one time, didn't he?'

'Laura, generals don't run armies, they lead them.'

She came and put her arms round his neck. 'Well, my handsome soldier, are we going to get ready for the party?'

'Will your friend Lizabeth be there?'

She shook her head. 'No, Papa doesn't like her much. Says she's common.'

Ray said nothing. Did Sebastian not feel the same way about Marilyn? Now, she was common. Beautiful but common. He didn't feel much like going to the party, mostly because he was uncertain about himself. Only knowing who he was and where he came from would build his confidence. He drew himself up. Best thing might be to get out there and meet a few people and perhaps a party was as good a place to start as any. No use sitting around Hilton Heights for the rest of his days. Strange, too, how the name Hilton Heights reminded him of something, but what?

'Ray, let's surprise everybody tonight and announce our engagement.'

He looked at the mischievous smile on her face. 'Sweetheart, I doubt that's a good idea.'

'Because of my Papa?'

'Yes, and because of Marilyn. It's their night. We'll have ours later.'

She snuggled up to him. 'Spoil sport. I wanted to see her face when I upstaged her.'

He watched as she trotted up the stairs to her room. When the door slid shut he poured a sherry and lit a cheroot. Minutes later, he began preparing himself for the evening ahead.

• • •

'Be a good idea if you publish these. I've got the go-ahead from the widow.'

Hubert Floyd dropped the diary on Lewis Wilson's desk. He had been back in Washington for almost a month and had only just gotten around to doing something about the de la Rey writing.

Wilson, sub-editor of The Independent, looked up. 'I'll give them a look over, sir.'

'Do so, soon as possible, Lewis. You'll publish, I can guarantee.'

Wilson picked up the pages and read the inside cover. 'Robert de la Rey. Rings bells.' He clicked his fingers. 'Got it. He had a political commission a couple of years back. We almost printed a story on him.'

Floyd raised an eyebrow. 'Yes, I agree it was frowned on at the time. He was accused of social climbing, not to his face, but behind his back aplenty. Officers appointed from civilian life, and all that. Knew the right people and so on and so on. Thing was, Lewis, he was a brilliant up and coming young fellow with an eye on a political future. We've lost a precious son, so Lewis, publish it.'

Wilson, a cynical grin on his face, flicked over the pages as Floyd consulted his pocket watch and made to leave.

'Take care of that diary. I aim to return it in one piece.'

Outside he hesitated before stepping into the snow-slushed street. It was freezing. February had been a wretched month. March might not be much better by the look of the threatening skies. He sighed. Time to see the President. He had consulted with Seward and Stanton in recent days about Lincoln's intended announcement on March 1st of a compulsory draft. It was a welcome turn of events. Rich young men who had bought their way out in past months could no longer do so. Which brought de la Rey to mind again. That young man would never have done that, would never have used his money to get himself out, despite Lewis's low opinion of him.

Hubert turned up his coat collar, pointed his walking stick in front of him and crossed the street.

• • •

It was a sad day, one of the worst in Ben's life. As he straightened his jacket and pulled himself into the saddle, his eyes slid to where he knew Susanne was watching behind the drapes, unable to be there for the final farewell, so distraught was she. Then there had been the tearful parting from Jo-Ellen and his Ma. It was more than he could bear.

'Walk on,' he said and without another glance backwards, he meandered the horse along the track leading from Highlands, cantering until they were no longer visible to any watchers at the house. In the clearing he reined in. All he had to do was turn back, stable the horse, walk into the house and discard his uniform forever. Up he would go to Susanne's room, take her in his arms and promise never to leave her again – just as he had before the soldiers came by. And that was the problem, for they would do so again. Therefore, wasn't it far better to do what he was doing than to be arrested and hauled back by them?

His decision had been made easier by Daniel who had spoken to him again about returning and facing the music rather than hiding away. And then there was Jamie to think about. One day she might learn how her father had refused to fight for his country, or that was how she might see it, despite his war record so far. He had to pray that Foley's death had not been looked into, that they saw it as just another casualty of war. Finally, Ben had learned that Daniel intended to buy Highlands and about this he had been delighted. It was a heaven-sent acceleration of his plans.

Hanging over all of this like an unmovable grey cloud had been his own situation and finally he came to realise that in order to stay alive and free, he had no choice other than to return to his division.

Ben took a long look around him, at the lake, the barn, and the trees he'd spent most of his boyhood climbing. There were tears in his eyes and his heart felt like bursting as he again said, 'Walk on,'

• • •

Jo-Ellen did her best to comfort her friend, knowing how she felt, the memory of when Rob had gone back to fight for the north still fresh in her mind. She took Susanne gifts of flowers and truffles, sat with her, reasoned, and comforted.

There was little time for her own problems and she was unable to miss Daniel as much as she thought, so taken up was she with the Plantation, Susanne, and her own Mama.

At night, though, when she lay her head on the pillow, her thoughts were with Daniel and she used that time to pray for him and for Ben. Alexander was able to run about now and she watched with pride as daily he grew and became stronger. How like Rob he was, especially about the eyes, and he laughed a lot, exposing dimples in his cheeks, just like Rob.

During the days that followed, Jo-Ellen worked as hard as she could to keep the Plantation going. Earl and Curtis did their fair share, both satisfied with their elevated positions. They got along well together, worked in harmony and Earl even brought along some acquaintances from his social life in Savannah to do some of the work, although new labour was increasingly difficult to come by. Gradually, Susanne took part in the day-to-day activities, content in the knowledge that at least she had a reliable buyer for Highlands, and Jo-Ellen was grateful that life was beginning to slot back to something resembling normality. A year from now, she told herself, casting her eyes round the countryside, they would be back on their feet and able to combat the declining economy. That was her dream and what kept her going in those early months of the year.

She had heard from Governor Floyd that the diary would probably fetch some remuneration for her and so she had readily agreed to its publication. Only one thing niggled at the back of her mind and that was the fact that no one had contacted her about Rob's body. Had it never been found? And if it had, why had she not been informed about it?

'Mama!'

She turned at the sound of Alexander's voice. His small face lit up, his smile huge. She lifted him and held him close, knowing that whatever she had lost in the past, there in her arms she still had everything. For his sake she would pressure Floyd about Rob's body. What did happen to all those victims of war?

The next time she was in touch with the Governor, she would ask.

• • •

Sebastian pulled on his dinner jacket and was pleased with the effect. It suited him, hid the tell-tale bulge above his belt.

Through the window he saw various guests arrive, heard the clink of champagne glasses and an increasing babble of voices. The only irritation was that Marilyn had not yet made an appearance, which was typical since she preferred the effect of entering last. That way, all eyes turned on her and she was the centre of attention. Not that she need go to such lengths. This evening, as the hostess, she would be her usual eye-catching self, which was why she should be there waiting. He tutted to himself and poured a drink.

Everything had been attended to efficiently; the food, the drink, the music. As they arrived, the guests looked animated. A gathering at Hilton Heights always went down well. He saw Jasper Lee and his cronies, could hear Jasper's loud laughter even from there. It would be a raucous evening once they had their fill of whisky. He was unsure of how many guests were expected. He'd left all that to Marilyn and her maid servant to organise. Best thing might be to go down there and find out, greet a few of them and stand in for Marilyn until she arrived. Where the hell was she?

The music began. He took a final look in the mirror and made his way down the spiral staircase. The marble hall was full. Carriages continued to draw up outside. Waiters busied themselves serving refreshments. He paused half way down, panned the scene before him. No Marilyn. Several handshakes later, he let himself into his study. A figure by the fireplace turned at the sound of the door closing and irritation replaced Sebastian's calm mood. Sidney Brewster. The man was an ass. How he managed an invitation was beyond Sebastian's comprehension.

'Good evening, Sebastian. Excellent party, excellent.'

Brewster puffed on a cigar and sipped at a glass of port wine. With an effort, Sebastian nodded towards him. Brewster had probably come on someone else's invitation. There was no way that Marilyn would have asked him direct.

'Evening, Brewster. I take it your visit to my house is a cordial one?'

Brewster frowned. 'Naturally. What else would it be?' Before Sebastian could reply, he went on, 'If you're referring to my generosity towards your good lady, it was with the best of intentions, I can assure you.'

Sebastian heaved a sigh. What was this stupid man talking about?

'Kindly explain, Brewster.'

'Explain?'

'How do I know you're not here to pressurise more money from Marilyn?'

The old man drew himself up to his full height, took the cigar from his mouth and eyed Sebastian coldly.

'More money? What are you talking about?'

'Yes, I wanted to pay you off, but she'd have none of it, bless her. I'd have got rid of you once and for all. It wears her down, you know, asking her for money – money that she doesn't owe and you know it!'

'Why, that's right, she doesn't owe me any longer. In fact, I wrote off that debt about a year ago. Told her to forget it.'

Sebastian fell silent. Was this old fool drunk?

'You saw her not so long ago, asked her for money,' he said.

Brewster chuckled and ambled past him out of the room. 'Water it down a bit more, Sebastian, there's a good chap. You're mistaken. I haven't seen Marilyn for over a year.'

Sebastian mumbled a half-hearted apology. Perhaps he'd had too much to drink already. Perhaps he'd made a mistake. He glanced at his pocket watch. He would handle that matter later. Where in hell's name was Marilyn?

• • •

'Hey, honey, ain't it time you got into that fancy gown and went to your engagement party?'

Marilyn came to and sat up in the bed. Next to her Vince lay, his eyes closed, his lips curled into a grin. Outside, it was already dark.

She switched on the light to look at the clock. It was getting late. The party had been going on for over an hour.

Pulling a gown around her, she went to the bathroom to freshen herself. The last thing she felt like was a party with Sebastian, not when she had Vince there in her bed. Their lovemaking had been sensational, the slow and pleasurable kind, and she wanted to lie in his arms and savour him. Reluctantly she dressed and concentrated on her face. Josie usually did all that for her but she daren't risk the girl finding Vince there. Servants tended to gossip.

When she returned to the bedroom, Vince was fast asleep, and she quietly let herself out. The drive to Hilton Heights took little time once the horses were whipped up, and when she arrived and made her way into the great hall, a hush descended on the guests and she gave that warm smile of hers as they came to greet her and began talking all at once. Out of the corner of her eye she saw Sebastian approach. He looked – what? She was unsure. She slipped her hand into his and allowed him to lead her forward.

'You're late, Marilyn,' he hissed. 'Everything all right?'

She smiled and assured him that all was well, that she had overslept that afternoon. He seemed satisfied, especially when she gave him a kiss and followed him on to the dance floor. Everyone stood around admiring her gown, which showed to effect her long neck and high bosoms. She felt and looked radiant. Vince always did that for her.

After two glasses of champagne, she felt better about the evening and with any luck she would be able to return to Vince quite soon. As soon as the music stopped, Sebastian stepped on to the podium and began his speech and Marilyn settled back to listen, knowing full well what was coming. Out of the corner of her eye she could see Ray and Laura together. Her spirits lifted. She would monitor that situation closely. The girl looked more grown up than ever and they were behaving like a couple in love. If she was right then everything might be working in her favour after all.

Sebastian was holding out his hand to her and she joined him, aware that he had announced their forthcoming marriage. His gregarious method of proposing suited her not at all, but she was careful not to show it. All smiles and charm, she eased through the evening with great success, delighting in the fact that those people who had once disapproved of her now seemed to have accepted her totally.

When the music started again, she slid into Sebastian's arms, pleased that his previous suspicious expression had been replaced by his usual jolly self.

When she again looked in Laura's direction she saw her wrapped in Ray's arms and swaying on the dance floor. Things certainly seemed to be moving along. Perhaps it wouldn't be too long, she decided, allowing Sebastian to whirl her around, before she, Marilyn Beauville, became the sole beneficiary of Hilton Heights.

•••

'Tell me what happened, then.'

Lizabeth stood, arms folded under well-endowed bosoms, wanting to hear from Laura all the gossip. Laura took her time, aware that Lizabeth was seething about not having been on the guest list. She had felt tempted to sneak her in, but finally thought better of it. No sense in annoying her Papa, not now when he was being so soft about Ray's being there.

All evening she had endured watching her Papa simper after Marilyn and it secretly sickened her. She did not trust that woman who seemed to Laura positively deceitful, nothing Laura could put her finger on, but her intuition was rarely wrong.

To Lizabeth, she said, 'It was delightful. Everybody had a wonderful time. They came and spoke to me and Ray. I felt almost married to him, Lizabeth. It was so romantic standing with his arm around my waist and him looking so handsome. You really must meet him.'

'What about your Papa and Marilyn?' Lizabeth cut in.

'They announced their engagement.'

'What was the ring like?'

'Large, a cluster of diamonds that gleamed under the lights. I'll probably have one like that when Ray and I…'

'Think he paid the earth for it?'

'Oh yes, Papa would have done.' Laura hated to think how much her Papa wasted on that woman.

They rounded the bend towards Hilton Heights. As they entered the house, Ray was coming down the stairs. His face creased into a warm smile. 'Laura and – no, don't tell me, this has to be Lizabeth.'

She was taken with him, Laura could tell and she stood aside while they chatted.

'Where is your brother, Lizabeth? he asked.

'I don't rightly know. He was at Fredericksburg, I believe. Could be he's still there. I hear they were delayed.'

'I expect you worry about him.'

'All the time. It's natural. You wait every day to hear news. I expect it was the same for you and your family.' She darted a look in Laura's direction, whose expression changed.

Ray chuckled. 'I wish I could agree. Until I find out who I am, I'm not sure I have a family.'

Lizabeth, aware of the warning look Laura was giving her, said, 'It must be awful not knowing.'

'In a way, yes, but on the other hand I'd never have met Laura had I not been shot that day.'

He slid an arm around Laura's shoulders and she leaned into him. Confound Lizabeth. Why did she have to bring up unpleasant things?

'I'll see you off, Lizabeth,' she said. 'Ray and I are spending the morning riding together.'

When they were alone, he drew her close. 'So, we're supposed to be riding? I had better ideas.'

'Oh? What were they?'

'I guess your Papa and Marilyn will be taken up with each other today?'

She shook her head. 'I doubt it. Marilyn left after the party. Said she was exhausted. Strange isn't it? Just announced their intention to marry and off she goes?'

He agreed.

'Marilyn worries me,' Laura said. 'Why would she marry my papa if she doesn't feel to spend time with him?'

Ray said nothing. He had long since made up his mind about Marilyn. Money was her god. Anything else took its place in the pecking order and Sebastian had the money – for now.

'Hey – how about we go back to bed?' he said.

She followed him to his room and lay on the bed where he took her greedily and passionately. It was quiet up there away from the rest of the house as Laura gave herself to the man she loved, feeling more confident than ever that he was now hers completely.

• • •

Daniel was eager to leave Fredericksburg, but days came and went with boring repetition and no sign of the army moving on. Even the Federal troops were quiet. Heavy rain had the Union Army bogged down and their General Burnside both unwilling and unable to move.

The winter weeks were depressing. There was little fighting for him to do, therefore much of his time was spent thinking about Jo-Ellen. He had received one letter from her in reply to two from himself. In it she penned her personal news and he, in turn, had written as much as possible about his own activities, all of which he wrote with great affection.

At the end of February, he went to the upper Rappahannock to see General Lee.

'Sir, I've come to ask for compassionate leave.'

Lee looked at him through the half light, his soft brown eyes questioning.

'Have you indeed? Nothing seriously wrong, I hope?'

Daniel did not hesitate. He had rehearsed his speech. 'I intend to court and marry a certain lady, sir. I thought that since we are at something of a stalemate here, I could go to Savannah and sort matters out.' With a grin, he added, 'And no, sir, nothing wrong at all.'

'Be seated, Major.'

As Daniel sat, the General rose. 'This lady, she's aware of your intentions?'

'Not entirely, no, sir.'

'I see. So you might be refused?'

'Yes, General Lee. I might be.'

Lee paced slowly to and fro in the silence. 'You recently had leave following your injury at Fredericksburg, I believe.'

'Yes, sir.'

'And you saw the lady then?'

Daniel nodded.

'How is the arm, Major?'

'Better, sir.'

Lee was silent again.

At last he said, 'I wonder – Longstreet is presently south of the James drawing provisions from Suffolk.' He paused and spared Daniel an apologetic grin. 'A move that will greatly benefit us, Major. We can't have the Army of Northern Virginia running out of supplies, can we? And then there's Fitz Lee, of course. He has matters well in hand elsewhere.' He stopped pacing and sat down. 'You're in luck. I can spare you – just. Get off to Savannah and secure your lady.'

Daniel's depression lifted in an instant. 'Much obliged, General.'

'Don't delay there too long, Major. I've a feeling this quiet period won't last. The enemy will make every effort to crush us between now and June. It'll require all our strength to resist him.'

Daniel saluted smartly and left. In his quarters, he finalised outstanding matters and prepared to journey south. He was jubilant. This time when he spoke to Jo-Ellen, he would not take no for an answer.

•••

Sebastian wasted no more time. He wanted an April wedding, whereas Marilyn had been deliberating on the necessity of having to marry at all after seeing how close Laura and Ray had become. If they were to marry in the near future, she reasoned, then surely any money belonging to Sebastian would be hers by right. Vince insisted that she was presuming far too much and that marriage was the only legal way of securing their future. Not if she had anything to do with it, she told herself, and began to believe it until one morning she arrived at Hilton Heights to find that Sebastian had already furthered the wedding arrangements.

'The invitations are being prepared and should be sent out in a few days,' he told her. 'Come here, darling, let me look at you.'

She gave herself up to his scrutiny and a bear-hug and would have been subjected to an indulgent kiss had she not said, 'Sebastian dear, how many are we inviting?'

He paused to consider, giving her time to step out of his embrace. 'Oh, at the last count it was nigh on one hundred and fifty.'

'What!' She tilted her face to his. 'That's so extravagant, sweetheart. Why not a quiet wedding with family and close friends?'

'Because it must be a day to remember. People from all over Maryland will want to come, and from Pennsylvania, too, providing they can get here. Why, darling, why are you so against a big wedding?'

Effecting a warm smile, she said, 'I'm not, honey, it's just that it's so much work for you and yours.'

'Now don't go worrying your lovely head about that.' His hand reached for hers and caressed it. 'Come here, I'm an impatient man.'

As he fondled her breasts and moved his hard body against hers, she said, 'Darling, why go to the expense of a wedding when we could simply live together?'

He roared with laughter. 'I'm delighted you want to save my money, Marilyn, but we must marry. How else will you and our child inherit?'

'Our child?'

'You know I want a son more than anything else, and I want you properly as my wife, not as a mistress. Then one day all this could be yours. Isn't that what you want?'

She turned on a doubtful expression. 'I thank you, dearest, but you can leave it all to me if that is your wish, whether we are married or not and I, as your partner in life, will try and carry on your good work here.'

His eyes widened in surprise. 'Absolutely not. No, my sweet, no marriage will mean no child.'

And no inheritance, she realised. There was no escape. She had to go along with it. His arms reached for her again and this time he was less gentle and she knew better than to resist or to make excuses. The last thing she wanted was to arouse his suspicions. His advances were rough, lacking any finesse and she endured them, thinking only of the reward at the end. Vince would help her, he had to!

When their love-making was over, Sebastian lay exhausted beside her, his breathing steady. Careful not to disturb him, she rose and went to wash her body, then dressed and brushed her hair. Sebastian's voice startled her.

'What are you doing over there, Marilyn? Come on back to bed.'

With false gaiety she chided, 'You naughty boy, Sebastian. I truly wish I could, but I have to go to my house. I asked Josy to wait for me there. We have so much to do.' Turning back to the mirror she proceeded to put the finishing touches to her face and hair, aware of his eyes on her.

'I saw old man Brewster at our party, Marilyn. You didn't invite him, did you?'

She tensed. Brewster! She had not seen him.

'Why, no, dearest. I can't abide him, you know that.'

'He said he hadn't seen you in over a year, said he'd written off the money owing. Is that true, darling?'

Her mind spun. 'He must have forgotten. I saw him just a few months back. He did say then that if I couldn't repay he would reconsider matters. I took that as a veiled threat when all he meant was he would waive the debt? What an unusual gesture of generosity. Perhaps he's not as bad as I thought.' She gave a delighted chuckle and twirled provocatively for him. 'There, what do you think, darling?'

His expression softened, his eyes on her breasts. 'Beautiful, come here to me.'

She moved quickly to him, bent to plant a light kiss then removed herself before he could entrap her in his arms. 'You lie and relax, Sebastian dear. I'll go and see Josy.'

Outside, she breathed a huge sigh of relief. Her body felt sore from his animalistic attempt at love making. In the buggy her mind went over the conversation concerning Brewster. Was Sebastian suspicious? He was bound to check out her story but did it matter now? She would keep denying everything. It would be her word against Brewster's and she knew Sebastian would sooner believe her, though she would have to be more careful in the future and think up better excuses for her absences.

Perhaps the sooner she married, the better, secure the money and Sebastian's good faith. Then if ever he were to find out how much she had lied to him, it would no longer matter. By then he would be dead.

Chapter Eleven

That winter turned into a nightmare for Ben following his traumatic return to Richmond. There he had been questioned at length by senior officers and had suffered the accusing stares of some of the men who had come to trust him.

With the oncoming spring, he was pushed out to Chancellorsville and after a bloody battle where he fought to redeem himself, he emerged unscathed though mentally battered after hearing that General Jackson had been shot and wounded by mistake by one of his own men. Although the Confederates won the battle, there was little for them to celebrate in the aftermath, for Jackson eventually died from pneumonia, leaving them stunned and General Lee inconsolable.

It was a tragic and dark day and Ben felt heavy with grief, initially for Jackson, but continually with his personal circumstances. Gradually he felt himself change, as though something had taken him over. His beard grew, his face altered, dark rings circled his eyes. Weight fell from his body and he barely ate the rotten food the division was given.

Susanne and the Plantation seemed a million miles away, in another life, another time. Moments of sanity returned with the thought of his baby daughter. Jamie was eight months old now and the thought of her sweetness kept him going, his main aim being that one day he would again lift her in his arms and the three of them would be free to get on with their lives.

The vision of Susanne's tear-stained face at the window as he left the Plantation that last day was ever present like a sword in his heart that twisted when he lay down his head at night.

After Jackson's funeral, when matters had once more settled, Ben tried to write some letters home. First he wrote to Susanne and Jo-

Ellen, and to his Ma he wrote a long, newsy letter. Lately, though, he had thought much about Rob, had reminisced about their youthful adventures and particularly about his friend's last visit. There had been no doubt about it, a gap had grown between them. Yet there remained that great affection, unspoken and solid. God, how he missed them all. Fighting had been almost a welcome activity to take his mind off the emptiness within that only reunion could end. When he got home, he promised himself over and over again, he would be more tolerant towards his sister. How she must have suffered, losing Rob like that and how unforgiving he, Ben, must have seemed about her journeying so far for so long away from her new baby and the folk who loved her.

Now he understood why. Had she not done so, she might never have seen Rob again and had those last precious months with him, might never have finally married him and given Alexander back his father.

He would make up for lost time with Susanne too, laugh more with her, tell her constantly how much he loved her, give her more children, first a brother for Jamie and a good friend for Alexander to grow up with and then, later, another girl.

These were the thoughts that kept Ben sane through the battles and skirmishes and he carried them around in his head like a Bible, leaning on them for comfort and warmth and most of all for protection.

One evening he received a letter. It was from Jo-Ellen telling him that Daniel Hunter had proposed marriage and that she had accepted.

• • •

The wedding took place mid-May and not in April as Sebastian had planned.

People from all over came to see the well-known Sebastian Hilton, popular with laymen and politicians alike, his forecast of 150 guests promising to almost double.

Marilyn bent to the pressure, going through the motions with a fixed smile and a false gaiety she had learned as an adolescent. Robbed of her parents in an accident at an early age, she had been brought up by an aunt whom she detested and from whom she had escaped at sixteen by running away and joining a vaudeville troupe in Oakdale, Louisiana. There she had grown up fast, learning about the hard facts of life, how to lie and deceive and, above all, how to survive by smiling and talking her way out of trouble. She had been blessed with immense charm and she used it as her main weapon in life and so far it had not let her down.

Marilyn cast an eye around the spectacle before her. It was the kind of gathering she usually enjoyed and it was a pity that on this occasion she was not doing so. Senators, judges, high-up members of the police force – many faces she did not know amongst the many she did – all there to see her marry one of the wealthiest men in Maryland.

The only face she wanted to see was not present. Vince. He had gone away on business again, promising to return when the celebrations were over and they could be together again. She could barely wait. Once the so-called wedding night was over – and she planned to get Sebastian so drunk that he would be incapable of sexual activity – she would arrange to see Vince and put their plan into action. She had waited long enough. Nobody would tie her in with Vince, they had always been so discreet, so careful, and lately he had not been around enough to cause suspicion. Sebastian's death would be made to look like an accident, and even if murder were suspected, they would never discover Vince. It would be seen as a crime by persons unknown and she, Marilyn, would be the epitome of the distressed widow – left with Hilton Heights and a huge fortune. Her aim in the meantime was to befriend Laura. It was essential to her plans to get the girl on her side.

'Marilyn, honey, time we left these good people to get on with their partying while we get on with ours.'

Sebastian's voice cut into her thoughts and she turned to him, dreading the moment when they would journey to Grange Manorhouse. It had been Sebastian's idea to spend their first night there, an idea she had contested fiercely since Grange Manorhouse was where she and Vince made love. But her several excuses had fallen on deaf ears.

'Why so early?' she asked. 'I was hoping to dance some more and have some of that fine champagne.'

The fact was Sebastian was far from drunk. He was behaving himself so thoroughly, it scared her.

'All right, darling. Perhaps an hour longer, but don't tire yourself now.'

He patted her bottom and she giggled and moved to where Ray and Laura were watching the other guests.

'Laura, my dear, you look absolutely delightful.' She turned on her most winning smile and was gratified by a blush from Laura.

'Thank you, Marilyn, and so do you, of course. It's been a wonderful day, hasn't it?'

'Yes, and I'm so pleased you are both here.' Another smile, this time directed at Ray. 'You know, I'd like nothing better than to see you two wedded. Sebastian's been telling me, I hope you don't mind.'

'Not at all,' Ray volunteered, returning her charm. 'We wouldn't miss this for the world. So many well-known people. The mayor, for instance, and one or two state governors in attendance. I must say I'm impressed.'

Marilyn gave a giggle. 'So typical of a man to notice such things, as opposed to us, eh, Laura? We notice the beautiful gowns and the fine jewellery, and, of course, the food and drink, don't we, Laura?'

Laura thrust her arm through Ray's. 'Why, yes, I'd say you're right, Marilyn.'

In that moment, the music changed. Laura tugged at Ray's arm. 'My favourite waltz.'

'You two go and enjoy yourselves. I must find my new husband.'

Armed with a bottle of his favourite whisky, Marilyn went in search of Sebastian. 'Come, dearest, you've hardly pressed a glass to your lips all evening. Let's drink a toast to our future.'

His arms encircled her and she smelt the foulness of cigars and onions on his breath. 'Pour them out, then, honey. We'll drink to the birth of our boy nine months from now!'

His laughter rang in her ears and she wanted to push him away and run off into the night, away from the hypocrisy, the lies and the play-acting. Yet, hadn't her life always been like that? The fact that it still was and she was again the reluctant star of the show appalled her. When would it all end?

With an air of happiness she did not feel she poured a large amount of whisky into a glass and added some ice. Sebastian generally preferred it that way. For herself she chose to have champagne, and raised her glass to him.

'To our future happiness.' She watched as he drank, hardly pausing for breath, and when his glass looked almost empty she topped it up and was delighted when he finished that also.

'I needed that,' he said. 'Come on, let's dance, show these youngsters how it's done.'

He swung her on to the dance floor and Marilyn was aware that he was unsteady and breathing heavily, aware also that many eyes were turned on them and that her every move was under scrutiny. When the music finally stopped, she delivered Sebastian to a group of his friends suggesting that he next dance with his daughter, then she contrived to be close to Ray and Laura once more.

'Laura, dear, why don't you and your father have the next dance?'

Tire him out, she thought, then another drink or two and perhaps she would get through the night untouched.

Laura glanced over to where Sebastian was taking his leave of the group and heading her way. Reluctant as she was to leave Ray she felt delighted that her Papa was about to afford her some time and affection and when he whirled her on to the dance floor, she was surprised at his dexterity.

Marilyn took full advantage of her absence. 'Ray, now I've got you to myself, tell me are you and Laura serious about each other?'

Curious, he replied, 'Yes, at least I am and I believe Laura loves me.'

'I do believe so, too,' she said. 'I'm so happy for you. We can expect a spring wedding, then?'

Ray sipped his drink, his eyes on her. 'As soon as you've tied the knot, Marilyn, we'll see what we can do.'

'But I have done so today.'

'Ah, by tying the knot means living together and being a real couple.'

She smiled. 'Yes, of course, but I really don't see…' She patted his arm. 'Make it soon, Ray.'

'We're in no hurry. We may wait out the spring.'

The smile froze on her lips. 'What a shame. Poor Laura. It's so obvious she longs to marry.'

'Really?'

'Why, yes. You men are so unobservant about such matters. Take my word for it, Ray. She's probably getting impatient.'

Laura and Sebastian joined them. 'Who's impatient?' Sebastian asked.

'I was saying to Ray, and I do so hope that Laura won't mind, a lady gets impatient to wed once she's fallen in love.'

Laura's eyes centred on her and Marilyn read clearly the message of gratitude in them. Her plan was working.

'Come, dear, let's have another small drink together before we go to the Grange Manorhouse.' She gave a final sweeping smile mainly in Laura's direction and followed Sebastian into the main hall, a bottle and two glasses in her hand.

'There's more than enough drink over there. No need to bring your own,' Sebastian chuckled, clutching the wall for support.

The journey to Grange Manorhouse was short and unimpeded and once inside the bedroom, he immediately began to strip off while Marilyn sat before the dressing table mirror slowly discarding her jewellery. Through the mirror she watched Sebastian, saw him stagger, but only slightly. He had been in a far worse state in the past and had managed to perform in bed. What was she to do?

His hands reached for her, his mouth claimed hers, wet, hungry, repugnant, reeking of drink, cigars and food. Her thoughts flew to Vince. Where was he now that she needed him? He would never have come to her unwashed and ungroomed. Always fastidious, his personal habits could not be faulted. She looked at the lumbering gait of Sebastian whose brow was covered in perspiration. And not only there, she thought, as his odour overwhelmed her.

'No – don't!'

The words flew from her lips. She could not, would not, go through with this. Enough was enough. For a moment he paused, his eyes registering surprise, then anger.

'What's that?' His hand clamped on her arm in a vice-like grip.

'Sebastian – it hurts!'

'Why, I don't mean you any harm, darling, but you're my wife now and you do my bidding, understand? Get undressed, there's a good girl.'

Marilyn fought back the tears. 'I can't. I don't want to. Not tonight.'

Humour lit his eyes. 'Not tonight? When, may I ask? It's our wedding night, we're in your home alone. No servants, no interruptions. And you intend making me wait?' His free hand fastened on the nape of her neck as he again forced his lips on hers.

Breathless from the struggle, she somehow managed to pull away. 'Leave me alone, please!'

'Ah, the lady wishes to spend her wedding night alone. Why is that, I wonder?'

Marilyn tensed. She had gone too far. All her good work in the past could be lost if she did not ease the situation.

'Sebastian, I have a headache. In fact, I haven't felt well today. I didn't say anything before because I didn't want to spoil your day.'

The silence that followed frightened Marilyn. It felt as though he was staring right into her soul. What fiendish ideas were lurking in his mind?

'All right, honey, but I'm not sure I'm convinced. You seemed fine earlier. You see, old Brewster said something that made me think and think hard but I've been too busy since then to pay it much attention. Something tells me you've not been honest with me. You've been late several times, always with an admirable excuse, only I think using Brewster as one of them was a mistake, eh?'

'What are you suggesting, Sebastian?'

'I don't rightly know – yet, but there's this feeling inside that keeps sneaking up on me of late.'

His expression hardened and so did his grip on her and she was thrown back on to the bed. In a frenzy he snatched at her gown and tore it away. She screamed, struck out at him but he was too strong for her.

'No one can hear you, darling, go ahead and scream all you like.'

The last garment between them finally thrust aside, he held her down at his mercy. 'Whatever you've been up to, you're my wife now,' he breathed close to her ear and he lowered himself, his erection huge. She struggled, her efforts only increasing his desires. Forcing her legs apart, he entered her and thrust and drove until she was bruised and humiliated. Above her, the carved ornamental ceiling that she knew so well, every crevice and mark etched in her mind from her love-making with Vince, now a cold and heartless spectacle.

When Sebastian fell into a heavy sleep she pulled herself off the bed and gathered up the torn gown. She washed her body thoroughly, scenting herself and dressing in a loose fitting skirt and silk blouse. Taking care not to disturb Sebastian, she let herself out of the house. The night air revived her. There would be no sleep for her tonight. She needed to think, to plan.

As soon as Vince returned, she would demand action.

• • •

The dream felt very real. Every night he was running across a field of blood, a gun in his hands, a sabre on his hip. The field would disappear and there was sunshine, a stream and an old barn.

Ray lay watching the sun span the wooden floor of his room, the dream vivid in his mind. It was recurring – or was it? What if it were part of his past?

He passed a hand across his eyes. Tiredness was well-deserved, and also well-earned. He and Laura had burned the midnight oil every night since the wedding. They had seen little of either Sebastian or Marilyn and this suited him well.

Rising from his bed, he went to the window to look out at the newly cut lawns, the trees stretching their limbs skyward and the flowers responding to the penetrating heat of the late May sun. Below, the gardener pulled some weeds and Ray watched a while until another activity caught his attention. Laura appeared and moved across his vision, strolling in that unhurried way of hers, obviously enjoying the morning. She was, as ever, lovely as the flowers she paused to smell or touch, her hair gleaming and taken up the way he liked it, and today she wore blue, his favourite colour. Had it always been his favourite? Perhaps because Laura often wore it. Yes, he thought. He did love her, and yes, he would marry her, but all in good time. Why was everyone in such a hurry? Everyone meaning Marilyn. She was the one person who would benefit. Get Laura out of the way and everything would be hers. Had Marilyn thought he had not worked that out? A grin lifted the corners of his mouth. She was a schemer. What was she up to now – being affectionate towards Laura suddenly? Surely not because the girl was now her stepdaughter? No- there was nothing maternal in Marilyn's makeup. As for her feigned enjoyment at the wedding, several times he had caught her off-guard. Those expressions of boredom, of exasperation even, fleeting though they had been and which she cleverly covered up with her smile, had not escaped him. Laura had not noticed, otherwise she would have said something, but he had read the signs well and wondered why a woman as beautiful as Marilyn chose to tie herself to Sebastian, when she could have any rich businessman this side of the Line.

'And the other side, no doubt. Beats me,' he muttered, as Laura made her way to the shed at the far end of the grounds. She paused by the open shed door, pushed it to and in that instant Ray experienced a sharp memory of another woman doing a similar thing, only the shed was a barn and it was surrounded by countryside instead of lawns and bushes. It was the barn in his dreams but where was it and who was the woman, if indeed she existed?

He went to bathe and prepare himself. What he fancied doing that morning after breakfast was either relax and read the papers, or go for a canter. Recently, he had felt guilty lazing about the house when he read how his countrymen were out fighting, yet he had no desire to go and get involved. This gave him doubts about being on the battlefield that day.

Downstairs it was quiet. He let himself into the breakfast room and picked up 'The Independent.' On the front page was a picture of President Davis. Ray read the caption. Jefferson Davis. Jefferson – the name meant so much, but what? Inside was a long article introduced by the editor. It was an account of the early days of the war. The words 'de la Rey' caught his eye. Written by Robert de la Rey, Major in the Union Army of the Potomac. Ray read on, his interest so intense that he did not hear Laura come in.

'Ray, come and walk with me. It's such a lovely day and you're missing it.' She put her hands out to him and, startled by her intrusion, he snapped,

'What is it, Laura!'

'Why Ray, is something the matter?'

He set aside the newspaper. 'No, nothing, my love. Yes, I'll walk with you but after breakfast.' He took her hand in his. 'You look lovely.'

Her kiss was warm, her body vulnerable against his yet he realised in those moments that something had changed. Not with Laura, not with the house, but with him. Something deep within had altered. Before, when he had no memory, he had felt nothing but contentment. Day one began on the morning he woke, with no recall, only what he had around him. Life was Hilton Heights, Hagerstown, somewhere in Maryland and with it came Laura to fulfil his emotional needs. He had everything and he was fortunate beyond his wildest dreams, having narrowly escaped death and been rescued by these loving people. Yet, something now nagged at him. The more flashes of the past he experienced, the more he felt torn away from the present. Something like a deep yearning, an indomitable ache within kept him from being entirely at peace. It screamed 'Remember!' and when he tried, his mind blanked. Only when he was not expecting it, did the flashes of memory return. If only he could hold on to them, make some sense of them. Instead they laid buried somewhere unattainable.

'Ray, are you all right?'

Her voice, sweet, concerned, drew him back.

'Yes, I'm fine. Will you join me for breakfast?'

'Of course. You know, when you go off in your head the way you do, I wonder where you are. I get worried.'

He squeezed her hand. 'I was reading about the war. There's an account of the early days in the newspaper.'

'Is *that* all?'

'All? When I read about it I feel something, Laura. I wonder if I might discover myself and then it all goes away again. And was I fighting? If so, I must have been fighting close to here, you said so yourself.'

She did not reply and linked her arm through his so that he could lead her in to breakfast.

As soon as he could, he would get back to the newspaper.

Chapter Twelve

Head north, that was always Lee's intention. Southern armies on Union soil would go a long way towards undermining morale.

June 31st was steaming. Daniel, riding alongside the General that morning, removed his hat and wiped a hand across his wet brow. He could barely breathe, the heat was so oppressive.

He had been back with General Lee for several days following the surprise attack by Union General John Buford on Jeb Stuart at Brandy Station. There, the Yanks had been matched man for man by Stuart's Cavalry and, reinforced by the Infantry, Stuart managed to force the attackers back across the Rappahannock.

Daniel paused to look at the high spirited Rebel army, pride thumping in his chest. Magnificent. They looked magnificent. Ready for what lay ahead, undaunted, enthusiastic. They would need to be, he thought. Word had come via one of Longstreet's scouts only two days before that the Army of the Potomac, now under the command of the newly appointed General Meade, was following Lee's army with all speed, and was presently concentrated south of Maryland and moving north.

Gettysburg. Lee had ordered his commanders, Ewell and Hill, to unite near Gettysburg. Daniel urged his mount forward. Caesar was tired, his stride sluggish. As soon as possible he would find water for the poor animal.

He glanced at General Lee. The old man had aged lately. Rumour had it he was sick, but Lee was not a man to give in to such a notion. His heart was apparently troubling him, yet he pushed on, albeit wearily and against the orders of his physician. Behind him rode William, his aide, his face lined with love and concern for his master.

Daniel turned his attention to what lay ahead. It was not difficult to estimate the import of this advance towards Gettysburg. It might well be the icing on the cake, was how one officer had described it and Daniel felt the familiar frisson of excitement that accompanied him before every battle, though on this occasion it was tempered by loftier thoughts of Jo-Ellen. Her beauty was always with him, no matter where he was. Her laughter and sensual voice kept him company during those long hours of riding. Strength flowed through him whenever he thought about her.

His arrival in Savannah recently had precipitated gossip on the one hand and sublime happiness on the other. The door had opened and there she was, looking as beautiful as in his dreams, and so surprised, that she had fallen willingly into his arms with a hug that turned quickly into passion. He sighed. Such memories. A hot day, Jo-Ellen in a light gown, fanning herself, her eyes dancing happily, her fair hair plummeting below her shoulders and that pert nose above a mouth both generous and kissable.

'How wonderful that you've come to see me again, Daniel,' she'd said, her voice sincere. When he told her why he had come, she listened intently, her eyes wide with expectation, her lips open slightly as though about to react in some way, yet she had said nothing to interrupt the words that came tumbling from him a little too quickly lest he might leave out something important.

'You love me – you really do?' she asked finally, and he had brought up his hands gently to her face, had claimed her mouth to his and embraced her soft body so completely that he felt her shake with emotion.

'More than words, my darling, more than life,' and their lips moulded together into a promise he knew they would keep for a lifetime. 'Marry me, Jo. I know I can make you happy.'

She had been silent for a few moments, then, 'Yes, dearest, I'll marry you.'

That was how he had re-played that scene over and over as he galloped back to rejoin his division. He cast his eyes upwards to give silent thanks. There is a God after all. Had he ever doubted it? Even in the bloodiest battle, amidst all the horror and stench of death, he had felt that presence, and now he had his prayers answered.

'Major – ride on ahead and see what's afoot!'

Lee's voice sent Daniel's stirrups into Caesar's flesh and he shot forward to investigate the ruckus ahead. Nothing could blight his day. Happiness, that rare commodity that in the past had spared itself so fleetingly, now stayed close to him as a true and earnest friend.

•••

'Do you approve, Mama? Oh, I do hope so. Tell me truthfully how you feel.'

Jo-Ellen braced herself as Constance raised what looked like troubled eyes from the book she was reading. 'I expect you find it all too soon, and so it is,' she went on, 'but what with this awful war and all, how can anyone afford to wait when we don't know what's going to happen?' She fanned herself rapidly. It was much too hot. This June had been hotter than most.

Constance smiled. 'Of course I approve. I think he's a fine young man and I'm happy for you both. He's just what you need, Jo-Ellen, someone with a similar background to your own.'

'You mean a nice southern boy, Mama? That's not why I'm marrying him, besides which Daniel hails from Maryland, I believe.'

'Whatever. He's so much better for you. I never did approve of Robert, as well you know.'

Jo-Ellen did not reply. Reference to Rob these days tugged at her conscience. She supposed it to be guilt. Ten months was not, after all, a very discreet space of time.

'When is Daniel coming to see you again?' Constance asked.

A question that Jo-Ellen wished she had the answer to. She knew only that he was moving north towards Pennsylvania, or at least that was the general rumour. The papers were full of it and people spoke of little else these days. Lee's aim was to conquer the north and thereby secure recognition from Britain, and the population waited with bated breath to see if he were successful.

She prayed often for Rachel and George up there amidst the fighting, had longed to write and empathise with them, yet how could she not let them know of her plans to marry? Would they understand after all that had happened? She had received a letter from them saying that they did not think Rob was dead, otherwise the authorities would have found the body. Until that happened, Rachel stressed, she would not believe her son was dead. Jo-Ellen sighed heavily. Poor Rachel. She had not accepted the truth. Jo-Ellen believed it now. Having heard what a bloody battle it had been at Sharpsburg, she wondered how anybody could have come out of it alive.

Soon – she would write and tell them soon. First she would wait to hear from Daniel that he was on his way home and then she would set the wedding date. Only then would she break the news to the de la Reys.

'I've no idea, Mama.' Rising to her feet, she left Constance under the shade of the tree and went into the house. If only Ben were there. She missed her brother dearly, so often she wanted to unload her fears and feelings, but instead had to keep them bottled up. She did not want to put pressure on her dear Mama, and Susanne had quite enough to worry about.

Louise was waiting for her. 'There's a package here, miss.'

Jo-Ellen did not recognise the handwriting. She took it to her room and tore it open. It was the diary and two newspapers. Attached was a letter from Governor Floyd. Flushed with excitement, she read it and then perused the newspapers. The entire diary had been printed, together with a small photograph of Rob. The governor had gone to much trouble. His letter promised remuneration at a later date. Slowly she read the words that Rob had so painstakingly written and a feeling of pride swelled within her. His account of First Bull Run brought tears to her eyes. She read on about the battle of Antietam and realised all over again how it must have been not only for Rob, but also for Daniel. Reaching for her notepaper, she penned a reply to the governor, thanking him for his trouble and the safe return of the diary. This time she remembered to ask. Would it be possible to know if her husband's body had ever been found? She sealed the envelope and called Louise.

Through the window she saw Constance set aside the book in favour of fanning herself. She would be pleased to hear about the diary and delighted to read the newspapers. As for being paid as well, Jo-Ellen could only guess at how much. Anything at all would be most welcome. She would let her Mama have it by way of a treat. It had been so long since she had been able to do that for her.

'Louis, post this for me but first bring us four scones and a jug of iced lemonade. I'll be outside with my Mama.'

• • •

The picture was small, slightly blurred, and familiar. Ray stared at it, studied it through a magnifying glass. The officer wearing the uniform of the Union Army looked remarkably like himself. Was this Robert de la Rey who wrote the account of three major battles, really him? Had he actually been in those battles or did he only write about them? Was that what he did – write about war? A war correspondent? No – he had been a major, probably only had an interest in writing. He must have been at one of the battles. Had he by some miracle survived a gun shot to the head, been removed from the battlefield by a person or persons unknown, and later left by the roadside to die? That would mean he commanded a section of the army at the battle near Antietam Creek. Somebody had since sent the newspapers his account of the war. Who had handed over his notes to the press? Someone close, perhaps a wife or a fiancee. Excitement throbbed through him as he read the second part of the battle. It was incomplete, finished off by the editor with a brief explanation about the possible fate of the author. He studied the picture again. If only he could remember.

A door closed somewhere and he guessed that Laura had come back from her trip to town. Laura. Dread suddenly filled him. She must not see the newspaper. Quickly he tucked it away as she entered and came to give him a hug.

'My, it's hot out there. Must be one of the hottest Junes on record.'

He kissed her cheek and held her to him, his head spinning from the new-found knowledge of his past.

'I saw the most gorgeous wedding gown in Hagerstown today,' she said. 'It had lace cuffs and was made from the most delicate of material. Next time you must go with me, Ray.'

He forced a smile. Right now he wanted to be alone.

'Sweetheart, I've a headache. Would you mind if I spend some time to myself?'

Her lashes lifted in surprise. 'You've been by yourself all day, surely. And no wonder you've a headache. I'll bet all you've done is read, read, read. Why don't we go for a canter, get some fresh air? That'll see off your headache.'

'Please, Laura, do as I say!'

His sharp tone startled her. 'Very well, dearest. I'll be in my room if you need me.'

He waited for the door to close and pulled out the newspaper again. More and more the person in the photo became him. Where was it taken and when? He turned the pages and found more pictures, this time an aerial photograph of the Confederate combat. Beside it was a picture of the Union troops. Did he know any of these men?

Had he been amongst them waiting to fire at the advancing enemy? He read the words beneath one of the pictures. 'Captain Benjamin Turner of the 20th Main.' Captain Benjamin, Why did that name sound so familiar? Probably read it somewhere. It was common enough. Yet he had seen it in a letter. Yes, but when? Was it possible that before he was wounded and dragged off to Hagerstown, he'd had a letter on his person with the words Captain Benjamin, or Ben? He stopped right there. Ben – Jefferson. Why did he know that name? Had he served with a soldier by that name? Whoever had stripped him of his clothing that day had also taken his letters and anything else that might help give him an identity. Someone out there possibly knew a darned sight more about him than he did himself. It would be a waste of time trying to trace such a person. What he had to do immediately was find out about this Robert de la Rey.

Scanning the small print, he found a name he thought he recognised. Governor Floyd. The diary had been printed courtesy of the governor.

Ray tucked the information away. Floyd. That's where he would start.

• • •

Gettysburg. Ben listened while his lieutenant outlined the latest strategy. God, he was sick of listening to it. This time it was shoes. Hell – a supply of shoes had arrived at Gettysburg and Hill had ordered the men to go in and get them. Lee's men were near Gettysburg, weren't they? Hill reasoned. The town was defended only by local militia, so go in and get the shoes. The army needed them!

On July 1st, Ben found himself riding towards the small prosperous market town, accompanied by a dozen cavalrymen. It was a pretty place, comprising some 25,000 people and served by several roads that converged from various points of the compass. As they neared the ridge about two miles northwest of their destination, the sound of gunfire brought the small band to a halt.

'Hold up!' Ben raised a hand, his eyes on the ridge. A bullet zinged into the ground beside him, causing his horse to rear. 'Take cover! Lieutenant, what is it?'

Lieutenant Makepeace threw himself flat, raised his field glasses and assessed the situation. 'Far as I can make out, sir, a brigade – maybe two – of Union Cavalry up on the ridge.'

'Any idea who?' Ben kept well down as bullets whined overhead.

'Sir, it's Buford!'

'Hell!'

The last person they needed to come across. Their surprise battle three weeks earlier at Brandy Station was still fresh in his mind. Ben shielded his eyes against the glare of the morning sun. This was not good news. Buford. Armed with Sharps single-shot breech loading carbines, Buford's men had been able to fire twice as fast as the Confederates. His men fought dismounted too, a tactic that had stood him in good stead so far. The Feds not only had Buford but the technological advantage as well. Ben looked along the track from where they had come. Somewhere behind, his commander, Henry Heth, led a division of seven thousand men. Should he, Ben, ride back and warn him or let fighting commence and take its course? His problem was answered immediately.

'Sir, Heth has arrived!'

'Give me the glasses!'

Ben peered into the distance. The Confederate army was advancing. They had heard the gunfire, were preparing for battle. A.P Hill led the line.

'Right, hold positions!' Ben shouted. 'And fire only when I give the order!'

• • •

Lee closed his eyes momentarily. The heat was unbearable. A low rumble in the distance made him open his eyes and turn his head sharply. What was that? Thunder? Or gunfire? How was he expected to know what lay ahead without his cavalry officer there to inform him? Confound Stuart. Where the hell had he got to, anyway?

Since the fracas at Brandy Station Stuart had disappeared. There would be questions asked, Lee promised himself. Jeb wasn't getting off so easily this time. For all he knew, the whole Federal Army were lying in wait up the road. He turned in his saddle. 'James! Move alongside!' Longstreet did as requested. 'Did you hear that?'

'Sounded like gunfire, sir.'

Lee frowned. 'Hope you're wrong, James, but I'm going on ahead to take a look. Bring up the rear and proceed with utmost caution.'

It took an hour and a half for Lee to ride, in penetrating sun, to where the action was. He pressed on at a slower pace and by 2 pm was looking down on a disturbing scene. There was no doubt that fighting had taken place already and two of Ewell's divisions were now engaging the right flank of the Union 1st Corps and two divisions of the 11th. Had Hill disobeyed orders? He looked back, hoping to see Longstreet not far behind. No use Hill going in again without back-up. Below, Ewell's attack was underway. Too late. There was no alternative. In an uncharacteristic change of mind, Lee rode in and gave Hill the order to engage.

At the sight of their division moving in, Ben urged his small team to do the same.

• • •

Longstreet galloped fast. Daniel followed. Something was happening. Hill and Ewell were meant to wait until Lee arrived with the entire force. Something had gone very wrong. They must join with Lee with all haste, though they would be lucky to get there before morning. They had the numbers but there was no telling what card Buford had up his sleeve, or Reynolds, or Howard.

Daniel spurred forward. There was no room for mistakes. Too much rested on this battle. For the first time that day he began to have misgivings. This attack was too finely balanced.

•••

Laura hardly dared think about it. For days she watched and waited, but her body did not lie and she had to admit that, subject to confirmation from her doctor, she was pregnant. At first she felt scared. So quickly had she taken on the mantel of womanhood. Was she ready for such a responsibility? Of course she was, she admonished herself, standing before the long mirror gazing at her still shapely figure. Wasn't she hopelessly in love? When would it begin to show? When should she tell her Papa? More importantly, when ought she to tell Ray?

She rode over to consult Lizabeth.

'Seems you'll have to get married sooner than planned, that's all. Your Pa won't mind once he's used to the idea. Anyhow, he's taken up at the moment, surely?'

Laura listened, hoping her innermost fears would ease. Why didn't she feel better? Marriage. It was what they both wanted yet she knew Rob did not want to rush things. Somehow the thought of rushing it seemed to cause damage. Only in my mind, she decided, checking what amounted to sheer panic.

Leaving Lizabeth's place, she proceeded towards Hilton Heights. As soon as she saw him she would tell Ray. Why, he would probably be delighted and would put her mind at ease.

As she approached the house, a servant came to meet her. In her hand was a letter. Laura tore it open. It was a note from Ray.

Dearest, forgive me for not waiting for your return. I have to go to Washington on urgent business. Will tell you all later.
All my love, Ray.

No! What business? Had something happened? She remembered their conversation the previous week. Ray had not been his usual self since that day. He had done the one thing he promised not to do – go away without her, or without telling her why.

Closing the door, she went up to her room and lay in semi-darkness, crying.

•••

A mist lay over the river as Vince turned his mount and galloped westward towards Hagerstown. He had risen early that morning reckoning that a punctual start was likely to bring him back into Maryland by mid-afternoon.

For the past few weeks he had travelled up and down the countryside, cleverly dodging the warfare and putting up anywhere he was able to until he could be with his Annabelle in Richmond, and all this combined with more business for his clients in Washington. His time had been well spent.

He thought about the men he had come into contact with in his business dealings. Some of them had made his flesh creep but there he'd been, smiling and shaking hands with the lot of them. What the hell was the alternative? He was in it up to his neck and lying and cheating was now a way of life. A man had to eat and drink and play and for that he needed money, lots of it. Not for him running around with a gun. One thing he knew he could never take to and that was to fight in a war. He was from the south but he told everybody he was from Canada and so far he had gotten away with it. If you were Canadian, you were neutral. Whoever won this war was going to deserve to, weren't they? Why get killed over it? His daddy had been the same, so it wasn't his fault. It was in his genes.

The wind fanned his skin in the afternoon sun. It was too hot. He would be glad to get his feet on good solid ground once more, lie in a cool bath with a cigar and a brandy.

'Come on, girl, faster!' he called, digging in his spurs.

They rounded a bend and Vince knew then he was on familiar territory as soon as he saw the start of Wilson's Mill and the farmland beyond. Wouldn't be long now before he arrived at Grange Manorhouse.

Not that he looked forward to what lay ahead on this occasion. In fact, his last conversation with Marilyn had kept him from returning more often than not. His mind had been in a turmoil since listening to her idea. Only being with Annabelle had calmed him down. There he had relaxed, got his thoughts in perspective about what was expected of him when next he was on the same soil as Sebastian Hilton. To this day he and Sebastian hadn't actually met, though he, Vince, had seen Sebastian from a distance on two occasions. Always careful to meet Marilyn at night, entering the house through the back way, out of sight of the servants, he was now expected to place himself in close proximity to the man in order to bring about this 'accident'.

How could he arrange such a meeting? Didn't Marilyn know how goddamned difficult it all was?

It was questions like these that had brought him forth the answer, finally. A brilliant idea occurred to him and he had left Annabelle's feeling lifted both in mind and spirit, not to mention body. Arriving early at the house might not be so clever, though. Perhaps he should go into town and wait out the darkness. But Marilyn had insisted it would be all right. Sebastian and she were going to be at Hilton Heights so there would be no fear of running into them. Therefore, he could sneak in and wait for her in her room. He only hoped that he had not left it too late.

Poor Marilyn. She was married to that ageing man whom she detested. Still, everything had a price. She had known that when she took the old fellow on. Now, she was relying on Vince to get her out of her predicament. He grinned to himself, gave the mare full rein and turned along the ridgeway leading towards Grange Manorhouse.

'Don't worry, darlin,' I aim to sort it all out for you. You need have no worry about that.' His voice was lost on the wind as he tore along the road he knew so well.

• • •

Governor Floyd read the message on his desk twice. A young man had come to see him. It was urgent. No name, no contact address. He rang for his secretary.

'Jessop, who was he? Didn't you ask?'

'Yes, of course, sir. He seemed not to want to tell me.'

Irritated, Floyd flung the message into the waste paper basket. 'I can't have my time wasted with mysteries. If he comes here again, insist or ask him to leave – for good!'

'Yes, sir.'

'Bring me some tea. After that, I'm off to the White House.'

The door closed. Floyd drew out a kerchief and dabbed at his brow. It was hot and the breeze had brought with it that day a stench off the sewers. He would give anything to put his feet up and rest. The last thing he wanted was to go and see the President. Lincoln had sounded optimistic about Gettysburg but had been demeaning about General Meade. That's what the meeting is about, bet my life on it, he thought. He was the last person to deny the President his optimism but a man needed a rest and the time had come for him to take one, if Lincoln would just leave him alone for a day or two.

Opening the door, he was brought up short. Standing outside was a man.

'Begging your pardon, sir, I did wait for your secretary but he's not around at present.'

The face was vaguely familiar. 'Who are you, young man?'

The stranger shrugged. 'That's why I'm here. I was hoping you'd know that, sir.'

Floyd frowned. Was this some kind of a joke? He stepped aside. 'Come in. I've very little time available, so we must be quick.'

Rob gazed around. The office, redolent in leather, was splendid, its walls lined with multiple books and files.

'I'll come straight to the point, sir. I wrote an article – at least I think it was me – and you published it. Robert de la Rey?'

Floyd's jaw dropped. 'You – but he died in battle – at Antietam.'

'I was lucky. Strangers found me and took me in. It was a close thing, apparently. Thing is, I lost my memory so I can't be sure about all this. I'm here because of the article and the picture you published. It's of me, I'm sure.'

Floyd waved towards a chair. 'Sit down, Mr de la Rey.' It certainly looked like George's son. At bit older, much thinner too, but the likeness, now he came to think of it, was incredible. Still, he ought to make sure before committing himself. 'You can't remember anything? Your parents, your wife…'

'My wife!'

Hubert leaned forward and pressed a buzzer in front of him. 'Jessop, tell the President I've been unavoidably delayed, a matter of extreme importance. And bring some Bourbon.' He turned his attention fully on Rob. 'Now, if you are who you say you are, you'll want contact with your nearest and dearest. Your father, George, hasn't been well so I think it better we don't bother him, but your mother, she can be sent for. As soon as we know for sure who you are I can fill in most of the other details for you.'

Rob felt the blood pound in his head. He was married? 'Sir, the name Jefferson comes to me. At first I thought it was the Confederate President, I've read so much about him but I see myself riding alongside a young man. It comes and goes often.'

'Your wife's name is – or was – Jefferson. Her brother, Benjamin, is in the Confederate Cavalry. Could it be him?'

Rob sat back. That was it. He felt comfortable with that. Ben Jefferson. He had a friend, a wife, and parents. If only he could recall faces.

Accepting the Bourbon Floyd poured him, he tossed it back, beginning to feel part of the human race once more. He belonged at last.

'I want to thank you for your time, sir.' He offered his hand and rose to leave.

'No, wait a while. I'm not letting you go so easily, Robert. There are matters to discuss.'

'Sir?' Sitting on the edge of the chair, Rob waited.

'I happen to know your father. It was I who pushed for your commission. Wrote to General McClellan myself and he was delighted to meet up with you again. You made quite an impression, young man.'

Rob frowned. 'I did? How? Did I fight?'

'Most definitely. How else did you get hit? But you have a political mind, you're bright, got ambition. You don't remember wanting to pursue a career in politics?'

Rob thought deeply. It would explain a lot. His intense interest in the subject while he was with the Hiltons and also the published diary. 'Not at present, but I will. Sir, where is the manuscript or diary now?'

'With your wife. I sent it back to her.'

'You met her?'

'Sure did. Went down there to see her myself.'

'Where is down there?'

'Savannah.'

Confederate country.

'She's...'

'A southern lady, as beautiful as they come. So is her mother. A delightful lady.'

Rob got to his feet. 'Sir, I request all details. I must know where to find my family, all of them.'

Hubert held up a hand of restraint. 'Sure you do, Robert, but I can't give out any details until I'm sure, you know that. More than my job's worth. I'll get your mother here soon as possible and we'll take it from there.'

They shook hands.

'Meanwhile, we'll keep this meeting between the two of us. I'd like your word on that, Major.'

Rob grinned. 'You've got it, Governor. Thank you for seeing me.'

'Where are you staying?'

'At the National.'

'Fine, I'll be in touch soon as I can.'

When he was alone, Floyd took up a pen and wrote out a quick letter to Rachel de la Rey. With any luck, the lady would be there within a few weeks. If necessary, he would go and bring her there himself. Not that he was free to do so at present. His thoughts once more on the President, he pulled open the door, gave Jessop the letter to post with all haste and took a carriage up to the White House.

Chapter Thirteen

The final attack had failed. Lee had rolled the dice and lost. He had also failed to heed Longstreet's advice to rather provoke an attack than launch one straight into the Union centre, and as a result had lost thousands of men. At last he ordered retreat and as it poured with rain on that fateful day of 4th July, he managed to escape with some of his men across the Potomac towards Virginia.

Lightning tore across the darkened skies. The roads were like quagmires, the going slow. Behind them, in pursuit and just as slow, was the Union Army. They got no further than north of the Potomac, having been trapped by the fords made by the rain and making the river impassable.

Daniel kept close to Lee's side, feeling dead beat not only from fighting for hours without rest, but from the oppressive heat and now the driving rain. They had advanced on the enemy relentlessly for the past three days and been pushed back finally by a force that had proved greater than themselves.

Daniel also felt wretched. He had seen great commanders, good friends some of them, killed or wounded at Gettysburg, and he had seen the disintegration of southern hopes and dreams in that last battle on the Emmitsburg Road.

His worse nightmare had happened. The tide had turned. The Army of Northern Virginia was in retreat.

•••

Ben pushed on through mud that almost reached his knees after a torrential rain burst. His small group had dispersed, most of them killed, their attack on Little Round Top having been well and truly repulsed. Word had reached him that Garnett was dead, and Armistead and Kemper were both mortally wounded. Others lay dead and dying around him as he pressed on in the wake of General Lee's small force ahead. Gettysburg had become a giant graveyard and he had to get away from it. Virginia – he had to get back to Virginia.

Rain stung his face as he arrived north of the Potomac to find pontoon bridges being thrown up by desperate Confederates. Morale was never lower. Most of the men were finished both physically and spiritually. He found a place to rest for a few hours. Only when he felt ready would he go in and offer his services.

Through the driving rain figures moved about like ants on a mission. Turning away from the scene, Ben turned his coat collar high and pulled his hat low over his face, then he slept a sleep so deep, so sound, that it was as close to death as he had ever yet come.

• • •

'My God, we took Gettysburg!'

'And Vicksburg! That was Grant, wasn't it. Papa, what does it all mean?'

Sebastian Hilton closed the newspaper with finality. 'It means, daughter, that we're winning the war. Can't be long now and them boys will be marching along the Avenue celebrating.'

Laura whooped with delight, her first feeling of happiness amid several days of gloom. Since Ray had gone she had felt lost and alone. With a baby coming – she estimated it would be close on December when it arrived – there had been days when she shut herself away barely able to cope with her situation.

There had been no word from Ray and everyone was asking questions. Her Papa never let up, neither did Lizabeth. To them she merely shrugged her shoulders and told them he had gone to Washington to find out about himself, that he would be back soon as he could and that such matters surely took time. Marilyn, on the other hand, seemed not to have noticed Ray's absence. She neither asked nor spoke of him, so taken up was she of late, which puzzled Laura, since Marilyn had been so concerned about their activities before his departure.

She wondered where Ray was, what he was doing. Was he staying in Washington, or had he learned something and gone searching for his roots? A pang of jealousy struck her and remained with her on a daily basis. If he had a family or someone special in his life, would he not have let her know by now? And she would always content herself with the fact that his silence meant he had found out nothing and that he was probably on his way back to her right this minute. And when he did not arrive, back she would go to her room to wait out a few more days.

'Now then, Laura, I want to talk to you.'

She looked at her Papa's expression, aware of what was coming.

'That young man of yours has not contacted us and I want to know what's going on.'

'Papa, he's busy. He can't very well write with the war going on and all.'

'Rubbish! Other people get letters, why not you? And don't use his condition as an excuse. He's as well as can be and might even have his memory back by now. Is that why he's not returned to you?'

She turned her eyes away, not wishing to hear the truth. How she wished she could talk to her Papa but how would he take it?

'Papa, I've something to tell you and I don't want you to be angry with me.'

'Well, what is it?'

She paused. It had to be done sooner or later. 'Papa, I'm pregnant.'

His eyes seemed to glaze over, his face reddened, his mouth opened and shut. Then, 'What? Pregnant? Is that why he went? He's got you in trouble and has left you?'

'Papa, calm down, it's not like that at all. Ray doesn't know. I was about to tell him, but he'd already left for Washington. I want you to be happy for us.'

Sebastian went to the drinks cabinet and poured a large brandy. 'Happy? Yes, I would be, Laura, if I knew you and he were about to marry, but how do we know he hasn't gone for good? I told you it might happen, remember? And now look at you. Pregnant and possibly without a man to take care of things.' He threw back the drink and poured another. 'Oh, I'm angry right enough. What father wouldn't be?'

Laura waited for him to get it all out of his system.

'Well, if he doesn't appear in the next couple of weeks, then you must get rid of the baby. I won't tell a soul, except Marilyn, of course.'

'No, Papa, I don't want anyone to know.' She didn't mention that Lizabeth already knew. Sebastian would never tolerate that. 'And I won't be getting rid of Ray's baby. What can you be thinking of?'

'You'll do as I say. What'll folk round here think if you produce a child and you're not married? Anyway, we'll leave it for now and see if he returns to you. That's all I've got to say on the matter.'

He finished his second drink and turned his attention to what was going on outside the window. The girl was positively wanton. Lillian would have been devastated had she been alive.

Laura went to her room accompanied by a feeling of relief. At last she had found the courage to tell her Papa. And she looked forward to the baby. It was Ray's, conceived with much love. There was no way she was going to destroy such a beautiful thing.

● ● ●

Marilyn was quietly beside herself with misery. Vince had not turned up when she most needed him and without word of his whereabouts, she began to doubt he would come to her at all. Would he give up everything and leave her to cope with Sebastian alone?

As she mulled over these thoughts for the umpteenth time that day, something told her to return to Grange Manorhouse. She had been there a couple of times but there was no sign of him and now she felt she had been at Hilton Heights for too long and besides if she did not go to her home often, how would she ever know if Vince had arrived? She called for the carriage and asked the driver to take her there.

As she entered, she felt his presence. Running up the stairs she called out and the door to her room flew open and there he was. She threw herself into his arms and in silence they kissed and touched and dragged at each other until they were on the king size bed and tearing at each other's clothing. Their bodies entwined and he took her over and over again, relishing the pleasure she always gave him.

He looked at her lying in his arms as she rested afterwards. This was when he loved Marilyn most, when she was his docile lover. No questions, no constant pressure.

'Darling,' she said, opening her eyes,' you were gone so long this time. I thought…'

'Then you thought wrong, sweetheart. I said I'd be here, didn't I? Couldn't promise when, that's all.' Dare he ask about the wedding? She read his mind.

'It was awful – the wedding, I mean. Sebastian got drunk, but not drunk enough. He was violent, Vince. Oh – I hate him!'

'Violent!' He sat up to face her. 'Honey, the man must be dealt with right away. I won't have my Marilyn treated that way.'

She snuggled into him. 'Are you going to do what I asked, Vince?'

'Of course. I said I would, didn't I?'

Relief swept through her. Her ordeal was coming to an end. Vince was back and he was going to make everything right.

'Let's do it all again, nice and slow this time, you know how I like it, darling,' she whispered, nibbling his ear.

He pulled her down to him and did what she asked. He was a champion in bed, she was always telling him so, and so did Annabelle who seemed never to get enough of him.

Things were beginning to come right for him at long last. His fortunes were about to take a turn for the better.

● ● ●

It was a strange request and at once Sebastian was suspicious. He had heard of the tricks schemers played and this message from a person who had withheld his name gave him much pause for thought. The words in the second line raised his curiosity, however. Something he would benefit from knowing – what could that be?

He need not pay any attention. All he had to do was throw away the note. On the other hand, he could attend the meeting on the other side of Hagerstown and he could go fully armed and accompanied by his driver. The note had stressed absolute secrecy and so he decided against telling Marilyn.

The door opened and he tucked it in his pocket as Marilyn came in from the garden. Her expression was tight, no different from usual. He knew she was angry with him and he loathed himself for his behaviour on their wedding night, but no amount of apologies had helped and she persisted in her cold attitude towards him. Had he been wrong to suspect her of having a lover? Jealousy was a terrible emotion and sometimes he couldn't help himself and he knew that if he was going to have her respect and love he would have to pull himself together and trust her. If only she wasn't so goddamned beautiful.

'Marilyn, you know Jason's coming over on the weekend? I hope you'll be here to welcome him.'

She raised her lashes briefly in his direction and continued to arrange the freshly picked flowers in the vase. 'I'll be here, I expect,' she replied, barely looking at him.

'Marilyn, honey, you're still angry with me. I've told you I'm sorry. What else can I do?'

She turned to face him. 'Do? You've done quite enough already. I've still got bruises, Sebastian.'

He fell silent. She made him feel so guilty. If only he could turn back the clock. Perhaps he could sweeten her with a visit to Hagerstown for the diamond bracelet he'd seen there. It had almost doubled in price in the past weeks but if it helped put a stop to the misery in his marriage then it would be worth it. After that, as soon as possible he would contact his solicitor and get the Will sorted out.

'You look lovely today, Marilyn.'

Her eyes met his. She did not reply and he couldn't read her thoughts in those few icy moments. She'd come round. He knew her. He would change his attitude, make her feel secure again and she would come round. It just needed some time. She had married him, hadn't she? If she was a mite disappointed so far, then it could only be his fault, not hers.

He watched as she gathered up the remnants of flowers and took them with her out of the room. Taking the note from his pocket, he decided there and then he would go. Perhaps this stranger had information of a financial nature. Might even be to his advantage.

Lighting a cigar, he called to his driver and told him to make ready for a journey to Hagerstown.

• • •

It was hot in the carriage. Sebastian drew a hand across his brow to wipe away the sweat. In his pocket was a small gun and his hand rested on it as though in readiness for what might lie ahead. It had been a good idea to take along his driver. He could trust him and knew that no harm would befall them with him there.

Hagerstown was busy as they left the carriage and made their way to the address on the letter.

'You wait outside,' Sebastian whispered. 'If you hear anything amiss, come in and get me. Bring help if need be.'

Cautiously, he moved up the rickety stairs. Half way up the second flight a door opened.

'Ah, Mr Hilton. Glad you could make it, sir.'

A young man stood there. He held out his hand. 'I'll not give my name, if you don't mind. Don't suppose you'd have heard of me, anyway. Now, if you'll just step this way, I'll enlighten you as to why you are here.'

Sebastian followed him into a sparsely furnished room. Before the door closed, he checked that his driver was not far away.

'I've only got cognac to offer you.'

'No, I don't intend on staying long. My driver's outside and we have only about ten minutes. So, let's get this over with.'

Vince grinned. 'Sensible. Never can be too sure of anything these days, can we? I'll be as brief as possible, Mr Hilton.' He poured himself a small drink and turned to face Sebastian. 'It's about Marilyn, your wife.'

Sebastian's brows rose.

'She and I have been having an affair for several months.'

The hairs on Sebastian's neck seemed to stand on end. 'What! How dare you, you...!'

'I dare because it's true. And I wouldn't do that if I were you.' Vince produced a gun before Sebastian could find his.

'What do you want?' His voice was little more than a whisper as he realised how he had been trapped.

'Look, I'm not here to scare you. If I tell you that Marilyn begged me to kill you so she could inherit everything and rid herself of her marriage, would you consider listening?'

Sebastian sat down heavily on the nearest chair, his thoughts on the Will he had just drawn up. What this man was saying had a ring of truth about it. 'Go on, I'm listening.'

Slowly, Vince went over every detail of his relationship with

Marilyn. When he finished, Sebastian, sweating profusely, said, 'And now you're going to kill me and hope to gain half of my property?'

Vince stood up and towered over him. 'No, sir. If I'd wanted you dead, you'd not have had the benefit of meeting me. I'd have killed you by now and high-tailed it to the gambling tables in Richmond. No, I decided I didn't want to spend my days running from the authorities as a murderer. Instead, I've a proposition for you.'

Sebastian licked his dry lips. He was mystified. 'A proposition?' He felt weak, hadn't enough strength to put up a fight. If what this man said was true, then Marilyn lied all along, had betrayed him to the last.

'Well, I reckon that you needed a break, and you ought to know what a double dealing witch Marilyn is.'

'Yes, but why? Why do this for me? Money?'

'Either way I'd have gotten money, I guess. And yes, I aim to make you pay, Mr Hilton, sir, but marrying Marilyn is not part of the plan. She would have had me kill you, marry her, and then lord it over me all my life, threatening to tell on me if I ever stepped out of line. Whereas this way she'll not inherit at all, but I will. And you'll live.'

A silence hung between them. Sebastian's mind raced. 'And if I refuse?'

Vince cocked the gun. 'I'll find you and do as Marilyn asked. And she'll believe me, not you. She's in love with me, you see.'

His expression told Sebastian not to doubt his words.

'What do you want in repayment?'

'You made a Will?'

'Yes, of course.'

'You'll change it. Hilton Heights will be left to me after you've passed on, and whatever money you were leaving Marilyn will come to me immediately.'

'No – I won't do it!'

Vince cocked the gun again. 'I think you will, Mr Hilton. You'll get it authorised and let me have a copy. I'll not be far away when it's all finalised. If I'm satisfied, you'll live.'

'But I have a daughter! She's to inherit!'

'Quite so. I said I wanted Marilyn's share of the money, not your daughter's'

Sebastian nodded. It was a clever plan. 'All right,' he said finally.

'I'll do as you ask.'

'Right. You won't say a word about this to anyone. I'll not be far behind you, remember that.'

'And Marilyn? Won't she wonder how I came to find out about you and her? Because I aim to let her know. She has to pay.'

'Tell her only when I've got my copy of the Will. Not until then.'

Sebastian passed a hand over his forehead. It would be very difficult to behave naturally in future when all he wanted to do was confront Marilyn and beat the living daylights out of her before he threw her out.

'One more thing,' Vince went on. 'Get the Will sorted now, this minute. You see, I promised Marilyn you'd be dead by now. When you turn up she'll ask me why and I'll have to keep her sweet as long as I can. Understand?' At a nod from Sebastian, he added, 'What you do with her afterwards is no affair of mine. Just see I get the inheritance.'

In a daze, Sebastian walked through the door that Vince held open for him. On the drive back his mind almost burst with all the murderous thoughts that passed through it. Two things stood out above all others. First, Laura must have her baby after all. It might be a boy and the only opportunity left for him to have a male grow up in his household. Second, and most important of all, Marilyn would not get a penny more.

• • •

Jo-Ellen tucked away the letter she had received from Daniel. It was post- marked Richmond, though she knew he wasn't there now, but much farther north. In the letter, he wrote of his longing for her, and also of his desire to finalise the purchase of Highlands. She knew already that he had written to Susanne outlining his plans in that direction and it was with uplifted spirits that she sat outside in the shade reading again the words he had penned. Everything was working out so well she could hardly contain herself. The sale of the house was going through, and the strangest part of all was that she was to live there, instead of Susanne. In fact, there had been no radical change. Highlands was to remain forever in the Jefferson family. What she had to do now was write to Rachel and inform her and

George of her intention to marry in the near future.

She felt a little tired after playing with Alexander that morning. At almost two years he was full of life and she was hard put to keep up with him. He was sleeping presently and Jo-Ellen thought she would do the same for an hour or so in readiness for her work-load later. Things were running smoothly on the Plantation, thanks to the combined efforts of all concerned and she tried to remember when she last felt so contented in all areas of her life as she did today. All but the war. That was always there, threatening to bring everything to an end.

'No, I shouldn't think like that.' Live for today and let tomorrow take care of itself, her Mama often told her. How else could she truly enjoy her life?

Hitching her skirts, she went into the house and up the stairs, careful not to disturb Alexander. Closing her door, she lay down and looked at the photos on the bedside table. One was of Rob, the other of Daniel. Rob would be pleased with her choice. Had they got to know each other, had he met Daniel under circumstances other than the war, she felt sure he would have approved. Perhaps they might even have become good friends. In many respects they were alike. Both were handsome and gentlemanly. Both rode well and had a love of horses. Daniel was a year older than Rob, but both were youthful and cheerful company; both had made her happy and both had loved her. She had been truly blessed, even though one wore blue and the other wore grey.

She lay back and closed her eyes, seeing behind the lids the day she would say 'I do' to Daniel, and gaze into his blue eyes as he promised to love and honour her all the days of her life.

It seemed like only minutes that she came to with a start. Alexander was calling for her and Jo-Ellen realised she had slept for almost two hours. The sun was still bright, though she knew it was late afternoon by now and quickly she rose and went in to see to her son.

Freshening herself, she prepared for work. Susanne wanted the horses seen to today and she also had some instructions to pass on to Earl and Jacob. She would have to hurry. Dinner was to be at seven thirty and she wanted to finish everything before settling down for the evening.

Calling Louise to look after Alexander, she hurried downstairs. On the hall table was a letter. It was addressed to her. Turning it over, she saw it was from Pennsylvania. She tore it open and looked at the signature. It was from Rachel.

My Dearest Jo-Ellen, I have the most wonderful news for you. My hand is shaking so much as I write because God has answered my prayers at last. I've seen and spoken to Rob. He's alive...

The words swam before her eyes and she gripped the edge of the table to steady herself.

'Jo-Ellen, whatever is the matter? You look as though you've seen a ghost.'

Her Mama's voice startled her. 'Mama, read this. It can't be!'

Constance took the letter and read it. 'Oh, my!'

Tears sprang into Jo-Ellen's eyes. She hardly knew what to feel. Joy that her husband was still alive after all, or sorrow that she and Daniel could never be together.

'What's going to happen? Oh, my!' Constance said again. 'Perhaps there's been a mistake. Daniel saw him on the battlefield that last day, didn't he?'

'No, it's no mistake. There was never a body. I should have listened to Rachel. She always believed he was still alive.'

She read the letter again. It told how Governor Floyd had asked Rachel to Washington and there waiting for her was Rob. They had spent an emotional day together and she finally returned home to tell George and to write to Jo-Ellen. It ended with words of enthusiasm that the couple could now be together and raise their son, hopefully up there in the north.

Stunned. She felt stunned. Constance put out a hand to her and she took hold of it. 'Mama, what am I to do?'

For once Constance was speechless. She hated the idea that Rob was going to come back and spoil her daughter's new found happiness. Yet, they were still legally married and she knew nothing could alter that.

'Poor, poor Daniel,' she muttered.

Jo-Ellen knew her Mama was right. As things stood, Daniel had no rights at all.

She retraced her steps up the stairs, tears beginning at the back of her eyelids. At the top, in a voice barely audible, she said, 'Please ask Earl to see to the horses. I've an urgent letter to write.'

∙ ∙ ∙

Rob could hardly believe his good fortune. His mother had been delightful and yes, he remembered her. The day had been a remarkable one. He had received a call from Governor Floyd to go to his house and when he arrived, there was Rachel de la Rey. The Governor had left them alone to talk and he had learned all about Jo-Ellen and Ben, and about this father, George, and how he, Rob, had gained a commission into the Federal Army. And he had a son, now almost two years old. Finally, he had promised he would bring his family away from Savannah to live in Philadelphia.

Since that meeting only one thing settled in his mind – Jo-Ellen. Packing the few things he had with him, Rob made ready for the journey south. Before leaving, he wrote a letter to Laura explaining what had taken place, but on reading it through, he tore it up. Nothing he said was going to alter the fact that he no longer wanted her, that he intended to walk away from her for good.

They would never find him, would they? Yes, an inner voice told him. When you are a senator and running for high office they would soon find you.

Rob pulled the door firmly shut behind him and handed in the keys. By then, though, Laura will surely have lost interest. Might even have met another soldier she could love and marry. Perhaps he would in time find the right words to say to her and make her understand. He was a married man. His memory was returning and his life had to be separate from hers. Surely she would see the sense of it all? Better to leave her now than later, when they might have married. The thought of what he had almost let himself in for sent a shiver down his spine

In the carriage he issued orders to the driver and settled back as the Washington streets slipped past. Soon he would be free, soon he would be happy. He would be with Jo-Ellen.

Chapter Fourteen

Luck, if it could be called that, was once again with them. The Confederate Army, having arrived north of the Potomac to find their pontoon bridges destroyed by northern cavalry, were trapped for several days while they waited for Lee's engineer corps to tear down buildings in order to construct a new set of pontoons. Meanwhile, Lincoln ordered General Meade to attack Lee and destroy his army.

The 'luck' was that the Union general and his men were so exhausted by this time, they could not do the President's bidding and while they hesitated, Lee was able to slip across the patched up bridge during the night and escape.

Daniel surveyed the surrounding countryside, his spirits deflated by the sudden down-turn of events in the Confederate fortunes. To hell with Jeb Stuart. It had been quickly rumoured that it was all his fault. Lee defeated; Sherman, Grant, and Meade the heroes of the hours. Daniel cursed silently. He'd give plenty to turn back the clock. Several of the men were already returning to Richmond and he decided to do the same.

Lee was on his way, and so was Ben, whom Daniel had by chance come across soon after the battle of Gettysburg. It had been a brief meeting. Both had looked up, seen each other and acknowledge with a nod or a salute. Daniel had been taken aback by Ben's appearance, thought he had looked wretched.

His thoughts returned to the one thing that kept him sane these last few days. As soon as he reached his quarters in Richmond, he would write to Jo-Ellen and let her know that he would be there as soon as he could be released from duty. The sale of the house was going through and he had to be there to sign the papers authorising it. Whilst there, they would set the date for the wedding.

Rain fell in sweeping sheets as he picked his way through the mud. In the background lightning streaked the landscape. None of this mattered to him. His sights were set fully on the journey to Richmond and thereafter on his arrival in Savannah.

● ● ●

Marilyn finished arranging the flowers and stepped outside for some air. God, she was bored. Sebastian had gone into Hagerstown and left her with only their maid for company and it simply wasn't enough. Life since her marriage had become dull, dull, dull.

Vince was nowhere to be seen. Had he managed to arrange Sebastian's little accident? He had promised her before he took off again. Had he too gone into Hagerstown? Was Sebastian in fact dead? She would only know the answer to that question if and when her husband returned. She said her usual silent prayer. Would God please rid her of that awful man and let her get on with her life in complete freedom and wealth?

Gazing off into the distance, she told herself that she could go to her own house and spend time there but what was the difference? It was even more lonely at Grange Manorhouse without Vince there. At least there was a chance of seeing Laura at Hilton Heights. Which reminded her. The girl was positively different when she had by chance crossed her path, quite withdrawn and morose, in fact. Not the sweet little thing she recalled of late. Why, not long ago she was the happiest face around, when Ray was there, of course. Ray – where had he gone, and why? Had he left her? It was a blow to Marilyn's plans. She'd had it all worked out and now she had to think again. Laura was still set to inherit. The day had to come when Ray discovered himself again. Sebastian had said so all along. The main thing was that the Will had been decided, and she, Marilyn, was to inherit money, lots of it. It was a start, and if Sebastian suddenly died, she would get the house, too. She might well get past the legal aspects of Laura's right to inherit, and would see the solicitor in due course to find out her rights as the wife. Not all was lost – not yet.

A noise drew her attention and she watched with mounting fury as a carriage carrying Sebastian rounded the bend and drew up outside. He paused to say a few words to his driver then made his way into the house.

He was alive. Marilyn had already decided that ignoring him as she had was futile. Besides, when he finally died, people might look in her direction for someone to blame were it to become known that they were not talking. So she wore her most charming smile as he stepped through the doorway.

'Sebastian, so pleased you're back.'

'Huh?' He eyed her coldly, she thought. 'Get me a large whisky, will you, Marilyn?'

She did as he asked and beamed at him as she handed it over. 'It got so lonely here today. Looks like I missed you, darling.'

Hardly looking at her, he downed the contents of the glass and went into the sitting room. She blanched at his dismissive manner. Something was not right. He was either in a foul mood over something or he wasn't feeling well.

'Honey, are you feeling all right? Your blood pressure up?' she asked, following him closely.

'Yes, you could say that.'

She left him sitting in the bay window looking out on to the freshly cut lawns. He was different today. Goodness, what was wrong with everybody? First Laura, now Sebastian.

One thing was certain. He had not met up with Vince yet. So where was Vince? All this time on her hands and it was wasting. Topping up the whisky glass, she took it through to Sebastian. 'Here, you look as though you need it. Have a bad day at Hagerstown?'

He glanced at her. 'No, it was good, very enlightening. What did you do?'

'I told you, I was here alone. That darned servant girl isn't exactly stimulating company.'

'You should have a hobby. Most women do.'

'Oh? Such as?'

'Crocheting, sewing.'

She did not reply. Sebastian's manner was too brusque and she was not interested in talk about such mundane matters. She waited, hoping he had brought back his usual small gift for her. Not once since she'd known him had he returned from Hagerstown without something for her. An hour passed, mostly in silence. He was totally preoccupied, staring ahead of him through the window and she wondered where his thoughts were. Had he forgotten about the present? Should she mention something to jog his memory?

'Did you do any shopping while you were there?' she asked, moving closer to him.

'No, none. I hadn't the time and I didn't go there for that.'

She was about to ask what in hell's name he did go there for but stopped herself in time. She must remember to remain calm and sweet to him at all times. When he eventually rose and left the room without a word, she knew better than to follow him. 'Goddamn it!' Marilyn stared after him in frustration. Perhaps it was better to leave him for a while until he was in a better frame of mind.

Behind the heavy oak door, Sebastian set about redrafting his Will and writing a letter to his solicitor. He arranged a withdrawal of money from his bank of thirty thousand Federal dollars. Finally, to cover himself, he wrote down all that had taken place in Hagerstown between himself and the man he learned was called 'Vince.' This he addressed to the Federal authorities in case of his sudden death.

When he had finished he gave the letters to one of the servants to send immediately and then went into the drawing room to join Marilyn.

'Ah, there you are, darling. You're looking exceptionally lovely today.'

Relief swept over her and she smiled at him, feeling better for his company, even though it was only his. She began to chatter and giggle as usual, only it was not the same. It wasn't anything she could put her finger on but Sebastian simply wasn't behaving as before. Something had changed and she had no way of finding out what it was.

• • •

Laura pushed open her bedroom door and listened. All was quiet, but it didn't mean that woman wasn't down there. Marilyn had hung about Hilton Heights most of the time since the wedding and frankly it was getting on Laura's nerves. Why didn't she go back to her own house?

The truth was Laura didn't feel like company, least of all Marilyn's. There would be question after question. Where was Ray, why had he gone, when would he be back? She had no idea if Sebastian had told Marilyn about the baby, but if he had it would provoke more questions.

It was very quiet below. Perhaps Marilyn had gone out. Closing her door, she crept down the stairs and stood in the hall, listening, unable to quiet the distressing thoughts that passed through her mind. She knew now why Ray had gone. It was Lizabeth who found out – Lizabeth of all people! The girl had taken great delight in confronting her with the newspaper article and the photograph of Ray, only it wasn't Ray. It was apparently 'Robert.' At first she refused to accept it. The picture was small, she pointed out, it could be anyone – until Lizabeth had thrust a magnifying glass into her hand.

'There – I'm telling you, Laura, it's him.'

And it was. There was no mistaking those eyes.

'Well, that don't mean anything. So he's gone to see who he is. He'll be back – he knows I'm here waiting.'

'Then why didn't he wait to see you before taking off like that?'

Why indeed? Laura had made a hasty retreat to her room. The two weeks her Papa had allowed Ray were up tomorrow. What was she to do? He'd had plenty of time to write to her but he had not bothered and she felt the impending misery of deceit and betrayal about to settle.

What she had to do was obvious. She would go and find him. Find out first hand why he had left and when he would be back. But how? She was in no condition to travel, and how would she fare out there on her own, with a war raging around her?

The idea appealed to her senses yet she knew that what she must do was bide her time, have her baby and make the decision later. Her priority was the baby, nothing else, and if Ray, or Robert, had forsaken her then she would at least have his child to bring up, and she would not even bother to tell him in that case. He must return to her because he loved her and not for any other reason. Having thus decided on the only course open to her, Laura straightened her shoulders and pulled open the French windows to let in some air. Sunlight poured into the house and lifted her spirits. No more hiding away waiting, she decided. That could go on forever. There were plans to make and much to look forward to. The pain of Robert's (she was already used to his real name) leaving would take a long time to heal but she had no intention of prolonging it by nurturing it. Change – things would have to change and she would see to it that they did.

Stepping outside, she inhaled deeply and lifted her chin in defiance as she set off on a brisk walk, the first for many days.

• • •

As soon as Rob reached the outskirts of Savannah, he began to remember and the thing that stood out most in his mind was riding in that day long ago and sweeping Jo-Ellen into his arms. It was all coming back, little by little, and most of it was very pleasant.

Urging his horse forward, he cantered through the town, glancing to the right and left, recognising first the hotel, then the whorehouse, and finally the alehouse. Wasn't that the place where he and Ben drank one night, got so drunk that they were thrown out and Ben had brought the lot up in the town centre right by the fountain there?

As he rode up the track that bordered Highlands, he felt the familiar frisson of excited anticipation. Susanne – that was the name – she lived up there at that big house.

What sort of a welcome would he get? These people all thought he was dead, didn't they? Their lives had progressed whilst his life had been placed on hold. What changes could he expect to find?

Ahead he could see the Jefferson Plantation and the house gleaming in the late afternoon sunlight and the sight of it did him a power of good. Stopping, he took that magic moment to look down on the calmness of it all. The war hadn't progressed to that part of the country yet. Everything was so still, so tranquil.

He had read as much as he could about the reasons for the war. There were varying accounts, yet Rob knew instinctively which side he was on. Those Confederates had been wrong – and Abe Lincoln sure had the sense to see that. Things were beginning to look better for the Union since Gettysburg and Vicksburg, and he, Rob, wanted to catch up on every last detail and put it all down on paper. His own part in the war was sketchy. He remembered George Custer and General McClellan, had read that Custer had been spiralled to brigadier-general in June of that year and had been in the thick of the fighting at Gettysburg. He was able to remember moments of his own time as Major Robert de la Rey but it flickered in and out of his mind only intermittently. With luck, he would not be required to go and fight again. Was he not a hero already? For him the war must be over.

All he wanted was to see Jo-Ellen and hold his boy in his arms. Alexander. He would bring him up properly in the north where he would thrive and grow in stature and have some chance of a future once the Union won this war. Big business, that's what he would train his son for, but only if he wanted it. Not for Alexander the claustrophobic environment that he had suffered. His thoughts now on his own father, he turned along the track that led to Jefferson House.

Below him was the old barn half hidden in the trees and the river that flowed beyond it. It was the barn in his dreams, where he had spent part of his childhood and certainly much of his older years. He dug in his spurs. 'Come on, let's go.'

In the fading afternoon beauty he entered the grounds of Jefferson House.

• • •

Jo-Ellen opened the door before Rob could lift the knocker and for a moment neither was able to move as they took each other in.

He was leaner, she thought, certainly fitter looking. His face was more lined, more manly, his expression harder but then he had been through so much. The eyes hadn't changed, though, their green as vivid as ever.

She held out a hand to him and he caught at it. She was a sight to behold, he thought. Lovely, adorable, his. With one gesture he swept her into him.

She drew him inside, shut the door and took him through to the drawing room where a cool breeze lifted the curtains and where she had given instructions to be left alone.

'Do you remember all this?' She motioned to the room.

'Of course. I remember mostly everything.' He held her shoulders so that she was forced to look at him. 'Who could forget you, Jo? I'm back, for good now. We'll get on with our lives, Jo. I've been making plans, you'll see. It'll come right for you, I promise.' He drew her close. 'Oh, my dearest, how alone you must have felt without me all this time! I want you so much – making love with you is the one thing I remember above all others.'

She felt his hard body, his need. 'Oh, Rob,' was all she could say in those desperate moments. 'Come, let me get you some refreshment. You must be thirsty in this hot weather.'

A chuckle escaped him. 'Dear Jo, such a charming hostess, and here I am panting for you.'

She pulled the bell rope. 'Louise – bring some cool drinks and let my Mama know that Mr Rob is back.'

Louise was looking at Rob with her mouth open. 'Mr Rob, sir...' Her eyes slid to Jo-Ellen as if to say, What now?

'Quickly, Louise!' said Jo-Ellen.

'She thought she had seen a ghost,' Rob joked. Pulling Jo-Ellen round to him, he said, 'Let me look at the woman I married. I must say I've splendid, no, perfect, taste.'

'And you're still as modest as ever,' she said, giving herself up to full scrutiny. Louise appeared with the refreshments, her eyes wide with wonder and when the door had finally closed, Rob said, 'At last I have you to myself. Let's take this up to our room, Jo.' With his fingers he skimmed her cheek, brushing aside the tendrils of silky fair hair, then lifted the tray and headed for the stairs. Jo-Ellen followed. What was she to do? He was her husband and he wanted her. Although she was delighted he was not dead, something had changed. Time had seen to that. There was Daniel now. Her life, her thoughts, her very being had progressed beyond where Rob had left her when he disappeared.

At the top of the stairs, she hesitated, her head in a spin. Rob turned and smiled at her. 'Come, dearest, let's not wait a minute longer.'

She stepped into the room and the door slid shut behind her.

● ● ●

His quarters in Richmond were a welcome sight. Without wasting a moment longer than necessary, Daniel refreshed himself in a bath, had a drink and a meal and changed into travelling clothes. General Lee had given his permission to journey to Savannah 'with all haste' and Daniel could barely wait to get on the road.

Packing some belongings, he fastened the carpetbag, pulled on a jacket and stood before the mirror checking himself with a critical eye. The last few weeks had taken their toll. Dark rings circled his eyes, his hair seemed greyer. Yet he knew that all would be well once he was with Jo-Ellen again. She brought back his youthfulness, gave him back the bloom the war had repeatedly stolen.

The journey to Savannah was urgent. Not only did he want to settle the wedding details, he needed to spend some time at Highlands to plan its redecoration, and Jo would most certainly want to be there to give her opinion. There were colours to consider, the reshaping of rooms. All this would require his urgent attention.

As for the war...Daniel heaved a huge sigh. The Confederacy were like a brave bull brought down by the picador and in its first throes of death. It was now just a matter of time unless a miracle happened. He looked off into the distance. Pray that they leave the south alone now, pray it was all over with before the Federal troops got as far south as Georgia. Sweat broke out on his brow at the thought of it – blue uniforms in their hundreds pouring like ants over the countryside. He'd seen it so often but could not stomach the thought of it happening in the State he'd come to love so much.

He opened the door to be confronted by an aide holding out a letter to him.

'Sir, this just arrived. You off now, sir?'

'I am, Cooper. Think you can manage without me?'

Daniel took the envelope and closed the door. It had Jo-Ellen's handwriting on it. Quickly he tore it open. The words danced haphazardly before his eyes as he read. Robert de la Rey was alive, he was returning to Savannah and by the time Daniel read this letter, he would be with Jo-Ellen. His hand shook as the shock of the words in the final paragraph took their toll.

'Daniel, my dear, I hardly know how to say this. I cannot see you, not as before, you must realise that. Rob and I are still married and I cannot change that. All my love, Jo.'

'Cooper!'

The aide came rushing in.

'Bring me a bottle of Bourbon!'

'Sir?'

'Bourbon, man, now!'

Clasping the bottle, a glass, and a cigar, Daniel sat outside on the porch. The evening was moonless. His jacket felt heavy with dampness, his shirt already soaked through with sweat. When he was almost halfway through the bottle, he placed it to one side and stared ahead of him. It had all gone – everything. The war, the thrill of glory, and now Jo and his future happiness.

'Sir, are you all right?'

He turned, grinned wryly at the concerned face. 'I'm fine, Cooper. You got a woman back home?'

'Yes, sir. I want to be with her, sir.'

'I know the feeling. Here, come and join me.'

Together they drank the night away, both to ease their very personal depressions. By the time Daniel went to his bed, he had made one definite decision. He was now the new owner of Highlands and no one and nothing, least of all Robert de la Rey, was going to stop that. He would still journey to Savannah, he would still sign on the dotted line. It was going to be very hard but was it any harder than what he'd so far endured? The deaths of many of his men and friends in a war that made no sense any longer. Men like George Pickett, whose assault at Gettysburg had been so thoroughly repulsed that the man was now a wreck. What Daniel was experiencing paled into total insignificance against that episode alone.

That night he slept fitfully. During the waking hours he kept telling himself one thing. He would go and secure the small part of his life still left to him. Highlands.

Chapter Fifteen

'Oh, my, what on earth's going to happen?' Susanne's voice was an urgent whisper when she heard the news.

Jo-Ellen placed a hand to her aching head. Sleep had not come easily lately and her body also ached from Rob's excessive use of it.

'I don't know,' she replied. 'I feel quite different and I've got to talk to somebody about it. I'd rather it not be Mama, so may I talk to you?'

Under the tree by the house that afternoon in late September the two women talked and when Jo-Ellen had finished, Susanne said, 'What an awful mess. I'd no idea. Not having seen you lately, I assumed you were taken up completely with the plans for your wedding and the house and all. Oh – the house! Whatever will happen to it now?'

It was too upsetting, so Jo-Ellen did not reply. Daniel would hardly want to carry out his promise to her now. To buy Highlands and move in right next door to herself and Rob would be torture for him. She felt so wretched. She had let down Daniel, Susanne, Ben, and her Mama and without the money for Highlands, they had little chance of survival at the Plantation.

'We must not think about the house,' Susanne continued. 'It won't help matters none, not when there are other more important issues to consider. Jo-Ellen, tell me how you feel. This must have been a dreadful shock for you. And Rob – how is he? Has he got over it all?'

Gradually Jo-Ellen unburdened herself. 'I do love Rob, but it's not the same any longer. When we lie together, I'm no longer eager.' She looked at Susanne for some sign of understanding. 'I cannot control my thoughts, you see. We can't take away what is, can we?'

'You mean Daniel?'

Jo-Ellen nodded.' I feel so guilty yet I'm caught up in a situation beyond my control. I can't just walk away and I don't want to hurt Rob after all he's been through. He loves me and I as his wife am bound to obey, but I do it more with my head than with my heart. Susanne, is there something wrong with me?'

'No, it's quite natural. You must not blame yourself.'

'Tell me what you're thinking, Susanne.'

Silence, then, 'You must ask yourself how you feel about Daniel and for what reasons, if you truly love him for himself and not for reasons of guilt or anything else.'

'Such as?'

'Possibly because of the promises you've made, and there's also gratitude. Just because you said you'd marry him does not bind you to him, regardless. Make sure you're not merely feeling sorry for him.'

'Go on.'

'Then ask yourself if it is possible that you feel unhappy because returning to Rob so suddenly has tested your sense of loyalty. You're a faithful woman, Jo-Ellen, and being thrust into the role of anything else may have caused some resentment.' Susanne paused to let this sink in. 'However, ask yourself also if, given time, you will not regain your feelings for Rob and he will replace Daniel, as Daniel replaced him.' She stopped as a look of horror came into Jo-Ellen's eyes. 'Forgive me, I didn't mean to sound so callous.'

'It's all right, I do understand.' Jo-Ellen leaned over and kissed her. 'Thank you, Susanne. My head feels much clearer. It's done me a power of good talking to you.'

'I'm pleased. One more thing, remember that what you decide will affect Alexander also.'

Jo-Ellen left her to go in the house. That afternoon she would spend with Alexander. Rob was out somewhere and she was glad. Alone with her son she could reflect on everything. She had much to decide and it was not going to be easy. She had Alexander's future to consider, not only her own. If she were alone in this, she knew what she would do. As it was, she was going to have to place her personal happiness second.

...

Susanne watched with a heavy heart as her friend disappeared from view. What was to happen now? One moment so very happy at the prospect of becoming Mrs Daniel Hunter and living at Highlands, the next thrust back into the role of wife to the man she believed dead. How would *she* have handled such a situation? It was all very well giving words of advice but could she take them as well as give them were it her instead?

At least Ben was alive and well but what if he were missing, believed dead, and she accepted that and got on with her life raising Jamie, and finally met another man whom she thought might make her happy? Of course, it was difficult to contemplate. The notion of meeting another was so outrageous as to be amusing. In fact, if she lost Ben, the chances were she would remain a widow and alone for the rest of her life.

Hitching her skirts, she made her way towards Highlands. The white pillars of the house in the sunlight dazzled her. Perhaps it was just as well it was not being sold since her Mama was still living there, although a portion of Jefferson House had been set aside for that reason, just in case.

She lifted the catch on the gate. The rest of the day she would spend with Jamie, who was growing bigger by the day. She smiled to herself. The child would soon be requiring her own quarters.

The letter lay on the hall table. She did not recognise the handwriting and tearing it open, she was surprised to see it was from Daniel.

'About the house,' she muttered to herself.

'*Just want to put your mind at rest, Susanne,*' it began. As she read, her spirits lifted. He would soon be on his way to sign the papers. He guessed she had heard the news by now, but nothing was going to change. The final paragraph warmed her heart. Her mother must remain where she was if she desired, and the money for the entire sale would be made over to Susanne at the earliest possible moment. Please would she convey his love to Jo-Ellen and let her know that he understood her situation only too well?

She tucked away the letter and made to rush back and tell Jo-Ellen. She paused in the doorway – Rob might be there by now. Far better to ask Jo-Ellen to visit her so that they could discuss the matter sensibly and in private. Daniel was going to be their neighbour come what may!

She went into Jamie and took her into her arms. 'It's going to be all right, little one. All we need now is to see your Papa come though that door.'

She sat down and hummed a lullaby, her eyes fixed firmly on the door that one day would open and deliver Ben back to her.

• • •

It had been several weeks since Gettysburg, but Ben could not dim the awful images he had seen there. The days blended into one another and he went through the motions of his job with mechanical ease, unaware of time and living only for the day when his Confederate colleagues realised the game was up and everybody could now go home.

He felt a lot better than when he'd first returned to his men. It had taken time to come to terms with the fact that he was no longer free to do what he liked, that the Plantation would have to get by without him and that life had to go on. Perhaps Gettysburg had helped. Perhaps it had been a catalyst in his life. Knowing that defeat was inevitable had come as a shock at first and then as a relief.

So the days were spent in quiet contemplation when he was able. He had regained some weight and was able to sleep at night, banishing his haunted mask-like appearance of past weeks. But when he was least expecting it, those awful sights crept up on him. Knowing that Garnett had been buried in a mass grave with his men, that General Louis Armistead had been killed and also Kemper, the secessionist general – all good men and all of them Pickett's brigade commanders - was a hell of a lot to take in. It would take time. You couldn't rub out something as awesome as that overnight.

A telegraph was coming through and he listened as his chief sent out his orders.

• • •

Patience was not one of Sebastian's virtues but he had so far managed to keep from Marilyn what he knew. On the day that he felt able to tell her, he was elated. He had received word that the man named Vince had collected the money and had taken off somewhere. To Richmond to gamble? That was what he had said.

As darkness came to the countryside he poured himself a whisky and lit a cigar. He would see Marilyn in there – no one would bother them and the walls were thick. To make sure, he rang for the maid and asked her to send Marilyn to him then go to Grange Manorhouse on an errand.

Marilyn entered looking well-rested and glamorous in her latest gown. That was the thing he always admired about her, her choice of clothes. He experienced a brief pang of regret. He was going to miss her.

'Ah, my dear, come in. I've something to tell you.'

She sat down, wearing her most charming smile, though inside she felt irritable. Either something had happened to Vince or he had decided against killing Sebastian.

'Yes, dearest, what is it?'

Sebastian stubbed out the cigar and tucked his hands behind his back.

'You must be wondering how it is I'm still alive, my dear. Well, I'm about to tell you.'

The smile disappeared. 'Sebastian – what are you talking about?'

'I'm referring to the deal you made with your lover, Vince, and the fact that he has double-crossed you as you did me, and decided to tell me what you planned between you. For this, he took a substantial sum of money, enough to set him up for some time, money that was to be yours. He will also be getting Hilton Heights when I die. You see, he blackmailed me to change my Will in his favour.'

The blood drained from her face, she made to stand but her legs felt weak. 'But how, why…'

Sebastian chuckled. 'I shouldn't try to reason why, my dear. The details are irrelevant.' He came round to face her. 'You'll not be getting a penny more from me, or the property now and if I were you, I'd not hide away at your house. You'll get little rest there when the neighbours find out about this.'

She shuddered at the thought of Jasper Lee and his cronies. Regaining a little composure, she said, 'You've been tricked, Sebastian, can't you see that? Yes, I did know Vince but he was nothing to me. He used me when I felt lonely one time and I'm sorry. I married you, didn't I? Why would I do that if I didn't care?'

'Please spare me the lies, Marilyn. You think me a fool? Yes, perhaps you do and perhaps I was. A man in love is little more than a fool. I wanted a son, remember? That's why we married, or have you forgotten? Now, Laura can produce for me. She's young, she's bound to marry one day. And the child she's expecting will get everything. I've other assets, you see, some you know nothing about. In the meantime, I aim to deal with you.'

Her mouth opened to speak. Before she could move out of his way, his hand came up and stung her cheek, causing her to reel sideways. Her other cheek took a similar punishment and she was pushed back against the wall as he gripped her hair and pulled hard. In defence she howled, finding her voice at last. 'Help me, someone, help!'

'No one can hear you. The servants are on the other side of the house and your maid is on an errand.' His fist struck her chin and her head jerked back. Dizzy, she gripped at him for support as his other fist struck her on the other side. He continued to slap at her until she slid down in a heap on the floor.

'Now, pack your bags and get out of my house! Go back to your boyfriend. You'll probably find him gambling his ill-gotten gains in Richmond! You're a fool, Marilyn. All the time he's had another woman there. All along he was deceiving you with a woman by the name of Annabelle.'

In a mist, Marilyn saw him leave the room, slamming the door behind him. Somehow she pulled herself to her feet and faced herself in the mirror. Blood poured from cuts to her cheeks and mouth. The gown was torn and stained. She managed to stagger out into the night air, hoping it would help revive her. Hiding her face, she ran with difficulty up the steps of the house, pain wrenching through her body. For a while she would be safe but for how long? When Jasper Lee and the other locals found out what she had done they would want their revenge, might even fire Grange Manorhouse.

She poured a large drink and dabbed some on her wounds. There was only one thing for her to do. She would rest up at the house and when her face looked anything back to normal, she would go and find Vince. Richmond – yes, that was where he often went. With all that money, he would surely go there to the gambling tables.

With an effort she discarded her clothes, sank into a hot bath, and sobbed her heart out.

• • •

It wasn't the same without Ben there. Rob gazed around the empty drawing room relishing the memories of how they had both stood by the roaring fire and toasted each other and their futures; how they had spoken about the then impending war and seeing themselves in very different roles.

As for his own situation, he knew he had to get Jo-Ellen and Alexander away. To remain in Savannah would be suicide with Grant and his men just outside the city waiting for the opportunity to march in, and Lincoln's Gettysburg Address on November 19th leaving no one in any doubt as to what the future might hold. Success for the north and failure for the south. As for himself, it sickened him to be in Savannah for many other reasons. As much as he might have loved these people in the past, they were Confederates. The enemy. Daily, he had to control his thoughts and feelings towards them. Under other circumstances, he would be justified in taking a gun and shooting some of them. But not Ben, not his friend, and there Rob felt torn in two. Therefore, the sooner he left Savannah, the better. Philadelphia was his home and that was where he and his family would live, although Jo-Ellen did not seem enthusiastic. She became very quiet whenever he talked about their future in the north. She was also not very forthcoming in the love-making department, either. Not like those women that he and Custer used to visit, which was why he recently began visiting the whorehouse in Savannah.

Spontaneity was not one of Jo-Ellen's virtues of late; it seemed to him that she went about her role as his wife in a mechanical, dutiful manner, rather than the enthusiastic, bubbly creature she used to be. He could remember that much. In fact, he had to inflict his will on her the last two occasions and take what he wanted because she sure as hell wasn't going to give it.

Straightening his neck-tie, he looked through the window at the windswept landscape and the dark clouds hovering overhead. November always made everything look so barren. Could it be an early snow warning?

Something attracted his attention. A buggy drew up outside. Sitting inside was a man. Rob waited for him to get out of the buggy, but he did not and sat looking intently at the house. Rob moved quickly to the door and opened it. As he stepped outside, the man saw him and rein-slapped the horse forward, leaving Rob looking down the track leading to Highlands.

• • •

That evening, alone with Jo-Ellen, Rob said, 'Honey, I think it better if we spend Christmas with my parents in Philadelphia. Get Alexander used to it, and of course, yourself.'

She tried to remain calm. 'No, Rob, I don't want to do that. We always spend Christmas with my Mama and I don't want to leave Savannah at such a time. Not again.'

He confronted her, his eyes narrowed. 'Don't you now, well it isn't up to you any longer. I've written to my mother that we're coming, so you'd best get used to it.'

Jo-Ellen felt her control snap. 'I'm sorry, I'm not going and that's final! I don't like it up there and I will not leave Savannah at this time. Besides, I've already made the usual arrangements here. What will my Mama do here all alone?'

'We'll take her with us. No problem.'

She stared at him as though seeing a stranger. It hadn't been her imagination – he had changed.

'No – Mama prefers it here.'

He placed a hand to his forehead in exasperation. 'What a goddamned family! What'll you do when we're living up there, Jo? You'd best get used to that idea, because you and Alexander are moving soon as I can arrange it!'

Tears sprang to her eyes. 'I'm not moving. We're staying here. Alexander's going to be raised a southern boy!'

His hand fastened on her arm. 'Now, listen to me and listen well. You're my wife, damn it, or have you forgotten? As for staying in Savannah, it'll be impossible come a few months from now, if not before.'

He released her and she glanced at the red marks on her skin. 'Impossible? Why?'

'Because Grant's men are ready to take this part of the country. The Confederacy is as good as finished and if you stay here, you'll be in danger. You want that for Alexander? Well, do you?'

'Of course not!'

She moved away from him to look out at the line of trees bordering the track leading from the house.

'Jo, I have to go back there. It never was my intention to live here. I want my boy to grow up there so he can have a good future. We've been over and over all this, so just do as I say!' He lit a cheroot. 'I've a career to consider.'

'In the Federal army?'

'No, as a Senator. I'm considering running for office, so I have to be close to Washington, don't you see that? I can't hide away down here for much longer. I fight for the Union, Jo, not the Confederacy.' This last was said with irony.

She did not reply. Her being a southerner had always been an issue with him.

'Why you wanted a southern bride, Rob, beats me!' She effected the southern drawl she knew he loathed.

'Stop that!'

She took a deep calming breath. 'I don't want to argue. But I can't go to Philadelphia for Christmas. If you want to go, then I'll understand.'

'Can't? Won't, you mean.'

'As you like.'

She heard the door slam behind him and his footsteps on the path outside the window cease as he climbed into the buggy and slapped the horses into action. She wiped her eyes and tidied herself. No use letting Mama see her in this state. A sense of relief settled on her. Her mind was made up. Rob could go to Philadelphia and so be it. She would not mind, she would remain in Savannah and try to make everybody's Christmas a pleasure, especially her Mama's. Too much time had been spent away from her family in the past. There was also Susanne. She would be alone that December for there was no sign of Ben returning in time for the festivities.

In Alexander's room, she sat with him and played with his toys. He was growing up so fast. Before she knew it he would be off to school and not long afterwards he would be courting. That was what happened, wasn't it? Time can overtake you – they grew up suddenly. How could Rob take the boy away from his true roots, from Jamie and all those who loved him? It just wouldn't work and if the boy was anything like her or Ben he would be land-loving and fond of the open countryside.

As she looked again through the window towards the trees, she saw a buggy draw up. Her heart missed a beat. Daniel! She rushed outside and called him over. In an instant, he was out of the buggy and hurrying towards her.

'Jo, I've looked and waited, hoping I'd see you.' His attention moved towards the house. 'Is it all right for me to be here?'

'Yes, of course. You're our neighbour now, aren't you?' Then, 'Daniel, can you ever forgive me?'

His hand brushed her cheek. 'Darling Jo, there's nothing to forgive, except a bad headache after a bottle of Bourbon. It was something beyond our control.' His eyes sought hers. 'Tell me, are you happy? I do so want you to be happy.'

She did not reply to such a loaded question but looked into his eyes as though wishing to convey her thoughts that way.

'You don't look happy. Is there something wrong?'

She shook her head. How could she tell him all the things that lay in her heart? How could she speak of her husband, of how he had angered her?

'Daniel, how long are you going to stay. Is everything all right at Highlands?'

He chuckled. 'As ever, a clever change of subject. Susanne is making ready to come and join you here any time now and has decided on leaving her Mama where she is. The old lady would hate to be uprooted at her time of life, I'm sure. As for Highlands, I'm making great strides with the decor, Jo, you should see it. When do I return to my men? I'm due back after Christmas. General Lee has been very generous indeed.'

'That's wonderful! You'll be here for Christmas Day. We'll all be together.'

He grinned. 'Is that such a good idea?'

'You mean Rob? Oh, he'll be all right. You'll both get along. Just don't mention the war and don't say who you fight for. You can do that for a few hours?'

'I can. Am I to take it he hasn't got all his memory back?'

She looked at him curiously. 'I'm not sure. That's something for the doctor to decide. Why?'

How could he continue the conversation? It would mean telling her about his meeting with Rob on at least two occasions and under what circumstances. When he had seen Rob at the door the other day, he hoped he had not been recognised. Until he knew how much he remembered, it was safer to stay out of the way.

'You know, your General Lee sounds very nice. I wish I could meet him.'

'I wish you could, too. He's a real gentleman and you would do him the world of good. He certainly needs cheering up. Things have gone from bad to worse and his health is now failing him. We all worry about him. Oh, I forgot – I saw Ben at Gettysburg.'

Her eyes lit up. 'You did? Is he all right? Did you speak to him?'

'He looked fine, though tired. We acknowledged each other and went on our way. I believe he went back to Richmond. I expect he'll remain at headquarters over Christmas.'

'Oh, Daniel, won't it be wonderful when we're all together again? You at Highlands, Ben and Susanne here with my Mama.'

'And you, Jo, where will you be?'

'Why, here, with my son...'

'And Rob?'

'Yes, and Rob, except...'

'What is it?'

'He wants to take us to Philadelphia for Christmas. In fact, for good.'

Daniel thrust his hands into his pockets. 'I see. Are you going? You said...'

'I meant it. I told him I wouldn't go. I'd miss Mama and Susanne.' She looked at him intently. 'And I'd miss you.'

'Jo – you know how I feel about you. Nothing can alter that. You know that I love you?'

'Yes, and God help me, I feel the same way.'

His arms swept her into him. His lips found hers.

'No, Daniel, it isn't right.'

'No, it isn't right, nor is it right that I crave for you every minute of the days that we're apart.'

She stepped out of his embrace. 'I can't, Daniel. It makes us seem cheap and our love isn't cheap. I won't accept snatched moments like this. It feels so wrong!'

'Yes, you're right. We must try not to meet. In fact, the sooner I leave Savannah, the better. Perhaps one day, God will bless us and bring us together but not like this. I'm so sorry, my dearest Jo.'

With one movement he pulled open the door and strode out to the waiting buggy. Without looking again in her direction, he urged the horse forward. As the buggy tore down the track towards Highlands, tears she could no longer hold back poured down her cheeks.

...

It was cold and dark on the morning that Marilyn set out from Grange Manorhouse. Careful not to be seen, she crept alongside the house and took the road leading to the station. The only person who knew about her departure was Josy.

'You're sworn to secrecy, Josy. Anyone asking about me, you tell them you've no idea where I am.'

She could trust Josy, but knew that in the hands of someone like Jasper Lee the girl would stand little chance and so Marilyn did not state her exact destination and gave no hint as to why she had gone. Of the bruises on her face and arms she merely said she had a fall. Josy had nursed her back to health and now she was ready to put her plans into action.

Pulling her cloak around her against the November wind, she gradually put the mile-long walk behind her. She still felt unsteady on her feet. The beating Sebastian gave her had taken much of her energy.

She boarded the train and tried to work out how long the journey would be to Richmond. The journey was not direct. She might have to change trains three times. Once in Richmond, she would make discreet enquiries about Vince and his woman, Annabelle. The chances of finding him were now slimmer because of the time lapse. He might well have completed his business there and gone to another part of the country.

Remaining in Hagerstown was dangerous. She could no longer avoid Sebastian or Jasper and so it was with trepidation that she set out on a mission that seemed futile but was all that was left to her. Once she completed her business in Richmond, she would head farther south before the festive season was on them. South was where she wanted to be even with the persistent threat of war. After that, she would re-think her plans.

In her head she rehearsed her new role as Madeleine Cecil, visiting her sick sister in Richmond. She pulled the bag she carried closer to her. Inside was a gown, various toiletries, some money and a gun.

The carriage door opened. A gentleman stepped inside. As he seated himself, he eyed her approvingly. She smiled. He was exceptionally good looking. Perhaps the journey was not going to be tedious after all.

• • •

She woke with a start. For a moment Marilyn did not know where she was.

'Have a good sleep?'

He was grinning at her and she felt a flush of embarrassment.

'Why, yes, thank you.' Her hand clutched at the bag, which had slipped off her lap onto the seat beside her. 'How long have I been asleep?'

'About an hour,' came the reply in a voice rich and deep. 'Name's Bradley K. Forrester. Brad to my friends.'

She straightened the front of her gown.

'And you are?'

'I beg your pardon?'

'I gave you my name. I'd like to know yours.'

'Madeleine – Cecil.'

'Hmm, nice. Looks like there'll be just the two of us, Madeleine, until we get to Charlottesville, at least.'

'That's where we'll be stopping?'

'Hard to say. But possibly. I hear the railroad's pretty clear until then.'

When the train stopped, many passengers got off only to be replaced by more, but none came into their carriage. Marilyn took out her lunch pack and bit into the sweet meats inside. She longed to get to Richmond and book into a hotel so that she could bathe and change her clothes.

'Will you be staying in Richmond?' Brad Forrester leaned

forward, his dark eyes capturing hers.

'Yes, for a while.'

'I know a very good hotel, not expensive and very cosy.'

Marilyn shook her head. 'It's all right, I already have arrangements.'

The last thing she wanted was company, not while she sought Vince, which was a pity as she liked this man, Brad. He was tall, slim, though broad shouldered. A neat moustache set off a fine mouth and his teeth gleamed when he smiled. Thick brown hair curled on to his collar and he looked her straight in the eye. His lips peeled back into a dazzling smile. 'Perhaps, then, you'll allow me to take you to dinner this evening.'

Off guard, she stammered, 'I – er- cannot. As I said, I have arrangements.'

'You're spoken for? Married, perhaps? There's no ring.' He grinned at her. 'Couldn't help noticing.'

She felt where her ring had been before she had taken it off. 'No, I'm meeting someone. My sister is ill and I'm visiting her.'

He gave a nod and leaned back in his seat, his attention transferred to the scenery outside. They stopped only once more and this time they had to change trains. This went straight through to Richmond.

As they were about to alight, Bradley Forrester assisted her and took hold of her bag, which he handed back once they were on the platform where he said goodbye and walked away.

She watched him go. What she wouldn't do for a good meal with this engaging stranger. Yet her entire time had to be given to finding Vince, if possible. That was why she was there and she could not involve anybody else.

She left the station and took a buggy, instructing the driver to find a suitable small hotel. On the way, she enquired about gambling casinos. The driver was most talkative and by the time Marilyn alighted outside Fairmount Private Hotel, she was thoroughly apprised of her whereabouts.

Booking in under her new name, she bathed, dressed in her new gown, took her hair up and made her face up similar to how Josy used to do it. She was pleased with the final result.

The main casino was in the town square. She would start there. As she went, snatches of conversation drifted her way about the war and about Lee's recent defeat.

The doorman asked who she was with.

'I'll be meeting my husband inside,' she said.

'And his name is?'

'Bradley K. Forrester.'

The doorman tipped his hat. 'Right, Mrs Forrester. Have a good evening.'

Through the cigar smoke she saw tables and decided to keep a discreet distance from the main venue. She selected a seat with a good view and waited. An hour passed. Doubts began to overcome her. How long could she get away with sitting there on her own? Perhaps Vince wasn't even in Richmond and if he was, surely there were other casinos he could go to? This was the main one, she had found out, the place one went to play the high stakes. And Vince would never settle for less.

She saw him then, accompanied by a blonde woman who gripped his arm possessively. Marilyn moved further back into the shadows and watched as they sauntered across the room, their attention on each other.

Vince reached inside his pocket, produced a cigar and lit the end. Seating himself at one of the tables, he engaged in gambling while Annabelle sat behind to watch. They had an air of wealth and grandness about them.

Not for long, Marilyn thought, not for long.

When it was safe to do so, she rose and left. Across the road was a doorway and there she waited until Vince and Annabelle emerged from the Casino and climbed into a buggy. She hailed one for herself and followed. It was quite late by this time and she wondered if Vince would stay with Annabelle, making it difficult for her to see him alone. Too bad, she decided. If she had to deal with the pair of them, so be it.

Their buggy stopped outside a building. He assisted her down, they kissed and Annabelle went inside, leaving Vince on the sidewalk. Perfect. Marilyn edged closer and followed as he walked down the street and turned into an alleyway. It was darker there. Producing a gun, she moved in behind him.

'Vince, stop there and turn around.'

His shock was apparent. 'What the hell – Marilyn! How in hell's name did you get here? How did you find me?'

'Shut up and don't come any closer. I'll fire this, I promise you.'

His face creased into a nervous smile. 'Now, come on, honey. You're mad at me for not killing Sebastian and I can understand that. I was going to explain it all to you. I was coming back to marry you…'

'I said shut up!' She pointed the gun at his head. 'You cheated me out of everything and you're going to pay.'

'You wouldn't – kill me, you can't.'

She levelled the gun.

'Look, I hit lucky tonight. Cleaned up at the Casino. You can have it all. Here.'

'I intend to. Keep your hands where I can see them.'

His hand flew to his pocket. Next thing there was a revolver pointing at her. She squeezed the trigger of her own gun. Nothing happened. She froze. Vince took careful aim.

There was a loud gun shot. Vince crumbled to the ground. 'Next time, Madeleine, get yourself a decent weapon.'

Bradley K. Forrester stepped out of the shadows, gun in hand. 'Come on, I've a buggy waiting. We must get out of here.'

'Wait!'

She bent and emptied Vince's pockets. He had been right. There were hundreds of dollars. They ran from the alleyway and Brad drove the buggy across town where they finally stopped. He turned to her. 'Now, what in hell's name is going on? I've waited hours for you and followed you only to find no one met you, there's no sick sister and I bet your name's not Madeleine. And when you said I was your husband, I knew you were up to no good, lady.'

She threw back her head and laughed. 'Hey, buy me that dinner, Bradley Forrester, and I'll tell you all about it.'

He drove to the nearest hotel and booked a room. She did not mind. She intended much more than dinner with him.

…

The arrival of Laura's baby on December 15th took Sebastian's mind off all his troubles. For those last few weeks he had felt the loss of Marilyn's company and had often wished he had not been so hard on her. When he found she had left Grange Manorhouse so suddenly, a feeling of isolation swept over him.

He looked with pride at his grandson lying in Laura's arms.

'What shall we call him, Papa?'

Sebastian was touched, noting the 'we.'

'Charles. I like Charles.'

She agreed. 'Charles Sebastian de la Rey. It sounds good.'

'No, no!' Had the girl taken leave of her senses? Did he have to remind her that she was not married? 'His name is Hilton. Always remember that, Laura.'

Shortly after that, the Christening took place and Charles Sebastian Hilton spent his first Christmas surrounded by enough love to last him a lifetime. Sebastian insisted on taking his grandson out at every opportunity to show his friends and neighbours. No one spoke much of Marilyn, or of the young soldier who had come to stay for a while. Attention at that time focussed mainly on the outcome of the war and what was to become of them all.

The New Year of 1864 was greeted with mounting trepidation.

• • •

Things had been happening at an appalling pace, things that most southern folk greeted with shocked despair. Following the Gettysburg Address that November, there had come news of the battle of Chattanooga, opening up the Union gateway to Georgia and signalling the beginning of the end for the Confederacy. To make matters worse, Britain had officially lost interest after Lee's defeat at Gettysburg.

Fear hung over Jo-Ellen as she went about her work during those final days of the year. It was as much as she could bear to think that any day now Union troops might come marching through the streets of Savannah. Ever since they had won at Chickamauga in the fall, the Federal forces had continued to threaten. Yet, their generals had it all in hand, hadn't they? Surely they wouldn't allow the Yankees to set foot in Georgia – would they?

There was one bright light in her despair. She had received news that Highlands had fetched a goodly sum from Daniel. He had insisted on paying the market price and she knew that this was as much for her sake as for Susanne's, and for the time being her family was safe and secure.

She looked along the track leading from the house, remembering the last day he had driven off to join the Confederate cause many miles away north-west of Atlanta. He had kept his promise; she had not seen or heard of him since. Susanne had moved in after that and it was to her that he wrote telling her that he had returned to his division early, and this news had left Jo-Ellen feeling the intense ache of missing him.

Christmas had been special now that Alexander and Jamie were a little older, and Susanne's Mama had been able to join them. Rob did not go away, and for those few days all difficulties had been set aside. Occasionally, Jo-Ellen was aware of Rob's expression as he watched her play with Alexander or laugh gaily with Constance and Susanne. It was as though he disapproved.

Standing by the tree on that crisp wintry day, wrapped in her thick cloak against a gusting wind, she could see in the distance the buggy bringing Rob back from Hagerstown. He was not at all pleased with her. Ever since cancelling his plans to visit his parents, he had been in a mood. She had tried to bring him out of it, but to no avail. When he had spoken in glowing terms of Grant, and the man called Sherman, they had further sharp words. Grant was nothing but a drunk, she had exclaimed, and Sherman – why, people thought him insane. Rob did not take kindly to hearing his heroes demeaned so, and her outburst led to further insistence from him that the sooner they packed up and left, the better.

She made her way towards the house as the buggy drew up outside. Rob got out and waited for her to join him. His expression told her that their rows were far from over.

• • •

'Matters have been accelerated, Jo. Governor Floyd wants me in Washington.'

They were sitting in the warmth of their drawing room. The lights were low, dinner had just finished, Rob had been drinking. Jo-Ellen, sleepy from the day's activities, closed her eyes to rest them.

'Did you hear me? I'm going away!'

'Away?' She snapped to.

'I've to go to Washington. Hubert Floyd contacted me. He wants to talk to me about our – my future.' He tipped more wine into his glass.

She sighed. It was getting closer. Any day now she would have to leave Savannah. She looked through the window at the January frost spread like a carpet as far as the eye could see.

'I'll go see him, hear what he has to say and then journey on to Philadelphia to my parents. Soon as I'm ready, I'll send for you and the boy.'

A slight reprieve. She did not have to go with him. 'When?'

'I'll leave first light tomorrow. Floyd won't wait forever.'

'Tomorrow.' She was secretly pleased.

'By the way, our new neighbour seems to be away. He never came in to introduce himself. Would have thought he'd done so by now. What do you know about him?'

She tensed. How much did Rob remember?

'Nothing much. Just someone helping out Susanne, apparently.'

'Hmm, mighty kind of him. I'd like to meet him some time. In fact, I'll try asking Susanne about him again.'

'Again?'

'Yes, she changed the subject last time. Ah, here she is now.'

Susanne came in at that moment. Jo-Ellen closed her eyes briefly. She had dreaded this moment.

'Susanne, this fellow who bought your house, how did you meet him?'

At the sound of his voice, Susanne coloured and glanced at Jo-Ellen for support.

'I'm in rather a hurry at the moment, Rob. Speak to me later?' She hurried off without announcing why she had come in the first place.

'You see? Tell me I'm making it up. She's decidedly evasive. So, tell me, Jo, what's the fellow's name?'

'Daniel Hunter.'

He frowned. 'Hunter – where have I heard that before?' He swung round on her. 'I have heard it before, haven't I?'

'I expect Ben mentioned it.'

'Ben? He's not been around for some time. You mean, this fellow's been here that long? He's not new around here?' Her silence alerted him. 'A Confederate, Jo?'

'I rather expect so. Most people around here are. Honestly, Rob, does it matter any longer what people are?'

'A Confederate officer?'

She averted her gaze. 'Yes.'

He turned to stare at the scene outside the window, though she knew he was not seeing it properly, not while his thoughts raced along the track she had set him on.

'What's been going on behind my back, Jo?' His eyes were narrowed, accusing.

'Nothing.' Her voice was without conviction, and she felt like a train without brakes hurtling towards a cliff edge.

'The officer I saw at Sharpsburg?'

Her lashes covered her eyes. 'Yes,' though she had no idea what he meant.

'It all comes neatly together at long last. Could he be the reason you don't wish to live in the north?'

'Of course not!'

'Has he kissed you? More to the point, have you kissed him?'

She looked away.

'Ah – I see I may have hit upon the truth. What does he mean to you, Jo?'

She placed her hands to her head. 'Rob, you were dead, for heaven's sake! You were gone!'

'And you found someone to replace me as soon as you could. Why, I was barely cold in my so-called grave.'

'Stop it!'

'This settles it. We're getting away from here. Where is this fellow now?'

'Away – I don't know where.'

'Away – killing Federal troops, no doubt.'

'Yes, of course – he'd hardly kill Confederate troops!'

He ignored her sarcasm. He remembered it all so well now. This officer was the one person who could destroy his political career, the one person who knew the truth about how he, Rob, came to be shot that day.

He took her by her shoulders and forced her to look at him. 'If he ever comes by again, I forbid you to see him. Understand?'

He turned on his heel and slammed out of the room. She burst into tears. She did not see him again. He went in the early hours before she rose from a sleep that left her exhausted from crying.

Chapter Sixteen

In the early hours of May 11th, 1864, a thunderstorm broke the silence of the night. Jo-Ellen rose from her bed and went to watch through the window. She enjoyed the sound of heavy rain and the fragrance of earth and plants carried on warm air. The earth around the Plantation was drenched, and billowing smudges moved swiftly across the sky as lightning stabbed in the darkness. She listened for any sound from Alexander's room. So far he had not woken up.

Lying down again, she closed her eyes and let her thoughts roam. Any day now Rob would be back, or so he had told her in his latest letter, though he had said as much in all his letters during those weeks away. She had expected him long before this. She took out his letter and read it again. After Washington, he wrote, he had visited his parents and thereafter tried to find a suitable home for her and Alexander. This had met with no success. Property had become very difficult to come by. His work had kept him occupied, he was meeting all the right people and he was well and happy in Washington. She folded the letter. So far, she had been lucky beyond belief. She was not expected to move yet.

Daniel had also written, but only once, to tell her he was near Atlanta. She had since read various accounts about General Sherman's advance and how he was progressing step by step in a bid to gain control of the southern railroads. It was all very distressing. Daniel wrote less about the war, she noted, and more about his personal feelings and hopes for the future and she prayed he would be kept safe and well.

A noise startled her and she strained to see in the darkness for any sign of those Yankees, in case some of them had reached as far as Savannah. But, surely that was silly. They wouldn't get that far. She looked towards the window as lightning lit up the scene outside. All the same, what would she do if they were to arrive? Kill them? She would have to. In war time, sentiment had no place. If they came as far as Jefferson House, she would have no option other than to protect her home and family.

Thunder crashed overhead and a cry came from Alexander's room. Casting aside the bed clothes, she went in, held him to her and carried him to her bed.

When they woke several hours later, the storm had passed and Louise was knocking on the door with a tray of tea.

• • •

That same morning a Confederate skirmish line, making ready to meet the oncoming Union soldiers, formed in the woods in the Wilderness, a rugged broken area of land that extended from the Rapidan to Spotsylvania. James Longstreet was their leader and his men, looking war-weary but determined, moved with all the prowess of tigers on a hunt.

Ben passed a hand across his forehead. His stomach grumbled. He had risen early, toasted a piece of old meat and washed it down with his canteen before getting on the march. Sleep had been fitful that night. Several of the men were ill, either with dysentery or pneumonia, several had coughed and wheezed, and this, amongst other things, had kept him awake.

As he marched with his men, a bright sun rose above the oak forest. The air was still cool. From the woods to the right came intermittent rifle fire. There was a battle up ahead and Ben guessed it was near the Brock Road where Longstreet's men waited. The smell of wood fire reached him, reminding him of better days at home, and then he saw that the woods nearby had been set alight. They pressed forward, joining with the skirmishers, who lurked behind trees firing briskly in the direction of the unseen enemy. Ben moved behind a tree and fired off several shots into what was rumoured to be the Union Sixth Corps. Cordite and gunpowder hung heavily on the air.

'Hey, soldier! Give me a hand here!'

He stopped firing and looked in the direction of the voice. In the undergrowth lay a Confederate captain, his face covered with blood. Quickly, Ben pressed a water bottle to the wounded man's lips.

'Thanks.'

'Where are you hurt?'

'My shoulder – everywhere, man.'

'Come on, I'll get you to an ambulance.'

An incredulous grin lit the captain's face. 'Ambulance? Out here?'

'Sure thing. Saw them way back on the road.'

'Good. Gonna need 'em. This place is full of dead and wounded. We've had it this time, sure we have.'

'You think so? There's been two assaults. You telling me we've been unsuccessful both times?'

The man nodded, his eyes closing. 'You got family? You from Georgia?'

'Yep – Savannah. And my family's there, too.'

'Then get the hell out of here, my friend. They're gonna need you. Stay here and you're dead. Hill's been repulsed. He lost thousands of his men.'

'That who you were with? Hill?'

'Correct, and if'n I had my way I'd be out of here back to my folks in Atlanta. Sherman's there, ain't you heard? He's got thousands of troops and if he gets a grip in Georgia, we'll be good as lost. And who knows what our folks will have to go through?' The captain winced in pain. 'Don't you worry about me. Get on home and save your skin. The fighting's finished.'

There was indeed a lull in the battle and Ben prayed that the captain was wrong, that their initial success in driving relentlessly into the Union ranks had not been checked and repulsed. Dipping a piece of his shirt in water, he cleaned the blood and muck from the soldier's face. 'Hey, you still with me?' He leaned closer to listen. The captain's hand slipped lifelessly to his side. It was no use. The man was dead. Ben stood up and looked around, exhausted and so hungry.

On the horizon, a glow signalled oncoming nightfall. With a last look at the dead captain, he walked away, accepting that the fight was over, that it was useless to remain. There seemed to be nothing more to be done towards the southern cause.

He guessed that if he walked in one direction, he would be taken prisoner and if he went in another, chances were he'd be shot at by Union stragglers. So he went in neither, but away from the bloody scene littered by hundreds of dead and wounded. The captain was right. It was time to quit for good.

He found a place where he could sleep for a few hours to regain his strength and well before dawn he got on the road. It was quiet as he set off, keeping out of sight and picking berries for breakfast. It had rained hard in the night and his clothes were damp, but his spirits were high. On the way he swam in a river and searched for anything that could substitute as food.

When he found a farmhouse, he approached with caution and let himself in, then searched each room to make sure he was alone.

'Owners either left or been driven away,' he muttered, heading for the kitchen a second time where he found a stale loaf, some vegetables, and half a bottle of brandywein.

Sitting at the wooden table, he surveyed his new-found home and ate the best meal he'd had in several days, content that very soon he would be on his way home to Savannah.

• • •

That June, when her baby was six months old, Laura approached Sebastian about the boy's future. He listened patiently. He had long been expecting this conversation. Since Robert de la Rey's departure from his house, Laura had been a model of restraint and he had come to admire her for that, but her announcement that she intended to find out where he was, disturbed him.

'Mind telling me why 'cause I see no reason to let that bounder in your life any longer.' He eyed her with concern. 'You still keen on him?'

She hesitated. Over the past weeks she had experienced various mood swings on the subject. Yes, she missed Ray, or Rob, yes, she sometimes felt warm toward him but on other occasions, and these were more constant, she felt anger, even hatred for him.

'No,' she said at last. 'It's not that, Papa. He'll never have contact with Charles, I'll see to that. I'd like him to know, however, that he does have a son but that he will no longer be welcome in our lives.'

This satisfied Sebastian. The girl had really grown up at last. She was thinking like him. Apply the knife, twist it slightly and withdraw. Make them suffer. It usually worked.

'All right, but I don't hold with you going off on your own. There's still fighting hereabouts. Never know where it's going to pop up next.'

'Papa, no one's going to bother me. I'm only going to Washington. If he's anywhere, he'll be there and if he's not there, I've a feeling someone will be able to tell me where I can find him.' Seeing his doubtful look, she added, 'Don't you worry, Papa, I'll be back before you know it. I'll feel better once I've done this.'

'So will I, no doubt,' he muttered. He gave a half-hearted nod. Women – they were all the same. Impulsive, wilful and never gave up until they got their way.

She put her arms around his neck and he didn't pull away. He never did these days. His feelings towards his daughter had mellowed and he actually felt paternal whenever she sought his affections. He placed an arm around her.

'God bless. I'll take good care of Charles, don't you worry.'

'I know you will, Papa. I'll only be gone a couple of weeks. It'll do me good, too.'

He watched as she walked up the stairs to Charles' nursery. Glancing at his time piece, he called for his driver. 'Bring the buggy, will you? I want to go in to town.'

● ● ●

From where Daniel stood he could see the long line of dead in grey uniform, mixed with the dead in blue uniform and he heaved a sigh as he looked on what was once a generous portion of the Confederate Cavalry and a sizeable section of Union Cavalry. Flies buzzed around the human cesspool, and unable any longer to stomach the stench of death, he pressed on, digging in his spurs to hurry to where his men waited in battle line. From out of the darkening June evening came the sound of rifle fire from the Union pickets. Tomorrow they were all going in to battle. Tomorrow it would start over again.

As he rode around his men, he sensed a depression, or was it only himself? Ever since he'd left Savannah all those months ago, he'd felt low in spirit. He had not written to Jo-Ellen again. How could he, knowing that Rob was there with her? His hands were well and truly tied.

He had heard from Susanne. She kept him in touch with as much news about Jo as she dared, though she never once mentioned anything personal, that being Robert or Alexander. She generally wrote that Jo was well, that the Plantation was holding its own despite the hardship in the south. She wrote mostly about Highlands and of her mother, who, despite no longer having her daughter there, felt happy and secure, come what may.

'*The house looks like new,*' she wrote. '*It's fresh and so comfortable. Mama adores it.*' And so Daniel had to satisfy himself with that.

He looked at the sunset and wished with all his heart that it was a Savannah sunset. Right now, he told himself, Jo-Ellen would be getting Alexander off to sleep then she would eat with her Mama and Susanne and take her evening stroll before bed. What he wouldn't give to be there one more time.

With a heavy feeling in his heart he urged his mount forward. It was no good wishing. He was now at Cold Harbour and he was expected to fight. But first, a good night's sleep because at daybreak he would have to lead his men into battle. Another day, another battle. How many more would there be? How much longer was he to risk his life? Would there come a day when a bullet might put an end to it all, when he would be unable to see his darling Jo again? The thought of death had never before held such dread for him. Now, because of his love and longing, he had to admit to a fear lurking within him, one he had never experienced before.

Rumour had it that the south was finished. Men really were turning their backs on the war and heading off home. Would the day come when he would do the same?

Handing his mount to his aide, he went to quarters and began a letter. This time he would send it. All he wanted was contact. Just a few words with Jo before he went into battle. As he wrote, the depression lifted and he felt more positive.

Taking a half bottle of Bourbon to bed with him, he knew no more until the silence was raked by the sound of the morning bugle.

• • •

Laura had been gone almost ten days and Sebastian missed her terribly. Daytimes he was fine. There were business matters to attend to and his presence was often required at this meeting or that conference. In the evenings, though, the house felt as empty as a shell.

His grandson filled in some of the time. Sebastian saw to it that the maid brought the boy to him every evening and he would sit and watch Charles with a great sense of pride. Whenever he could, he took Charles out with him and daily he watched for Laura's arrival or at least a letter announcing it.

When none came, he began to worry. She had sent only one letter when she first arrived in Washington. She spoke mainly of the sights and the people and that she was staying in a small hotel in the centre of the city and that she would contact him again soon. There was no mention of Robert de la Rey and he had to assume she had not begun looking for him yet.

Sebastian poured a whisky and stood by the window to watch the sun go down. Yes, he missed his daughter. Even his evening drink wasn't as enjoyable. No one poured a drink like Laura did.

As week three came with no word from her, a sense of morbidity settled on him.

• • •

'That just about sums it up, I guess.'

Hubert Floyd's words brought to an end their final meeting and Rob stood to stretch his legs, longing to get home to his small apartment on Nineteenth Street where he could eat a good meal and try out the new whisky he had found.

'Drink? I think we deserve one, don't you?' said Floyd.

Rob ordered a Bourbon, drank it quickly and accepted a second.

'What'll you do now, Robert? Go to Savannah or back to Philadelphia?'

A good question. For weeks he had pondered the problem. It was no use expecting Jo-Ellen to come to Washington of her own accord. He would have to go and physically bring her there.

'I intend to join my dear wife and child. I aim to bring them here. Got my eye on a nice little house for us.'

Hubert nodded his head approvingly. 'Good, good. If you need any help with finding a suitable home, always ask me. I've got contacts, you know that. But of course, if you're requested to, and depending on your condition, you might rejoin your men?' It was more of a statement than a question.

'Naturally, Hubert. That's always been my intention, be sure of that.'

A lie. He had told several lately to keep Floyd sweet. Rob gave his most charming smile. 'Better get going. I'll be at my apartment a few days longer then I'll be heading south.'

Hubert held out his hand. 'All the very best, Robert. Give my regards to your wife. I look forward to your joining us soon as you get back.'

It was not until he was striding along Pennsylvania Avenue that Rob let out a huge sigh of relief and felt an enormous rush of elation. Business matters were finalised. His career was on its way. His foot was on the ladder and he would keep on climbing. And all thanks to Hubert Floyd.

• • •

Laura had arrived in Washington feeling irritable after all the delays. It had taken longer than she expected. Trains were unreliable, connections often didn't exist.

After sending a letter to her Papa, she began making enquiries about Rob. Apparently he stayed a while at the National then found himself a small apartment somewhere on Nineteenth Street. For several days thereafter, she wandered up and down hoping to see him. When she eventually saw a carriage draw up and Rob step from inside, she could barely contain herself. He looked wonderful. Dressed in a dark suit, and carrying a brief case, he looked every bit the successful businessman. Gone was the downcast and confused expression. His countenance was cheerful, positive, and she knew he had fully recovered.

She followed him into a nearby building, waited until she heard his door close, then went and knocked.

He opened it immediately.

He was shocked to see her. What the hell was she doing there? How on earth had she found him?

'Laura! How? When?'

God, what do you say at a time like this? For once he was lost for words.

'Hello Ray, or shall I call you Rob? Aren't you going to ask me in?'

He hesitated then stood aside to let her pass. She looked different, more mature, and certainly more beautiful. He closed the door.

'How did you find me?'

She smiled. 'It wasn't easy. I located Hubert Floyd's office here, made some enquiries and found out you had an apartment on Nineteenth. After that, all I had to do was wait.'

'I see.' He gave that grin she had missed so much. 'Clever girl. How long have you been in Washington?'

'Just over a week.'

He turned to the drinks cabinet. 'What can I get you?'

'Please, the usual.'

He fixed her a Martini dry and poured himself another Bourbon. 'Are you here alone?'

'Yes, Papa didn't like the idea, but I insisted.'

Rob gazed thoughtfully into his drink. 'You waited a long time to search for me.'

'Yes, I've been rather busy with other matters.'

'And Sebastian obviously doesn't know yet that you've found me?'

'No, only that I'm staying in Washington. I'll write to him tonight, I expect.'

'I see. Laura, I'm so very sorry, running out on you like that. I can imagine what you and Sebastian thought. Once I thought I'd found out about myself, I had to follow it up. It became the most important thing in my life.'

'I know, and I do understand, truly. However, it would have been nice to hear from you during all this time.' She paused. 'I take it you found your family?'

He nodded, looked at her grimly. 'Yes, my wife, my child and my best friend in Savannah, and my parents in Philadelphia.'

'My, you have struck lucky. I can understand why writing to us was the last thing on your mind.'

'No, Laura, it's just that...'

'Please, Rob, leave it.'

He gave a half smile. 'Well, now that you know, I guess we can still be friends?'

'Yes,' she replied, 'why not?'

'Good. Let's go out for dinner. I'm ravenous. Been stuck inside government offices far too long and now I want to celebrate.'

'Oh? What are you celebrating?'

He raised his glass. 'I'm about to enter the political arena. It'll be the Senate for me and then one day, who knows?'

'You'll run for president?'

'What do *you* think?'

She moved closer to him. 'Well, well, that certainly seems like something to drink to. Here, may I have another?'

He took her glass and refilled it.

'You know, Laura, just because I've found out who I am, doesn't mean that things between us have to change. You're a very beautiful young lady, you know that?'

She sipped her Martini, her eyes never leaving his. 'Except that I'm to share you now?'

He chuckled. 'Well, I can't marry you, of course, but as I say, nothing else need change.' His hand came up and caressed her shoulder. 'What do you say?'

She turned away from him. 'I say this, Rob. What you're suggesting disgusts me. In fact, you're the last person I want near me right now.'

His eyes narrowed. 'Is that so, little lady? Miss High and Mighty! What the hell are you doing here, then?'

Her gaze met his across the icy chasm. 'I'm here to tell you that our son, Charles, was born a few months ago. I'm also here to let you know that you'll never have contact with him. You'll not be welcome.'

He was dumbstruck. 'My son?'

'And please don't ask me how, or when!'

Silence. She guessed what he was thinking. 'An inconvenience, to say the least, isn't it? Not the sort of thing a future Senator would want in his background, is it?'

Quickly, he refilled his glass, spilling some as he did so.

'You've turned quite pale, Rob. Whatever will you do now?'

He smiled. 'What can I say – it's wonderful that we have a son, Laura. And I'm sorry you had to go through it alone.'

'No need. I managed.'

'Yes, of course. Look, I'll see to it the boy's taken care of financially. Only, we have to keep this just between ourselves. For several reasons, you understand.'

She gave a wry grin. 'I understand perfectly well.'

'Promise me, Laura. I'll see you both all right if you promise me never to tell anybody.' He was up against it, he knew that. Could he ever trust this woman? He doubted it.

'And what about my Papa?'

'You must tell him what I've said.' Sebastian was a real danger. Once he knew, all hell would be let loose. He would have to think of something.

'You'll see him all right, too? One of the richest men in America?'

Rob closed his eyes briefly. The bitch – she was laughing at him.

'I'll want to see my son. It's natural, Laura.'

'No, you'll never see him. I mean it. And as for not telling anybody, you think I'd agree to that? I'm going to tell everybody I come in contact with as soon as I leave here. Robert de la Rey fathered a boy and has denied both mother and child. That'll look good on your report, will it not? I wonder what the President will think when he hears. And Floyd? What'll he make of it? So much for your future as a Senator...'

She got no further. His hand came up and she was thrown backwards with the sheer force of it.

He moved quickly to her side. Blood oozed from the back of her head. He felt for a pulse. There was none. She was quite dead.

• • •

He waited for the dark of the moonless night, left by the back way, placed the body in the buggy and covered it with a blanket. She was unusually light to carry. He drove fast through the night to a woodland area several miles outside the city, and lifting her into his arms, laid her against a tree. Suppressing the noise as much as he could, he fired a bullet into her. With a spade he began to dig into earth that was soft after a heavy downpour. Forty minutes later he had dug a hole large enough for her to lie in. It was only when he was on his way home that his appetite, put on hold, returned. He called into a roadside Inn, ate a hearty meal and drank a bottle of wine.

When he arrived at his apartment, he entered by the back way and checked that everything was in order. There was no sign of blood or even that he'd had a visitor. Had he missed anything? Laura's enquiry at Floyd's office had obviously not been documented, since they would have told him. And no one would have seen her entering his apartment. Or would they? There was the janitor. He might have seen her, might even have spoken to her. Foolish of him not to have thought of that before.

With this in mind he hurriedly packed a suitcase. What he had to do was leave Washington immediately. The sooner he got to Savannah, the better. By the time he and Jo-Ellen returned, the whole thing might have died down. What he could not allow was time in Washington to elapse, time in which he and Laura could have met. For two hours he slept then, in the early hours, he prepared for the journey.

Leaving by the front lobby entrance, he went out of his way to speak to the janitor. 'Thought I'd go earlier than planned.' He grinned. 'Missing the wife and boy.'

'Sure thing, Mr de la Rey, sir. Don't you worry none. I'll take care of things this end. You'll be coming back here?'

'Soon as I can. And thanks for your help.' Rob passed him a huge tip and made a point of checking the time. 'Six fifteen. Nice and early. Hope I get good connections. By the way, were there any messages for me?'

'No, sir. It's been very quiet.'

'Only I was expecting a visitor last evening. A colleague from my office. He was due around eight. You were on duty?'

'Yes, sir, but not at that time.'

'Who stood in for you?'

'No one. We're short-staffed. I went off for forty minutes. Doubt if anyone came for you in that time, sir. And they would have waited, surely.'

'You're probably right.'

'Can I get you a car to take you to the station, sir?'

'No, I need the exercise. I'll walk.'

Almost giddy with relief, Rob stepped outside. The morning was fresh. A slight breeze accompanied him as he strode through the almost empty streets to the station. He was in luck. A train was due and would be stopping only once on its way to Georgia. It was then that he felt that enormous rush of adrenalin. Laura was dead and he was free.

• • •

Daniel rode flat out along the road that would take him to Johnston's command. The news was not good. Word had reached him that Sherman's armies had crossed the Chattahoochee River, a few miles from Atlanta, and Daniel at once realised the seriousness of the threat upon that city. Its capture would deprive the Confederacy of sorely needed arms and an important rail centre.

Greatly outnumbered by Sherman's troops, General Johnston had been forced to retreat and, tired as he felt, Daniel pushed his horse almost beyond limits in order to rejoin his men.

He arrived on July 17th, the day chosen by President Davis to replace Johnston with the more aggressive General Hood. Under this new command, Daniel took part in many strikes against the Union armies. These would have succeeded had the attacks been coordinated, but good fortune deserted them and although Hood turned his full attention on preparing Atlanta for siege, Sherman had already sent a strong force towards the city. The Confederates were far too late.

The siege continued for five weeks. August came and went, hot and sultry, and Daniel's men sweltered daily in the trenches and at night were invaded by another enemy, the mosquito. Food was in short supply, except for beef, such as it was. The poor animals that supplied it were little more than bare bones when they reached the army.

Sherman's troops devastated the countryside on their march to Atlanta, and the Confederates were unable to prevent it happening. On 2nd September, Sherman arrived in Atlanta and in his determination to see that the city would no longer serve as a major supply centre for the Confederacy, he razed it to the ground. When Daniel later learned that the ensuing intention was to march through the State to Savannah, he was struck with terror.

There was only one thing left for him to do. He had to make the journey south. Towards Highlands, towards Jo. Towards home.

∙ ∙ ∙

Rob watched the events of the war with increasing expectancy. Any day now, he kept telling himself as he watched the Savannah sunrise, the Confederacy would fall completely, the war would come to an end and he would return with his family to take up his career.

Daily he checked the press to see if there was any mention of a woman's body having been found on the outskirts of Washington. As time passed he worried less about this. They were at war. Women got killed. Another woman found in such circumstances would not raise any suspicions.

Weekly he kept in touch with Floyd by any means at his disposal. The Governor expected him to return to Washington soon and Rob had no intention of letting him down. Besides, he was getting impatient himself, wanting to settle matters concerning the new house.

His arrival in Savannah had not been met with enthusiasm. Jo-Ellen was dutiful, though distant. She watched the post with regularity and he never doubted that she awaited word from the Confederate officer. When he mentioned it, she refused to talk about it. Well, he was a patient man when needed. She would soon forget all about the fellow when she was living in Washington and what use would he be when the Confederacy lost the war? He grinned to himself. He also knew that the fellow had not written, nor had he been anywhere near Jefferson House. This he had learned from Louise.

Word finally arrived from Floyd reminding him of their previous conversation. 'Seems you'll be needed by General Sherman,' he wrote. Rob's initial reaction was reluctance. The last thing he wanted was to get shot again. Yet, a final involvement would certainly ease his present boredom and elevate his reputation. The war was all but over, the real danger had surely passed. Rejoining his men would be a mere formality and so he had a change of mind and sent word that he was fit and ready for action.

When he told Jo-Ellen, she hardly said a word.

• • •

Constance was worried sick. Jo-Ellen wasn't herself lately and she knew why and couldn't do anything about it. She could hardly interfere in the affairs of matrimony. Robert had come back full of his future plans about how he was going to one day run for the presidency, how he was going to have published the book he was working on about the war and his personal experience as a victim of it. Then there was the house he intended moving his family to. He was not aware of the effects this news had on his wife, and he seemed not to notice their son who was approaching three years. The boy needed his father now and Robert paid him so little attention.

As for Jo-Ellen's moods, she was either sharp in her speech or completely silent. Where had her fun-loving daughter gone to? Then there was Susanne's mother. Elizabeth Montgomery was living at Highlands on her own and Constance often had a mind to either go and join her there, or bring her to Jefferson House to live. Susanne was worried too, she could tell, having to divide her time between the Plantation, her baby, Jamie, and visiting her Mama almost daily.

Constance peered through the window along the track that wound its way into the distance. There had been no word from Ben and this told her that something was wrong. Last she had heard, he was at the Wilderness somewhere. That was some time ago.

Matters at the Plantation were worsening. Curtis and Earl worked their hardest but Constance could sense it was all shuddering to a halt. All their plans to grow food had gone up in a puff of smoke. The pending loss of war had changed people's attitudes, she thought, directing her attention to the spot on the horizon. As soon as it was all over, she guessed the black labour would pack up and go.

The spot had moved. She blinked. 'God save us,' she muttered. 'The Yankees are here!'

Automatically she moved to one side out of view. Once she fathomed out who it was, she'd decide whether to fetch the gun. The spot was getting closer, and now it was either limping or running. Certainly it was heading towards the house.

'Jo-Ellen, are you there?' she called, feeling the effects of fear in her stomach.

'Yes, Mama, I'm right here.'

She beckoned. 'Come quickly. There's someone coming. Best get the gun in case it's one of Sherman's raiders.'

Jo-Ellen looked along the track. 'Yes, it's a man. Probably hunting around for food and drink. I'll deal with it. You stay right here.'

Taking the gun with her, she pulled open the door and waited.

'Be careful!'

'Yes, Mama, don't worry.'

The hand she was holding the gun in shook and she steadied it with the other. Let the man get closer and she would caution him. If he didn't stop, she would shoot.

Constance held her breath as the seconds ticked by, and watched her daughter advance a few steps holding the gun out before her.

'Mama, you know who that looks like?'

Constance had no idea and no interest other than hoping it was not the enemy. What would they do? He would certainly have a gun. What if he shot first?

'Yes it is! It's Ben! Go get Susanne!'

Constance found herself running through the house in search of her daughter-in-law. Looking back, she could see Jo-Ellen running along the track. The figure had stopped and then they were locked in each other's arms. By the time she and Susanne got there, the pair of them were crying.

That evening was the happiest they had known for some months. Jo-Ellen and Susanne were beside themselves with joy. Ben was home at long last. What a difference, thought Constance, between the arrival of Robert and the arrival of Ben. It was very noticeable and she watched with concern Robert's reaction to it.

For that one evening there was no mention of the war. Everything was placed on hold while they scraped together whatever food and drink they could and gave Ben a welcome home party.

Constance watched her son cuddle first Susanne then Jamie, and gaze on them as though they were miracles. And they were, she thought, unable to keep the tears from her eyes. It was only Ben's appearance that gave cause for concern and this had brought a reaction from Susanne.

'Oh, my, he's so thin and, and...'

'And what, Mrs Jefferson?' Ben came up behind her.

'And so very, very wonderful!' she cried, as he wrapped her in his arms.

Robert seemed delighted to see his old friend. 'It's great to see you,' Constance heard him say, as he tucked an arm around Ben's shoulders. Yet she hadn't missed his expression as the others fussed over Ben. Especially Jo-Ellen, whose eyes constantly filled with tears of joy that her brother was back. There had been no such happening on Robert's return from Washington. In fact, Jo-Ellen had withdrawn into that silent world of hers.

Certainly, Constance had considerable cause to worry.

Chapter Seventeen

The letter arrived just as Rob was leaving the house. There was no doubt in his mind who had written it and, pushing it into his pocket, he strode out to the buggy, his attention on the upstairs window where he could see Constance moving to and fro.

Jo-Ellen closed the front door behind her and hurried to join him.

'Mama would have come along with us had you not insisted on going so early,' she said, settling down beside him.

Without a word, he motioned the horse forward and turned along the track towards town.

'Mama said she saw the postman call by.'

Still Rob said nothing and urged the beast into a gallop.

'Well, who was the letter for?' She turned to him. 'Was there a letter? Mama thought she saw one in his hand.'

'Yes, there was a letter.' He pulled the envelope from his pocket. 'It's for you.'

'Well, now, you *were* going to give me this, weren't you?'

'It's from that Confederate. I was in two minds, I can tell you.'

She read the words slowly. There was little about the war, nothing about where he was. His words were warm and she could sense his feeling of isolation. His final words heartened her. He missed talking to her, wished he was back in Savannah, his home. All in all, the letter was guarded. She tucked it back in the envelope.

'Well?'

She glanced at Rob's tight expression. 'Well what?'

He halted the buggy. 'Am I going to see it?'

'No, it's addressed to me.'

He snatched it from her and began to read. 'Hm - a nice cosy letter.' He glanced at the front of the envelope and chuckled. 'Atlanta. That'll be the last you see of him, I suspect. Sherman's boys'll sort out the remaining Confeds, if they haven't already done so. This letter's almost three weeks old!'

His look of triumph drove a final wedge between them. As he urged the horse forward again, she said, 'Stop the buggy, Rob. I want to get off.'

'What?'

'I'm not coming into town. I'll go another time – with Mama.'

'Sure thing. I can't stand a sulking woman.'

She alighted and snatched at her bag. 'I'm not sulking, Rob, but I see no reason to put up with your disgusting comments any longer. And I'll not be going to Washington with you. I'm staying here with my family!'

He leaned back and ran a hand through his hair. 'Right, I agree. It suits me, actually. I'd thought to have a good wife would be an asset, but you? You're more of an obstacle. You stay here in the south, Jo, and see how it'll be.'

'Is that all I am to you? An asset? Someone to show around to enhance your career?'

'Perhaps you'll see what you're giving up when I'm on my way to the White House and Alexander and I are living in luxury.'

Her composure snapped. 'Now, wait a minute! Alexander's staying right here with me where he belongs! You'll have no right to him!'

'No right? He's my son. When folk hear that you've been carrying on with a Reb behind my back, who will they sympathise with? Me, not you. And I think the law will side with me as to where Alexander will be happiest.'

Before she could reply, he took off and left her alone in the middle of nowhere. Hitching her skirts, she began the long walk back, the dust flying into her eyes, her thoughts racing. Tears of anger rolled down her cheeks. She was caught in a situation she could see no solution to. If Rob took Alexander away, she would be powerless. Not even Daniel could help her with this one.

An hour later she strode into the drawing room and threw herself into a comfortable chair. Constance set aside her book.

'My, you look terrible. What happened? Why aren't you with Rob?'

After explaining, Jo-Ellen added, 'Mama, we've got to send

Alexander away. Rob must not take him!'

'Away? Where? How?'

Jo-Ellen had by now come up with an idea. 'You remember that doctor you and Papa used to visit? The one in Charleston?'

'Doctor Wellesley? What about him?'

'Is he still there?'

'Who knows? That was years ago.'

'Could you find out?'

Constance shrugged. 'I've no idea. He and his wife settled there in the forties. We've heard from them from time to time, the last time being about three years ago. Why?'

'Mama, find out and then go visit him. Take Alexander with you. Once there, you can explain everything and ask if he and his wife will look after Alexander for a while.'

'I can't just turn up and ask them that.'

'Please, Mama. It's our only chance. Then as soon as Rob has left Savannah, I'll go and fetch him.'

Constance moved to the window, her thoughts in turmoil.

'All right,' she said at last. 'I'll do it, but on one condition.'

'Yes, anything!'

'That the Wellesleys let me stay with Alexander. I simply couldn't leave the boy behind.'

Jo-Ellen prayed the conversation would go that way. That night she lay in her bed turning over everything in her mind. A noise outside told her that Rob had returned. She heard him go up the stairs and prepare for bed. Soon, she told herself, he would have to leave. Floyd was expecting him. Tomorrow she would urge Constance to contact Doctor Wellesley and as soon as they knew he was in Charleston, then they would set their plan in action. She would not contemplate the Wellesleys not being there. They had to be there.

● ● ●

'I'll pay any man any price if he finds her and brings her back to me!' Sebastian thumped his fist hard on the table. 'You hear me, Jasper?'

Jasper Lee sprang to attention. 'I hear you, Sebastian, and I'll do anything in my power to find Laura, you can depend on it.'

'Of course, the girl might be having the time of her life, but why hasn't she written? She knows I'd worry. And she'd not stay away longer than necessary from her son. That I do know!'

Jasper did not reply. The whole thing was a mystery to him. Had Laura got caught up in the war? Hardly. Not where she was. Had she run into Marilyn or that blackguard, Vince? Probably not, and why would they want to hurt her or even delay her? Didn't make sense. What he didn't voice was his secret dread – that Laura had found Robert de la Rey and had taken up with him again. But surely, if the rumours were true that de la Rey had recovered his memory and returned to his family, the fellow would want Laura out of his life as quickly as possible, wouldn't he? Jasper sighed. This one was beyond him.

Sebastian lit a pipe. He had given up cigars on his doctor's orders, along with his heavy daytime drinking. He glanced at his time piece. Almost six o'clock. That counted as evening, surely. Going to the drinks cabinet, he threw some ice into a long glass and had his first whisky. It was smooth and soothing.

'Help yourself, Jasper.' Through the window he watched the sun sink lower towards the horizon. 'You know, Laura and I used to stand here every evening and watch that miracle out there but it doesn't hold the same magic now.' He turned to watch Jasper fill his glass with Bourbon. 'I miss her, Jasper. I miss her terribly. I might not have shown it much but I do love my daughter. In fact, I've come to feel very proud of her and I want nothing more than to have her back here with me. Should never have let her go off on her own like that.'

Jasper nodded patiently. Here goes, he thought. Time he said something constructive.

'I was thinking, you don't imagine she caught up with de la Rey and they got back together?'

'You think I haven't thought of that one? The answer is no, because she was adamant that it was over between them and that de la Rey would not have access to Charles. She wouldn't go back on that, not after all she's been through.'

Jasper was silent. Sebastian of all people surely knew that women changed their minds.

'Go on, I can see you're bursting to speak. Say what's on your mind, for God's sake!'

Jasper blinked. 'You sure?'

Sebastian merely glared at him.

'Right – she might have had an accident. It could go unreported nowadays.' He waited. Sebastian said nothing. 'Then again, her letters to you might have gone astray.' Again he paused. Still nothing. 'If she met up with de la Rey, he might be stopping her from returning.'

Sebastian's head came up. 'How?'

'Well, what do we know about him?'

Sebastian's eyes widened. 'You mean – no, I doubt, it Jasper. You've seen the papers. He's well thought of. Floyd has him earmarked for a post in the Senate. The fellow's not going to put a foot wrong, is he?'

Jasper poured another Bourbon. 'Things happen, things beyond our control.' He swallowed the contents of his glass and collected his coat. 'Try not to worry, old friend. I'll be in touch if I hear anything.' He grinned. "I'll be in touch even if I don't.'

Sebastian waited until the door had closed then decided to send another wire to Governor Floyd. This time he would enquire directly about de la Rey.

• • •

It was some time before Daniel could leave his command. In fact, he'd begun to wonder as October faded away and November arrived with its undecided climate, whether he would be able to go at all. Hood had decided to shift the army to the south-west in an effort to outflank Sherman, and this effort had met with miserable failure and inevitable delay for Daniel, exacerbated by the 62,000 strong Union Army's march to the sea.

On their way, they destroyed stores or provisions, standing crops and cattle, cotton gins and mills, railways and bridges. Georgia folk were stripped of all their possessions and the State was reeling. Savannah was next in line for Sherman's savagery and as Daniel finally made his way there, he could feel the depression that had settled everywhere. He rode carefully, always aware of the hidden dangers surrounding him. There was a sense of unreality about the place. Fields were empty, towns were quiet, depressed. Fresh graves lay around. He put up at the only Inn he could find, and set out refreshed the following day, putting behind him as many miles as he could until he reached the more familiar sights of the Savannah countryside.

Twelve hours later he reined in and was looking down on Highlands.

• • •

'I tell you, Jo-Ellen, I don't like it, I don't like it at all!' Ben thrust his hands deep into his pockets. 'What the hell will Mama do if Sherman's men arrive there?'

She hadn't considered that. 'All I want is to keep Alexander out of Rob's reach. It'll only be for a short while.'

'Huh! Really? I know about your short whiles. Let me see, the last one lasted about six months, didn't it? This time it could be several weeks, especially if Mama gets stranded there. Christ – it could be dangerous, Jo-Ellen!'

She sighed. Ben was right. She hadn't thought it through at all. 'What alternative have I? If Alexander goes to Washington I'll probably lose him forever!'

He felt great sympathy for his sister, despite everything. Truth was, he felt scared for his family. With them all under one roof, he had some control, with them scattered elsewhere, he had none.

'What in hell's name is Rob up to? He's behaving like a lunatic or something. When's he due to leave for Washington?'

'End of this week. He's all packed up to go. The house isn't quite ready but he has an apartment in Washington for the time being.'

'And the Wellesleys, have they agreed?'

'Yes, we heard yesterday. Please, Ben, this is very confidential. Rob must never know.'

He nodded, impatient at her even saying the words. Did she think he would say something and jeopardise his nephew's future? 'Don't you worry about me,' he said.

She smiled. 'You're looking much better. Putting on some weight, at last.'

'Think so? I sure feel better.' He took hold of her hand. 'Come on, let's go see if Mama needs our help.'

• • •

While Rob was away shopping for some last minute things, Constance and Alexander bade Jo-Ellen, Ben, and Susanne a tearful farewell at the station. They had chosen a good time to leave and by the time Jo-Ellen got back to the house, she felt a sense of relief she had not felt for so long.

Two hours later, Rob drew up outside. She waited in the drawing room for him and when he entered he went first to pour a drink then mumbled a greeting.

'Had a good day in town?' she asked.

'Not bad.'

'Dinner's in an hour or so.'

'Good. I'm hungry.'

He placed his drink down and went into the hall. She heard him go upstairs, heard Alexander's door open and close. Seconds later he was back.

'Where's Alexander? He's not in his room.'

'I was about to tell you. He's away.'

His eyes narrowed. 'Away? Where?'

'I sent him on a short break away from here.' She smiled. 'I thought he should go. It might not be safe in Savannah much longer.'

'What the hell do you think you're up to?' he snapped. 'Not safe? Of course it's bloody well not safe. Not here, not anywhere. There isn't a place within five hundred miles of here that's safe!' He grabbed her arm and held it firmly. 'You didn't ask me, you didn't tell me first!'

'No, there was no time. Mama thought it better to go immediately.'

'Mama! She's in on this, too?' He let go of her. 'Why the hell am I even asking. Of course she is. Jo – I want to know where my son is.'

'He's in a safe place. That's all I can tell you.'

'And you think this will stop me from taking him to Washington?'

She did not reply.

'I'll find him, I'll track him down. He won't remain forever where he is and as soon as he gets back, I'll send for him. You'll not have him, Jo!'

She felt faint with fear. Rob took the stairs two at a time and she could hear him moving about overhead. He was more angry than she had ever seen him. There was no use in her arguing any longer. All she wanted was for him to leave.

She was about to get her wish. When he came down he was carrying a large bag. 'I'm leaving today, now, tonight. There's a late train through to Washington.' He looked at her long and hard. 'Don't bother to see me out.'

She heard the buggy take off, heard his last command rent the air as the whip lashed against the horse's rump. Then the silence. Jo-Ellen realised that she was shaking. She was also alone, except for Louise. Quickly she pulled the drapes, wishing her Mama were there. Had she done the right thing? Would they be safe in Charleston?

At that very moment, Yankee soldiers began pouring over the Savannah countryside.

• • •

He was home and Daniel felt a surge of great relief. There was no cannon fire here, no horrors of war, only the foliage that had been brilliantly green that summer, some still lingering in places, and on the soft breeze as he picked his way towards Highlands, the aroma of wood fire and fresh earth.

The house, set against a mauve and red sky, was elegant and worthy of the pride he felt. As he approached, determined to drink in as much of the surroundings as possible, a rider cantered from the direction of the house and Daniel reined in behind a tree. For several seconds he watched, his heart thumping in his chest.

'Jo!'

She stopped. Impulsively, he rode forward and reined in beside her and she slid from the saddle into his waiting arms.

'Daniel.'

He felt her small body quiver against his. He smoothed her hair, kissed her forehead, feathered tiny kisses down her cheeks, his lips finding hers in a moment so passionate, he felt dizzy with desire and longing. If this was a dream, then it was a beautiful dream and one he did not wish to wake from.

'Daniel, I can hardly believe it. It is you, isn't it?'

'It's me, Jo, and I thought you were an illusion.'

'No, no illusion. Are you home for long?'

'I'm not sure. I came because of the news about Sherman's men.'

Her eyes widened. 'What about them? Are they here?'

'Don't be alarmed. Yes, they're in Savannah by now.' His arms enfolded her again. 'And what may I ask are you doing riding out alone?'

She shuddered at the thought. Yankees on Savannah soil and she was taking the equivalent of an evening stroll!

'I went to see Elizabeth Montgomery. She's all alone since Mama left for Charleston. Susanne visits but not for long.'

'Charleston!'

He listened as she explained that Rob had gone to Washington for good and that he had tried to take Alexander with him. None of this surprised Daniel. Rob was simply living up to his expectations. He remained silent, lest he should say something he ought not.

'You are definitely not going to join him?' He tipped her chin so that her eyes met his.

'No, it's over. He's not the man he was. He's changed so much, he can be so...' She stopped, about to say that the love they once had was destroyed. The admission startled her. But it was useless to lie to herself any longer. What she'd had with Rob was entered into history.

Daniel took her hand in his. 'Come on, we can't stay here. It isn't safe.'

Leading the horses, they walked down the hill and Jo-Ellen automatically followed him in to Highlands.

● ● ●

Hubert Floyd felt impatient. Sebastian Hilton might be a force amongst business colleagues and social circles but he had little pull where Floyd was concerned. Twice Hilton had called, twice he had been fobbed off by the secretary. Now he was outside again and Hubert was in a hurry to get to the President to discuss Sherman's final thrust into Savannah. Seemed the only way to get rid of the fellow once and for all was to see him and be as brief as possible.

As Sebastian was shown in, Hubert expressed a welcome smile.

'Glad to meet you at last, Mr Hilton. So sorry I wasn't available before.'

Sebastian grunted something beneath his breath. He had tried for weeks for an audience with this man. He accepted a small whisky.

'So, tell me what it is you want of me, Mr Hilton.'

Finding himself centre stage all of a sudden, words failed him. 'Hard to explain, Mr Floyd, hard to explain. Bear with me a while.'

Hubert suppressed a sigh. Something told him he was going to be delayed.

'I'm here about Robert de la Rey – and my daughter. Seems de la Rey was in Washington a while aback and my daughter went searching for him.' Sebastian hesitated. How much could he tell this man? Would Laura want the world to know about the baby?

Hubert waited.

'Truth is, my daughter's missing. Been missing now for weeks. She's not written, I haven't heard a thing and I'm worried, Mr Floyd. I thought as you know de la Rey, you might know where I can find him.'

It had all come out in a rush. Hubert raised surprised brows but said nothing. When he did speak, he said, 'I'm afraid I can't help you, Mr Hilton, much as I'd like to. You see, Robert de la Rey is on government staff now and we are not at liberty to discuss personal matters. Now, if you'll excuse me...'

'No, you don't! I realise you're busy, Governor, but this matter is urgent.' Sebastian paused. How could he put this? 'I have reason to believe that my daughter's life is in danger.'

Hubert's head came up sharply. 'Have you, indeed! What evidence is there of that? There's a war on, Mr Hilton, people might conceivably go missing.' He shook his head. 'The age we live in.'

'I also think that de la Rey has something to do with it.'

Hubert chuckled. 'Been philandering, has he? Well, he's a mighty handsome fellow – women adore him. However, this isn't government business...'

'Yes it is.' Sebastian was losing patience. 'De la Rey and my daughter were going to marry. She's had his child. I'm afraid that if she confronts him with this, he might harm her.'

Hubert drew himself up. 'I think you should be guarded about what you say, Mr Hilton. You're levelling accusations against a war hero, a young man who's gone through torment, but then you know that. I'm sorry to hear about your daughter, but I think you're wrong.

Robert's a fine man, he wouldn't harm a woman, least of all one he probably has feelings for.' He gave a cynical grin. 'We must not forget the wife. Robert won't want this to get out, now, will he?'

Sebastian made to reply but Hubert continued, 'He's been two people because of his lost memory. Two lives. Both included fine women – his wife and your daughter. It's obvious one has to be sacrificed for the other. I would appreciate it, sir, if you would forget the entire matter and allow Robert his future free from all this nonsense.'

Sebastian took a deep, steadying breath. He had hit a man for much less than that in the past. 'My concern is for my missing daughter. I want to know if she has been here asking for him, or if she's contacted your office at all. That had been her intention and I cannot envisage any reason why she might not have arrived in Washington.'

Hubert pressed a buzzer on his desk. The door opened.

'Has a young lady been here in the past few weeks asking for Mr de la Rey?'

The secretary thought for a moment. 'There was somebody, sir. She came asking for an address. Of course, I didn't give it.'

Hubert felt himself go pale. 'What in hell's name did you tell her?'

'I felt sorry for her. She looked worn out, apparently had trouble getting here.'

Sebastian stepped forward. 'Where did she go? Tell me!'

With a cautious look in Hubert's direction, the secretary said, 'I told her that Mr de la Rey lived in the vicinity of Nineteenth Street. She was satisfied with that and left.'

'Did you log this visit?'

'No, sir.'

Hubert glared at him.

'Was she a beautiful young woman with auburn hair?' Sebastian asked.

The secretary smiled. 'Yes, sir. I'd not forget that.'

Hubert gave a light cough. 'Thank you, I'll talk to you later.'

'I knew it!' cried Sebastian as soon as the door closed. 'She found that bastard. Something's happened, Mr Floyd, I know it.'

'Now, don't go jumping to conclusions. She might have come in contact with the Rebs, or she might have had an accident. Robert probably doesn't know anything about her.'

Sebastian shook his head. 'No- I'm certain of it. I'll not stop until I find out the truth. I've to return to Hagerstown soon. I can't leave Charles too long.' He paused. 'Charles, that's Laura's baby. Got large green eyes just like his papa.' With a satisfied grin, Sebastian held open the door. 'You've not heard the last of me, Mr Floyd, not by a long way!'

Hubert hurried to his side and pushed the door to. 'Mr Hilton, let's not be too hasty here. I can understand your concern and suspicions but shouldn't you wait until you know for certain?'

'Worried about your new boy? The so-called war-hero? He got shot – so what? Thousands have – they're not heroes, just unfortunate souls doing a job for their country. All right, Mr Floyd, I'll not let the press know – yet. But I will in time, be sure of that. If I find out he's had anything to do with Laura's disappearance, I'll personally see to it he gets nowhere in your government, or anywhere else. I'll ruin him!' The door slammed behind him.

Hubert stared at the space Sebastian had occupied. Goddamn Hilton. How was he, Hubert, to explain all this to the President, after all the glowing accounts of Robert's character? Time and money and not least, hope, had been invested in the young man who Hubert hoped would become a symbol of the future of the Union.

He glanced at his time piece. As usual, he was late for the President.

Chapter Eighteen

A harsh winter settled quite suddenly in Savannah. Under an icy pale sky, frantic winds surrounded the house and Jo-Ellen worked hard to keep the rooms warm.

Food had become a major problem. There was barely enough on the table each day as supplies were cut to a minimum because no railroad could bring them through. The little they had been able to grow for themselves had dwindled almost to nothing.

She tried not to show how it worried her. Something had always turned up in the past, hadn't it? Besides, she reasoned, Daniel was back and she had so much to be grateful for. She had also made the journey to Charleston to bring back her son and Constance. The Wellesleys had been delighted to see her again, remembering her only as a child, and Jo-Ellen had remained there overnight so that she could spend some time with them.

As Christmas approached she told herself that as long as they were all together, nothing else mattered. Neighbours were always so kind at this time, and as yet there had never been a year when the Christmas dinner table was bare, yet this year may well be different. Even people with money found food hard to come by.

Curtis and Earl also helped. Curtis often went out looking for rabbits and Earl knew somebody in town who seemed to have a goodly supply of milk and nuts. They had little money, however, and gradually Jo-Ellen saw that these kind folk were not charging their usual and pledged to herself that one day she would go in person and repay everything she owed.

Most days she either went to visit Highlands or Daniel came to see her. He never once wore his uniform and she secretly prayed he had hung it up for good. He spoke little of the war, but she sensed his growing concern at the hardships that had come upon them of late.

She heard several reports about what had happened in Atlanta, how all the residents were moved out by Sherman's men so that they could take over the houses and then when they finally left, how Sherman had ordered the town torched. By the time the Confederates got there to reclaim it, there was little left to reclaim. Many people had died either from shock, or illness, or exposure. Jo-Ellen dreaded that Savannah might suffer the same fate, and daily reminded herself to put the thought from her mind and pray they would all be safe. Meanwhile, that November, Lincoln was re-elected to office, with Andrew Johnson as his vice-president. The Union was riding high.

One thing was certain. She was not going to leave Jefferson House. Let the Yankees come. She'd get all her family out and then stay right there and defend her home.

In the weeks that passed since Rob left, she heard nothing from him and it surprised her that she was not too bothered. Feathering his nest, probably, she thought, cow-towing to Governor Floyd or perhaps even to Lincoln.

There were also times when she felt a tremendous sadness for her marriage that had failed miserably despite all her efforts. Then there was Daniel. What of the future with him, for not so long ago she had agreed to marry him. Neither had spoken of it since his return. It seemed that the war had robbed people not only of their past by its destruction of livelihood, but also of the present and future, for who in the south could consider either logically? It was insane to contemplate beyond the hour.

She had so much with Daniel, she knew, and even though he was only next door she missed him when he was not there with her. With him she enjoyed that greatest of virtues, the shared laughter. They delighted in each other's comments and wit and it was this that helped ease the burden of the war and make their relationship, such as it was, so rounded.

That December morning, after settling Alexander, she hurried downstairs to find Daniel waiting for her.

'Hello – I wasn't expecting you,' she said, and enjoyed his look of approval as she approached.

'I have a confession.'

'And what is that?'

'I'm unable to get you off my mind. I wake up and there you are.

I prepare for the day and you're still there and all through my work you're sitting beside me. When I was in battle it was a Godsend, but now? Jo- do you think I'm sickening for something?'

She laughed at this and gazed into his steady blue eyes. As she put out a hand to touch his hair she felt in that moment so much love, words were inadequate. It had been said that one should control one's passions but that lesson was lost on her as she allowed him to kiss her and the kiss leaving him in no doubt as to how she felt.

'I want to stay here and make love to you,' he whispered, and she felt the tears prick at the back of her eyelids, for that was as far as they ever got, both always remembering she was still a married woman.

'Daniel, how long must we put our love on hold?'

He did not reply.

'Suppose I never get free of Rob? Suppose he never lets me go? What will happen to us?'

He made to speak but she went on, 'Then there's the war. Yankees are just down the road. Does either of us know that we even have a future?'

She felt his grip tighten. 'You present a very compelling case, my love,' he said close to her ear.

They climbed the stairs and entered her room. She pulled the drapes and turned to him. 'We're alone, except for my sleeping son. Mama's in town with Louise. Susanne is visiting Highlands. And I love you.'

His mouth bore down on hers, his arms wrapped around her and he swept her beneath him.

• • •

Jo-Ellen heard the noise upon waking. Daniel had long gone, and the book she had meant to read slipped to the floor. She picked it up and straightened her gown.

'Mama, is that you?'

The noise that came from the back of the house sounded like a door slamming. With pounding heart she edged from the room and looked through the cavernous hall to where the back door swung to and fro in the wind. Silly, she thought, Louise probably left the door unlocked. I'll have to talk to her about that. She shook her head at the manner in which she and others behaved at the slightest sound these days.

As she turned, a figure stepped out in front of her. Tobacco stained teeth leered at her and she felt the blood drain from her face.

'Right, ma'am, don't move till I tells you.'

Jo-Ellen stared at the gun pointing at her chest. Move? She wished she could. 'Who are you?' Silly question. He was a Yankee soldier and not a very respectable one at that. Hat tilted at an angle, uniform mud-spattered and torn, and he smelt bad.

'Never mind that. Where's the food and I want a Bourbon, right now!'

'Food is something we don't have. I might have Bourbon, though.' She motioned with her head and he followed her into the kitchen. There she found some old bread and the little meat they had.

'The Bourbon, ma'am. And bring me the bottle.' He grinned. 'You weren't considering bringing me a glass, were you?'

She did as he asked and he tossed the contents of the bottle down his throat. Oh, God, what if he gets so drunk he shoots me? she thought. She had heard what some desperate soldiers did when they drank.

'My, you're a pretty little thing. You here all alone?'

'No, of course not.'

'I beg to differ. I saw the other lady take off down the track a while back and there ain't been a soul coming or going since.'

She tensed. So he hadn't seen Daniel leave.

He tipped the bottle again. 'Mighty fine Bourbon, since we're all alone why not join me?' His hand snaked out and caught her in a vice-like grip. 'I ain't had a woman in an age.'

'Let go of me, you Yankee bastard!'

The smile left his face. He spat on the floor beside her. 'Now, I ain't about to take that from no Reb, not even a female one. What I will take, though, is this.' His hand grabbed the front of her bodice and she felt her gown fall away. His eyes roamed over her. 'That's better. Nice, very nice.' His hand felt her bosoms. 'I advise you not to fight, ma'am, since I'm the one with the gun.'

'Touch me again and I'll scream There are people around, believe me!' she cried as he pressed her against the wall. His foul breath made her nauseous.

'Try it. I'll use the gun and you'll never know if anyone heard you. Be a pity, eh? But I don't want to kill you yet, not before you put that lovely body my way.'

His hands sought her breast and then she felt his hand between her legs. She tried in vain to push him away and any sound she wanted to make was prevented by his mouth over hers. His strength amazed her. She wriggled and tried to bite, but he merely laughed.

The shot, loud and accurate, got him in the back of the head. Jo-Ellen felt him tense, release her and fall backward. Blood spattered over her face. She gave a sharp scream. Daniel ran to her.

'My darling, are you all right? Did he hurt you? Thank God I came back.'

She clung to him, hardly able to breathe, her body shaking uncontrollably. Seconds later they heard someone shouting. Ben reined in and then he was running, wildly calling her name.

'I was praying you were here, Daniel, too. Get Alexander and leave immediately. The Yankees are here. Thousands of them!' He stopped when he saw the dead soldier. 'What the hell happened?'

'It's all right, Ben, we had to kill him. As you say, they've finally come. We'd best hide the body…'

'No time for that now.' He grabbed her hand. 'Come on, we must hurry!'

She pulled away from him. 'No – I'll not leave the house.'

They stared at her. 'What? There's no time for heroics now, Jo-Ellen. Didn't you hear me? They're here and killing anyone who stands in their way.'

'I'll not leave the house to that load of savages. They'll not burn my house!'

She was swept off her feet into the strong grip of Daniel's arms and draped over his shoulder. 'Ben – go get Alexander, fast as you can,' he ordered.

'Put me down – Daniel, let go of me! If you don't let me go, I'll, I'll…'

'You'll what? Live longer? Not die at the hands of a hoard of Yankees? You drive a hard bargain, darling.'

She stopped struggling. Behind her came Ben with Alexander wrapped in a blanket. They climbed into a buggy and took off.

'Where are we going?' she asked, as trees and countryside

whipped past at a speed she was unused to.

'We'll make for the old Church. Most folk will have gone there. It's probably the houses the Yankees want, not us, and certainly not the Church!'

Daniel's voice became lost on the wind. The Church lay less than a mile away.

Jo-Ellen imagined the Rev. Charles Biddell scurrying about as the local inhabitants descended upon him. As they went, Yankee soldiers came into view. Jo-Ellen saw them clearly at the top of the rise near Highlands before they were obliterated by a bend in the road.

'Here we are.'

'Is Mama safe? Where is she and Susanne? Oh – and Jamie!' Jo-Ellen rushed about rounding up her family.

Ben took her hand in his. 'They're all fine. I saw to Mama earlier.'

Susanne ran to him. 'My Mama – where is she? I can't find her.'

'Isn't she here with you?'

'No – I thought – Oh, Daniel, I thought she was with you!'

He shook his head. 'I went over to see Jo-Ellen, then we came straight here.' He turned to Jo-Ellen. 'Those Yankees, Jo, you definitely saw them near Highlands?'

'Why, yes. Might they go to the house?'

He did not reply. His eyes scanned the horizon. 'What in hell's name is that?'

'It looks like fire. It's coming from that direction. If Mama's there, she'll be so frightened.'

Daniel leapt into the buggy.

'Wait, I'm coming, too!'

'Me, too,' Ben said. 'Come on, let's go!'

The pungency of smoke became intense as they neared Highlands. Flames shot into the air. Jo-Ellen glanced at Daniel's face set in a determined pattern, his shoulders hunched. Sweat poured down his face.

It occurred to her that she had not seen Curtis at the Church and wondered if he had found some means of escape. Perhaps he had saved himself and Elizabeth and managed to get away. She prayed he had.

'It's the only house they've fired!' shouted Daniel as they reined in. 'Jo, you keep well back. You can help with the water. I'll go in and look for Mrs Montgomery.' He quickly sized up the task before him. The flames had gathered momentum. Putting something over his head, he ran into the house, up the stairs and into the top bedroom. The smoke was thick, he could hardly see.

He called her name several times. No sound came and he feared the worse. Pushing open her door, he was forced back by the heat. In he went, hardly able to breathe. He saw her then, lying at the foot of the bed. He covered her face, and hurried her down the stairs to safety.

He laid her down and felt her pulse. She looked so still, so lifeless. He thought he saw movement and when her eyelids flickered open, relief soared through him. A slight smile played at the corners of her mouth when she saw him.

'Mrs Montgomery, Elizabeth, ma'am,' he said. 'I think you're going to make it.'

• • •

'It's Curtis - I've found him!' Ben advanced on them out of the smoke. 'Susanne's going to be devastated. Shot through the head. I imagine he stayed put to try and defend Highlands.'

Jo-Ellen buried her face in her hands. 'And where's Earl? I haven't seen him or Jacob!'

'Jacob's at the Church. I'm not sure about Earl.'

'Oh, they're going to kill us all. They're going to destroy Savannah. What can we do – what can *I* do?'

Daniel held her, stroked her hair, felt her body tremble against his. He had seen to Mrs Montgomery, taken her to safety, he had also watched his house burn. He was past knowing the answer to any questions. Savannah would never hold up – there were so few men left there to fight.

'We'll stay and fight,' he found himself saying and her head came up, and there was hope in her eyes.

Between them they managed to douse until the fire at the back of the house was under control. Daniel concentrated on the front area. Jo-Ellen paused only to wipe her face with the back of her hand. That was when she saw them – three Yankees approaching.

'Ben!'

He grabbed her and they ducked out of sight. 'We can't stay here, they'll see us,' he whispered. Behind were some thick bushes and they edged into them. Jo-Ellen was curious. Daniel had said the Yankees wanted the houses for themselves, so why set Highlands alight? From what she could tell, no other building around there had been torched. She listened to the Yankees talk amongst themselves, as they came to stand about a hundred yards away.

'Ben, did you hear that?'

'No – what?'

'That voice...'

She suddenly stood up in full view of the men. Ben made to grab at her hand to stop her, but was unable to. She was walking away from him. As she neared the men, one of them said, 'Hey – lookee here, we got ourselves a perty little thing.'

Their leader turned to face her. A grin curled the corners of his mouth.

'Hello, Jo.'

It was as she thought. 'Rob!'

● ● ●

'I've come back, Jo. Had orders to and it suits me. I've come for Alexander, and this time I'll not leave without him.'

Shock at seeing him struck her motionless for the moment. 'He's not here – I told you.'

'Ha! Good try, but I don't believe you.'

Anger wrenched through her. 'Rob, you almost killed Susanne's mother...'

'Yes, I was sorry about that but it couldn't be helped. Went right out of my head that she lives at Highlands still.'

'How can you? How can you turn against us all?'

He shrugged. 'Had to, dearest. You see, The Union means much more to me, as the south does to you.'

'And Curtis – did you kill him?'

'Poor Curtis. He tried to stop me from firing Highlands. I had to, Jo.'

He pulled a gun and held it on her. 'Now, stand back while we make our way out of here. Nothing will happen to you, I promise.'

A footfall had him spinning round, gun ready to fire.

'Stop right there, Reb, place your hands where I can see them!'

Daniel raised his arms, glancing at Jo-Ellen, and the two soldiers who had their guns on him.

'Had an idea it might be you, de la Rey. Taken up murder and arson now, have you?'

Rob motioned with the gun. 'Where have you taken my boy?'

'Somewhere you can't touch him.'

'We'll see about that. Think you can take over my family, do you, Reb? Think I'd let my boy be brought up by a dirty Confederate...'

Ben leapt from the bushes, bullets flying, at the same time that Daniel dived at Rob. Both soldiers went down. Rob fired, but the bullet missed. He and Daniel wrestled each other to the ground, rolling around in a tangled heap until Rob got free and sprang to his feet. His fist connected with the side of Daniel's head and sent him flying. Daniel was on his feet in an instant and tackling Rob in a massive dive that winded them both.

Ben and Jo-Ellen watched, horrified and unable to assist.

'On your feet!'

Somehow Rob got to the gun and held it on Daniel.

'What are you going to do now, de la Rey? Shoot me?'

'Probably.'

Daniel said in a low voice, 'Yes, that would ease your problem, wouldn't it? At least I wouldn't be able to tell any of your little secrets...'

'Shut up! You think they'd take note of anything you tell them?'

Daniel gave a wry grin. 'Don't worry your head, I've said nothing. Do me a favour, though, keep out of politics and things might well stay that way.'

Rob brought up the gun to head height. 'One more word and I'll kill you.'

As Rob took aim at Daniel, Ben's hand moved to his back pocket for a gun. It all happened so quickly. Ben's gun went off, and Rob fell to the ground, clutching his leg.

'Sorry, old friend, I had to stop you.' Ben turned to the others. 'Come on – we must get out of here. Every Yankee within miles will be swarming here soon!'

Jo-Ellen made to go to Rob who was dragging himself forward, his leg bleeding badly.

'Leave him,' Ben said. 'He'll live. I only shot him in the leg.'

'I can't – he's hurt!'

'You saw what happened – he would have killed Daniel. I did the only thing. Leave him. He'll get help soon, you can depend on it.'

She moved to Daniel's side. 'What did Rob mean – he would deny what? What's going on, Daniel?'

'Leave it! Just let it be, Jo!'

She was startled by his tone. She had never seen him so angry before. She had overheard the muted conversation and this was obviously upsetting to him. As they took off to the Church, Jo-Ellen, her face blackened, her throat so dried out with the heat and grime she found it almost impossible to speak, went over everything in her mind. Rob had purposely fired Highlands, regardless of who might have been inside. He had also killed Curtis. What had driven him to do such things? Surely he couldn't dislike Daniel so much because of the side he fought on? Or was he still jealous? No – there was something else. His hatred went deeper than north against south or Union against Confederate.

Daniel whipped up the horses to go faster. His expression was fierce, sweat poured down his face. It was unsafe to remain where they were, he told them. Rob's men would come and find him and the two dead soldiers. When that happened, the Yankees would come looking for them all. To remain at the Church would endanger all who sought refuge there.

They had to get away. Somewhere safe, somewhere that Rob would never find them.

• • •

The semi-circle of faces surrounded Daniel as he stood to address them.

'Listen to me, friends, me and my family aren't staying here with you. It won't be safe for any of you if we do. What we need is somewhere to go. Has anyone any ideas?'

There was a silence. Furtive glances passed from one to another. Daniel tried again. 'Please, try to think. We need somewhere to hide out in quick.'

Again silence, then a voice from the back of the room spoke up. 'Old Jonas Danby over at the Pike – he's gone, so I hear. Family just upped and left. You could try there!'

There was a rippled murmur of agreement.

'Thanks.' Daniel was relieved. 'We're grateful. And remember, you haven't seen us and you don't know where we are, okay?'

They prepared to leave and waved goodbye to the Reverend and his group.

'Think we'll be safe at the Pike?' asked Ben as they sped off in the buggy.

'As long as theYankees haven't found it, yes.'

'And if they have?' asked Jo-Ellen, clutching Alexander to her.

'Then we continue looking,' he replied. 'There are probably several empty houses hereabouts.'

Jo-Ellen knew he was only trying to comfort her. She glanced at Susanne, huddled in the corner with Elizabeth, Constance and Jamie. And poor Elizabeth – the sooner they got her to a doctor, the better. Susanne looked exhausted and stressed and Ben was staring ahead, finger taut on trigger, ready for a fight. She reached out to hold Alexander's hand. His eyes were frightened. How she longed for the ordeal to be over. He had not long been back from Charleston and now he was being taken across country to yet another strange destination.

Almost an hour later, Daniel reined in at the top of a hill.

He gazed around, looking for any signs of soldiers. 'There, that's Jonas's place. We'll wait here a few minutes, see if there's any movement.'

He jumped down and walked a short distance to where he could watch without being seen. Several minutes passed and he returned and slapped the horses forward.

'Seems we're in luck. Just pray that Jonas left some food behind.'

The house was spacious. Ben and Susanne took the room overlooking the main approach road and Daniel situated himself at the back. Elizabeth and Constance were made comfortable in one of the upper bedrooms while Jo-Ellen chose the room next to it. In the room on the other side from her, she put Alexander.

When she was settled, she put her hair in a chignon and went into the kitchen to see what she could find. In the larder she found, wrapped in muslin, a joint of meat. It had been covered in salt and smelt fresh and she placed it in a tray to cook. In another section she found some home grown potatoes and beans. There wasn't much, but it would serve to stem their hunger for now.

The aroma brought the others downstairs. 'Can you believe they left this behind? It might seem as though we're stealing but I'm sure old Jonas would rather we ate than starve,' she said as Ben and Susanne joined her. Daniel came in minutes later with a bottle in his hand.

'Bourbon, anybody?'

They prepared food for the children and Elizabeth and settled in the kitchen around a long table which reminded Ben of the house he'd sheltered in on his way home. For those few hours they put their problems behind them. Every so often one of the men would slip out and scout round to check there were no Yankees about then they would continue talking and laughing as the drink mellowed their mood.

When they were finally on their own, Daniel took Jo-Ellen's hand in his.

'Fortune is smiling on us, Jo. The Yankees haven't found this place.'

'And thank goodness you're here,' she said, nestling into his arms. 'What would we have done without you?'

A frown creased his brow. 'That's just the point, had I not come home, had I not become the new owner of Highlands, perhaps none of this would have happened.'

She was startled by this. 'No, I won't have that. Rob would still have pursued Alexander.'

He did not reply. He had his own views on the subject.

'Daniel.'

'Yes?'

'Is there something you're not telling me?'

He looked away. 'Nothing. I think you over-reacted to what was said out there.'

'I got the impression I wasn't meant to overhear.'

'Forget it.' He drew her to him and planted a kiss on her lips. 'And now, Miss Jefferson, I think it's time you had some sleep. The day hasn't exactly been lazy.'

'And you?'

'Nope. I think I'll stay here a while, keep a lookout. I'm not tired and I want to think about everything, make a plan for us.'

She rose to her feet. 'What will happen to Elizabeth? Is she strong enough?'

'I think so. She's tough. When I can, I'll ride in and find the doctor. Goodnight, Jo.'

He watched her out of sight before pulling his gun and loading it. Making himself comfortable, he sat in the dark facing the window and listened to the extraordinary silence outside. No one would be able to approach without attracting attention, he thought. Laying the gun to one side, he stared into the inky blackness beyond the window frame. He now had his own private war to fight. Rob was not going to let up, not while they had Alexander. Clearly his aim was to see Daniel six feet under, Jo-Ellen his possession, and Alexander living with him in Washington. Meanwhile, he would rise ever upwards in the world of politics.

He sighed. He was in a difficult position. As much as he wanted personally to put a stop to the de la Rey career, he was going to find it almost impossible. For how could he be the person to stop this man? Whatever he did or said would be construed as at most murder and, at the least, the action of a jealous man.

In the meantime, he had the unenviable task of staying out of Rob's reach and of merely staying alive. He had to, at all times, watch his back.

• • •

That period leading up to Christmas would remain in Jo-Ellen's memory forever. Not only were they living in a neighbour's deserted house, but during the daytimes they had to stay out of sight. This was difficult. The children became restless, they cried more than usual and both Jo-Ellen and Susanne began to feel stressed as a result.

After dark, Daniel and Ben went out and scouted around for food. With their bare hands they killed rabbits. Around them was an air of despondency. Winter set in, harsh and unrelenting, and Sherman's men with it. They heard news from the doctor they sought assistance from for Elizabeth. Savannah had fallen, he told them. Many folk were homeless, many of their old friends now dead. Jo-Ellen longed to get back to Jefferson House. Was it still standing - was it occupied by those savages? She also missed Louise, wondered where the girl had gotten to. She had apparently been with Susanne that day at the Church but must have run away. Was it possible she had found safety with a neighbour?

Meanwhile, Jo-Ellen did her best to prepare for 25th December and make it special for everyone. While she was busy in the kitchen Daniel came up behind her.

'My dearest.'

She turned to look into troubled eyes. 'What is it, why so gloomy on such a special day?'

His expression softened, a smile lifted the corners of his mouth. 'Gloomy? I don't mean to be. In fact, I feel blessed that you and I are together. It's just that I lay awake last night wishing I could gallop off to town and buy you something special for Christmas.'

'Oh, is *that* all?' She tucked her arms around him. 'I have all I want right here, Daniel. There's nothing on earth you could buy to improve my day. Besides, I thought about the same thing for you. But, here we are, prisoners in this house, yet I don't mind, not today, and you shouldn't either.'

'This damned war!' he said.

'Yes. But it can't go on indefinitely and when it's all over, we'll go back. We'll rebuild. We have that to look forward to.' Still his expression remained serious. 'Is there anything else on your mind, my darling?'

Then she understood. As soon as he was able to, he would have to return to his command. He was still a major in the Confederate Army.

As he made to speak, she placed a finger to his lips. 'No, let's not talk about the war and when you have to go back. Not today. Promise?'

His look of relief gladdened her heart. He had obviously been dreading telling her.

'Come on, Mama and I have performed miracles for today. Let's forget about everything and enjoy it.'

And they did. The truly magnificent news that emerged was that Savannah was still standing. Sherman had spared it from fire. Only the crops had been destroyed. The City had been given by Sherman to

President Lincoln as a Christmas gift and at first Jo-Ellen thought this disgusting and arrogant, but later during the days that followed into the New Year, she hoped that Lincoln might return the City to its people and gradually allow them to return to their homes. After all, what good was it without its inhabitants?

As January 1865 swept in, Sherman moved his army out to begin his campaign of destruction in the Carolinas.

Jo-Ellen began to feel a cheerfulness and optimism she could not explain. Deep down inside, something told her they would all be returning soon to Jefferson House.

Chapter Nineteen

The pain was still there. Rob eased himself into as comfortable a position as his leg would allow and waited for the orderly to join him. The wound had only partially healed, he'd been told. An infection had set in and this had to be dealt with.

The room he was in smelled strongly of blood and urine and he was impatient to get on his way.

'Hey, orderly! Where the hell are you?'

There was no reply. Christ – how long had he to wait? According to the notice outside the building he was somewhere south of Savannah, having final checks on his condition before being allowed to return to his duties in Washington. Trouble was, it was taking time. His leg was giving him trouble, and all because of Ben, his greatest friend, who had seen to it he was immobilised for almost a month and that the Confederate major was still alive.

He sat up slowly, leaned heavily on his stick and pulled himself to his feet. He couldn't go anywhere at all until he had sorted out that matter. With the Reb alive, his future would remain uncertain. His plans for himself and Alexander would be thwarted from the word go.

The door opened.

'Apologies, sir,' said the orderly. 'Got delayed. Now, let's take a look at you.'

The treatment was painful and took forty five minutes. Eventually Rob left the dismal building and was taken back to his temporary quarters in Savannah, where his aide handed him some papers.

'Both men were killed, sir, as you know. It's been seen as unnecessary killing.'

Rob nodded grimly. They had both been his friends. 'That's right and I want that logged. We were leaving the area, having done no harm to a soul. We saw a house and went to investigate. It had been fired, so we tried to put it out. Found some Rebs there and they killed my men and almost killed me.'

The aide made notes. 'Right, Major, we'll need your evidence of this, of course. Meanwhile, you're returning to Washington? To rest up?'

'Yes, but not immediately. I want you to search for those Rebs. Look everywhere. They're hiding out somewhere.'

The aide frowned. 'Sir? We've no idea where to begin...'

'Haven't you! Then make a note of this. The woman...'

'Woman?'

'The woman is my wife. The major is her new lover and the captain is, or was, my friend. You see what the war has done – divided friend against friend. They'll never get away with this. Never!'

The aide wrote furiously. 'I see, sir. I'll make sure this gets to the right quarter.'

'You do that. Search and find them. You hear me? Then report to me.'

The aide paused at the door. 'When we find them what do you want us to do with them?'

'Do? What you usually do with someone who tries to kill a future member of the Senate. They knew full well it was over for them yet they refused to give in.' Rob leaned heavily on his walking stick. 'I want you to treat them as you would any other murderer.'

The aide's eyes widened. 'A trial, you mean?'

'No – it's war time, we won't bother with all that. Kill them. I want them dead. America will be better off without them!' He paused. 'But not my son. I want him for myself. Find the boy, regardless.'

...

When word reached the people of Savannah that Sherman had finally gone, they cheered. At last they could emerge from hiding, at last they could resume their lives. Gradually, they filtered back to the homes that had been poorly used by the Yankees. Crops had been destroyed by fire, businesses ruined. Most of the black labour had gone. Houses had been left to gather dirt and their surrounding acres were in a dilapidated state. But with hard work and renewed spirit folk began to right the wrongs and the town buzzed with activity once more.

During the third week of January, Jo-Ellen decided to return to Jefferson House.

'Are you sure it's safe?' asked Susanne as she tended to Jamie.

'If we're to believe the rumours, the Yankees have gone. We're going home.'

'I was meaning Rob. How do you know he isn't still around?'

The thought had tormented Jo-Ellen constantly. 'I don't but he's still under orders and will most probably have gone with Sherman.'

'He's injured, remember.'

Jo-Ellen prayed she was right, that Rob had gone away. To contemplate otherwise was almost too much to bear. Daniel agreed. They should return, he told them, begin again, show the Yankees they were not beaten. As for himself, Jo-Ellen learned that he had to go back.

'Highlands is no use to me in its present state so it might be a good time to go,' he told her.

'Where will you go?' she asked, her spirits low. She had been expecting this.

'Sherman's heading for Columbia. Could be there – wherever the fighting is, Jo.'

The very next day they set about moving. As they drove up to the house Jo-Ellen felt a sensation of excitement and apprehension. She watched carefully for any movement that might warn them of strangers approaching but as that first evening arrived, she told herself not to worry, that she was over-reacting. She soon realised that the Federal soldiers had taken everything; jewellery, food, and from others sometimes even the clothes they were wearing. They also stole from the black people. What they couldn't take and make use of, they destroyed. Some people, she noticed, were left with nothing at all.

That night a storm hit them. It lasted well into the early hours. She lay in Daniel's arms listening to the rain hit the windows with force as lightning forked amongst the trees and thunder penetrated the silence. She felt Daniel stir in his sleep, could hear his even breathing. Somewhere distant a door banged.

Carefully, she freed herself from his grip, took the gun, and made her way down the stairs. The front door had sprung open and was swinging to and fro in the wind. She remembered the last time this happened, and shuddered. She closed the door securely and went up the stairs to Alexander's room. The darkness inside blinded her momentarily and she crept towards his bed and leaned over to look at him. It was empty. On the floor lay his jacket. Frantic, she opened one of the cupboards. His clothes had gone. She rushed to the window. All was quiet outside. She let out a scream, then another and another. Daniel and Susanne were beside her in an instant. 'It's Alexander. He's gone!'

• • •

Sebastian thought he might experience delay in returning to Maryland but not for the reason that presented itself quite suddenly.

Opening his newspaper on the morning before he planned to depart, a short news item caught his eye. A woman's body had been discovered in a shallow grave about two miles outside Washington. Immediately, he contacted the editor for any further information and was put on to the Federal office in charge of the investigation.

'Investigation?'

'That's right,' replied the editor. 'Seems there's more to it than meets the eye, but don't quote me.'

First Officer Reilly listened carefully to what Sebastian had to say, eyed him quizzically over the top of thick spectacles.

'Of course, it's a long shot, Mr Hilton. This woman must be one of many found in such circumstances. Best thing we can do is go along and see if it's your daughter.'

Sebastian was thereafter driven to the mortuary when he should have been catching the train back to Maryland. The scenery rushed past and then they stopped outside a tall building. Sebastian had never seen so many corridors as he was led down several to a room at the far end.

'In here, sir.'

The officer pushed open the door. Lining the walls was a stack system of huge filing cabinets but which were in reality where the bodies were kept. Sebastian pressed a kerchief to his face.

'Over here, Mr Hilton.'

An assistant pulled out one of the cabinets and drew back the cloth covering the body inside. Sebastian recoiled in horror.

'No – it's not possible!'

The officer held his arm in support. 'Is this your daughter, sir?'

The room swam momentarily. He felt sick. He wanted to wrap his arms around her, tell her he was there for her, that he was taking her home with him. When he found his voice, he whispered, 'Yes, it is.'

The assistant covered her face and Sebastian was led away.

'Wait!'

'Mr Hilton, I'm sorry it's your daughter…'

'What happened to her?'

Reilly shook his head. 'I'm afraid I can't discuss the details, not yet.'

'Oh, no? When?'

'We have to finalise our investigations.'

'Which could take weeks, even months. No – I want to know now.'

'It's out of the question.'

Sebastian moved closer to Reilly. 'Do you know who I am?'

'Yes-yes, sir. I know who you are.'

'Good, that will save precious time.' Reilly turned pale under Sebastian's close scrutiny. 'Have you any idea who the murderer might be?'

'We don't know that it was definitely murder, sir.'

'Oh, it was murder, all right. And the murderer's name? De la Rey.'

Reilly grimaced. 'Fine, we'll look into him.'

'Good. Start with Governor Floyd, start with the Senate.'

'Floyd? The Senate?'

'That's right. I hope you can see I mean business, Mr Reilly. So, shall we now talk about what happened to my daughter?'

Sebastian learned that afternoon much of what he needed to know and it did not take long to work out in his mind what must have happened to Laura. Her injuries sent shock waves through him as he listened to Reilly speak.

'I realise that what you say is a possibility, Mr Hilton, but we need proof. You can't go around accusing the likes of this Mr de la Rey without evidence. And as far as I can see, there is none. We cannot even be sure yet it's murder, not in these times.'

Sebastian felt his temper rise. 'Somebody hit her, somebody drove her to that wood and buried her. Agreed? I mean, she didn't do it herself.'

Reilly nodded reluctantly.

'That same person also shot her to make it look like she was in cross fire or something. It sure as hell is murder! Sort of devious plot that bastard would come up with. I took him in, gave him everything in order to make him well again, and how does he repay me? Kills my only daughter.' Sebastian looked towards where Laura lay. 'If it's the last thing I do, I'll bring him down, so help me.'

He strode from the room and accepted a lift back to the hotel. He did not hurry to leave. First he wrote to Governor Floyd about his findings then he contacted the newspaper to publish his own news item. De la Rey would see it, and he could sweat it out wondering how safe he was now that Sebastian Hilton was back on the scene.

• • •

Governor Floyd was delighted. With Robert's recent return, complete with leg wound, walking stick and son, the young man was sure to be given the welcome of a true hero. Why, hadn't he put himself in the front line yet again to fight for the Union? And the diary – de la Rey had continued right along with it and soon there would be a complete account of the whole war for publication. His further account of Antietam, or Sharpsburg, in which he had almost lost his life, would capture the hearts and minds of all those who believed in heroes and heroism. When the President heard, he had expressed great interest.

It would not be long before Robert took his place in the Senate. With the election just over with, a new government had been formed and it was not yet fulfilled completely. Hubert could see Robert filling one of those seats. His background, ability, and charm would see him into a career headed in only one direction. He was sure to gain a place on several important committees and he already had powerful colleagues in Congress. His service to the people of the Union was without doubt exemplary and Floyd knew he would have unanimous party backing. There was the small matter of the wife, however.

Seems Mrs de la Rey had not accompanied her husband and son on this occasion. Was there some trouble there? Possibly.

He rubbed his hands together. The war was all but over. The Confederates were struggling whilst the Union went from strength to strength. It was only a matter of time and then his own career would take a giant step forward with young de la Rey by his side. All he had to do was sell him to the people. It was just what they needed, a new role model, someone to take them out of the doldrums of four years of fighting and into a new era of peace and expansion. One day Robert de la Rey would be a presidential contender and he, Hubert Floyd, will have put him there.

As for Sebastian Hilton, the man was clearly overwrought and apt to imagine things. Hubert had dealt with such matters many times in the past. Hilton would soon soften up with time. Besides all this, he had no proof to back up his outrageous story.

He poured a drink and stood looking down on the street below. The late January sun was trying to get the better of heavy cloud and not succeeding. Rain was forecast.

The telephone rang disturbing his daydreams. It was his secretary. A letter had arrived. It looked urgent.

'Bring it to me, Jessop.'

Hubert looked at the postmark. Washington. The handwriting was familiar.

It was from Sebastian Hilton.

• • •

The driver whipped up the horses, pleased to be free of the southern countryside as more familiar Virginian surroundings loomed into view.

He turned his head to check on the young woman in his care. She was a real beauty. Picked her up in Columbia, South Carolina, and she had ridden with him ever since. She seemed very distant, very preoccupied, had hardly said two words to him in all that time. Just gave directions. Where was she going – Hagerstown? Well, that suited him, anything to get away from the war-torn south, especially now that Sherman was in Columbia. It was too dangerous to stay around long. Sherman had seen to that.

He wielded the whip again, dreaming of his next hot meal and

Bourbon.

Marilyn stretched her body as much as possible as the carriage sped through the Virginian countryside. Soon she would order the driver to stop at an Inn. She was hungry and tired and longed for sustenance.

It had been a long journey, up from New Orleans, across the Mississippi and on through Alabama and Georgia. Dangerous too, for Sherman's men had not been very far away the whole time she was on the road. Then she had gotten lucky and found the driver who would take her all the way to Hagerstown.

She longed to see the house again. Was it still there? Would Sebastian have left it there for her? She sighed. Sebastian. She was still married to him and he was no doubt still angry, but she would face all that rather than continue moving endlessly around the countryside. One thing she had learned and that was that time heals and anger subsides.

She leaned towards the window. 'Driver – pull in as soon as you can. It's time we stopped to eat, don't you think?'

He did not need reminding. The whip cracked again. Thirty minutes later they stopped at a small Inn just outside Richmond.

● ● ●

'It's Marilyn, she's back.'

Jasper waited for the explosion. He had been deliberating on when was the best time to tell Sebastian but he couldn't keep it to himself any longer.

'Back? How long?'

'Couple of days, I think.' He waited while Sebastian, himself only just arrived home, wrestled with this piece of news. 'Listen, I'll go tell her to keep moving. We don't want her sort round here…'

'No – tell her to come see me.'

Jasper's eyes widened. 'What's that? You want to see her?' He looked at Sebastian closely. Had he been drinking?

'You heard me. Tell Marilyn I want her here now, soon as possible. We're still married, you know. Everyone seems to have forgotten that. How is she?'

'Fine – she's fine. Looks lovely as ever. But she won't have changed…'

'I'll be the judge of that. I'm tired, Jasper, worn out. I could do with a friendly face round here. Apart from yours, that is.' A weak smile with this.

Jasper was bowled over. Sebastian was different. What had happened in those few days he'd been away?

'How was your trip? Did you find out anything? Did you see Laura?'

Sebastian motioned with his head. 'Sit and listen.'

The story came out falteringly and Jasper listened, amazed that the hard-headed Sebastian Hilton was as close to tears as any woman and despite himself, Jasper felt his own eyelids moisten when he heard what had befallen Laura.

'That swine,' he uttered. 'So you think it was definitely him?'

'Who else? Trouble is, I can't prove it. She went to see him, told him about Charles, they probably argued over the boy, and then he got scared she would go telling everybody. With Laura out of his life, there's no proof, is there?'

Jasper frowned. 'You mean he killed her just because of what she might have said?'

'Right.' There was a silence. 'Goddamn it, Jasper, who the hell else could have done it? No one knew her. De la Rey had opportunity and motive. If he didn't do it himself then he ordered someone else to, but I think that's unlikely.'

'How do you know they didn't argue and he hit out and it was an accident?'

Sebastian glared at him. 'I don't. But she's dead, isn't she? Whichever way I look at it, she'd still be alive if she hadn't gone to see him.' He glanced across at Jasper. 'You've gone quiet. Don't tell me you're having doubts.'

'No, of course not. What you say adds up, but whatever we say or whatever we do, there's no basis to it. And we've got to go careful here. This de la Rey is no ordinary person.'

'And he's not royalty all of a sudden, either!'

'No, but have you seen the news? Pictures of him, Floyd, and the President all on the same page. De la Rey's a hero, returned from the south wounded, and bound for high office. To suddenly go accusing him of murder at such a time might go more against you than him.'

Sebastian plunged his hands in his pockets. 'I take your point, Jasper. What the hell can I do?'

'Bide your time. Sooner or later de la Rey will put a foot wrong and then you'll be able to make your move.'

'Think so? How the hell am I going to wait so long? But you're right. I'll try and do that.' His face softened. 'Tell Marilyn I want to see her now. I need to talk to her. And Jasper, see she's settled in comfortably at the house.'

• • •

'But I have to go. I have to find him!'

Jo-Ellen was beside herself with frustration. No one was listening – did they ever? Tears welled up for the umpteenth time, while Constance, Ben, and Susanne tried to give their support.

'He must have been here all the time,' said Constance. 'What can we do to save Alexander? To think of it, my grandson in the hands of that…'

She was about to say 'monster' for that was how she saw Rob now, but managed to stop herself.

'Going up there, Jo-Ellen, isn't the answer. It'll get you nowhere,' said Ben.

'I agree,' said Daniel. 'What point would there be in you turning up in Washington, Jo, just to find they've all closed ranks against you?' He wanted to say much more, wanted her to know that Rob would stop at nothing in order to get what he wanted and that he also probably lied and cheated without conscience. He glanced at Ben. How long could they keep all this to themselves? And why should they? Yet he knew this was not the right time. Jo had clearly shown great concern when Rob was shot in the leg, and therefore it would be wrong to damage her illusions about her husband to soon. Daniel was also convinced that she might find herself in danger if she were to pursue Rob herself. Far better that she remain there in Savannah. He was also cursing himself that he had not been more alert to the fact that Rob and his men had remained in the vicinity all along watching and waiting for their opportunity to snatch the boy. He realised, too, that he'd probably had a lucky escape himself. So far, de la Rey had not found the opportunity to silence him.

None of this could he say and instead he held Jo-Ellen to him, feeling suddenly powerless to prevent what might befall her and Alexander when he was no longer there to take care of them.

'We'll leave you both in peace,' Ben said. 'Jo-Ellen, you can be sure that Alexander is safe. Rob would never harm him.'

He glanced at Daniel and an unspoken acknowledgement passed between them.

'Let me get you a drink, Jo,' Daniel said when they were alone. He poured two whiskeys and they stood together on the veranda and watched the sun sink in the leaden sky.

'Not cold?' he asked, tucking an arm around her.

'No, not cold.' She realised she was trembling still, more from shock than anything. The whiskey helped and she drank it down and accepted another.

'You know, my parents used to stand on this very spot and watch the late evening sun. Papa loved this time of day. He'd pour a drink and look out there to his acres and he was so very proud.' She smiled. 'And now we're doing it.'

'Yes. I feel as though we belong here, Jo, you and I. I'd give anything not to have to leave you now. Not at this time.'

'Not at any time. But it won't be for long. Not now. The war will end soon. That's what they all say.'

'When it does, we will have lost.'

His words saddened her. 'Yes, it seems that way. I suppose only a miracle could turn things round.'

'One hell of a miracle.'

'Then why go back? Only to be captured and be taken prisoner perhaps?'

'I've no alternative. Lee wants me there. I've been away long enough.'

She leaned into him. 'Of course, my honourable Confederate Major.'

'Do you know I have three wishes, three prayers for you and me?'

'Tell me what they are.'

He thought for a few moments. 'One, to have done with fighting. To know that when I come back next time, it will be for good.'

'Yes, and the other two?'

'To find Alexander, safe and well, and return him to you.'

'Oh, Daniel, if only!'

'Jo, while I'm away, I'll do all I can to find him. Someone will know something. Rob's in the public eye now.'

Hope sprang into her eyes.' Yes, he is. You think that will help us?'

'I believe so. That's why I want you to make a promise to me.'

She looked up at him. 'What is that?'

'Not to do anything impulsive. Stay down here and fight for Alexander. You can do it through the newspapers. It might take longer but we must be cleverer than Rob. Wait until I can help you sort things out.' He stopped. He must not say anything he might regret. 'What do you say?'

'All right,' she said. 'I promise. You had a third prayer – what was it?'

'Can't you guess? I want you to be free so that we can be married, that's if you still want to.'

'Just try and stop me. It's what I want more than anything.'

He placed his empty glass to one side and lifted her in his arms. As the fading light of day gave way to blackness of night, he carried her up the stairs and into her room.

• • •

'Well, now, just look at you!'

Startled by his voice, Marilyn turned and at the first sight of Sebastian after so long, was surprised by her own reaction. No longer afraid, no longer guarded in her response, she smiled with genuine fondness. Perhaps that was because Jasper had been there recently and helped her settle back in, and had hinted strongly that something had happened in her absence, something that had contributed to this change in the man who was still her husband.

It was not only that. Sebastian looked fitter, healthier. And he was smiling at her with a softness in his eyes she had not seen for so long.

'Jasper said you were more beautiful than ever and I have to agree with him on that,' he remarked, his eyes taking in the top of her exposed breasts and her long hair falling elegantly round her shoulders.

She moved towards him, took his outstretched hand and planted a kiss on his lips, which took him by surprise.

'Have you kept well?' he asked.

'All the time, Sebastian, except for once when I was in Missouri down with a mild influenza.'

'Missouri? That where you ran off to?'

She gave a mischievous grin. 'Only one of the many places. I've been around, I can tell you.'

'And did you catch up with that blackguard Vince?'

Her lashes covered her eyes briefly. 'Yes, we were able to settle up nicely.'

Sebastian chuckled. 'I won't ask how, but I'm pleased to hear it.'

She motioned him to a chair. 'Sebastian, thank you for being so nice about my coming back. Jasper gave me a lot of help.'

'That's fine, Marilyn. Forget it, least I could do.'

She waited while he settled and she poured him a whisky and one for herself.

'Here's to past times, and to the future. I expect you've a great deal to tell me, Sebastian.'

He said nothing, gazed into his glass as though for inspiration.

To jog him forward, she said, 'Did Laura have her baby?'

A momentary smile flickered over his face. 'Yes, a boy. We named him Charles. You'll love him, Marilyn.'

'And Laura. Is she well? Is she happy? Did she manage to find Ray, or whoever he was?'

The questions were ready to come, one after the other, but something in Sebastian's manner caused her to hesitate.

'I hope – Sebastian, if you don't want to tell me, I understand. I guess I shouldn't ask so many goddamned questions.' She gave a nervous chuckle. 'Always was my problem.'

'No – it's all right. I want you to ask, and I want to tell you.'

She listened while he began his story of how he had become closer to Laura and how they were bringing up the child together when Laura decided to go looking for Robert de la Rey.

'So, that's his name. I've read something about him somewhere, I'm sure. Something political, I believe.'

Sebastian continued, and she felt a strong sensation of icy shock when he told of Laura's death.

'And you think that this Robert whatsisname killed her?'

'Yes, Marilyn, I do. It's a feeling I have right here in my gut. He killed her all right.'

His hand suddenly shook and he placed the glass on the table, which he clutched with his other hand for support.

'Sebastian, my poor darling, what have you had to go through?'

She let him cling to her and then she saw that he was crying. Tears rolled from his eyes and his body wrenched with great shuddering sobs.

'I miss her so much, I miss her, Marilyn!'

'Come, come with me.'

She led him into the bedroom and closed the door. 'Take off your jacket,' she said.

'Now, lie down next to me. I just want to put my arms around you.'

He did as she asked and then nestled into her, closed his eyes and cried himself out.

After he had slept, she left him in the semi darkened room and took herself out for a walk in the night air.

Chapter Twenty

As the grey light of day gave way to the blackness of night, Jo-Ellen pulled the drapes and shut out the chilly March wind that surrounded the house. The silence was welcome. She could focus her thoughts more clearly on her predicament. Shortly, Daniel would be returning to duty, and she would be left with the aching gap in her life of having neither him nor Alexander.

She had cried, lost sleep, tried to reason it all out, but had failed. She wanted her son back, nothing more, nothing less. Even the knowledge that life in the south, were the war to come to an abrupt end, would no longer be as it was before, did not change her mind. Deep inside she knew that leaving Alexander with Rob to bring up made her feel very uneasy, as though she could sense some kind of danger for him. She could not explain it, and even Ben's words of reassurance had not helped.

Daily she had to steel herself against ignoring her promise to Daniel and making the journey to Washington. It was hard. Her common sense told her it would be of little use to go there, but her heart urged her to go. If she located Alexander, what then? Go in there and steal him back? Hardly. Yet, how could she go about fighting for him, and through the media? Rob was probably right when he said that public sympathy would be on his side.

On her mind more than anything else were the questions that flooded her thoughts whenever she let them drift back to the encounter Daniel had with Rob. There was so much she needed to know and she decided that the questions could not remain unanswered.

Daniel had been behaving strange ever since that day, was more on edge, ever watchful with a loaded gun at his side. The Yankees had gone yet he acted as though they were still there. Was it them or was it Rob that kept him forever on the alert? In which case, she had to know why. Why did Daniel warn Rob of running for office? What secret had he referred to? That much she had overheard that day. Therefore, why did Daniel continually brush aside her questions as though she were overreacting and imagining everything?

Pausing before the mirror to check herself, she pulled open the drawing room door with determination. It was now or never.

A door banged somewhere. She stopped at the sound of footsteps. Coming towards her was Daniel. He was in full uniform.

'Jo, there you are, I was just coming to see you.'

'Daniel – what's happened?'

'I had word from General Lee. I'm to make haste to join Johnston. I'm to leave now, Jo.'

•••

The aroma of baked bread drew Ben to the kitchen where he found his wife absorbed in her work.

'Smells good, Susanne. Now, why does bread always make me feel ravenous?' He wrapped his arms round her and kissed her lightly on the lips. 'How's our daughter, today? I haven't seen or heard her yet.'

'Only because you've been so busy. As soon as you left this morning, Jamie made her presence known. Thank goodness she's sleeping now, so I can get on with some baking.'

He grinned. 'Oh, oh, I can take a hint. I'll leave you in peace.'

He pulled the door to behind him and went to the drawing room intent on pouring a drink and relaxing with the newspaper. Jo-Ellen looked up as he entered. As soon as Ben saw her he guessed all was not well. He knew Daniel had gone and had volunteered to keep an eye on Highlands in his absence. Something about his sister's grave countenance, though, warned him it was not only Daniel's going away that was on her mind.

'I'm having a drink, Jo-Ellen. Want one?'

She shook her head, barely looking in his direction.

'Daniel get away okay?'

'Yes, I believe so.'

She rose and moved to the window, looked out at the scene on the other side, then returned to her seat.

'Why is March always so chilly? Bright but chilly. Is someone cooking? Mama, perhaps?'

'No, it's Susanne. She has one of her baking moods at present. Says it relaxes her.'

He tried to get eye contact, but Jo-Ellen kept her head turned away.

'Want to tell me about it?' he asked, finishing the drink and pouring another. His eyes took in the newspaper lying on the table. The headline did not promise well.

'There's nothing to tell.'

'Well, I know you're worried about Alexander...'

'It's not that.'

Ben made for the newspaper. 'Right, just asking.'

'Except...'

He paused.

'...that Dan and I had an argument.'

Her face creased as she spoke, then composed itself. He settled beside her. 'I see. You need to talk. Agreed?'

She nodded and a tear rolled down her cheek. 'It was all my fault – at first. You see, I had to know. That day when he and Rob fought, things were said and I overheard them. Daniel has been avoiding the issue ever since.'

'And you demanded an explanation before he went away?'

She again nodded. Another tear was released. Ben sighed. How typical of Jo-Ellen to make demands.

'What happened?'

'He told me not to bother my head about it.'

'And you wouldn't leave it at that.'

'No.'

'He got angry?'

'Very. I was surprised, well shocked, really.'

'Yes, Daniel rarely loses his temper.'

'I didn't mean it!'

He looked at her. 'What? What didn't you mean?'

She buried her face in her hands. 'Well, I suppose I pestered him to tell me why he doesn't trust Rob. Oh, I know they are both in my life and are possibly a little jealous, but it's not that, is it? There's something else, something he's keeping from me.' She gazed up at Ben, her eyes red from crying. 'I'm afraid I lost my temper. I said he hadn't given Rob a chance, had pre-judged him. I said that if he'd got to know him he'd see a different side to him. Oh, Ben, I accused him of being jealous of Rob's success in government.'

'You did what?' What the hell was his sister thinking of? 'What did he say to that?'

'Nothing - he said nothing. Just stared at me…'

'Speechless, I expect. Really, why'd you say it at all? None of it's true.'

'I thought it might be at the time – Oh, I don't know what to think. I was so upset at losing Alexander.' She looked into his eyes. 'Ben do *you* know? If you do, tell me!'

He thrust his hands into his pockets. Why was Jo-Ellen so goddamned curious about everything? Thank goodness Susanne wasn't like that. His thoughts flew to the moment he had shot Rob in the leg. Had Jo-Ellen forgotten that he was about to shoot at Daniel? He remembered how concerned she had been about Rob when she saw the blood. Did she not realise that it could have been Daniel lying there, only he would probably have been dead?

How could he explain the hatred that had grown between these two men? Each wanted the other out of his life. Ben could remember how that felt, to hate like that; the loathing and the yearning to pay back, to kill if necessary, a feeling he had never dreamed of experiencing – until he killed Sergeant Foley. He recalled the overpowering sense of relief, of the power it had given him, and he relived the smell of death that day and the longing to be anywhere other than on that battlefield.

Since then, he had carried the inevitable guilt with him, for try as he may, nothing could convince him it was an act carried out within the confines of war during which soldiers were expected to kill each other. What he had done to Foley was nothing less than murder, there was no other way to look at it. Earl had disagreed on that long walk home, had tried to tell him he'd had no alternative in the heat of the moment but Ben knew full well how long he had carried the lust for revenge in his heart.

'If you know anything, Ben,' Jo-Ellen was saying, 'I'm asking you to tell me. Daniel confided in you, as I do. He trusted you and you may not want to break a confidence, but this is different, don't you see? This is the rest of my life, mine and Daniel's.'

He rested a comforting hand on her shoulder, felt her tremble and his heart went out to her.

'Just hear me out,' he said.

She said not a word as he told her what Daniel had said to him. How that day at Sharpsburg he and Rob had met up, and Rob's maniacal desire to kill him. And how Rob had since then sought to silence Daniel, the only man who could destroy his political career.

When he had finished, Jo-Ellen took a deep, steadying breath, stood up and went to look through the window again. 'It's all beginning to make sense, that conversation, everything.'

'So you can see, can't you, that Daniel was all along protecting you from the truth so as not to hurt you, or Alexander. He could so easily have told you everything. The trouble was that Rob lived with that fear. Still does.'

'Yes, I see that now.' She turned, her eyes brimming, a smile on her lips. 'Thank you for telling me, for breaking that confidence. I can see how harsh I've been and it's too late now.'

'No, it's not too late. Daniel will be home again. Time will heal, it always does.'

If only she could believe that. 'Yes, he'll be home but will be still feel the same? I feel that I've damaged our love.'

'No, you haven't. I think he'll realise what a truly loyal woman you are. Let's face it, during all the trauma, you still felt concern for Rob, you still cared. You were his wife, despite everything, even though he pushed you away. I think Daniel will come to appreciate that eventually.' He grinned. 'Not sure I've put all that correctly.'

She raised hopeful eyes. 'What would I do without you, Ben?'

She let herself out and he made to pour a drink then changed his mind. He took up the newspaper and read. Lee's army were outside Petersburg facing Grant. The Confederacy were running short of much needed supplies and they were painfully short of men. He felt a pang of guilt, tossed aside the newspaper and went into the kitchen.

∙ ∙ ∙

No word came from Daniel. Jo-Ellen prayed daily. She wrote him a long letter, poured out her heart to him. She did not get a reply.

She was unaware that he had left General Johnston, had moved from the Carolinas and gone to join General Lee to fight against Grant in Richmond.

∙ ∙ ∙

The press were full of it. Lee had surrendered. Daniel could scarcely believe it. It was all over. What now? He would have to await orders from Marse Robert, the man he would move heaven and earth for. How strange it all was now. His job was done, he would be going home. His hand touched the letter that had been forwarded to him. He would reply to Jo in person.

He turned the page of the newspaper and his attention fell on a picture of Rob. Below, the headline read: 'Senator-in-waiting questioned about missing girl.'

He snatched up the paper and read and for the first time in weeks felt a surge of optimism.

'Got you, de la Rey. Got you at last! You're about to hang yourself and you're doing it all on your own.'

He read on as an idea that wouldn't go away formed in his head.

∙ ∙ ∙

'I tell you, it's true. It's over!'

Everywhere the cry went up. Rob felt a rush of power and contentment as he stood fixing his necktie and listening to the shouts outside his window.

His eyes took in the newspaper lying on the chair. There were pictures of Lee riding tall and proud on his horse, Traveller, pictures of him sitting opposite General Grant at Appomattox Court House and many pictures of foot-sore men returning home.

Rob helped himself to a drink and kicked off his shoes. His feet hurt today. April had been blessed with much sunshine and his feet hurt as a result. Gently, he rubbed his toes and slipped into a pair of soft moccasins.

'Alexander, come here and sit by Papa.'

The boy took no notice, his attention on the toy cannon Rob had given him.

'Alexander, do as you're told. Come sit by Papa.'

His patience had snapped twice already. The boy was positively annoying at times.

'Papa, you play with me!'

Rob rubbed at the blister just forming and swore. 'I'll not ask you again, come here!'

Alexander did as he was told. 'Papa, when is Mama going to come?'

'Soon, I told you – soon.'

Alexander picked up the cannon and hit the floor with it. 'I want Mama!'

Rob shot another whisky into his glass. He'd had enough. What with the Federal authorities asking him questions about a girl's body found in woodland outside Washington. That had been a shock. At first he wondered how they had traced him then he realised – Sebastian. He was back on the scene. He expected it. No use, therefore, denying ever knowing her. Now it was all in the newspapers, not helpful at this time when he was about to go forward in his career. Not that it would harm him, he would see to that. Give them all the help he can, write an article if need be. He'd had enough clout to get through this – and he had Floyd behind him all the way.

'Papa – I'm hungry!'

'For God's sake!'

He drank in one gulp and went to the kitchen to fumble for some food. Perhaps that woman he'd met at the party the other night would come over and help out. She'd been very forthcoming in sexual matters, maybe he could dump Alexander on her for a while.

• • •

They waited in the shadows of an old church in a street not far from the White House. Washington looked splendid as darkness came to claim it. Moonlight lit the rooftops, its beams spiralling along the tree-lined street. There were few people about and Daniel knew they had chosen a perfect night. Dressed in leather pants, dark shirt and an old slouch hat, he neither looked nor felt like a major of the Confederate Army. No one would recognise him.

Once he had been released from his duties for good in Richmond, he had taken two of his best men and journeyed to Washington. That was the easy part. Finding de la Rey was not. His purchase of the grand looking house they now closed in on had helped find him. They waited now for him to emerge, preferably with Alexander.

'The boy's probably asleep now,' whispered Dougall. 'What if we don't get to see de la Rey before morning?'

Daniel gave the stocky Irish man a reassuring grin. 'Be patient, my friend. I've a mind to go right in now and surprise him.'

Patience was not one of Dougall's qualities, he knew, but they had come this far and Daniel was not going to waver now. To his left Ethan Foster, his ex sergeant, bent low beneath a window where a light had gone on. Cautiously he raised his head and gave Daniel the signal that de la Rey was in residence. Another signal told him that Alexander was there with him.

'Perfect. We go in,' Daniel muttered to himself. 'Perfect.'

He preferred it that way. He wanted to confront de la Rey, not merely steal the boy. They moved forward, Foster skirting to the back while Dougall went in the front with Daniel.

The house was in complete darkness, except for the light from the window. With one swift movement, Daniel kicked in the door.

• • •

Rob whirled round to face them as they stepped inside. 'What…! You've destroyed my new door! Who the hell are you?' He teetered backwards as they advanced on him. 'How dare you break in here…' He saw Daniel. 'So, it's you, Reb. You've gone too far this time. I'll see you in prison for this.'

Alexander, who had run behind the sofa, smiled at Daniel and pointed. 'Uncle Daniel!'

'That's right, Alexander.' He bent down to him. 'How about coming to see your Mama? She's waiting.'

The boy's eyes lit up. Rob stepped forward. 'Now, listen here...'

'Yes? You got something to say?'

The colour disappeared from Rob's face. He took in the build of Dougall, who was presently flexing his muscles. 'Let's talk about this,' he offered. 'Have a drink and let's come to some agreement.'

Ignoring him, Daniel lifted Alexander with one sweep of his arm. He motioned to Ethan. 'Go get the boy's belongings.'

'You can't do this – it isn't lawful. He's my son!'

'Lawful? What would you know about the law? Was it lawful what you did to that poor girl in Hagerstown?'

'You surely don't believe that I...'

'Oh, I believe all right. The newspapers are fully on the story.'

'The papers. They've got it all wrong. The girl's father is down on me because I'm the obvious choice. I can prove I haven't seen Laura Hilton for several months.'

Daniel eyed him coldly. 'She had your child and then you walked out on her.' He handed the boy to Dougall and turned his back on Rob. 'I've come for Alexander. That's all I want. You can deal with your other problems yourself.'

Ethan appeared, clasping a box of clothes and toys. Daniel headed for the door. 'I hope we don't hear from you again, de la Rey.'

'Hear from me! You'll have the full force of the law on you, Reb,'

'Very foolish. If I were you, I'd sink into the background. After all, you'd not want the whole of America to hear how their new so-called hero really behaved at Antietam, would you? And it's no use getting rid of me because you'll have Dougall and Ethan here to deal with.'

Rob glanced at the two men. 'You forget that you killed two of my men at Highlands. The authorities are looking into that right this minute.'

'Let them. They'll be interested to hear that you all fired the house, killed the overseer, almost killed Susanne's mother and had guns trained on us. Shall I go on?'

'You'll have to prove it.'

'I will, have no doubt of that. I've got Ben and Jo as witnesses and besides, it won't look too good on your record.'

'I should have killed you when I had the chance,' Rob growled.

'Yes, you should have.' Daniel motioned to the others and they took the boy and disappeared into the night. He made to follow, then hesitated.

'One more thing, de la Rey. When Jo asks for her freedom, be a good fellow and give it to her. We plan to marry.'

Rob lunged at him, his fist connecting. Daniel fell backward, recovered, and they went into a clinch. Regaining control, he managed to scramble to his feet, and hit out first with one fist then the other. Scooping up his slouch hat, he stood by the doorway, his eyes on the barely moving figure at his feet.

When Rob regained consciousness minutes later, all he could see was bright moonlight throwing strange long shadows across the room.

• • •

Standing side by side, Ben and Jo-Ellen, each holding a newspaper, read out the news to Constance and Susanne. Not for the first time, for they had all gathered in the drawing room of Jefferson House when news came of General Lee's surrender, and now the two women listened in awe as Ben told of the increase in crime and violence in the States and went on to relate the horror of the assassination of President Lincoln. April 1865 was becoming a month to remember.

'Oh, my, I can't say I ever took to him, but I certainly wouldn't wish that to happen,' said Constance, and Susanne discreetly wiped a tear from her eyes as Jo-Ellen took up the story and related the events of the night when the President attended a play at the theatre and suffered death at the hands of actor John Wilkes Booth.

She longed for news of Alexander. Daniel had written only once, a short note, following the surrender to say that he would come back to Highlands as soon as possible. That had been over a month ago and he was still not back. She missed him.

Every day she went to Highlands to sweep and clean and try and make it habitable again. Every day she missed Alexander and it felt like a dagger in her heart. Daily she sought news of the political arena in Washington and she read with horror the news of the woman named Laura Hilton from Hagerstown. The papers stated that Rob might have known her and that it was rumoured he had fathered a child with her. Here Jo-Ellen fought to understand. He had not been well then, he had lost his memory and taken on a different personality. That he had taken up with another woman and formed another life, was surely not his fault? Had he not returned to her as soon as he rediscovered himself?

None of this had affected his popularity, it seemed. He was hailed as a hero and Jo-Ellen had no power to oppose that. Twice she had started a letter to Governor Floyd, both times she had torn it up, knowing that what they would see in her words were the rantings of a bitter woman, one who had failed in her marriage, one who was not worthy to bring up her son.

And so she awaited word from Daniel. The days passed into weeks and suddenly it was May again.

• • •

Sebastian bought every newspaper every day and kept those articles about his daughter, and the political career of Robert de la Rey. Daily he looked for a way to accelerate de la Rey's downfall but so far had met with little or no success. The public was by now aware of Laura's suspicious death; they knew that de la Rey had been her lover and that the child, Charles Hilton, was his. They knew also – and here Sebastian had been most diligent – that de la Rey was being questioned concerning Laura's death and that he was under suspicion. Yet, there seemed to be no sign of a lessening of his popularity. It was almost as if they were prepared to forgive him anything at all, even murder.

Sebastian read the latest news item and looked at the picture of the young politician on the front page. Good looks will get you anywhere, he thought. And de la Rey had those aplenty. Women fawned over him and men admired him. This turn of events was enhanced by the loss of President Lincoln. That man had left a giant gap and there was no one of stature to fill it – except the likes of de la Rey, or so the vulnerable public thought.

He thrust aside the newspaper. Perhaps it was time to up the pressure. A private detective, perhaps? Someone under cover who would spy on de la Rey and help bring him to justice? He brightened. The idea was a sound one. Next time he saw Jasper, he would sound him out. Jasper would know who to contact. Then there was the family of de la Rey. He obviously had one. Wouldn't they know a thing or two?

He poured a drink and stood in his usual spot near the window to drink it. It was beginning to rain, yet it was warm, almost humid outside. He would not wait. A walk to Jasper's house would surely do him good.

Wrapped in a rain coat, he strode down the hill in the pouring rain. It fell slantwise and stung his face but he did not notice, nor did he slacken his pace. He had at last found the solution to his problems.

• • •

Roused from sleep by the song of morning birds, Jo-Ellen looked out at the day, feeling that the sun was going to climb high and hot, and slowly she stretched her invigorated limbs.

The previous day heartening news had reached her and Ben that Earl and Louise had been located. She had made strenuous enquiries about them since settling back at Jefferson House and had found out that Earl had taken refuge at a friend's home somewhere on the outskirts of Savannah, and that Louise had been taken in by an elderly relative whom she had rediscovered whilst hiding in the Church. Jo-Ellen had sent word and now Louise had contacted her to promise she would return to the Plantation. Earl had done likewise but owing to more complicated circumstances, his return was to take longer.

Almost back to normal, she thought, looking at the failed crops through the window. The cabbages they had planted had been either stolen by the Yankees or had failed to grow. There had been few potatoes and beans. It had become a way of life to always feel hungry. On rare occasions strange tasting eggs and scrawny chickens were all they had to eat and these were now dwindling to a minimum. Jo-Ellen longed for the taste of real meat, any meat, to ease the grumbling in her tummy.

She rose and dressed. On that lovely morning she would go for a canter. After breakfast she led out the Grey and mounted, turning its head in the direction of the sprawling meadows, away from Jefferson House and away from Highlands. Today she wanted to leave it all behind, to blend with nature, to 'smell the roses' as Constance always urged her to do.

Reaching the top of the rise she stopped to survey everything around her, for up there she could see for miles in any direction she chose. It was so good to feel free from fear. There was no war. Life was good again as far as that was concerned. She had far-sighted plans. The Plantation had taken devastating punishment in recent months but that did not mean that she and all the others, and this included Earl and Louise, would not be able to set matters straight again. She saw the day when the fields were once more thriving, when food was once more abundant, and that long lost feeling of security and contentment returned.

'It's possible – we'll make it possible!' she called into the breeze.

Around her there were still traces of the ravages of war, but they had been more fortunate than most. Savannah was spared. They would capitalise on this, turn it all to their advantage.

What would her Papa feel now? She knew the answer immediately. In that blunt manner of his, Samuel would dismiss any negative feeling, delegate work, rebuild, and never give in.

She smiled to herself. Did she take after her Papa or her Mama? A bit of both, no doubt, but probably more after Samuel. The word 'rebuild' remained in her mind and her eyes slid away to Highlands in the distance, its side a twisted wreck. Poor Daniel. All the time and money he had invested had come to nothing. Yet she knew he would not see it that way at all. He had begun a love affair with Highlands and even in its present state, would see only beauty.

She sighed. He had also begun a love affair with her and she had turned him away, no doubt a confused and disappointed man. Had he received her letter? He had not said so in his short note. She knew that none of her well laid plans would give her happiness if he were not there beside her. Would she ever forget the expression in his eyes that day they had argued? Would he want her now? Had she lost him?

A sharp breeze tugged at her free flowing hair and she tried to turn her thoughts to glory in the freshness of the air. What was Alexander doing – where was he? If only she knew. With a click of her tongue she motioned the horse forward, negotiating the meadows until they came to a creek where the water gurgled around small rocks and trees and occasional moss. Not long ago, enemy forces had crossed this very creek and raided small houses. Now everywhere was quiet and she wondered how long it would take the good people of Savannah to come to terms with their new situation and resume their lives; how long before children laughed and played and men broke in new horse flesh and the familiar sound of music and dancing, combined with aromatic cooking on fires, once more became the norm?

And what of her? Would she also be part of that new life force she longed to see happen? Because within her was that incessant pain which started the day Alexander was taken from her. How long was she expected to sit idly by, doing nothing? Her family had fallen silent on the subject and there was no word from Daniel on the matter. It was her own fault. Lately she had listened far too much to the advice of others instead of acting on her own inclinations. What had happened to her these past months that she had not gone after the most important thing in her life? Daniel – Daniel had happened to her and she felt incapable because of her own inadequacy. She'd had everything and now it was all gone.

'I'm going up there and I'll face Rob and demand my son be returned to me!' she vowed.

Digging in the spurs, she raced across the meadow, jumped a fence, tore alongside the stream, took a steep incline, flew over another fence and finally came to a halt on the rise again. The Grey reared, grateful for the exercise. It had also done her some good, had taken away some of the anger.

Something ahead caught her attention, as she ambled home. Caution still her watchword, she stopped. She was riding around with no possible heed to danger lurking. She heard hoof beats and turned her head toward the sound. A rider came into focus.

Jo-Ellen watched. He seemed to be heading for Jefferson House. She noticed then he was not alone. She strained to see but the rider had turned slightly, blocking her view.

He stopped then, dismounted and lifted his companion down. When he removed his hat to wipe his hand across his forehead, she dug in her spurs, her heart and spirits so lifted that tears of joy sprang to her eyes.

The rider turned on hearing her approach. She stopped a short distance away.

'Daniel!'

He smiled, took the hand of the small boy beside him and led him forward.

'Hello, Jo. I said I'd be back.'

∙ ∙ ∙

'Sausages!'

'And meat!'

The family celebrated, cooking on a bonfire the food that Daniel had managed to bring with him. They rounded up their neighbours and even the Rev. Charles Biddell attended.

Jo-Ellen stood watching. Someone played music, several danced and sang and Ben's voice could be heard above everybody else's. Constance moved amongst them all, happy and animated, and Susanne carried Jamie in her arms and chatted gaily to old friends. Jo-Ellen sighed. All their friends had arrived – all except Daniel. She looked constantly towards Highlands willing him to make an appearance. Everybody lingered well into the late hours, not wanting the evening to end. Jo-Ellen turned away. The magic was gone for her. The night felt old and tired without Daniel there.

Pouring a drink, she stood in the porch under the glow of the moon and wondered if she was destined to always look back on this time with regret. Daniel had given her back her son, as promised. And she thought that day was the happiest of her life. Seeing him ride in with Alexander had squeezed her heart almost beyond endurance and she had run to him, thrown her arms around him and he had held her tightly. Yet, she felt instinctively that he was different, that something was wrong.

'You look beautiful, Jo,' he'd said. 'It's good to see you again.'

They had made their way to Jefferson House and all attention turned instantly to Alexander. The boy looked well, was happy to be back with his family and none the worse for his experience in Washington. She had waited, impatient to be alone with Daniel so that they could talk, so that she could explain, but as soon as all the greetings were over, he had taken up his bag and hat and climbed into the saddle and she watched, her heart pounding, as he coaxed his horse along the track to Highlands.

'Jo-Ellen?' Her mother's voice startled her. She turned to Constance who was smiling and frowning all at the same time.

'What are you doing here alone in the dark? Come and join us. And where's Daniel – hasn't he arrived yet?'

'No, he hasn't arrived.' She swallowed visibly.

Constance took her hand in hers and searched her daughter's face.

'Ben told me about the argument. I'm so sorry, dear. If there's anything I can do…'

'No, Mama, it's all right.' Her fingers tightened on her mother's hand.

'Jo-Ellen, you must go and find him. Nothing's going to be resolved with you here and him there.'

Try as she may, Jo-Ellen could not prevent the tears from spilling down her cheeks.

'Yes, have a good cry. Best thing a young woman in love can do.'

Jo-Ellen smiled through the blur of water. A woman in love. The words heartened her.

'Well, are you going over there?'

She shook her head. 'Daniel will come when he's good and ready.'

Constance tutted. 'You think so? Why must you always be so stubborn? Suppose he doesn't come. Suppose he's over there waiting for you? You went tearing after him before, remember?'

'Mama, that was different.'

'Was it? Seems to me that young man's as disappointed and confused as can be. Why on earth should he feel welcome now?'

Jo-Ellen frowned. 'What do you mean? It was only an argument. People have them all the time, they don't always break up over them, though.'

'Men are very territorial animals, you know. Very few can accept sharing what they believe to be theirs. And Daniel now considers you his.'

There was a silence while this sank in.

'Don't you see, he thinks that part of you still wants Rob,'

These words startled Jo-Ellen. 'You think so? But that's not true.'

'He doesn't know that, does he?'

'Goodnight ladies, it's been a pleasure.' Charles Biddell advanced on them, his hand outstretched. Jo-Ellen realised that the music had stopped and so she put her feelings on hold to see the Reverend off and make an effort to talk to those remaining.

When they were alone again, Constance said, 'When are you going to stop being so stubborn, Jo-Ellen?'

Jo-Ellen turned away. Her Mama was right. Deep inside she knew that. But what if he wouldn't see her? There was only one way to find out. Her mind suddenly made up, she turned back and smiled, a shimmering hope growing in her heart. 'Yes, I'll go and see him right away.'

As she let herself through the gate, she said, 'Thank you, Mama.'

'For what?'

'For being here when I needed you.'

• • •

Highlands was in darkness when she got there. A light wind rustled the trees as she tethered the buggy and made her way to the house. She peered through the only lighted window. Inside it was empty. A sudden despair shot through her. What if Daniel had gone – for good this time? What if he had decided to give up Highlands after all?

A sound came from behind. He stood there, dressed in a black suit, white shirt, black tie and hat, and she thought she had never seen him looking so handsome.

'Hello,' she said, and surprised herself by feeling a sudden shyness.

'I was about to come over...,' he began.

'It's all finished by now. You missed it.'

'Never mind. I was only coming to see you and now you're here.'

'You look – beautiful,' she said, and he gave a low chuckle.

'I've been trying to leave here for almost two hours but I couldn't.' He grinned. 'Too much going on in my mind, too many questions, you know.'

'Yes, I know. I want to explain everything. You see, Ben told me everything. You mustn't blame him for that. He was just thinking of us – I'm so sorry, Daniel...'

He strode over to her and swept her into his arms. She knew then by the way he kissed her and the way his fingers touched her skin that he still wanted her, that he still loved her.

'Daniel...'

He placed a gentle finger to her lips. 'No more apologies. Just listen to me, Jo. I want you to be sure. I'll want you forever, not just a part of you, but I want you to have my children, I want to grow old with you…' He stopped, his eyes on hers with a message in them that was unmistakable. 'It has to be the same for you.'

'It is, Daniel. Surely, you know that?' His strong arms fastened under her and she was lifted and carried to his room.

Hours later, as she lay beside him, she could see through the window low clouds massed in the distance. The horizon was bright and the rising sun promised to be brilliant as it found an opening and emerged in that flood of colour she had seen so often before, and never tired of.

Together they watched the dawn of a new day.

END

Printed in the United Kingdom
by Lightning Source UK Ltd.
103410UKS00001B/230